Rebel's Fairytale

Howlers MC Series Book 7

Rebel's Fairytale

Howlers MC Series Book 7

T.S. TAPPIN

Rebel's Fairytale
T.S. Tappin
Published by T.S. Tappin
Copyright © 2022 T.S. Tappin
All rights reserved. In accordance with the U.S. Copyright Act of 1976, the scanning, uploading, and electronic sharing of any part of this book without the permission of the publisher is unlawful piracy and theft of the author's intellectual property. Thank you for your support of the author's rights and work.
This book is a work of fiction. Names, characters, places, and incidents are the product of the author's imagination or are used fictitiously. Any resemblance to actual events, locales, or persons, living or deceased, is coincidental.
Cover Design by: T.S. Tappin
Editing Services: Elisabeth Garner & Kimberly Ringer
ISBN: 9798362882082

Dedication:

You bit him... so it's your fault.

Other works by this author:

Under the name T.S. Tappin
Howlers MC Series:
Bk1: Axle's Ride
Bk2: Trip's B*tch
Bk3: Pike's Pixie
Bk4: Siren's Flame
Bk5: Bullet's Butterfly
Bk6: Dragon's Kiss
Bk7: Rebel's Fairytale
Bk8: Rex's Release

Tiger's Claw MC Series:
Bk1: Crush's Fall

HTC Related Anthology Story:
Bride's Bail Out (coming Spring 2023)

Through Newsletter
Coming soon:
Rock's Reward: A Howlers MC Series Novella
Joker's Second Chance: A Howlers MC Series Novella

Under the name Tara Tappin
On the Clock: A Spicy RomCom Novella Charity Project

Acknowledgements:

My PIC: For pushing the *publish* button for the first time for me. I Heart You.

My family: I appreciate your support and believe in me. You are my reasons why.

Elisabeth: Your time has come. He's yours. I hope I gave you all that you asked for, but none of this would have been possible without your support and knowledge of the grammar, O' Grammar Chosen One! HGS 4 Life!

Kim: Dragon may be 'bigger,' but Rebel has more girth. We have to give her that, but you are the Howlers Wiki, and that deserves a certain level of respect. Hats off to you, Ma'am. Thank you for all your help and support! HGS 4 Ever!

The HypeGirlSquad Discord: For keeping up my spirits each and every day, I thank you.

My Beta team: If not for you, none of this would make sense. Thank you for wading through the mess to find the good stuff.

My ARC team: Thank you, thank you, thank you for taking a chance with my work! You are one of the most important parts of the publication of my books. Without you, none of this would be possible.

Dear Reader,

There are themes in this book that may affect readers negatively.
The following are those themes:
Death
Violence
Weapons
Hostage Situation
Domestic Violence
Possessiveness
Controlling behavior
Cussing/strong language
Explicit sex
If you encounter something that isn't listed and feel it could negatively affect a reader, please email me at booksbytt@gmail.com

Thank you!
T.S. Tappin

T.S. Tappin

Chapter One

Bri

Brianna 'Bri' Jeanne Cooke's brain was unprepared for what she saw when she stepped up behind those young men at the open back door of the library and looked out into the alley. She had expected to see Rebel fighting with someone or even a gun battle. *A shoot-out?* She had heard a few shots, so she was prepared for that, and at first, that was exactly what she saw. That hadn't surprised her at all.

What surprised her was when Rebel turned from a man to a large wolf in less than a second. *How?* She couldn't even begin to process… That wasn't true. Her book nerd brain could come up with a thousand ways to explain *how*, but she wasn't living in a book. She was living in the real world, and things like that didn't happen.

Right? Right?!

After he tore that man to shreds *as a wolf* and turned back into the man she knew, he approached her and the two younger men. She just stared at him, her mind attempting to process what she had seen while he spoke with the men. After a moment, the two young men stepped past her and entered the library. Rebel's gaze shifted to her, and he uttered, "I'll explain that later. Okay?"

She was curious, but she could see that he had more important things to take care of, so she just nodded. Although she had a million questions and was beyond curious, while also stunned, her brain had begun screaming, *Now is not the time!*

He looked as if he wanted to say so much, but he only lifted his hand, clocked the small amount of blood on it, and lowered it. *How was there only a small amount? No! Not the time.* She watched him as he walked away, pulling his phone out of his pocket, and typing something out on the screen, most likely a text message.

She had a flash of thought about how his phone was able to make it through him turning into a wolf and back, but she shook it off. *Again, not the time!* As she did, her eyes dropped to the mess of blood, bones, and tissue on the asphalt of the alley.

Why was she not more freaked by the dead man torn to shreds? Probably because she was stuck on the wolf's appearance. It would hit her — The shock and the freakout. When? Bri didn't know, but she knew it would, eventually.

She called out, "Should I call the police?" Bri watched as he turned around to look at her.

Rebel shook his head. "I'll take care of it. Just… let me take care of it."

She nodded again and started to back into the library. Glancing back down to the mess of human pieces, Bri held a surety in her gut that the man deserved what Rebel gave him. As much as she didn't like violence, she somehow knew Rebel wouldn't have done it without it being a last resort.

Closing the emergency exit door, she sighed and rolled her eyes at herself. She didn't know the man. Bri was a responsible, logical person who should be calling the police after witnessing a murder, but how would she explain what she saw? *Um, yes, officer, I said the man turned into a large wolf and tore the other man apart. No, officer, I don't need to talk to a therapist.*

"He's not a freak," one of the young men said as she turned to head back to her desk. *Ryker?* He was leaning back against the wall, approximately ten feet from the emergency exit. "We're… we're not freaks, Ruby."

She smiled at his use of the nickname Rebel had given her. When he showed up with the women, children, and the two young men, Rebel introduced her that way. To her surprise, it didn't bother her at all. She actually liked it, which was another thought for another day.

"Yeah, Rubes," the other young man, Ross, added. "We were born this way."

"I believe you." She shrugged and offered a smile. "I'm a librarian. By nature, I'm a book nerd. It's almost impossible for me to *not* think anything is possible."

Ross snorted a laugh. "You know that was full of all kinds of confusion, right?"

Bri grinned. "What can I say? I have a way with words."

It was a few hours later, when the truth of what she saw in that alley finally hit Bri. She knew she wasn't losing it. She actually witnessed a man turn into a wolf and tear another man apart. Bri saw the blood and the gore, heard the growls and the screams, smelled the unfortunate scent of death. It *had* happened, and she needed answers.

Bri thought about getting in her newish Camaro and heading over to the Howlers MC compound to find Rebel and get those answers, but she didn't. After what she saw in that alley and on the news, she knew he had a lot to deal with. He didn't need her needling him with questions.

Instead, she curled up on her couch in her two-bedroom townhouse, with a cup of hot peppermint tea and her favorite shifter romance. Okay, it wasn't her favorite, because picking a favorite sounded like torture to Bri, but it was *one* of her favorites.

The way the author wrote about the shifters was hilarious. She leaned into the typical animal clichés. All the male lions were particular about their manes. The she-wolves were strong and aggressive when provoked, and the wild dogs loved chocolate, but it had an adverse effect on them. The author made you wish you lived in that world. She made you love the dangerous shifters, even though they could rip your throat out. Bri needed that.

As she read about the male wolf, who just happened to be a biker, finding his mate, and helping her come into her own power, her thoughts drifted back to Rebel.

Bri's brain still wouldn't let her even approach thinking about the scene in the alley. Instead, it brought her back to the day they met and how sweet he was to her when he saved her from choking on a gummi bear. That was the day he dubbed her *Ruby*. He said it was because of the pretty red color of her cheeks when she blushed. When he said those words, her heart skipped a beat.

Then she thought about the day he stopped by with coffee *and* tea for her. He had been so nervous about getting it right. For being a rough, badass biker, he was awfully cute when insecure. He didn't realize that she would have drunk anything he brought her just to make him feel better. Rebel asked her out that day. She'd said yes, of course, but they had yet to have their date.

And the kiss... *Oh, that kiss!* When he showed up at the library to ask if the women and children could hang there, she immediately agreed. She wouldn't be the reason a group of women and children he cared about were unsafe. His immediate response had been to kiss her.

It was the single most perfect kiss she had ever had. It wasn't a deep one. There was no tongue or teeth involved, just a simple press of lips against lips, but it lit up her body. Her blood heated and her heart raced from the contact. Every time she thought about it, she wanted to do it again, wanted to feel his mouth on hers, wanted to feel that sizzle that ran through her body.

Rebel was sexy with that blond hair and beard on top of that fit body, but he was also sweet and kind. He was protective of the people he loved. He was smart and giving. As crazy as it sounded, Ruby knew he would never harm her. She was beginning to think he was everything she had ever asked for… and more. She didn't remember asking for a man who grew fur, but hey, everyone had their quirks.

Rebel

Sitting on his bike outside the clubhouse, Rebel was rocked by the reality of what had happened that day. It was hard to wrap his head around it all. On top of him killing his uncle in front of the man's children, his club family had literally had to fight for their lives. The war that had been brewing between them and the Hell's Dogs MC had finally come to fruition.

In a field outside of town, hundreds of bikers and their allies fought to the death. When members of your family are killed or kidnapped and your businesses are blown up, you have little choice than to face the enemy and end things.

The Howlers and the Tiger's Claw MCs weren't the type to call the police when faced with adversaries. They were the type to handle their business and protect their family. Unfortunately, they failed too many people that day.

More than anyone else, the loss of Georgia, the beloved sister of the Howlers MC president's mate, would reverberate for years. She was the best of them. Her kind soul, gentle manner, and love for life made it impossible not to love her.

After hearing how Emerson reacted to the loss of his mate, Rebel's heart broke. How could it not? The thought of Emerson having to watch Georgia get blown up was inconceivable. He wasn't a Howler, but he was part of the HTC family. They weren't sure Emerson would ever recover.

They also lost Darlin' and Dragon's dad. He was killed while saving his son. While they all knew it was the way Griff would have wanted to go, it didn't make the loss easier to take. Rebel was glad Dragon and Darlin' both had their mates, Kisy and Trip, along with the rest of the club members and family, to help them through.

And Rock... *Fuck.* He and Lace may have been divorced for years, but they didn't end things because Rock didn't love the woman. Once upon a time, Rock was head over heels in love with the girl. He jumped into their relationship with both feet, married the girl as soon as she'd let him, and knocked her up. He thrived in fatherhood. Motherhood didn't have the same effect on Lace. She fell into addiction, and the situation deteriorated until Rock had no choice but to end things with her and take full custody of their two children. He never stopped loving Lace, but he was a father first. She was shot before the major battle, and the drugs and alcohol in her system didn't allow her shifter genes to heal her like they normally would. He had to say goodbye, and Rebel knew that brought Rock to his knees.

And that was just the tip of the iceberg for the injuries and deaths they experienced. The Tiger's Claw MC, the ally female club to the Howlers, had lost three members. With the losses of others who had fought alongside the Howlers and the Claws, that brought the number of dead to eight and the injured to double digits. The effect would linger. The enemy was gone, but that didn't mean they weren't still hurting.

Starting his bike, Rebel took a deep breath. The situation at the library alone was enough to stress him the hell out. He was almost positive he scared Ruby off. Frankly, after what she had seen, he couldn't blame her if she ran from him. Seeing him murder someone after turning into a predatory animal wasn't something a person usually considered a turn-on. At the same time, he didn't really regret it. His uncle was a piece of shit who deserved what he got.

Life was fucking complicated.

Breathing out slowly, he pulled out of the parking lot and headed for home. As much as he would have liked to track down Ruby and explain everything, it was more important for him to check on his cousins and make sure they were okay after watching him tear their father to pieces. Even though his cousins were grown, he had made a commitment to them, and he planned to honor that. It would take a lot to make up for killing their father.

He knew one thing for sure. He'd never qualify for cousin of the fucking year.

T.S. Tappin

Chapter Two

The Next Day... Bri

Sitting down at the dining table in her high school best friend's kitchen, Bri took a sip of the spicy mango margarita Liz had just handed her. More than a decade of friendship had Liz recognizing Bri's need to talk as soon as she stepped through the door.

Liz had told her to get comfortable and went to make the margaritas. Bri knew she was curious about what was on her mind, but they were waiting for Allie to arrive.

Allie was Bri's friend from her pole dancing classes, which she decided to take for exercise but also to feel sexy and show off the side of herself she was forced to tame for her career. Outside of her workday, there was no reason she couldn't embrace her sensual side. They had sparked a friendship after class when a group of them went to have lunch and had spent the lunch talking and laughing. The friendship just came easily to them.

After a particularly bad day, Bri had needed a download day. She invited Liz to come to town for the night. While they were having drinks and airing out all the crap they had been dealing with, Allie showed up at Bri's townhouse with the stuff for margaritas. Since then, the three of them made it a point to meet up once a month and have a margarita download day.

This time, it was being held at Liz's cute, little, light blue house about an hour from Warden's Pass, in Bri's hometown. The outside was whimsical, without being over the top. She decorated her house and yard with various stone and glass structures. The light from the sun, or even the porch light, filtered through the glass and sparkled, creating a magical world where you fully expected a fairy to open the front door.

After her third sip of her margarita, Liz's front door swung open, and Allie stormed into the room. Allie was a force of nature who stormed into every room, demanding the room's attention, and radiating love, light, and did so with absolutely no filter. She could be sweet and supportive but could also throw hands and cut you with her words if you deserved it. That dynamite personality mixed with her dark brown hair and eyes, beautiful smile, and curves made her the center of attention at all times, whether or not she wanted to be.

Liz was quieter, but she also had a way with words that would make you regret crossing her. Her effect on the room was softer, but no less potent. She was the more levelheaded of Bri's friends, but she was also the queen of pushing Bri to step outside of her box, *and* the reason Bri even gave pole dancing a shot.

"Okay. Okay. I'm here!" Allie plopped down in the chair across the table from Bri and smiled. "Girl… we have some shit to tell her."

Liz set a margarita in front of Allie before she took a seat and a sip of her own drink. Pulling her blond hair back and securing it with a clip, Liz's blue-green gaze shifted back and forth between the two of them. "I can see in Bri's eyes that she is shooketh. I noticed it when she walked in. So, spill, both of you."

Bri didn't even know where to start, so she started at the beginning. "Well… like a week ago I was at the library, reading that book you insisted I read." Looking over at Liz, Bri noticed the smile grow on her pretty face. "Yeah, you were right. I loved it. Anyway, I was reading and heard the cat, Bleu, that keeps getting into the library make a noise. Then I looked up, and there was a man reaching up to pet her. When I tell you he was hot, I mean he was *hot*. My brain instantly put him in a pink hand towel, and I choked on a gummi bear. Because he's *perfect,* he saved me. Then, a couple days later… I still can't work it out in my head. He brought me coffee, tea, and gummi bears and asked me out."

Allie and Liz were staring at her with goofy grins on their faces.

"He's tall, has longer blond hair, golden green eyes, and a full beard. He's a member of a motorcycle club. He loves to read and is so damn sweet."

That's when Allie started laughing. "A Howler? You're dating a Howler?"

"What's a Howler?" Liz asked.

"I'm not dating him… Okay, yes, we're supposed to go on a date, but—"

"No buts," Allie interrupted. "That's dating, and I'm here for it! Which one?"

"Excuse me." Liz waved a hand in front of their faces. "What is a Howler?"

"Howlers MC are based in Warden's Pass," Allie told her. "They are a motorcycle club of eye candy perfection." She waggled her eyebrows at Bri. "Which one did you snag?"

Bri took another sip of her margarita and then a deep breath before she replied, "Rebel."

Allie shook her head, but she looked to be in awe. "Of course. If there was one of them who liked books and was sweet and thoughtful, Bri would be the one to find him. Nice, Bish. Nice." Then she held her fist out to Bri across the table, to which Bri immediately hit it with her own.

"Okay. Hold up. I need to know more," Liz said. "So, he's a biker who reads, is sweet and thoughtful, wanted to pet Bleu, and saved you from choking on a gummi bear?" She narrowed her eyes on Bri. "What's wrong with him? No one is *that* perfect."

"I haven't talked to him except the few times he came into the library."

Allie took a drink before she blurted, "Can we just talk about the fact that these are the men who can change into animals? Did you see that on the news?" She looked over at Liz, whose eyes went wide.

"Yes!" Liz's gaze shifted back to Bri. "Is he one of them?"

Bri nodded. "A wolf."

"Holy batman," Liz began, "you stumbled into a shifter biker romance."

"Isn't it fantastic?" Allie giggled and took another drink of her margarita.

Liz narrowed her eyes. "But she doesn't look happy."

Allie gazed at Bri with curious eyes. "Does it have something to do with the bombings and stuff that happened in Warden's Pass?"

Bri held up her hands to stop her friends from bombarding her with questions. After another sip of her margarita, she told them the story of everything that had happened since she met Rebel. When she was done, she let out a deep sigh. "And now I have all these questions. They are nagging me, and I don't know what to do."

Liz reached over and gave her hand a squeeze. "Sounds like he has a lot going on. Maybe you should give him a moment to breathe."

Allie nodded. "Then, when you see him again, tell him you have questions and see if he's willing to answer them."

"I like this plan," Liz said.

"I don't want to wait," she grumbled.

Her best friends laughed, and Liz uttered, "That's because your curious brain needs *all the information*. Make your list of questions… or at least add the new questions to the list I'm sure you've already started."

Bri took a large drink of her margarita as she lifted her pinky finger in the air — Their secret way of flipping each other off.

Rebel

Two days after the scene in the alley behind the library, Rebel walked into the auditorium at the high school and his eyes instantly scanned the crowd for the prettiest librarian he had ever met. Hell… she was the most beautiful woman he'd ever met, but he didn't see her.

Disappointment filled him as he took a seat at the end of the roped-off section of the second row. The Howlers and Claws seats were sectioned off with caution tape, like they were diseased or dangerous. If they were actually a danger, did the town really think caution tape would stop them? Rebel rolled his eyes and yanked the tape down. That wouldn't help their cause.

His brothers and the Claws filed in and took seats, except for the ten who would be on stage. Crush decided on Pinky, Ginger, Shortcake, and Kitty to join her. It made sense. Just like the Howlers had Skull, Top, Rex, and Siren join Axle on stage, Crush chose the most notable members who already had a presence and a good reputation in the community.

As he waited for the rest of the townspeople to enter the room and take their seats, Rebel's thoughts once again turned to Ruby. After what she saw him do in the alley of the library, he hoped she wasn't afraid of him. He didn't regret it, but he didn't want her to think the worst of him.

His wolf snarled at him. Yeah, his wolf was pissed that he might have pushed away their woman, but it wasn't like Rebel wouldn't do whatever he needed to do to fix it.

"Why the frown?"

Rebel jolted at the sound of her voice. He turned his head to the right, and there she was, sitting next to him, giving him a sweet smile. Her beautiful blond hair was half-pulled back in a simple braid, and she had on simple make-up that allowed her beauty to shine through but also accentuated her gold-flecked blue eyes.

"You're here." He cringed as soon as the words left his mouth. *No shit, Sherlock!*

Ruby giggled. "I am. Figured I ought to get to know more about the man who is going to take me out for tea."

He bit the inside of his lip to stop the grin that threatened to appear, not wanting to look more like an idiot. "So, you aren't planning to lose my number?"

"Considering you have yet to give it to me…"

"Oh, shit!" He took out his phone and asked, "What's your number?"

She rattled it off, and he called her. When her phone rang, she pointedly added his number to her contact list and showed him.

"Now, to answer your question… No way."

Rebel let the grin grow as Ruby's face turned the lovely shade of red that made his cock twitch. "That makes me happy." He reached over and took her hand in his, lacing their fingers together. "Just so you know, we aren't a danger to you or anyone else in this town. You'll always be safe with me."

She gave his hand a squeeze and replied, "I know."

Her acceptance of that made his wolf let out a low howl of approval, and Rebel wanted to do the same. There was so much more he wanted to say, but the mayor was approaching the microphone in the middle of the stage. Instead of saying the words in his throat, he turned his head and leaned toward her. He pressed a kiss to her temple and stayed close to her as they listened to the town hall meeting. The content sigh that slid from her lips had him doing a mental happy dance.

Bri

The Howlers and the Tiger's Claw MC spent two hours taking questions from the audience. Axle was more patient than she would have been as the townsfolk asked everything from how they shift to whether they knew anything about aliens. The point was to prove to them that the shifters weren't a threat, as if they hadn't already proved that from their decades of service to the community. Bri had spent most of the meeting stopping herself from rolling her eyes at the questions.

Once the last question was answered, Axle motioned to where the other members were sitting. Rebel kissed her temple again, and whispered, "Duty calls. Be right back."

Then Axle held the microphone to his face and uttered, "We will now show you. Keep in mind that while we're in our animal forms, we are still us. We still think as humans, for the most part. We recognize people we know and remember what happens while we are in animal form. If anyone is interested in touching our animals, we ask that you form a line and remain respectful. While we're willing to do this to make you comfortable, we're not a circus show."

As he put the microphone back on the stand, half of the town began to line up at the edge of the stage, while the other half either remained in their seats or left the building. Axle motioned toward a large black man, and the man joined Axle and the others on the stage.

Bri watched as two women and three men were lined up at the edge of the stage and shifted into a tiger, a mountain lion, a wolf, a lion, and a brown bear. After a collective gasp from the crowd, the rest of the members, the mayor, and Hawkin congregated on the stage as the townsfolk walked up the steps and crossed the stage. The reason for their presence was obvious — cross a line, and there would be consequences.

Ruby's eyes rarely left Rebel. He was so handsome with his medium blond hair pulled back in a man bun and his thick reddish beard. She loved it was long enough to get a grip on, but also trimmed and neat.

He must have felt her eyes on him because he looked over at her, smiled, and winked. She felt her cheeks heat, but she couldn't pull together enough embarrassment to care. She liked the way he looked at her.

Most of the townsfolk didn't touch the shifters. They just looked and seemed to be curious, and the few dozen who touched them had remained respectful.

After the last of the line crossed the stage, the shifters returned to their human forms. Axle approached the mayor, and the others started to file out of the room. Rebel jogged down the steps from the stage and returned to her side.

When he reached her side, Rebel lifted a hand and ran his knuckles along her cheek. "Fuck. I love that."

Ruby shrugged and smiled. "It's your fault."

The smile that grew on his face made her clit throb. She was surprised that her body reacted so easily to him, but she couldn't say she hated it. There was something about him that called to her in ways no man had before.

"That's blame I'm willing to claim," he said under his breath as he took her hand in his.

Rebel

With Ruby's hand in his, Rebel led her outside the high school and over to her car in the parking lot. As they walked, he noticed Rock and Mary over by Rock's bike. Rock's face was hard, and his body was tight, his movements mechanical. The expression on Mary's face was what had Rebel worried. There was a fear in her hazel eyes that had his gut clenching.

"That looks serious," Ruby softly commented from his side.

He swung his gaze around to look at her. "Yeah. That's my brother, Rock. Club brother. Uh... the mother of his children died the day before yesterday. The woman with him is his new woman. Well, not new... They've been together for like a year or something. I imagine he's struggling with how to deal with all of it. It's got to be hard for both of them."

Ruby's brow creased and her eyes softened with the compassion she was obviously feeling for his brother. Without allowing himself to question it, he leaned toward her and pressed his lips to hers. The kiss wasn't deep or wet. There wasn't a deep, urgent passion, but he meant it all the same.

When he pulled back, Ruby looked at him with amusement and a hint of lust in her pretty blue eyes with the gold flecks sprinkled throughout. "Not that I'm complaining, but what was that for?"

"Someday, you won't have to question it. This time, I'll fill you in." He pressed his forehead to hers. "You showed care for my brother. That means something to me." It meant everything that she cared for the important people in his life, even minutely.

Her smile turned playful. "So, is that all I have to do?"

She was quickly taking over his heart, piece by piece, and she had no idea. Rebel closed his eyes as he pulled her into his arms and held her tight. He would gladly hand the thing right over to her. All it would take is for her to ask.

Niles

Standing in between two large vehicles in the parking lot of the high school, Niles Flynn watched as his ex-bitch wrapped herself around that Howler asshole on the back of his bike. If it wasn't for those fuckers, his kids and his wife would still be at home where they belonged.

Niles knew it was wrong to put his hands on her, but she knew better than to talk to other men, and she still did it. She tried to tell him it was just that a guy approached her at the gas station, and she had done nothing wrong, but he didn't trust the lying bitch. He taught her that lesson, or at least he thought he had, until she disappeared on him.

When he found her at her friend's house, he was pissed. She knew she wasn't supposed to hang out with that bitch. The bitch's husband was always in their business. Niles didn't like that shit. He planned on coming back for her after she calmed down.

Unfortunately, the day he showed up to get her, he found her with those fucking bikers, and they were taking her somewhere with a moving truck. He tried to follow them, but an hour into the drive, he was ambushed by two people he'd never seen before and knocked out. He woke up naked in his sister's car, parked in front of a church, with the words *child abuser* written on his forehead in permanent marker, and the police were tapping on the window. That was not a fun night in jail.

He had never abused the children, like the bitch and her new bodyguards accused him of doing. Whooping their asses when they needed it wasn't abuse in his book. If they just followed the rules and stayed out of adult business, everything would have been fine.

In court, they wouldn't let him address her. They just gave the bitch everything she wanted — a divorce, sole custody of his kids, and a no-contact order for all three of them.

Seeing her looking even better than she did the day he met her pissed Niles right the hell off. How dare she give that fucker a better version of her than she gave her fucking husband? There was no way in hell he was going to stand by while she rode off into the sunset with some biker trash *or* let that man raise his kids.

With a plan forming in his head and his jaws clenched tight, Niles turned and headed for his mom's car.

T.S. Tappin

Chapter Three

Rebel

After agreeing to pick Ruby up the next day for their brunch date, the two of them said their goodbyes and headed their separate ways. Rebel wanted to walk her to her car, but she had refused, letting him know she was a big girl and would be fine. He still didn't like it, but he didn't push her on it.

After mounting his bike, Rebel headed back to the compound for the memorial. As much as he wanted to honor their dead and spend a few moments with his dad before he left town, Rebel wasn't looking forward to the ceremony. The individual loss of any of their family members would have been enough to make it a heart wrenching experience, but there were several losses. On top of that, he was dealing with his own guilt and grief that he didn't fully understand.

His uncle was unsavable. He had been too far gone into his world of violence and addiction to come back, but part of Rebel wished he would have found another way to handle the situation.

When his uncle mentioned Rebel's deceased brother, Patrick, something in Rebel's brain short-circuited, and his wolf took over. Normally, he was still in control when he was shifted, but that day he had been too overwhelmed with his own anger and the need to protect the twins to hold back.

If he was being completely honest with himself, it wasn't killing his uncle that he felt guilty for. A part of him felt like he had avenged his brother's death, as horrible as he knew that logic to be. No, his actual guilt was rooted in the fact that he had done it in front of his cousins.

Ross and Ryker had been through a hell that he didn't even know all the details to, and it was all because of their father. Even though he had put them through so much heartache and trouble, he was still their father, and they would always care about him. It wasn't their fault they were born to that man, and he didn't blame them for loving their father. Rebel wouldn't have blamed the twins if they hated him for taking their father away. They were insistent that they didn't, but he wondered if Ross and Ryker would come to have hard feelings about what he did someday in the future.

All Rebel could do was be there for them and try to provide them with the stability they had never received from their father. Their mother had taken off when they were just boys, unable to deal with their father's addictions. When she abandoned them, the parent they were left with had barely made sure there was bread and lunch meat in the house.

Rebel couldn't count how many times his father had picked the twins up and brought them home with him. A few times, the twins had been at their house for weeks before his uncle even realized they were gone.

His father had talked to a lawyer about suing for custody of the twins, but Ross and Ryker had insisted they wanted to live with their father. Rebel had suspected it was to make sure he was eating and looked after when he went on a bender.

That suspicion was confirmed by the fact that they basically submitted to servitude to a drug lord in order to pay their father's debts and to keep him safe.

The anger that boiled up inside of Rebel at the memory of finding them in that warehouse made him wish he could bring his uncle back to life only to kill him again.

He just wished he could have avoided hurting his cousins in the process.

After the memorial, Rebel shook off the thoughts as he climbed on his bike outside the clubhouse and headed for his house. He had offered to let the twins stay home during the memorial, but they had insisted on being there for Rebel and his club family. They had driven over in a truck Rebel had bought them and were already heading home.

What Rebel really wanted to do was ride over to Ruby's and just spend time in her company. Something about her made him feel like he wasn't a murderer and an asshole. She made him feel like a good man.

He may have taken the life of his uncle for a good reason, but that didn't erase the fact that he murdered him in front of the man's children. Nothing could erase that.

How Ruby accepted that without being afraid of him, he didn't know. The fact that she didn't balk at shifters being real was mind-boggling to him. Oh, he knew she had questions. He could practically see the wheels turning in her pretty head when she looked at him, but she didn't run. She wasn't afraid of him, and that was a damn miracle.

Halting at a stop sign, Rebel gazed ahead. If he continued on a couple blocks and took a right, he could stop at Ruby's. The urge to go to her was strong. He didn't examine whether it was right to have their resident hacker, Keys, get him her address long before she gave it to him. It was wrong, but it was done.

With a deep sigh, he took a right and headed for his house. His cousins were waiting for him, and he could wait half of a day to see her again.

Reginald

Being on the town council, Reginald Smith and his wife, Gladys, wanted what was best for Warden's Pass. In his opinion, the Howlers never should have been allowed to run businesses in their town. If the business licenses weren't approved, the trash would have had to find somewhere else to operate.

Unfortunately, Joker Weber had connections and fast-tracked every document he ever had to file for. At the time, Reginald didn't have enough power to do anything about it.

"We need to do something," Jeffrey White huffed as he took his seat in the back room of the hardware store owned by Charles and Daniel Williams.

Jeffrey and Sharon White were farmers who owned a large section of land on the edge of the town line. They were in their seventies, and rumor had it that Sharon once messed around with Joker before he had his boys.

Sharon's sister, Dorothy Jones, a seamstress, had followed those men around with her sister for years, trying her best to nab one. When it was clear it was never going to happen, she stopped helping them with their patches and started acting like they were the scum of the earth.

Reginald didn't much care what her motivations were for being at the meeting, as long as she was on their side. They needed numbers, not quality members.

Elsie and Elfie Kirsh were there for reasons well known to the rest of the members. It was rumors or whispered gossip. Their son, Ernie, was beating his wife, and the Howlers helped get her to a safe place. In the process, Ernie ended up with a broken arm, three broken fingers, and a face that was more black and blue than it was not. Reginald couldn't say he cared that they helped the wife, but Ernie's condition when they found him was more than Reginald thought he deserved.

"I agree," Charles said. It wasn't a secret that Charles had been dating Minx from the Tiger's Claw MC. They had been seen around town together for a few months. Charles was spotted at the jewelry store, scoping out wedding rings, but Minx ended things the next day.

His brother, Daniel, had a thing for Nova, also a member of the Tiger's Claw MC, but Nova had never let him have a shot.

Daniel shook his head and sighed. "They are good customers, Chuck."

"So it's okay that they are monsters?"

"I won't sit here and pretend to know anything about that animal stuff, but I don't feel right calling them monsters when they've never done anything to warrant that," Daniel insisted.

"They tortured my son," Elfie shouted, his face beet red with anger.

Daniel looked over at the man and replied, "Your son *tortured* his wife and got what he deserved."

When Elfie opened his mouth to argue, Reginald stepped forward into the middle of the circle of chairs and said, "The fact of the matter is they are criminals. We now find out that they can *somehow* turn into animals, capable of killing anyone they choose. How are we supposed to feel safe?"

Sharon added, "And the children! I heard parents talking about how the librarian was holding hands with one of them! The library isn't even safe for our babies anymore!"

"We need to band together and make it uncomfortable for them to be here. Make them move on to another place, somewhere far away from Warden's Pass."

The owner of the auto parts store, Nicholas Brown, shook his head. "You're asking me to put my business at risk, for a *possibility*."

"Do you not care about the children?" Sharon looked at him like he grew a second head.

Reginald couldn't stand the sound of the woman's voice, but she was helping his cause, so he would let her rant and rave in that ear-splitting tone.

Nicholas sighed. "The only thing I've ever seen when it comes to children and the Howlers is the Howlers *and the Tiger's Claw MCs* making sure the children of Warden's Pass aren't mistreated."

"You either keep the Howlers business, or you keep the business of the citizens of Warden's Pass," Reginald stated. "You choose."

Rock

After the memorial, Rock drove Mia and Logan over to Brute's parents' house. Since he was a kid, they were the only parental figures he could count on. As far as his kids were concerned, they were the only grandparents they had.

Mama Nia was the woman who saw the anger and distrust inside of Rock as a teenager and did what was needed to get him on a better track. She made sure he had food, shelter, and a safe place to exist, and never asked him to be anything other than himself.

Pops, Brute's dad, was the one who taught Rock about engines and also how to treat women. He talked about the importance of protecting the people who weren't in a position to protect themselves, but he made sure to make it clear that women were stronger in every way that mattered. Pops was basically the reason for Rock's drive to help the weakened find their strength again and the mistreated to find their justice.

Mama Nia and Pops loved Mia and Logan just like they did the rest of their grandkids. Rock and his children were in all the family photos and invited to the family reunions. It didn't matter one lick to them that he and his children were white, just like it didn't make a bit of difference to Rock that they were black. Family was family, especially when you chose them.

"Wes," Mama Nia said as she opened her front door. The warm smile she gave him right before she wrapped her arms around him dulled the ache in his heart. She was what he needed at that moment. Her guidance and unconditional love would help him navigate the heart-wrenching situation he found himself in. "Let me greet my babies, then you and I are going to talk about that look of despair I see in your eyes."

She pulled away from him and gave his kids attention, while Rock moved on to give Pops a handshake and a hug.

"Boy, I'm sorry to hear about Lace."

Rock gave a nod and backed up, clearing his throat. "We knew it was coming," he mumbled as he watched Mama Nia point the kids toward the kitchen, where there was no doubt a mountain of baked goods waiting for them.

"Wes, don't you even begin to tell me not to spoil those babies." She waved a finger in his face. "They have had enough heartache to kill the baddest badass, and I will heal them with baked love if I want to."

Rock couldn't stop the smile from growing on his face. "Mama Nia, I would never stop that, and you know it."

Pops chuckled. "That's only because he's scared you'll come after him with a wooden spoon."

They all knew that was bullshit. Rock and her biological children were scared of her, but it wasn't because of her spoons. It was because the thought of disappointing her would hurt them more than any ass-whooping could.

"Now, I know you're going through some hard stuff, Wes, but why do you look so conflicted?" Mama Nia crossed her arms over her chest and stared him down, daring him to try to not answer her question.

"Lace… uh… you remember me telling you about Mary? Well…"

43

Mama Nia nodded. "She told you to go after that woman and seal the deal, didn't she?"

Rock nodded. "And... I dunno. I feel like that would be... unfair to Mary, somehow."

Pops shook his head as Mama Nia replied, "You're thinking Mary will think you are only doing it because Lace told you to? Boy, if you haven't made it clear to that woman you want her yet, that's no one's fault but your own. Now, I get that you didn't want to jump into anything, and I even understood that you didn't want to disrespect Lace by bringing Mary into your world. I knew you felt like that would be rubbing it in her face. I am not telling you to hitch your ride to Mary just because Lace told you to, but we all know you've been in love with Mary for a long damn time, now. It's time to shit or get off the pot, son."

Rock sighed. She wasn't wrong, but he worried about the timing. "But Mia and Logan—"

"Want their dad to be happy," Mama Nia cut in and finished for him. "They've lived through years of seeing their dad unhappy and watching the most important woman in their life teach them how *not* to live. It's time they saw a smile on your face that actually reached your eyes. It's time they saw a mother who put her kids first and would make sure your kids felt that same kind of love. Everything you've told us about Mary tells me she is *that* mother."

Rock nodded. "She is." Mary would walk through fire and move mountains to prove her love for her children.

He had no doubt that she would do the same for Mia and Logan.

"Great. Now, I expect her over for dinner soon." Mama Nia lifted up on her toes and kissed his cheek. "Pops will see you out. I have grandbabies to spoil."

As they watched her head for the kitchen, Pops patted Rock on the back. "You know you have to claim that woman and bring her over for dinner within a couple weeks or Mama Nia will just invite her herself, right?"

Rock chuckled and nodded. "Yes, I know."

"Good." Pops cleared his throat. "The kids will be fine. You aren't dealing with this alone, Wes. I think Mary being in their lives will only help them through this. It would help if you let her in to help you through it, too."

Sighing, Rock turned and walked to the front door. "I get it, Pops." Then, with a wave of his hand over his shoulder, he opened the door and headed for his truck.

He had to lay everything out for Mary and hope that she still wanted to be around. She knew a bit about Lace, but he had yet to tell her what happened in Lace's final moments. He worried she would think he was finally letting her in just because Lace told him to or that he was only accepting her as his just because Lace was gone. It wasn't the truth, but love and grief were complicated, confusing bastards.

Mary

After dropping Mia and Logan off to his parents' house, Rock had switched out his truck for his motorcycle at the clubhouse. He had Mary climb on behind him and took them back to his house. It was the first time Mary would get a glimpse into his personal space. Sure, she had seen his room at the compound, but there was something more intimate about Rock allowing her to see his home, the space he shared with his children.

He told her they needed to have a long, serious talk, but she wasn't worried about whatever it was he wanted to discuss. It didn't matter what he said to her. She knew who he was, and she had no intentions of walking away from him. Mary was in it for the real deal, not the easy shit or rainbows and unicorns. She would hold his hand and face his demons at his side, the same way he did for her.

Every struggle she'd had in the several months since her move, she leaned on him to help her navigate through it. He was good about not taking over and fixing everything, but he also didn't leave her out on a ledge without a hand to grab.

It was her turn to be the hand to grab, and there was no way she was falling down on the job.

Not that it was hard to do. He was such a good man, which made emotionally supporting him easy to do. Add in the fact that Rock had dark hair the right length for her to get a grip on while he did fantastic things with

Rebel's Fairytale

his tongue between her legs, and it became even easier.

And those eyes of his… *Damn.* They were deep set and brown, the kind of brown that drew you in. Soulful and intense, they were eyes that saw right through your shields to the person you were inside. They were also compassionate and kind.

Below them was the mouth she was in love with. Sweet words and sensual promises fell from those lips. Rock's tongue was talented in *so very many* ways. And his mouth was surrounded by scruff that just added to the appeal and the experience when he was using that mouth on her body.

If you dropped below his neck, you ran into a body that made you want to lick and nibble on every inch, follow his tattoos and muscles with your tongue, see how many different ways you could get him to curse in the deep, rough voice of his.

Yeah, supporting this wonderful man was not a hardship for her, neither was holding onto him on the back of his bike.

Once they reached his house, she wasn't at all surprised to find that it was a white, two-story house with a wide, covered front porch and a white picket fence out front. Rock was all about being a dad, a family man, and his house was the house of the *ultimate* family man.

She would almost bet money that he had a shed full of the best engine-powered toys and a jungle gym in the backyard. Hell, it wouldn't surprise her in the least if there was a treehouse back there, too.

He rode his bike into the open garage and cut the engine. She glanced to their left as she climbed off and almost giggled when she caught a glimpse of a go-cart lined up next to a dirt bike behind a few boxes. Yup, he had all the fun stuff a family man would have for the children who were the center of his world.

"What's that smile for?" he asked as he got off his bike and took her hand.

"Oh… just thinking about how you are the ultimate *dad*."

Rock looked at her and cocked a dark brown eyebrow. "What is the ultimate dad?"

"You have a go-cart."

"I do." He clearly didn't understand her meaning, and she wasn't sure she wanted to fill him in.

As he opened the door to his house, she patted him on the chest and cuddled up to his side. "Just know it's a turn-on."

He led her inside and gave her a crooked smile. "Then, thank you."

"You're welcome."

He gave her a peck on the lips before he made his way over to the refrigerator and grabbed a couple bottles of beer. He opened them both and handed her one.

"So, it can't be too heavy of a talk if you're handing out beer instead of whiskey," she commented as she took the offered beer and slid onto a stool at the island in his kitchen.

The room was nothing fancy. It had light wood cabinets and white walls, and the tile was a mix between light gray and white. It was obvious that Rock liked things clean, but home decor was the least of his concerns.

Rock took a drink of his beer and set it on the island before he crossed his arms over his chest and sighed heavily. "No, it's heavy. It's a lot, but... I just have to say it."

Mary gave a nod. "Lay it on me, Wes." She switched to his given name in recognition of the fact that the man she loved was about to lay his heart open.

"You know everything I went through with Lace over the past few years... and what my kids have been through."

Mary nodded and kept quiet, letting him get it out.

"Now that she's gone, I'm... almost relieved. I hate that she's gone because I cared about her and my kids loved her, but... I feel like a jerk for being relieved."

Mary felt for him. It was difficult to have a spouse with addiction issues. Having kids with that spouse and having to help them grieve while you also grieved was overwhelming. Having to witness someone slowly killing themselves and knowing there's nothing you can do to stop it would make anyone feel a bit relieved when it was over. She didn't take that to mean he was heartless or cold. It just meant that he had been suffering with Lace and was grateful they weren't in that seemingly endless cycle.

"Wes," Mary began softly, "it's okay to feel what you're feeling."

"I still love her. I probably always will. And I hate her for not putting our kids first, for not putting me first, but I'm sad that my kids will grow up without her." He huffed out a breath. "I sound like an idiot."

Mary slid off her stool and made her way around the island to his side. She cupped his face in her hands and forced him to look at her. "You are *not* an idiot, and I don't appreciate you talking about my man that way."

A sexy smirk appeared on his face. "Your man?"

"Well, aren't ya?"

"That depends on whether or not you still want me when I'm done telling you everything I have to tell you."

Mary shrugged and dropped her hands to her sides. "Then it's settled because I'm not walking away *regardless* of what you tell me. And want you? Wes… there hasn't been a day since I met you that I didn't want you."

He pressed his lips to hers and gripped her hips, pulling her against him. When he broke the kiss, he said against her lips, "Maybe we should shelf the conversation and do something else."

"No." She extracted herself from his hold. "Let it out, so I can prove that I'm in this. Then you can strip me down and have your wicked way with me."

The lust that flashed in his eyes had her backing her way around the island.

"I told you about the gods and the war."

"Yes," she answered as she took another step back.

"I told you about Ol' Ladies and what that title means to my club." He started around the island in her direction.

"Yes." Two steps back.

"In her last moments, Lace told me to embrace our relationship and allow myself and our kids to have you."

"Okay." Mary was unsure where he was going with his statements, but she knew what his intentions were when he reached her, so she took another step back.

"I want to honor her last wishes, but not just because they are her last wishes."

It all clicked into place. Her heart clenched at the thought that he would think she wouldn't understand his intentions. She stopped in her tracks and smiled at him. "Wes, I know you love me. I know you love Lace. And I know that you can do both at the same time. You can honor Lace's wishes and *also* put your all into our relationship because *you want to*. Is that what you're trying to say?"

Rock visibly swallowed hard and nodded. "And I want you as my Ol' Lady."

Mary's smile shifted to a grin. "About damn time."

And that was how she ended up naked on Rock's kitchen floor.

T.S. Tappin

Chapter Four

Rebel

When Rebel's alarm went off, he wasn't surprised by the fact that he was already wide awake. It was the day he would take Ruby out for tea. Their first date. He couldn't fucking wait. His wolf and his gut were telling him she was his mate, his happily ever after, and he wanted to get on with it.

With more spring in his step than was probably appropriate the day after a family memorial, Rebel threw the covers aside and headed for the bathroom. He took a quick shower, toweled off, and brushed his hair back, making sure he looked appropriate for a date with a respectable woman. He considered pulling it back in his usual man bun, but he decided that might be too casual of a look.

Telling himself he was a grown ass man and not a pimple-faced teenager, he forced himself to leave his bathroom and get dressed. He pulled on a pair of jeans and a dark gray Henley. After putting on his boots, he slipped on his cut and headed for the door. Before the teenager in him decided to rethink his outfit, he stormed outside and to his bike.

After mounting his bike and starting her up, he rode over to Ruby's townhouse a handful of blocks from the library and parked at the curb. He got off the bike and took a couple deep breaths to steel himself.

Relax! Fuck, Rebel! She's just a woman… a woman who could make and break his happiness… and his future. Who was he kidding? She was more than just a woman. She was his mate. He knew it. His wolf knew it. Now, Rebel just had to do what was necessary to get her to realize it.

You've got this. Now, don't fuck it up.

With one last deep breath, Rebel made his way up her front walk and onto her little porch. In front of the door, she had a tan mat that had writing on it. He tilted his head to the side in order to be able to read it and read, *You look really silly doing that with your head…* Chuckling, he looked around her porch and noticed she was one who liked to decorate for the seasons, or at least for fall. To the right of the door, she had a collection of small pumpkins and gourds. On the left side were a few pots of what looked like mums on a multi-level plant stand. Situated in front of the pots were pumpkins — one large pumpkin and two small ones.

Pressing her doorbell, he began to feel a little more comfortable and less stressed. Rebel knew he had been freaking out a little too much. She was laid-back and wasn't at all judgmental. It was his desire to keep her that had him tied in knots. He just needed to breathe and remind himself that everything would be okay.

After a few moments, the door flew open, and a breathless goddess stood just inside the doorframe. Her hair was done, and she was dressed, but there was something *undone* about her appearance. It got his wolf's attention, causing it to begin to growl in low tones and shoot the word *Mine* into Rebel's brain.

"Come on in. I'm almost ready." She took a calming breath and gave him a sweet smile.

He stepped inside and shut the door behind him.

"Be right out." Then, she was gone, heading up a set of stairs along the wall to the left of the door.

As visions of following her up those stairs filled his brain, and Rebel began to lecture himself about cooling it. To give himself something else to think about, he strolled around her living room. She had a simple, dark blue couch and a matching chair at an angle at the other end. In front of the couch sat an old chest with a wooden tray on top that she seemed to use as a table. In the center of it was a large candle surrounded by fake fall leaves.

Across from the couch was a flat screen television mounted on the wall, flanked by two floor-to-ceiling bookcases on each side and two waist-high bookcases under it. All of them were jam-packed with books. Rebel could picture them cuddled up on that couch, wrapped up in blankets and each other, with books in their hands. Honestly, it was how he wanted to spend every evening for the rest of his life.

On the far end of the room, in a corner, he saw the most comfortable looking chair, in the same blue as her couch. It was large and slouchy, no hard edges, with an oversized ottoman pushed up to it. Next to it was a small table with a lamp, a couple books, and a notepad. It was obvious by the way things were piled next to it that she spent most of her time in that chair. Curious as to the books she was reading, he approached and caught a glimpse of his name at the top of the notepad. Unable to resist, Rebel glanced at the notepad.

Questions to ask Rebel
Does it hurt?
How long can you stay shifted?
How often can you shift?
What happens to your clothes?
…

Rebel grinned as he read the questions. The list was neat and organized, but the questions were all over the place. There were sixteen items on the sheet, and he assumed it wasn't complete. His woman was a curious creature, and Rebel loved that about her.

"Okay. I'm ready," he heard Ruby say as she jogged down the stairs.

Keeping his eyes on the list, because he knew his brain would short-circuit once he got a glimpse of her, Rebel began answering her questions, "No, shifting doesn't hurt. I can stay shifted as long as I want to. I can shift whenever I want to. Nothing happens to my clothes when I shift. They're just there, and then they're not. No, we can't change people into shifters. We're born this way. The moon is interesting to look at, but it doesn't affect us any differently than it affects you. If I eat in wolf form, it's what a wolf would eat. Werewolves are the half-wolf, half-man creatures you see in movies. We shift into a full animal, so we are shifters. I don't necessarily clean my fur. It's just clean when I shift. Axle is our alpha, but we don't have to have one. The mate thing is most definitely a real thing, and we will get into that more later. No, our mate doesn't have to be a shifter. Our mate bond is about the person, not the animal, so tiger shifters can mate lion shifters, for example." He grinned and raised a brow. "Sex works the same way it works for everyone else on the planet. If my mate is human, which she is, our kids would be wolf shifters." He set the notepad down on the table. "Any other questions?"

Rebel finally looked at her, and instantly, his pants got tighter. He couldn't look away from her, and it became harder to breathe. She *literally* took his breath away.

Damn, she's beautiful.

She was wearing a pair of black slacks that were fitted in all the right places, accentuating her hips and that ass he just wanted to bite into. Her blouse was light gray and simple, but it looked like it was made to wrap around her curvy body. She paired the outfit with a black and gray scarf that looked to be made out of some type of sheer material, and a pair of light gray heels that would most certainly make her as tall as him.

She looked how he expected her to look for work, which made sense, since that was where she was going after their date, but it was probably the sexiest thing he'd ever set his eyes on.

Fuck! Pull yourself together, Rebel. Your first date!

He swallowed hard and gave a shake of his head, trying to push his lust to the back of his mind. "You look beautiful."

Ruby smiled that sweet smile she always gave him and tucked a bit of her blond hair behind her ear as the blush grew on her face. "Thank you, Rebel."

He crossed the room to where she stood and cupped her face in his palms. Running his thumbs over her reddened cheeks, he stared into her gold-flecked blue eyes. "I want to kiss you."

"What are you waiting for?"

Her breathy question sent his banked lust into overdrive, bringing it right back to the front of his mind. With a low growl, he pressed his lips to hers and moved one hand from her cheek to her hip. As he pulled her closer, his other hand slid into the hair on the back of her head, tilting it, and as she gasped, he deepened the kiss.

She wrapped one arm around him, under his cut, fisting his shirt, which made him growl. Her free hand slid into his hair, taking a grip of it the same way she had his shirt, eliciting another growl from him.

Rebel moved both hands to her lower back, forcing her body up against his. His wolf was growling his approval and urging Rebel to claim their mate, but Rebel told him to *shut the hell up*.

A whimper came from Ruby as Rebel broke the kiss and made his way across her cheek to her jawline. He nipped the skin there, before he whispered into her ear, "As much as I fucking love what we're doing right now, we should stop."

It took everything in him to step back. He didn't want to. He wanted to press her against the wall under her stairs and show her exactly how sexy he thought she was in that outfit, but there were a number of reasons why he couldn't.

Rebel didn't want to go too fast and ruin things. He was in it for keeps. That meant he couldn't treat her the way he would treat a woman he picked up at a bar. She deserved better than that. She deserved *the world*, and he intended to be the one who gave it to her.

Not to mention, if he started down that path, he wouldn't want it to end for hours, and she had to go to work. The real world couldn't wait on him to get his fill of her. If that were the case, they'd never leave the townhouse.

She cleared her throat as her arms dropped back to her sides. "Yes. You're probably right." Another throat clearing. "Tea. We were going for tea." He wasn't sure who she was trying to convince with that statement.

After taking in her mussed hair and her lust-filled eyes, Rebel's gaze drifted down to her kiss-bruised lips. Her lightly tinted lip gloss was smeared, and her lips were plumper than they had been before he kissed her. Rebel wanted to mess her up more, have her completely undone on his bed, the couch, hell, the floor.

"Rebel, if you don't stop looking at me like that, we're not getting our tea," Ruby warned with a smirk.

He grinned as he ran his hands through his hair. "I think we should probably pull ourselves together, unless you want to go to work with your hair looking like my hands had spent some time in it."

Giggling, Ruby took his hand, pulling him a few yards away and into the guest bathroom. It was through a door in the dining area of the open-plan space of the first floor.

In the bathroom, Rebel pulled out the hair tie he always kept in his cut pocket. *So much for the no man bun look.* Standing next to each other, he pretended he was just pulling his hair back, when really, he was staring at her out of the corner of his eye. He knew she was doing the same thing, sneaking glances at him, as she leaned forward a bit and began to fix her lip gloss.

Once he was done with his hair, and she started fixing her own, he crossed his arms over his chest and allowed himself to take in every one of her curves. His wolf was doing all the snarling and growling that he wanted to do at the visual.

"Rebel," she uttered in a warning.

His attention returned to her eyes in the mirror. "What?"

"You know what."

He grinned. "Can't blame a man for enjoying the scenery."

She snorted a laugh and shook her head. "Shifter or not, you're still a man."

He shifted until he was behind her and wrapped his arms around her waist. "That I am, Ruby. That I am."

After she was done fixing her hair, he followed her back into the living room, where she grabbed her glasses off a side table and slipped them on her face. That alone was enough to have Rebel's lust sparked again.

Fuck. He was in trouble.

Bri

Because she had to go to work after their date, Rebel rode his bike to the diner and Bri followed behind him in her car. The entire way, she was able to take in the sight of him straddling the machine and in complete control of its movements. And, what a sight it was. He wasn't the nervous man he was at the library when he was on his bike. He was a confident man with a bit of a bad boy and a lot of a sexy biker mixed in. To be honest, it made her wish she could just call off work and spend the day with her arms wrapped around him on the back of his bike.

Wondering what it would be like to take a ride on a motorcycle, she followed him into a parking lot behind a brick building a few blocks from the police station that held a diner, a shop that sold men's attire, and a nail salon. Bri had been to the diner before and knew she loved their pastries. She smiled as she got out of her car. *Rebel and apple fritters?* It was almost too good to be true.

"I like that smile," Rebel commented as he strolled up to her and gave her a kiss on her cheek.

"I love this place," she told him honestly.

Sliding his arm around her shoulders, he began leading her toward the back door of the diner. "Good. We have a diner at the compound, TC's Diner, but we would have no privacy if we went there, so I figured this was a better bet."

"I'm curious about the compound. You've mentioned it a few times. I've driven past it, but I've never been there."

Rebel let out a sigh, but a smile grew on his face. "You'll spend time there soon enough. For now, though, I'd like to keep you to myself."

As they crossed the parking lot, Bri thought about her list of questions he found and answered for her. She was happy to hear shifting didn't hurt him, but some of the other answers only created more questions. *How could his clothes just disappear and reappear? How did he change shape like that without any pain or discomfort? Was his gene makeup different from hers? Were they a different species?*

Rebel's Fairytale

Why did he say they would talk about mates more later? What did he mean by, 'If my mate is human, and she is,'? How did he know his mate was a human?

Her brain was running through questions as he reached to grip the handle of the door. Then, he just stopped.

She glanced up at him to find his attention fixed on her. He pressed his forehead to hers and gazed into her eyes. "Listen. I will answer all the questions about shifters I know are swirling around in that gorgeous mind of yours, but for now, can we just have a normal date and do the typical get-to-know-you stuff?"

Feeling a bit bad about focusing so much attention on the wolf side of him, Bri sighed and nodded. "Sorry. When something sparks that part of my brain, I tend to go into overdrive with the research."

He gave her a peck on the lips. "Don't apologize for being curious, Sweetie. Being around you makes me happy, and I could use some happy. Can we have just an hour where we're just a man and a woman?"

Bri reached up and caressed his stubbled cheek with her fingertips before she ran her fingers through his full, thick beard. "I think we can do that." Her inner girl was squeeing that she gave him happiness just by being near him. For a big, bad biker who could turn into a terrifying predator, he was such a sweetheart.

He gave her another peck, before he pulled the back door open and led her inside the diner. Calling out a hello to the older server behind the counter, he chose a booth in the front corner of the place.

Bri slid into one side while he slid into the opposite side of the booth. The server came right over and took their orders. She ordered a vanilla chai latte and an apple fritter. Rebel ordered a black coffee, a maple glazed donut, and a custard-filled cherry pastry. She was curious about the last item he ordered but decided to wait until it arrived to see what it was.

The server returned quickly with their drinks and left them to chat while they waited for their food.

Bri took a sip of her beverage and let the flavor and warmth flow over her. After taking a moment to appreciate it, she looked across the table at Rebel and asked, "So, what do you do for a living?"

After a sip of his coffee, he set the mug down and wrapped his hands around it. "The club owns several businesses. Like quite a few of my brothers, I work wherever it's needed on any given day, but I spend most of my time either doing maintenance on the rentals or I bartend. Sometimes, I do security. Considering our club was blown up, I'll be doing construction for a while." Rebel took another sip of his coffee. "You saw the disaster that is my blood family. Tell me about yours."

Bri wanted to ask about the club and about the story of his family, but she figured that might be too deep for a first date. "Well, my parents met when they were seniors in high school. They dated for a few years and got married. A year later, I was born. Four years after that, my brother, Brandon, arrived. My childhood was… comfortable. We didn't have everything, but we had everything we needed. My dad is a construction supervisor and has been for as long as I can remember. When my brother was old enough to start school, my mom took an admin job at the construction company my dad works for. We had a decent home and my parents drove decent vehicles. We were happy."

She sighed and sipped her latte. "I had friends who struggled, and it made me appreciate what we had. Seeing my friends worry about whether their parents could pay their bills for the month, or where their next meal was coming from, made me understand that I may not have had the best of the best, but I was lucky."

Rebel's smile was sweet. "I'm glad you had a good childhood." That smile faded. "My brother followed my uncle down the drug path and ended up overdosing when I was a teenager."

Bri's heart broke at his words. Drugs were so destructive to more than the person using them.

"When my mom found out, she had a heart attack. We rushed her to the hospital, but…" As he trailed off, he shook his head.

Bri reached across the table and took one of his hands in hers. "I'm sorry to hear that. That had to have been rough."

Rebel gave a nod. "My sister… She couldn't handle it all and took off. Dad keeps an eye on her, but she doesn't want anything to do with us, and I can't say I blame her. She's living in Colorado, working at a store that sells local goods. I hear from her around my birthday every year, but that's about it. She seems happy."

"Rebel..." She gave his hand a squeeze, unsure of what to say. She hated that his family seemed to have fallen apart at the seams.

He winked at her. "It's okay. Really. I always wanted to have a family that was supportive and *there* for everything. That's why I joined the Howlers. They gave my dad a place to belong, since his childhood wasn't much better. I knew how the club operated and the way they rallied around their members. I saw it, firsthand, when Mom and Patrick died. So, as soon as I was old enough, I prospected."

"Prospected? I think I know what that means, but will you explain that?"

He nodded. "It's basically like the period of time where you're proving yourself to the club, and they are evaluating whether you're a good fit. You do all the shit jobs and anything else they order you to do, with the intention of proving your loyalty."

"If he'll do all of this, he'll do anything for the club."

"That's the idea," Rebel confirmed. "When you patch in, you get your cut, but you also get a family. We're not just friends and business partners. Every member is my brother and would do anything for me, just as I would do for them. And their women are my sisters. Their kids are my nieces, nephews, etc. We depend on each other in ways that are hard to explain unless you're a part of our world. You'll see what I mean."

She raised a brow and stared at him. "I will?" While she liked the idea of spending time with him and his club family, she thought it was awfully presumptuous of him to assume they would make it to that point.

He tried to hide his smile behind a sip of his coffee, but she caught it. "Yeah," he confirmed as he set his mug back down, "you will. So, besides books, what are you into?"

Bri debated on whether or not to tell him the truth about her hobbies. On the one hand, it was a way to show him another side of her, but she worried it would make him look at her differently. With a mental roll of her eyes, she reminded herself that it didn't matter. He had two choices — accept her for who she was or move on to someone else. What she wouldn't do is change or hide herself to please a man.

Lifting her chin a bit, she looked him square in the eye and answered, "I take pole dancing classes for exercise."

She didn't think you could actually see a man's brain shut down, but the expression on Rebel's face proved her wrong. He blinked twice, shook his head, and looked at her like she lost her mind.

"Wait. What?" Another hard blink. "But you're a librarian."

Bri narrowed her eyes on him, not too happy with his words, because they sounded a lot like judgment. "And you're a biker who reads romance novels and can turn into a wolf. If we're going on stereotypical assumptions, would you even be able to read?"

Rebel's brow raised. "Fair enough." A smile slowly grew on his face. "So, pole dancing… okay."

Her ruffled feathers were smoothed a bit by his easy acceptance and admission that at least his phrasing was bad. "I was taking classes at Heat, but I guess I'll have to find somewhere else, now."

"Heat? Really?"

Still not completely appeased, Bri rolled her eyes. "Yeah. And?"

"Give me a minute to process, Sweetie. My brain is recovering from the visual of you swinging around a pole." As she laughed, he lifted his mug and took another sip. "And it's a good thing we can't leave until after we eat, because I can't stand up from this table just yet."

"Oh really? Why would that be?" Bri smirked at him as she took a sip of her drink.

Rebel's gaze met her own and lit with lust as he replied, "Reasons."

Chapter Five

Messer

Stella Messer was surprised by the speed at which the Black Forest Academy was put together. Within a day of the first video being released, maybe eighteen hours, she had received a call from a well-known billionaire about teaching and working for a security group he was putting together. The goal was to do what was necessary to keep civilians safe from the monsters that had come out of the shadows.

She was aware that her job duties would cross the line of what was considered legal, but she had never felt those lines were solid. To Stella, those lines were opaquer than most people knew. If you knew the right people and had enough of the population on your side, your ability to break the law grew at an enormous rate.

In the world they were all living in, money talked. Working for a billionaire whose mission was to keep humanity safe blurred those lines like nothing else would. Did it matter if it was right? Stella shrugged. It was a job, and a well-paying one at that.

When she had arrived at the address that was given to her in the packet of paperwork, she was impressed. It was an old boarding school. It had the pretentious columns and arches with the outdated decor and gaudy wallpaper. None of that really mattered, though. What mattered was the state of the gym, dorms, and utilities. The water was clean and hot, and the radiators seemed to heat the place well enough. The rest could be changed if the owners decided to do that in the future.

Being one of the lead hunters, she was given a larger suite on the first floor of the women's dorm. It had a full kitchen, bathroom, living/dining room, and a bedroom. She couldn't complain.

Accommodations had never really been important to her. When she took the job to teach and go on missions, her biggest concern was whether they would be able to find worthy recruits. Judging by their first training sessions, six of the eight women they assigned to her were able to be trained. She was still unsure of one. The last one she recommended for dispatch duty to her commanding officer, Xavier West.

West was a no-nonsense, grumpy bastard, but he was smart and trusted her judgment. He could be a prick as long as he didn't get in her way or think he could hit on her. She didn't do the cocky, inflated-ego assholes. Messer stuck with men she could control, so she could screw and shoo. No hanger-on men for her.

Rebel's Fairytale

No relationships or strings. She wanted to get off and get out.

After being discharged from the military and being fired from her job at her hometown police department, she needed this job. Hopefully, it was one she could stand to do.

She'd find out at her afternoon meeting. Supposedly, the higher ups at the Black Forest Academy were going to fill them in on what exactly they were facing and how to defeat them.

All Stella knew for sure was she couldn't see how someone could turn into a wolf or a tiger and *not* be a monster.

Pixie

Once all the Ol' Ladies had arrived at TC's diner, Pixie had them take seats around the two tables she had pushed together in the back. When she mentioned to Kitty that she wanted the space because they needed to have church, the woman grinned, raised an eyebrow, and told her to have at it. As a member of the Tiger's Claw MC, Kitty knew what church meant.

She was glad Pike hadn't seen her push the tables together. Since she was preggo, he would have flipped his lid. The man gave a whole new meaning to being overprotective.

The women took their seats. Pixie was surprised not to see any of the kids in attendance, but it would make all of it go a lot smoother. She sat at the head of the table, with Sugar to her right and Gorgeous to her left. Next to Gorgeous was Darlin' and Peanut. To Sugar's right was Harlow, then Kisy.

There was a seat at the other end of the table that would be occupied for Mary, but Rock still hadn't settled everything after his ex-wife's death and hadn't fully embraced Mary as his Ol' Lady. He would get there. It was just going to take time.

"What's this about, Pix?" Wearing her Tiger's Claw cut with the newly attached *Property of Dragon - Howlers MC Enforcer* patch on the bottom right corner, Kisy rested her elbows on the table and looked over at Pixie.

"Yeah, Pix," Gorgeous said with a smile, "the text sounded like you had juicy stuff to tell us." She jogged her eyebrows, making Sugar giggle.

Pixie looked around to make sure none of the Howlers were in the diner. If they heard her plans, they would try to shut them down. They would tell her to mind her own business, and maybe she should, but what was wrong with a little fun?

When she saw the coast was clear, she faced the women again and told them of her plan. "We need to go on a stakeout."

"Ooooo," Darlin' crossed her arms over her chest and leaned closer, her auburn messy bun bobbing on top of her head with her movements. "What are we staking out? Or who? Whom? I don't remember which one it is."

Butterfly snorted a laugh. "It's 'who'."

"Thanks." Darlin' smiled at Butterfly, then she returned her attention to Pixie.

"The library." When they all just stared at her, she huffed out a breath. "None of you have wondered why Rebel brought us there? Or why he keeps making frequent trips to the library, by the library, near the library?"

"Because he likes to read," Gorgeous mumbled, but Pixie could see her gears turning.

"Yes, we all know he likes to read, but he practically has a library in his room here and has a million books piled up at his place."

"So frequent trips would be excessive," Gorgeous surmised as her eyes widened. "Ruby?"

"I asked her where the name Ruby came from, expecting her to say it was a grandmother or aunt's name." Pixie grinned. "She said, 'Rebel.' That's it! Just… Rebel."

"Oh, my goodness," Sugar breathed.

Peanut laughed. "It's happening again!"

"Okay. So, Rebel might have found his mate," Butterfly said. "Why would this make us stakeout the library?"

Pixie opened her mouth to explain, but Kisy beat her to the punch. "To get proof. Rebel is so damn private. If another woman is joining our crew, we need to know."

"What are my chickens scheming about, now?" Mama Hen strolled over to their table. Her hair was teal and cut short to her head. The woman pulled off the color better than any woman Pixie had ever seen.

"Pixie is organizing a stakeout of the library. We think Rebel is falling for the librarian," Kisy told her biological aunt.

Kisy called her Auntie Hen, but the rest of them called her Mama Hen. She claimed every person in the neighborhood as family, except for the snooty ones. She didn't do snooty, and she refused to surround herself with it.

Mama Hen slipped into the empty chair at the end of the tables and gasped. "No… really?"

"Yup." Darlin' ended the word with a pop.

"So… when are we doing this?" Mama Hen looked around the table. "The library closes at nine during the week and seven on Saturdays, I think."

"Tonight," Pixie said. "We just need to figure out how we're getting out of here without our men knowing what we're doing. They will try to shut it down."

Pixie absently rubbed her baby bump as she watched an evil grin grow on Mama Hen's face.

"Leave it to me, chickens. Meet me at the hotel at seven-thirty and wear your biker boots." Mama Hen winked at them as she stood. Then, she left the diner, walking like a woman on a mission.

"What is Mama Hen going to do?"

Pixie looked over at Sugar as she answered her question, "Take care of business, like always."

Mama Hen

Mama Hen stepped into the clubhouse and looked around the space. It was what you would expect from a group of men in their space where they drank and bonded — lots of nicked and blemished wood, old leather stools, tables that probably should have been replaced a decade ago, and lots of neon and beer signs.

She spotted Ranger talking to Trip and Bullet across the room. As she made her way over to them, Trip and Bullet wrapped up the conversation, gave her a nod, and walked away. *Perfect.*

"Mama Hen," Ranger uttered and wrapped her up in his strong arms. "Looking beautiful as always. I like the teal."

"Well, thank you. I got a favor to ask ya."

Ranger slowly released her and looked down to meet her eyes. "What are we doing? Robbing a bank? Burying a body? Painting *I'm a good boy* on Dragon's bike?"

Mama Hen chuckled. "You really do have a death wish, don't you?"

"I just don't fear it the way most do," he replied with a grin and a shrug. "No, seriously, what are we doing?"

"I need to borrow your night-vision goggles. My ex-husband got our stakeout equipment in the divorce."

Ranger blinked at her, then blinked again. "I'm sorry. Wait. Why did you have—"

"Don't ask questions you don't want to know the answers to, Ranger." She raised a brow at him. "The goggles?"

He narrowed his eyes on her, studying her like he was trying to decipher all her secrets.

Locked safe, my boy. Locked safe. Good luck!

"If I'm going to let you borrow them, I need to know why you need them." He crossed his arms over his chest and stared her down, but she saw the twitch at the corners of his lips. The man was enjoying the conversation.

After glancing around and seeing that the room was empty except for the two of them, Mama Hen mimicked his position and began negotiations. "I will tell you… *if* you promise to not share with the rest of the Howlers."

"I can't promise that… unless I'm going with you." It was his turn to cock a brow.

"You drive a hard bargain, soldier." She thought for a moment. Considering his playful nature, Mama Hen determined Ranger would probably be the best Howler to include in the mission. And it would have the added benefit of keeping the men of the Ol' Ladies from being too curious. "Then, you will tell the others that you are bringing the Ol' Ladies to the hotel at seven-thirty."

Ranger's eyes widened. "The Ol' Ladies are involved? This was Kisy's idea, wasn't it?"

"No," Mama Hen replied, but she grinned, because usually Kisy would be the ringleader. "This is Pixie's idea."

"Pike's Pixie?" He shook his head but immediately continued, "Okay. Fine. I agree. Now, what are we doing?"

Mama Hen looked around again to make sure they were still alone. When she determined they were still the only ones there, she answered, "Pixie suspects that Rebel has fallen in love with the librarian. The Ol' Ladies want to do a stakeout. We need proof."

Ranger just stared at her for a long moment. Then, he threw back his head and laughed. "Count me in."

Rebel

Still riding the high of his first date with Ruby, Rebel finished making dinner for Ryker and Ross. He stuck with something simple since the twins were still getting used to eating more than just a sandwich for each meal. He went with the only recipe he remembered from his mother. A beef stew with chunks of potatoes and carrots. She always told him it was full of nutrients but wouldn't be hard on the stomach.

He decided to pair it with buttered toast. After preparing a stack of that, he moved everything to the dining table and called out to the twins that dinner was done.

Throughout dinner, he put aside his thoughts of Ruby and kept an eye out for any concerning behaviors from the twins. It was odd to him that both of them seemed perfectly okay with everything that had happened. The fact that neither of them seemed angry or confused made Rebel more concerned. He made a mental note to ask Siren again about family therapists they could trust.

For a while after their rescue, the twins went to a therapist, but they had decided to stop when it was clear it wasn't going to work unless they could be completely open about everything. They needed a shifter or someone who knew about shifters.

With the war and all the drama, it had gotten pushed to the back burner. However, it needed to be addressed, especially after they witnessed him killing their father.

"So, Chris, you heading back out to meet up with Ruby?" Ryker asked and took another bite of stew.

Rebel nodded. There were very few people on the planet he allowed to use his real name. His name was Port Christopher, but only his cousins and his sister called him Chris. To everyone else, he was Rebel.

He nodded and swallowed his food. "I won't be gone long."

"Take as long as you need," Ross commented. When Rebel shot him a glare at the insinuation there, he added, "We are adults, Chris. We will be fine without a babysitter. That's all I meant."

Ryker shrugged. "And we like Ruby. She's good for you. We're glad you found her."

"You don't know her."

"Yet, we still know she's too good for you," Ross shot back with a grin.

Relieved to have a relatively normal interaction with the cousins he always thought of as little brothers, Rebel chuckled and shot them the bird. "Fuck off."

Ranger

At twenty after seven, the Ol' Ladies started gathering in the clubhouse. Ranger cleared his throat and approached where Axle and Gorgeous were talking, the keys to the Howlers MC's van in his hand.

"Where are you going again?" Axle had his hands to his hips and a scowl on his face as he talked to Gorgeous.

"We're just going to have a girls' night with Mama Hen. We won't be gone long," she replied.

"Don't worry, Pres. I'm taking them, and I'll hang out," Ranger uttered and stopped next to them. "I'll bring them back when they're done doing whatever they plan to do."

"If you don't keep them safe," Dragon said as he joined the circle, "I will—"

"Yeah. Yeah. We know," Gorgeous uttered. "You'll cut his balls off with a rusty butter knife dipped in citric acid."

Ranger winced.

Dragon shrugged then nodded.

Axle sighed. "Fine. Be safe. Listen to Ran—" He looked over at Ranger, scowled again, and Ranger tried not to be offended. Then Axle looked back at Gorgeous. "Just stay safe."

Ranger rolled his eyes and called out to the room, "Ol' Ladies, let's roll."

As the women said goodbye to their men and headed toward the front door, Axle stared hard at Ranger. "I don't know what the hell they have planned, but I don't believe this girls' night shit. Keep them safe."

Ranger gave a nod and high-tailed it out of there. If he stayed too long, the other men would join in, and they would try to pressure him into revealing their plans. And Ranger was looking forward to their stakeout mission. His boy, Rebel, had been holding out on him, and he wanted all the information.

Rock

Holding himself up on bent elbows, Rock slid his naked hips between Mary's thighs and pressed his lips to hers. Her legs wrapped around his thighs, and she used her feet to try to pull him closer. Nipping her bottom lip, he slid one hand up, tangling his fingers in her curls. The sight of her caramel curls laid out across his pillow took his breath away.

"Wes," she gasped against his mouth as he pressed his erection against her core, letting her feel the effect she had on him.

Taking advantage, Rock deepened the kiss, caressing her tongue with his own as his hand fisted in her hair, and his other hand moved between them. He circled her opening with his middle finger as his thumb flicked her clit, making her moan into his mouth. He

Rebel's Fairytale

loved how responsive she was to him. She didn't hold anything back.

Sliding his finger inside of her, he broke the kiss and moved down to her jaw, nipping the skin there. "You're always so damn wet for me, Angel," he growled against her neck. He slid his finger out of her and added another on the next glide inside.

"Wes," she panted as her hands went to his back, one holding on, the other sliding up to his hair, "I need you."

"I'm right here." He kissed down her neck to her chest and nipped the inner swell of her left breast. "And I have no plans of going anywhere."

She gripped his hair in a fist and yanked his head back. Looking up at her, he grinned at the almost feral look in her eye. "You've been teasing me for an hour," Mary whined. "Fuck me already."

When she let go of his hair, he chuckled and kissed his way back up to her lips. "How many days until your birth control takes effect?"

"Nine."

"So, I'm assuming you want me to use a condom." He stared down into her gray-green eyes and waited for her to make a decision.

Her brows came together. "Do you think *now* is the right time to even consider making our family larger? We don't even live together. Hell, we don't even live on the same side of the state. Do you even want more kids?"

Rock rested his forehead against hers. "You're right. Now isn't the time, but just to clear up any confusion on the subject, I would *kill* to see these curls on a little girl of my own."

When he saw the tears well in her pretty eyes, he pressed his lips to hers and reached over to the bedside table to grab a condom from the stash he had left on the top. Breaking the kiss, he used his teeth to open the packet. Mary took the condom from him and reached between them.

He waited for her to finish rolling it on his hard length and wrap her arms around his shoulders, before he said, "When I'm done making love to you, we'll talk about our living situation."

Before she could react to his words, he slid inside of her. They couldn't get enough of the sensuality and affection they shared. It was that way every time they were within reach of each other. If Rock had to pick a favorite moment, though, it was the glossy-eyed look on her face every single time he entered her. She made him feel like a god.

He pulled out and slid back in a little harder, tilting his hips just right on the end of the stroke to make sure he hit the spots her body needed from him. He kept up the pace, making sure to build the momentum just the way she liked it.

With his forehead pressed to hers, he held her gaze, letting his guard down and letting her see all the love and desire he had in his heart and body for her. No one had made him feel as deeply as she did. It was as if she reached the bottom of the well and just kept digging, allowing his capacity of love to grow.

"Wes," she whispered as a tear streamed from her eye and across her temple, before it disappeared into the corkscrew curls that had mesmerized him for over a year.

"I love you," he told her. His voice cracked as he said the words, but he knew she understood him when her legs and arms tightened around him.

"I love you, too."

He kissed her lips and picked up the pace, desperate to hear her cry out with pleasure. Mary's nails dug into the skin of his back, amping up his lust and making the snap of his hips a little erratic. Rock broke their kiss and made his way to where her neck met her shoulder.

He wasn't a shifter. He was as human as they come, but that didn't mean he was without desire to mark his woman. When her core began to contract around him, and Mary cried out his name, Rock latched on, giving the skin there a sucking loving bite that would surely leave a bruise. It was that bite that sent them both over the edge.

Slamming home, he released inside of her as her pussy milked his cock, and Mary held him in a death grip.

He waited for the waves of pleasure to ease and his breathing to slow before he kissed the area he had bitten. "I want you and the kids to move in with me."

She took a few panted breaths before she replied, "So, you thought you would fuck me into submission?"

Rock barked a laugh and leaned back enough to look into her eyes. "Do I need to?"

She cupped his face in her palms and let out a sigh. "Wes, my dream consists of us in the same house, with all of our children, and having this connection with you every night. I'm not turning you down, but I won't move my kids back to this town until you're in this all the way."

Rock's brows pulled together as he tried to figure out what she was trying to say. "Angel, I'm literally as *in all the way* as I can possibly be, and I don't mean my dick."

Mary rolled her eyes. "I'll tell you what. I don't need a ring or a wedding or any of that, but I do need to be acknowledged as yours in front of the important people in your life."

Understanding dawned and Rock smiled. "You want to be my Ol' Lady."

"Duh."

He kissed her lips. "You want my property patch."

"Again… duh."

"You want your name tattooed into my skin."

"That's not a necessity, but yes, I want that."

Still smiling, Rock pulled out of her and climbed off the bed. As he headed for the bathroom to take care of the condom, he called out over his shoulder, "Well, get dressed, Angel. We have a meeting to call."

"Now?"

He tossed the condom and proceeded to clean himself up. "Well, it will probably take a couple hours to get the guys together, but yeah, *now*."

Looking in the mirror as he washed his hands, he saw Mary standing in the open doorway, wrapped in his white sheets.

"It's that easy? Decision made?"

Rock chuckled. "Angel, I knew a year ago that you were my Ol' Lady. So did my brothers. Now, we just gotta make it official. You got a reason to put it off? Because I sure as hell don't."

"What if the kids aren't okay with us?"

He knew what she meant. She meant what if *Mia and Logan* weren't okay with their relationship. "You've been having phone conversations with Mia and Logan for months. Despite what we call each other to them, they aren't stupid. They know you aren't just a friend of mine." He grabbed the hand towel from the towel rack next to the sink and began drying his hands. "And if the phone calls didn't confirm that for them, the fact that you rushed here to be with us in the darkest moment of our lives sure as hell did. They like you. They'll like us together. And they'll enjoy having more siblings to play with and fight with." He tossed the hand towel in the sink and turned to face her. "I'm not saying it will be easy or problem-free. I'm just saying we can do it, and our kids will grow to love our family."

The tears in Mary's eyes told him it was what she needed to hear.

"Well, if you don't start hanging up the hand towel when you're done with it, you might regret asking me to move in with you," she grumbled in an obvious attempt to shift the focus off of her overwhelming emotions.

Rock laughed as he picked up the towel and hung it up on the towel rack. "Better?"

"Much." She huffed out a breath and sniffled. "Now, I want you to take me back to bed, but we have a meeting to call."

Chapter Six

Pixie

When they arrived at the hotel, Mama Hen directed them to go into the first conference room down the hall. It was one of the rooms people could reserve for a small party or business meeting.

In the center of the room, there was a large conference table surrounded by chairs. The walls and carpet were done in various shades of blue. It was a gorgeous room, if a bit formal for Pixie's taste.

On the table were black tote bags that looked to be full to the rim. Pixie was curious, so she walked closer to get a better look. When she saw the words *The Shifty Sisters* in a badass font on the side of the bags, she busted out with laughter. "The Shifty Sisters?"

Mama Hen shrugged and approached the table. "You bitches needed a name. Like the Howlers and the Claws, you work together and always have each other's back in the same way. You should have a name."

T.S. Tappin

Kisy chuckled. "I like it."

"Me too," Gorgeous said with a smile.

Mama Hen started handing out bags to each of the women. All the women ooo'd and ahh'd over the tote. Pixie took hers and opened it. She saw a black cloth item on top. When she pulled it out, she saw that it was a black turtleneck. Under the turtleneck was a camo face paint kit, a black beanie cap, a pair of black gloves, a pair of black cargo pants, and a flashlight.

"Mama Hen, you didn't have to do this," Sugar said as she laid out all the stuff on the table.

"If we're going to do this, we're going to do this right," Mama Hen insisted and handed a tote bag to Ranger. The side of his said Honorary Shifty Sister.

Ranger's laughter filled the room, but he took the bag and headed back for the door. "I'll find somewhere to change. Be right back."

When he left the room, Pixie began to change along with everyone else. She was glad to see that Mama Hen took her baby bump into account when she was putting together their outfits. The turtleneck was stretchy and loose enough to easily go over her bump, and the cargo pants had a drawstring.

All the women were fully dressed in their black outfits and beanie caps when Ranger returned to the room. He was dressed just like them, but he slipped his cut over the turtleneck. He helped them put the camo make-up on their faces. The flashlights were small and had a carabiner clip, so they could attach them to their pants.

Pixie was about to load the clothes she had just removed into the tote when she noticed it wasn't empty. She peered inside and found a baggie containing two dill pickles in separate packaging along with a beef jerky stick and a tinfoil wrapped, still warm, burrito.

With tears in her eyes, she hugged the tote bag to her chest as she approached Mama Hen. "I love you," she mumbled as she wrapped Mama Hen up tight with her free arm.

"Get your hormones under control, girl. Can't have you blubbering during a stakeout." As she spoke, Mama Hen gently patted Pixie on the back. "Now, wipe your tears and eat your burrito."

Pixie nodded and sniffled as she wiped away her tears. Mama Hen was sent by the gods.

Ready to go, Ranger loaded them back up in the van and they were on the move.

Mama Hen

As they sat in the van down the street from the library, but in full view of the parking lot, Mama Hen was about to pull her hair out. She loved her chickens, but the bitches didn't stop clucking for long.

Darlin' was complaining about the floor of the van being too hard, when in all reality it had more to do with the fact that her ass could use some fluff. Kisy was having a hard time sitting still. She kept flicking the carabiner against the side of her flashlight. Gorgeous kept yawning because Axle had a tendency of waking Nugget up every time he wanted to snuggle his baby girl, and Gorgeous ended up having to put the little girl back to sleep. Moral of the story: She was tired. Sugar questioned whether or not they should be invading Rebel's privacy. Butterfly explained that it wasn't invading his privacy because they would be watching him in public. Peanut thought everything was hilarious. And Pixie kept crunching on her dill pickles.

Good thing they didn't need to stakeout for long.

Just as the thought crossed her mind, she noticed the door to the library swing open. Peering through the night vision goggles, she saw Rebel step out with a beautiful woman.

"Show time, Ladies," Ranger said.

Rebel

Rebel followed Ruby around the library as she closed things up and turned off lights. He picked up any stray books he found along the way and put them on the cart she had next to her desk. After she locked the front door, he took her hand and walked with her across the parking lot to her newish metallic mint Camaro.

Bri pushed the button to unlock the car, but when she went to open the door, Rebel stopped her. She turned to face him with a question in her eyes. He couldn't wait any longer. The forty minutes he had spent in the library with Bri was enough to have him on edge. He needed to kiss her like he needed air to breathe. Rebel reached up and cupped her head in his palms, sliding his fingers in the hair on the sides of her head, and pressed his lips to hers.

The sweet taste of her lips sent shocks of pleasure through his body as his wolf howled his approval. She gasped, and Rebel took advantage, sliding his tongue inside her mouth and caressing hers. He knew the moment she decided to go with it, because she dropped her bag and slid her arms around his waist, pulling him closer.

Rebel broke the kiss with a growl and was about to move down to kiss along her neck, but a raucous noise came from the street. He turned his head and groaned when he saw the van owned by the Howlers parked under a large tree that was blocking the glow of the streetlight. With his shifter vision, he was able to easily see Mama Hen in the driver's seat and Ranger in the passenger's seat. Standing outside the van were all the Ol' Ladies, dressed in all black, with camo paint on their faces.

"Squeee!" Kisy was up on her toes, her TC cut shifting with her movements.

Sugar was giggling with Peanut and clapping.

Darlin' and Gorgeous were hooting and hollering.

Pixie was whooping and fist-bumping the sky.

Then, Ranger rolled down the window and stuck his head out. "I can't believe you went and fell in love and didn't tell me! I'm supposed to be your closest friend!"

Rebel rolled his eyes and let out a sigh. That's when he heard the giggles coming from Ruby. He glanced down to see her eyes shining up at him with laughter.

"You think that's funny? They are all my brothers' women."

She nodded. "They love you. They want you to be happy and are happy for you. That's never a bad thing."

He was just about to suggest he follow her home when he felt his phone vibrating in his pocket. With a quick glance at his group of *loved ones*, he saw they were all looking at their phones. *Shit*.

Rebel pulled his phone out of his pocket and read the text from Axle.

>EMERGENCY CHURCH. ROCK AND MARY REQUEST. NOT BAD.<

Rebel knew what that meant. Rock was *finally* making Mary his Ol' Lady. As much as he wanted to spend more time with Ruby, he needed to be there to support his friend and his new sister.

Shoving his phone back in the pocket of his cut, he pressed his lips to Ruby's, retrieved her bag from the ground, handed it to her, and opened her car door. "Can you do dinner with me and the twins tomorrow?"

She nodded. "I work the early shift and will be out by three."

Once she was situated in her seat, he bent down and kissed her again. "I'll text you my address. Be there around six?"

She smiled and nodded. "Can't wait."

Rebel's Fairytale

With a wink, he closed her car door and watched as she drove away. Then, he shot his family the middle finger as he made his way over to his bike. He couldn't help but chuckle at the sound of the laughter they shot back.

Dorothy

Dorothy Jones was disgusted. She couldn't believe what she was seeing. Out on her nightly walk, she stopped across the street from the library and stared. In the parking lot of the library, she saw that sweet librarian with one of those hooligans, and he had his tongue down her throat! Dorothy thought the woman should know better. She was supposed to be a role model for the children of Warden's Pass. Instead, she was behaving like a loose woman out on the prowl.

The sound of shenanigans off to her left brought Dorothy's attention around. She spotted a group of the other women the men of that club had convinced to climb in their beds. Disgusting behavior.

Yes, she had thought the men of the club were attractive when the club was first established and had spent many days trying to get their attention, but she was young and that was before she was aware of their wicked ways. Sending up prayers she didn't get wrapped up with the filth that was the Howlers all those years ago, she took a deep breath and exhaled.

Reginald was right. They needed to push these men out of their town, get rid of the trash and the debauchery. Hopefully, they would be able to save these women in the process.

Rock

Sitting in his usual spot at the table in the room they used for church, Rock waited for all of his brothers to settle and for Axle to start the meeting. He expected to have some nervousness or anxiety as he made the most important decision in his relationship with Mary, but all he felt was a calm determination.

Once his brothers were in their seats, Axle slammed his fist down on the table and said, "I'm assuming the reason for this meeting has to do with the love bite on Mary's neck."

The grin on Axle's face had Rock lifting his hand from the table and shooting his president the finger.

"That's an affirmative," Brute graciously translated.

As his brothers chuckled, Rock took a deep breath and announced, "I want to claim Mary as my Ol' Lady. It's time."

"It was *time* a year ago," Pike said, "but we get why you waited."

"Do we need to vote?" Axle looked around the table.

The chorus of 'Fuck you and your vote,' 'She's been family forever,' and 'fucking no,' had a grin growing on Rock's face. He loved this group of guys more than he could ever put into words.

"Well, it's a good thing I ordered her cut a long damn time ago. I took the liberty of picking an Ol' Lady name, but if you don't like it, I'll order a new patch."

Rock was curious about what name Axle picked, but Axle was the president for many reasons. One of them was because of how intuitive he was regarding all the people he considered family.

Axle stood and walked the few steps to the only shelving unit in the room. He used a key to unlock the doors and opened one, reaching inside and pulling out a leather vest. After relocking the cabinet, he tossed the cut down on the table to Rock.

Rock held the thing up in front of him and had to choke down the lump in his throat. The Ol' Lady name Axle chose was perfect for Mary. *Diamond*.

He nodded and cleared his throat. "Yeah."

As he stood, he felt various brothers give his shoulder a squeeze. He knew they were happy for him and excited to officially welcome Mary into the family.

Mary

"Is this for what I think it's for?" Kisy asked as she plopped down in the chair next to Mary. Mary didn't know the woman well, but she liked what she'd seen. Kisy didn't hide behind pretty words and polite chatter. She was an out-with-it type chick.

"Yeah, you getting your Ol' Lady status confirmed?" Butterfly took the seat on the other side of Kisy.

Gorgeous, Darlin', and Sugar filled out the rest of the table, until Pixie made her way over. Then, Sugar stood and gave Pixie her chair, since Pixie was obviously pregnant.

All of them looked like they had just washed their face, or they just had a shower. Their faces were clear of make-up, and they looked to all be in comfy clothes.

"Am I supposed to say that?" Mary looked around the table. "What if I jinx it, and they don't approve? Don't the brothers have to approve?"

Gorgeous waved off her worry. "Let these men try to deny our sister her due and see what happens. They aren't going to deny you, Mary. You've been one of us for a long damn time."

Hearing the matriarch of the Ol' Ladies call her *sister* made Mary's eyes fill with tears.

"Aw shit. The water works are already starting," Pixie commented as she eyed Mary and sniffled.

"I see our boy Rock doesn't need shifter genes to get all bitey," Darlin' said with a grin.

Mary blushed and smiled as she lifted a hand to the love bite Rock left on her neck.

"Good for him… and for you." Kisy nudged Mary with her elbow. "Congrats."

"Don't mind her," Butterfly said with a laugh. "It turns her on that Dragon gets all marky and bitey and caveman."

"LA LA LA LA LA," Darlin' shouted as she plugged her ears.

Dragon barked out, "Kisy, are you torturing my sister?"

Kisy huffed and popped up to her feet. Shooting Dragon a glare, she replied, "No, you bossy accusing bastard. It was Butterfly."

As the men filed back into the room, they were all chuckling.

"My plans to worship those tattoos some more can change, Love," Dragon said as his eyes flashed a green light in Kisy's direction.

She watched as Kisy swallowed hard, and the sass drained right out of her, leaving Kisy speechless.

"Huh. Looks like he found her off button," Sugar giggled.

"Or the right *on* button," Pixie retorted as she stood.

"Fuck all you bitches," Kisy grumbled, not meaning a damn word of it.

Rock approached Mary and bent his head down to kiss the mark he left on her shoulder.

"Did they agree?" She whispered the question to him, scared of the answer.

"Angel, most of them are shifters. They can hear you when you whisper."

As her cheeks reddened again, she looked around to see that the group had gathered in front of them, with all the brothers in the center.

Axle stood in front of the others and was smiling at her. "It's been a while since I've had the honor of doing this, but it *is* an honor, Mary. By tying yourself to Rock, you tied yourself to us and to our pack. By having his back, you have ours. By protecting him, you protect us. By loving him, you love us." His smile intensified. "We're a package deal. And we understand we're getting more out of the deal than you are."

Her eyes filled with tears again, and her breathing quickened as she realized what was happening. They were accepting her, welcoming her. She was one of them.

"You will never need for anything for long. You will never want for anything for long. You will never suffer. And if for some reason you do," his eyes flashed a silver light, "the one who caused it will suffer far more for their efforts." There was a pause in his speech while growls and hisses filled the room. "I'm honored to call you my sister." He held out his hand to her and in it was a leather vest, much like the one each of the Howlers and their women wore.

Mary slowly reached out and took it from him, choking out, "Thank you, Axle." She held the cut up in front of her and began to sob as she saw the name they had given her. *Diamond*. They thought she was strong and came out of pressure stronger and more resilient. "I love you guys."

As Rock chuckled, he pulled her into his arms and kissed the top of her head. "They love you, too, Diamond."

A cheer went through the room and someone, one of the Ol' Ladies, she thought it might have been Sugar, shouted, "Shots!"

After her sobs subsided, Rock helped her slide the cut onto her shoulders. She looked down at the patches again. On the left, there were two patches. One of them said the name they had given her. The other just simply read *Rock's OL,* which might have been the most beautiful patch she had ever seen.

As the rest of the room began to drink and party, and music was turned on, she felt Rock's breath on her ear. He nipped her ear lobe and whispered, "Fuck. That looks so damn hot on you."

"Rock," Gorgeous shouted as she headed their way with the other Ol' Ladies in tow and a tray full of shots in her hands, "you can fuck her later! We have a new sister to initiate."

T.S. Tappin

Chapter Seven

Rebel

After spending a few hours down at Heat assessing the damage and how to attack cleanup, Rebel stopped by the library to ask Ruby what she wanted for dinner. He made sure to stomp as much dirt and debris as he could, not wanting to make a mess of the place. When he entered, he spotted her at her desk, but she was on the phone. He shot her a wink and decided to explore a bit while he waited.

It was in the third area he was perusing, when he rounded the corner into the next row and noticed a kid halfway down. The young man looked to be in his younger teens. He was holding a book and studying the back of it, but something about his expression told Rebel he was troubled.

Rebel glanced around and didn't see any parents milling about. Deciding he would try to help if he could, he casually made his way down the aisle and stopped a few yards away from the boy.

"Hey," Rebel softly said. "What's that? I don't think I've read that one."

The boy glanced up at Rebel before dropping his gaze back down to the book. "I doubt you've read any of these." He motioned to the young adult section in front of him.

"Try me." Rebel took a couple slow steps in the boy's direction.

"It's a fantasy book for young adults. I'm trying to see if it has any romance, because… it can't."

Rebel's brows drew together in contemplation. The wording of the boy's statement set off warning bells for him. "Are you not into romance? It's not for everybody."

The boy shrugged. "It's not… cool to read it."

"Says who?"

The boy's gaze shot back up to Rebel's face. "My friends said… They said boys don't read romance."

"Huh… Well, I'm a boy, and I read romance." Rebel shrugged. "I think it's cool."

"You… *you* read romance?"

Nodding, Rebel smiled. "Yup."

The boy slid the book back onto the shelf and grabbed another. He held the book out to Rebel. When Rebel took it, he said, "A friend of mine… Jasmine, she said I should read this one, because it has the paranormal stuff I like, and the mystery stuff. So, I was reading it. Then, my other friends saw it and started saying I shouldn't read it."

Rebel studied the cover. It had a dagger through a heart with purple and blue decoration around it. The title was *Forgotten Life*, written by Angel M. Johnson. As Rebel read the blurb on the back, he asked the boy, "What's your name?"

"Derrick," the boy said.

"Nice to meet you, Derrick. I'm Rebel."

"Rebel?"

"That's what they call me." Rebel finished reading the blurb and nodded. "Okay. Derrick, forget about what your friends said. You liked this book?"

Derrick nodded.

"Cool. Okay. You liked it because it had the paranormal and mystery stuff. Did you like how the author wrote the romance, too?"

Rebel watched as Derrick shrugged and looked away.

"I bet I'd like it. I find that most books I read are centered around a romance or have a romance in them. In my opinion, it doesn't make you anything but better if you're trying new things and having an open mind."

"You don't think… I'm… like… weak because I read the same stuff girls do?"

Rebel snorted a laugh. "Weak? Nope. Do you think I'm weak because I do?"

Derrick looked over Rebel's cut and shook his head. "No. You're a Howler. You… you're like a tough guy. And you ride a motorcycle and stuff."

Holding up the book, Rebel smiled. "I'm going to check out this book because my friend, Derrick, told me it was good. I want you to remember some things, though. If your friends pick on you for something you enjoy, they aren't your friends. Read what you want. And if you ever need some book recommendations, Ms. Bri up at the desk will set you up. She can also get you in touch with me if you need to chat. Deal?"

Rebel held out his free hand and waited. Derrick took his hand and gave it a firm shake.

"Nice, strong handshake. Nah. You aren't weak."

After laying those words on Derrick, Rebel turned around and headed back toward the end of the aisle, where he spotted Ruby watching him. When he reached her, he leaned forward and kissed her cheek.

"Are you spying?"

She shrugged and smiled at him. Quietly, she replied, "I didn't want to intrude. You handled that really well, Rebel."

Rebel shrugged. "I don't like bullies."

"And you like helping others. And you are proof that reading is cool. And you were trying to feed that boy's love of reading and his open mind. And—"

Rebel shut her up with a kiss to her lips. "Yeah. And that."

"Would you be willing to lead a book club for teens? It would be like an hour or two a week? There's been a request for it, but I don't have the staff to dedicate to the book clubs, and I've had trouble finding someone to lead that one."

With a shrug, Rebel agreed, "Yeah, I'd like that. Don't know if I'm qualified, but count me in."

Ruby raised a brow. "That interaction was proof you are qualified enough. You free next Monday afternoon? I'll post about it on our site and start building interest. There probably won't be many kids the first few meetings, but…"

"Like I said, count me in." He smiled and held up the book. "I need to check this book out. I also need to know if you're okay with grilled steak, potatoes, and asparagus for dinner."

"Uh… Heck yeah, tech yeah!"

Chuckling, Rebel followed her back to her desk.

Mary

Rock wouldn't let Mary go with him to get his tattoo, instead insisting she go down to the diner and have lunch. Pouting a bit, she agreed.

When Rock saw her protruding lip, he smiled and sucked that lip between his own before giving her a heart-stopping kiss, a smack on the ass, and a playful shove toward the diner.

Pushing down the desire to drag him to his room at the compound and have her way with him, she stomped down to the diner and took a seat at an empty table near the back.

She had just ordered a turkey on Rye with a side of potato salad when two women slid into chairs at her table. Pixie sat across from Mary, and Sugar sat to her left.

Mary smiled at them. "Hey."

Sugar returned her smile. "Hey. Thought you might like some company."

"And I'm starving," Pixie added with a laugh as she waved down Kitty.

Kitty strutted over to their table on her stilettos, wearing her short shorts and a *TC's Diner* shirt, looking like a tasty meal. "What can I get ya both?"

Mary envied the confidence Kitty had. From what Mary could tell, she was who she was, and she didn't apologize for that. It was the type of woman Mary aspired to be. She wanted to exude confidence, but she also wanted to feel it. *Someday*, she told herself.

Sugar and Pixie put in their orders. They spent the next couple of hours talking about everything from kids to the guys to what their dreams were.

As Mary laughed and chatted with the girls, she realized it was the first time in a long time that she felt comfortable just being herself around other women. She didn't feel like she had to lie about her past or adjust her personality to fit them. She was completely open and honest, and she didn't feel one ounce of judgment coming from Pixie or Sugar.

It was refreshing and empowering in a way she hadn't expected. She felt accepted, welcomed, a part of something. The Howlers, and even the Tiger's Claw members, had welcomed her with open arms. She couldn't wait to be closer and return the favor, and she desperately wanted to give that to her children.

Her ex had systematically cut her off from the majority of her friends and family, leaving her solely dependent on him. It was part of the reason she hadn't left sooner. She'd felt trapped. It wasn't until after she had reconnected with her friend Mallory, behind her ex's back, that she felt like she had somewhere to turn when things got out of control.

When Mallory's man, Stone, heard what Mary's ex was up to, he gave Mary and her children a safe place and called in Rock and the Howlers to help keep them safe.

Now, she realized she had Mallory, Stone, Rock, and all of his family. Her eyes filled with tears as she listened to Pixie talk about baby names and felt the comfort of knowing she and her kids would never be on their own again.

"Why is my woman tearing up?" Rock stopped across the table from Mary with a scowl on his face.

Mary's eyes landed on the ink on the left side of Rock's neck. In beautiful, flowing script was *Mary*. It was large and left no room for misunderstanding. He was hers and he was proud of it.

"Diamond?" Rock started around the table, his eyes never leaving her.

Mary gave him a smile as the tears spilled over and ran down her cheeks. "I'm okay, Wes."

His hands reached up to wipe away her tears, and that's when she spotted the other new tattoo. It was a simple outline of a diamond on the ring finger of his left hand.

She told him she wanted proof that he was all-in, and he was making sure she knew he meant it. The joy that filled her heart overwhelmed her. She shot to her feet, wrapped her arms around his waist, and face planted against his body.

"Mary?" Rock wrapped his arms around her and held her tight. "What's wrong?"

She shook her head. "Nothing. Everything is perfect."

And just like that, she was sobbing into his chest again.

Rebel

Still smiling from seeing Ruby, Rebel parked his bike in a spot near the front of the local grocery store and headed inside. He couldn't wait to have her in his space and to have his cousins get to know her better. He had no doubt they would love her, but it was important to Rebel that Ross and Ryker had more than an acquaintance relationship with the woman that was going to be in his life.

Ruby was his mate. His wolf had made that fact very fucking clear. Now, it was just about building the relationship, so it didn't freak her out when Rebel started to plan their future out loud instead of only in his head.

He grabbed a basket from the holder near the entrance and made a left. As he perused the produce, he let his mind wander to what Ruby would look like first thing in the morning. He wanted to know what her eyes looked like heavy with sleep and what her version of bedhead was.

Grinning, he grabbed two bundles of asparagus and dropped them in the basket as he thought about what she would wear to dinner. Would she be buttoned up librarian, or would he finally get to see her in a more casual outfit? What did she look like when she was reading in her chair?

Fuck. He wanted to be able to picture her in every situation and every place, not because he had a good imagination, but because he'd witnessed it, and he had an excellent memory.

As his wolf began to pace inside him, Rebel assumed it was because of their shared urgency to build that history with Ruby. It wasn't until he made his way to the meat section that he began to notice how people would change course to avoid getting too close to him.

He'd never been treated like that before in Warden's Pass. Usually, the town was very accepting of the Howlers, knowing the Howlers did a lot of good things for the community, but things were different after the truth of shifters had been announced to the world.

The general world population was a mixed bag of people who believed and those who thought the video proof was altered in some way. It wasn't. However, the residents of Warden's Pass had experienced shifters, firsthand, just a few days ago and knew it all to be true.

Axle had warned they would probably experience some push back. He had told all of them to expect awkward or frightened glances. His orders were to not react any differently than we would have before. Our mission was to prove to the town nothing about us had changed. It was the truth. The only difference was in the knowledge of the residents.

Rebel shook off the avoidance and grabbed a large package of high-end steaks. Dropping them in his basket, he turned and headed for the aisle that held the tinfoil. Once he had that in his basket, he moved over to the spice aisle.

He was trying to pick the best seasonings to put on the steaks when he glanced over and noticed a woman heading down the aisle he was in. She was on the city council and had been fighting to revoke the liquor license from Heat, the Howlers MC owned strip club, for as long as Rebel could remember. She was what Rex's teen daughter, Neveah, would call a *Karen*.

As she got closer to him, he gave her a polite nod as he usually would. She scowled at him in return. When she walked past him, she hissed, "Somebody should call animal control."

Before Rebel could formulate a response, she was gone, turning down another aisle. Shaking his head, he picked up his favorite steak seasoning and marinade, and dropped them in his basket.

Rebel's Fairytale

Remembering he wanted to make her his grilled potatoes, he headed back to the produce section and grabbed the first bag of potatoes he came across. He needed to get out of the store before he snapped and told all of those judgmental assholes what he really thought of them.

With the basket in one hand and the five-pound bag of potatoes in the other, Rebel headed for the front of the store, trying extremely hard not to let his annoyance show on his face.

Keeping his cool was important in this situation, probably more important than ever before. The Howlers and the Claws didn't need to give the citizens of Warden's Pass any reason to rise up against them.

They were already receiving reports from the champions of the gods about a group of hunters that had sprung up with the mission to eradicate any paranormal creature. They didn't have solid evidence of the group or where they were located yet, but it was still on their list of problems. The last thing they needed was to grab the attention of the hunters or their band of idiots.

When he reached the front and attempted to get in line behind a few other customers. Those customers moved to a different line. Gritting his teeth, he moved forward and started unloading his basket.

The cashier was polite, but she definitely wasn't friendly as she rang up his purchases. When she was done, he wished her a good day, and all she gave him in return was a forced smile.

Deciding that having groceries delivered was probably a good idea next time he was having a good day, Rebel returned to his bike and loaded his purchases into his saddlebags.

Before he started his bike, he sent Axle a string of texts, informing him of the reception he received at the grocery store. The reply text told him to stop by the compound, so that was what he was going to do after he dropped the groceries off at his house.

As he rode out of the parking lot, he made a promise to himself that their asshole behavior wouldn't ruin his day. Ruby was coming to dinner, and that was something to be happy about.

Chapter Eight

Rock

Loading Diamond into her Jeep and watching her drive away was one of the hardest things Rock had to do. He wanted to go with her and help her pack everything up, but he had responsibilities he had to take care of before he could do that.

First, he had to pick up his kids and spend some time with them. He didn't enjoy being away from them for more than a day or two at a time. They had already been gone for two nights. Before he took off for Detroit to load up the rest of his family and bring them back, he needed to have quality time with Mia and Logan.

Second, he needed to explain to Mia and Logan the status of his relationship with Diamond, and also that they were expanding their family by three. He wanted to gauge where they were at, emotionally, and make sure they were ready for what he and Diamond had planned.

Lastly, he needed to arrange for a babysitter and for a few of the guys to join him when he went to pick up Diamond and the kids. It would be faster and more efficient if he had his brothers with him to help load the truck. There was no way in hell he was letting Diamond carry furniture, no matter how capable she was.

He figured he would ask a few of the unattached brothers. Rebel was in the middle of his own love story. Pike had a pregnant woman, so he'd want to stay close to her. Not that Pixie wasn't completely healthy, she was. It was just that when you take a protective, alpha male and add a pregnancy to the mix, you end up with a paranoid, protective, alpha male. Besides a mother protecting her children from danger, you would be hard pressed to find a more dangerous creature.

Yeah, he'd ask Ranger, Brute, and maybe Rex.

Once Diamond's Jeep was out of sight, Rock got in his truck and headed over to pick his kids up. Pops had golf plans with his buddies, but Mama Nia was at their house waiting on him.

He parked his truck in the driveway and made his way up to the front door. He barely stepped onto the front porch before the door swung open, and Mama Nia was standing there with a grin on her face.

"What's that there on your neck, Wes?"

Rock cracked a smile and held up his left hand, palm facing him. "I might have went and sealed the deal like I was told to."

He was not surprised at all when Mama Nia reached out and grabbed his hand, pulling it closer to her face so she could get a good look at the diamond tattooed on his finger.

She let out a low whistle. "You sure did listen."

"I know an order when I hear it." He leaned forward and kissed her cheek. "She's heading home to pack as we speak."

"Good. I'll expect her and my new grandbabies over for dinner as soon as they get settled. I assume you're heading over to help her."

Rock nodded. "In a few days. Just want to spend some time with the kids and talk things over with them, first."

Mama Nia nodded. "I might have broached the subject. Don't you scowl at me, boy. You should've talked to them about this already."

He didn't realize he began to scowl until she pointed it out. He wasn't happy she talked to his kids about Diamond, but she wasn't wrong. Rock knew he had put off the inevitable for far too long.

"You should have cleared it with me."

Mama Nia let go of his hand and put hers to her hips. "And you shouldn't have acted like they didn't know their daddy had another woman in his life. They've been asking me about Mary for months, Wes. I don't lie to my babies."

Rock cringed. "Okay. I get it. I fucked up." He kissed her cheek again. "Where are my kids?"

"In the living room." She patted his chest with her hand before leading him in the house.

"Dad!" His baby girl jumped up and ran to him with her arms outstretched and a grin on her face.

He scooped her up and kissed her cheeks. "How's my girl?"

She cupped his face in her five-year-old palms and let out the sigh of a stressed adult. "Hunter wouldn't let me pick the shows. Mama Nia had to tell him to share." She shook her head. "It was annoying."

Rock swallowed down his laughter. "I bet it was."

"Why is Mary's name on your neck?"

Rock looked down at his seven-year-old son, Logan Hunter. Two years ago, he declared his road name was Hunter since he wanted to be a Howler like his uncle Brute. Rock didn't take offense that his son idolized his brother. There were worse things.

Taking a deep breath, Rock set his daughter on her feet and took her hand. Putting his free hand to his son's back, he led both of his kids over to Mama Nia's couch. When they sat down on the couch, Rock perched his ass carefully on Mama Nia's solid wood coffee table in front of them.

He could see her lingering in the entryway just off the living room, but he didn't mind. It wasn't as if he kept her out of his business. She wouldn't have allowed that if he tried.

"Listen, kiddos. You remember Mary, right?"

Hunter rolled his eyes. "We just saw her like two days ago, Dad."

Rock nodded. "Right. And you've talked to her on the phone." He saw his daughter smile and nod her head. Mia loved her girl talks with Mary. "Well, remember how I told you she was my friend?"

"But you looooove her," Mia cooed with a little giggle. "I heard you say it, and Mama Nia said that it's not like I love my friends."

Rock took a deep breath and tried to remember that he loved Mama Nia more than life itself. He also reminded himself that it was his own damn fault he was in that position. With a nod, he confirmed, "I do love her, and no, it's not like you love your friends. It's like… how Pops loves Mama Nia."

"Like… you loved Mom… but more," Hunter guessed, his expression guarded.

"Yeah, Hunt, like that but more." He ran his fingers through his hair and scrubbed his face with his palms. "Okay. As for your mom, I will always love her." He rested his elbows on his knees and clasped his hands together in front of him. "I will always love her for the person she was when I met her… and because she gave me you two. I know that's confusing, but it's true. With Mary… I love her because of who she is as a person, for how she is with her kids, for how she takes care of me… all the things that *should* come along with a relationship. Do you understand?"

When both of his kids nodded, he let out a sigh of relief.

His daughter was kicking her legs out and bringing them back, over and over again. "Mama Nia said she wouldn't be our new mommy, but she would treat us like her kids."

Rock nodded, hating that his cheeks were heating with the embarrassment of how poorly he handled the situation. "Mama Nia is right. No one can take your mom's place, and no one is expecting you to call her *Mom* or anything. *But* if you needed to talk to her about anything, she would listen and talk you through whatever it was. You would be expected to listen to her, just like you would listen to Mama Nia or Aunt Ginger."

Hunter nodded and was quiet for a moment. Then, he asked, "Are we going to have to share rooms?"

Rock kicked himself again for not even thinking about room assignments and did a quick mental evaluation of his three-bedroom house. "For now," he answered. "As you get older, we'll figure out how to build a couple rooms in the basement. Fair?"

After huffing out an annoyed breath, Hunter grumbled, "I guess."

Rock sighed. "Her son, Miles, is nine. He would room with you, Hunt. Her daughter is six, and her name is Jenna. Mia, baby, you'll have to share your room with her."

Mia clapped. "Yay! Sleepovers!"

Chuckling, Rock reached out and gave his daughter's hand a squeeze. Then, he looked over at his son. "I'll build you a room in the basement as soon as I can, Hunt. I'll let you decorate it however you want. I just need you to have some patience. Okay?"

Grudgingly, Hunter nodded. "Yeah, Dad. Okay."

Rebel

When Rebel walked into the clubhouse, he wished he could say that his mind was on the conversation he had to have with Axle, but it wasn't. His mind was on Ruby and his lust for her. The woman was driving him crazy in the best possible way. He couldn't stop picturing her bent over her desk or his kitchen island or his bike. All he could do was imagine coming up behind her and sliding inside of her, fucking her until they were both sweating and panting. He'd never wanted a woman so badly in his life. His wolf wasn't much help either — growling, snarling, and demanding Rebel claim their mate.

Crossing the room, he didn't even acknowledge his brothers. He just rounded the bar, poured a shot of tequila, and threw it back.

"Hey brother," Rock uttered as he set his daughter down on her feet. As soon as Rock let go of her, she was running off with her brother to greet their uncles, scattered around the room. "You good?"

"No," Rebel growled and poured more tequila. "I'm trying to be a gentleman and take this slow. I don't want to fuck it up or push too hard, but…"

Rock gave a nod. "And who said she wanted you to be a gentleman? Did she tell you that?"

Rebel looked at Rock and wondered if he lost his damn mind. "What?"

"Rebel, look... I get you want to be a gentleman. There's nothing wrong with that, but what makes you think she isn't waiting for you to make a move?"

Rock's words hit Rebel like a ton of bricks. Was she waiting for him to take things further? Would she be open to more? Were they at that stage of their relationship? He *had* been the one to stop things every time. It was something he would have to ponder.

"For fuck's sake, *literally*, stop thinking so damn much," Rock said and took Rebel's glass. He shot it back, winked at Rebel, and walked away.

"If you want my opinion, and I'm sure you don't, but here it is..." The prospect behind the bar stopped at Rebel's side and said, "The worst thing that could happen is she stops you."

Rebel glared at him, but he didn't really mean it. He wasn't annoyed with the prospect. He was annoyed with himself. Ruby had him tied up in knots, and he suspected it was him that caused it.

"How long have you been a prospect?"

The prospect shrugged. "This time? Eleven months and seven days."

That surprised Rebel. He would have said six or seven months. Then again, a lot had happened over the past year, and time was something they hadn't been tracking as well as they usually would. The Howlers had been too worried about safety to worry about what month was at the top of their calendars. He would have to bring it up to Axle, since the prospect was close to the year mark where they usually made a decision on whether or not to patch them in.

Rebel reached out and gave the man a pat on the back. "Thanks for the advice."

"Sure, Rebel. Yeah."

The pride on his face solidified it for Rebel. He was trying to be as helpful to the Howlers as he could. It was obvious he just wanted to be part of the team. That loyalty and brotherhood was what the Howlers were about. Add in the fact that he was the biological brother of their club brother, Brute, and he probably should have already patched in.

Making a mental note to bring it up to Axle, Rebel stepped out from behind the bar and made his way down the hall to Axle's office. He'd do the rundown with Axle, mention the prospect, and head home to take a shower before Ruby arrived for dinner.

Bri

Bri had an hour before she had to be to Rebel's house for dinner, and she had yet to decide on her outfit. Standing at the foot of her bed, she stared down at the options laid out there. She could go with her navy wrap dress with a knee-length hem. It made her eyes pop. Or she could go with a pair of dark blue skinny jeans, a loose-fitting white V-neck tee, and her wine-colored asymmetrical zip leather. *Hmm... choices.*

Readjusting the sash on her light blue satin robe, she contemplated those choices. The dress gave off work vibes, and the last thing she wanted was to feel like she was at work while she was sitting at Rebel's table. Although it complimented her curves and accentuated her eyes, it just didn't seem like the right pick.

The other outfit was comfy and more relaxed than her usual attire. Besides, it was starting to get chilly at night, so the jeans and the jacket would help in that area. Not to mention, it would be in line with what Rebel and his cousins would most likely be wearing. She did not want to be the only dressed up one in attendance.

She tried to picture Rebel in a suit, but all it did was make her dissolve into a fit of giggles. Bri didn't think Rebel would be in a suit anytime in the near future, but that was okay with her, because he looked delicious in a pair of jeans and a Henley.

Decision made, she grabbed the dress and hung it back in the closet. After putting on her *Awesomesauce* playlist, Bri started shimmying and shaking her way around the room as she got ready for her date.

She decided on a natural make-up look. Besides a little shimmer on her eyes and the color on her lips, she stuck with the neutral tones. On her lips, she used a tad darker shade of red lip-stain than she would normally wear with a clear gloss. Bri left her hair down in the vein of keeping things casual. For footwear, she went for the spicier side and slipped her feet into a pair of black, stiletto-heeled ankle boots.

Looking over her outfit in the full-length mirror on the back of her closet door, she grinned. She looked damn

Rebel's Fairytale

good. Feeling hot and excited, she grabbed her small, black clutch and her keys, and headed for the door.

The drive to his place didn't take long. Like everything else in Warden's Pass, it was less than ten minutes away. Checking her phone to make sure she had the right address, she nodded to herself when it was confirmed.

She was in the right place, wearing an outfit that made her feel sexy, and in the house in front of her was the sweet, sexy, intelligent biker that had made her heart race with a look.

You got this, Bri. Why was she so damn nervous? She knew Rebel liked her at the very least. It was just dinner. Dinner wasn't a forever commitment, so why was she just sitting in the damn car staring at the door? *Dammit, Bri.* Taking a deep breath, she threw the car door open and stepped out. Shutting the door on her car, she looked up at the house and butterflies erupted in her stomach. Then she finally made herself move.

Making her way up to the front porch, she smiled as she saw the front door open and the twins looking out of the screen door at her. They smiled back at her and one of them swung the door open. If she wasn't mistaken, it was Ryker.

As Ryker swung the door open, Ross put his index finger to his lips in a *shh* manner. Bri didn't know what was going on, but she decided to go with it. She pressed her lips together and gave the twins a nod.

She followed them into the house, and Ryker closed the door behind her. Bri looked around the room, taking in the dark wood tables and the deep brown leather couch and chairs. It was definitely a masculine household, but it was clean, if a bit sparse. There wasn't much in the form of decoration. It was obvious that he had focused on making sure the necessities were provided, though.

Across the space was the kitchen and dining area. Separating one from the other was a large island with a few stools pushed up to one side. From what she could see from where she was standing, the kitchen looked to be pretty updated, but it was as sparse as the living room. She didn't see any personality in his space. Making a note to ask him about it, Bri followed the twins to the island and took a seat on one of the stools.

Ross moved over to the other side of the island and began preparing the asparagus to go on the grill. Ryker was doing the same with cut up potatoes.

Ross shouted out, "Your dress Henley is perfect! Your hair is perfect! And I'm sure your jeans are perfectly pressed and hug your ass perfectly! Come out of the damn bathroom!"

In an attempt to keep her presence a surprise, Bri whipped a hand up to her mouth. It was the only way to stop the snort of laughter that had worked its way through her.

They heard a door swing open right before Rebel's voice rang out. "Keep it up, and I'm kicking your ass! It's not child abuse once you're eighteen! The most I'd get would be a month of… Oh. Hey." Rebel stopped at the mouth of the hall and stared at her.

Smiling at him, she gave a wave.

"I didn't… You're… They didn't… You're here."

"Wow." Ross shook his head. "It's his intelligence that does it for you, isn't it?"

Rebel took a few steps into the room, reached out, and gave the back of Ross's head a smack. "I'm glad you're here." He rounded the island and approached her.

"Fucking, ow," Ross grumbled.

Ignoring him, Rebel bent forward and kissed her cheek. Into her ear, he whispered, "Nice leather, Sweetie."

Feeling her cheeks heat, Bri cleared her throat and replied, "Thanks."

"Can I take that for you? Get you a drink? We got wine, some whiskey, and beer. Or pop and water if you're not feeling the other stuff."

"'Hi. I'm a rambling, nervous wreck because a pretty girl looked at me twice.'"

When Rebel turned and glared at Ross, he looked down at the asparagus and became really focused on prepping it *just right*.

Giggling, Bri slipped her leather jacket off and handed it to Rebel. "I'll take a whiskey on the rocks, please."

"On it," Ryker said and turned. He approached the cupboard next to the refrigerator and grabbed a short glass before he opened the freezer to get the whiskey and ice.

Rebel walked away long enough to hang her jacket on a hook to the right of the front door. While he did that, she got a good look at his backside and determined that, yes, his jeans *did* hug his ass perfectly. The snort laugh that came out of her had Rebel turning around to look at her with an arched brow.

"What?"

"Nothing," she choked out and shook her head.

When the twins busted out with laughter, she knew they had spotted where her eyes had been focused and were well aware of what she had been thinking.

Chapter Nine

Rebel

He didn't know what the three of them were laughing about, but Rebel liked that she seemed to be bonding with the twins. They were important to him, and Ruby was well on her way to be important to him, too. If making fun of him was the catalyst for that bond, he was all about it.

It was the way of cousins to pick on each other and crack jokes. He didn't take any offense to it, really, but he also didn't want Ruby to think he was a fuck up. He worried she might misunderstand his jokes and think he would really hurt his cousins. It wouldn't be a stretch since she witnessed him killing his uncle.

His wolf began whimpering at the thought.

"Whatever thought is putting that scowl on your face, stop thinking it," Ruby ordered as he stopped at her side.

Shoving his negative thoughts aside, he looked down at her and sighed. "Sorry. I just… Never mind.

It's not important." He glanced down at Ruby's outfit and had to bite back a groan. So much about the outfit had his jeans fitting a little tighter, but it was the boots that sealed the deal. He couldn't help but picture them biting into his ass as he… His eyes flashed a greenish-gold light for just a split second, before Rebel was able to shut down his thoughts and get himself back under control.

Ruby gasped at the sight of the light, but he couldn't address that until he was back in control of himself. Not to mention, he didn't really want to talk about it with the twins around.

What the hell is wrong with me? It's like I'm thirteen again and turned on by everything.

"For fuck's sake, we're getting ready to make dinner." Ross threw a towel at him, and it hit him square in the face. "Don't make me lose my appetite."

His eyes shot open, and he glared at Ross. "I swear to all the fucking gods that I will make you clean every toilet in the apartment building, every single day, when you become a prospect, if you don't knock it the fuck off," Rebel growled at his cousin.

"Anyway!" Ryker set Ruby's drink in front of her from across the island and asked, "How was work?"

Rebel shot Ryker a grateful look as he took the stool next to Ruby. When he glanced over at Ruby, he saw the questions in her eyes. He mouthed the word *later* at her as he put his hand to her back and ran it up and down. He wanted to do much more, but just like

Rebel's Fairytale

answering the questions in her eyes, it would have to wait until they were alone.

"It was work." Ruby shrugged. "It wasn't bad or good, just… was."

"Do you like being a librarian?"

Ruby nodded, and Rebel noticed that she had shifted closer to him. He was able to slide his hand around her opposite hip, and he did with the full intention of bringing her closer.

Her phone vibrated as she answered the question. "I do. Not only is it filled with my favorite thing, books, but I also like that I get to help others, serve my community, inspire young people to keep their minds open, and all the other things." She turned it over on the island and glanced at it. Not wanting to be nosy, he avoided looking to see who it was. She quickly sent a text and turned the phone back over. Then, she was smiling at his cousins.

The smile on her face had him smiling with her. It lit up her eyes and drew him in, like a moth to a flame. She very well could be his undoing, if she wanted to be. Lucky for him, his Ruby wouldn't do such a thing… not in a negative way, at least.

"That's so cool," Ryker replied. "Did you know that Rebel was a straight-A student and also had a short story published when he was in high school?"

Rebel groaned, out loud this time, and dropped his gaze to the tile top of the island. The last thing he wanted to talk about was that damn story. Everyone told him how great it was, but he knew he could have done much better. Now, it was an embarrassment to him.

"No, I didn't." Ruby nudged him in the ribs with her elbow. "Where do I find this story? I want to read it."

"Oh! Hold on!" Before Rebel could stop the little brat, Ryker rushed out of the room and came jogging back with the magazine in his hand. He set it down on the island in front of Ruby and said, "It's on page twenty-three."

"Ruby, you don't have to read it," Rebel said, quietly, and tried to take the magazine.

She swatted Rebel's hand away and began turning pages to find his story. While she did that, he got to his feet. He kissed her temple and headed for the back door.

"I'm going to get the grill going."

The last thing he wanted to do was sit there while she read the story. He would focus on getting the grill ready for the steaks and pretend it wasn't happening.

For the next ten minutes, he avoided being in the kitchen. He only reentered the house to get the steaks from the refrigerator. When he stepped through the door, he glanced over at her and found her gazing at him with a grin on her beautiful face.

Fuck, she was beautiful. For the first time that he'd noticed, she was wearing red on her lips, making Rebel want to nibble on them, but also making him want to see them wrapped around his cock. His wolf let out a growl and began to prowl inside of him. Their mate was the prettiest girl they had ever seen, and his wolf was impatient to claim her.

I know, buddy. Soon.

"Rebel, that was a great story," she told him and got to her feet. She came around the island and stopped at his side. Wrapping her arms around his waist, she pressed her body against his side.

He let out a growl, unable to stop it, at the feel of her pressed against him. It was getting harder to keep his brain off of thoughts of taking her and giving her pleasure.

She stiffened at the sound, but when he looked at her, he didn't see fear. Her beautiful gold-flecked blue eyes were laced with lust and her teeth were latched on to her bottom lip. Taking advantage of the fact that her heeled boots made them equal in height, he leaned his head forward and took her mouth in a slow, deep kiss.

He growled again when he felt her hand fist his shirt at his abdomen and she tilted her head just enough to give him better access. He had just wrapped his arms around her and was about to lift her into his arms to take her to his room, when they heard someone loudly clear their throat.

Shit. The twins.

He broke the kiss and pressed his forehead to hers. "Uh… oops."

The giggle she let out made him grin.

Looking into her eyes, he promised, "Later."

She nodded in response and bit her bottom lip again.

Fuck. If she didn't stop doing stuff like that, no one was getting dinner.

"Down boy," she breathed.

He fully expected commentary from his cousins at that since they could hear her just fine with their shifter hearing. Surprisingly, the most he heard was a swift intake of breath before he saw in his peripheral vision Ross turn and walk out of the kitchen.

"I think I'll put the steaks on and… uh… give you two a minute," Ryker mumbled before he stepped around them and through the back door.

Giggling, she told Rebel, "I really like your cousins."

"They like you, too," he told her and gave her a soft kiss. "I do, too."

With his hands on her hips, Rebel stepped forward, making her walk backward, and kept going until her back was to the wall on the far side of the dining room.

He reached out and opened the door to her left. "Come on," he said and took her hand. He led her inside and flipped on the light. After pulling the door closed, he pressed her against the back of it with his body.

"Rebel?"

"I just need a few minutes," he whispered and pressed his lips to hers. Running his hands up and down her sides, he slowly, softly kissed her lips, letting his tongue caress hers as he felt her hands travel up his chest under his cut.

Rebel's Fairytale

He broke the kiss and wrapped his arms around her. Hugging her close, he let out a deep sigh, loving the feel of her in his arms.

"Are we going to talk about how in the hell you have lights behind your eyes?"

Rebel chuckled into her shoulder. "It happens when we feel extreme emotion. Rage, love, passion."

"Okay… So, if your eyes lit up when you were looking at my boots, that means…"

Rebel lifted his head from her shoulder and looked into her eyes. "It means I was picturing things that I liked a little too much." When her cheeks reddened at his words, Rebel smiled.

"Oh," she breathed.

"Yeah." He stepped back enough to look her up and down. "Now that we're alone, I can finally say what I wanted to say when I saw you."

"Wh-what's that?"

"You look fucking amazing. You should wear these jeans every damn day. I like seeing you more casual, even if I really do like your librarian look. And those fucking boots… God *damn*." He cupped her face in his hands and ran his thumb over her bottom lip. "This… short-circuits my brain."

Those lips curved into a smile. "Thank you," she replied, dropping her eyes to his chest.

"After dinner, I'd like to take you on a ride… on my bike. You up for it?"

Her gaze flipped up to his. "I'd love that." She smiled. "I have to go change my boots though. I…" She stopped talking and blushed further.

"What?" He was curious what had her blushing this time.

"I… I was driving down main street, the other day. I saw some boots in the window of that one shoe store near the west side of town." She waved off her explanation of the location. "Anyway, I stopped and went inside. I bought a pair of boots I thought were cute but the store clerk had also told me they would be good to wear on a motorcycle."

Rebel grinned. "You bought boots so you could go on a ride with me?"

She shrugged.

"That's so damn cute." He chuckled and kissed her lips. "Sweetie, there are pegs to rest your feet on. If you wanted to wear these boots, you could, but we'll go get your biker boots. I've gotta see 'em, now."

"Rebel," she uttered as she playfully smacked his chest.

"I'm not teasing you. Okay… maybe a little. Keep in mind, Ruby, I'll want these boots on you when we do other things." There she went, blushing again. He caressed her cheeks with his thumbs. "Damn, I love this."

"Kiss me again, Rebel."

And he did.

Messer

Hunter Messer received the summons while running her recruits through their paces in hand-to-hand training in facility one, the first of three training facilities on the west side of the compound. They weren't the worst group of soldiers she'd ever come across, and they had potential, but she was working with bare bones skills. It would take them months to be ready for any kind of fight with a human, let alone whatever these shifter monsters were.

The summons told her she had a meeting with Commander West and one of his associates. That was vague, but they hadn't really set up policies and procedures yet, so it didn't surprise her.

When she reached the main building, Messer took the stairs on the west side of the building up to the second floor and the hallway down to Commander West's assigned office. She knocked on the door and was immediately granted entrance by a shouted command from Commander West. Messer opened the door and stepped inside.

Commander West's office was pretty bare. The navy walls were empty as were the built-in bookshelves behind his desk. He had a dark wood executive desk, three dark brown Queen Anne style chairs, and a white board. She didn't doubt that it would be filled with bullshit before long.

"Sir." She stopped just inside the door and stood at attention, staring straight ahead, an old habit from the military.

Commander West snorted a laugh. "For fuck's sake, relax."

Hunter Messer relaxed and looked over at her commander who was standing to her left with another man she had never met. He was shorter than Commander West and had graying hair that looked to be thinning. He had a large gut and was wearing an ill-fitting blue suit.

Commander West was a large man with dark brown skin, a muscular body, and a permanent scowl on his handsome face. He was grumpy as hell and rarely found humor in anything, but he seemed to be a good boss so far.

"Messer, this is Ambrose C. Thompson. He is the owner and investor of this academy."

She walked over and held out her hand. "Nice to meet you, Sir."

The older man shook her hand. "You as well. Your name is Messer?"

"Stella Messer. Yes, sir." She yanked her hand from the man's grasp, since he didn't seem to have the intention of letting it go anytime soon.

Commander West cleared his throat. "Stella is our most skilled Hunter, which is why we are giving her Elite Hunter status. Messer, you will from now on be referred to as Elite Messer. Your crew will be Strike Team One, once you get them trained and ready.

Before that, we have a special mission for you, personally."

"Yes," Mr. Thompson said with a nod, "we do. We have been informed that there is a large enclave of these… these monsters in a small town a couple hours north of here. We need you to go there and gather as much information about these creatures and their habits. We have all the weapons and facilities we need, but we don't have as much intel as we would like."

She nodded. "Absolutely, sir. I will do my best. Do I have a departure date and time? Do I have a return date?"

Commander West crossed the room and grabbed a navy folder from his desk. He handed it to her and answered, "This mission is about information, but if you have the opportunity to eliminate any of the creatures, you are under orders to not hesitate. You will leave this evening. Elite Cox will handle your recruit's training while you are gone. We expect daily updates. Your return date is two weeks from today."

"Do I report directly to you, Commander West?"

He gave a nod. "Yes. However, if you need resources, there is a list of contacts in the folder for you to reach out to. Most of them are stationed here. Add them to your phone and memorize what you can."

"Will do. Am I dismissed?"

Commander West sighed. "This isn't the military, Messer," He waved a hand toward her, "but yes, you are dismissed."

She turned on her heel and left the office. As she made her way to her suite, she looked over the information she had and added the contact list to her phone. *Where in the hell is Warden's Pass, Michigan?*

Bri

Spending time with Rebel and the twins was the best way to spend her evenings, Bri decided as she drove back to her townhouse. Remembering the way Ross teased Rebel and Ryker talked him up made Bri happy. They obviously loved their cousin, and Rebel made it clear he felt the same way about them.

She didn't know a lot about the family dynamic, but from what she gathered, Rebel was giving them a stability they had never had, and if she was being honest with herself, that was probably the sexiest thing about the well-read biker. The concern for his cousins and determination to give them a safe place to be themselves was evident in his interactions with them and also in the home he provided them.

As she pulled into her driveway and pushed the button on her visor to open her garage door, Bri wondered how she would fit in their dynamic. Would the twins still be as welcoming if she were a more present figure, or would they balk at the idea of having to share Rebel's time and space with her? It was something to keep an eye on, she decided.

After parking in her garage and getting out of the car, Bri made her way to the door that led from the garage to the kitchen. She waited there as Rebel dismounted his bike and headed for her. Once he was in the garage, she pressed the button on the wall to close the garage door and turned to use her key to unlock the kitchen door.

They had barely gotten inside before he had her pressed against the wall, face first with her palms against the surface next to her, and his hand was moving the hair away from her neck. She felt his lips and tongue there and gasped at the pleasure that shot through her.

"The things you do to me," he whispered into her ear before he nipped at the lobe.

Bri didn't say a word. She didn't know what to say. She just tilted her head to the side and closed her eyes, allowing him to kiss and suck along her neck. When she felt his large hands on her hips, pulling them back against him, she let out a moan. The proof of his desire for her was obvious and pressed against her ass.

He kissed back up to her ear and ordered, "Get your biker boots, Sweetie."

Then, he wasn't pressed against her anymore. The sudden disconnect from his body had her feeling a strange sense of loss. It wasn't like he was gone. He wasn't. He was only a few feet from her, but that didn't matter. She wanted his touch back.

As she turned to look at him, he chuckled. "I know. I want to. I *so* do." His eyes flashed that light again as he absently scratched at the beard on his chin. "I don't want to rush this, though. I want to do things the right way." He huffed out a breath and smiled at her. "I'll wait here, because if I go any further, I'll be carrying you to your bedroom."

Feeling sassy, Bri put her hand to her hip and replied, "Yeah… and? I'm not seeing the problem."

A low growl came out of Rebel, and his eyes flashed again.

Giggling, Bri headed down the hall that led to her living room, putting a little extra swing in her hips. When she heard a louder growl come from Rebel, she knew he noticed.

She was quick when she went upstairs and changed into her biker boots, as Rebel called them. She couldn't wait to take a ride with him on his bike. Seeing the Howlers on their bikes around town had always made her curious about why they loved the machines so much.

After she grabbed the important items from her purse, she slipped her debit card and her driver's license in the back pocket of her jeans and carried her keys in her hand as she made her way back down the stairs. When she returned to Rebel's side, he kissed her cheek and whispered in her ear, "Yeah, my Ruby looks good in any fucking thing."

She couldn't stop the shiver that ran through her at his words. "You… so… you like them?"

He chuckled and reached for the doorknob. Pulling the door open, he nodded and waved her through. "Yeah, I like them."

"Lock the handle behind you," she mumbled, distracted by his words. Stepping out into her garage and descending the few stairs, Bri looked down at her boots. They were black leather, with a very low heel, and a laced leather strap up the outside of the calf over a leather panel. The strap zigzagged down to her ankle where it stopped with a silver buckle. They were simple, but cute. She loved them.

"Ruby." When she looked over at him coming down the stairs and stopping at her side, he grinned at her. "I *really* like your boots." He winked at her. "Ready to go?"

When she nodded and smiled at him, he took her hand, and they headed for the exit door to the left of the garage door.

Once they stepped through the doorway, Bri used her key to lock the door before sliding her keys into the zipper pocket on the side of her jacket and zipped it closed. Excitement grew in her gut as they approached his bike. She couldn't wait to have the experience, but more importantly, she couldn't wait to share it with him.

T.S. Tappin

Chapter Ten

Rebel

As much as Rebel loved the way Ruby fisted his shirt in her hands, every single time she did it, if she didn't stop, he was going to pull over a lot sooner than he planned. It combined the feeling of her touch with an I-don't-want-to-let-you-go vibe that sparked his lust and sent his imagination flying.

The giggle she gave when he started the bike and the way she held on tight as he took off made him smile. She liked it, and that was important. If she was going to be with a biker, and she *was* going to be with *this* biker, then she had to enjoy being on the back of his bike.

He liked the feel of her thighs surrounding him and her chest pressed to his back, but it was her hands fisting in his shirt that drove him insane. He'd been hard since they passed the town line. Every time he cranked up the speed, she tightened her grip, making him think of her gripping other things.

An hour into the ride, he saw the sign for the state beach, and relief coursed through him. Finally, they had reached their destination. He slowed the bike and took a right into the parking area. After backing his bike into a spot near the end of the lot, close to a copse of trees, he killed the engine and looked at her over his shoulder.

Under the rim of the helmet she was wearing, he could see the exhilaration and joy in her eyes. Yeah, his Ruby fucking loved being on a bike. "You good?"

She unhooked the helmet and pulled it off her head. With a smile, she nodded. "Yeah. That was… awesome."

Rebel chuckled and climbed off his bike. He took the helmet from her hands and stowed it away in one of his saddlebags. When she started to climb off the bike, he stopped her. He loved watching her braid her hair before she got on the bike, but now he wanted it free again. She had the most beautiful golden hair, and he wanted access to it.

Standing at her side and gazing into her eyes, he reached up and slid the hair tie from the end of the braid. Maintaining eye contact, he slowly undid her braid, running his fingers through her hair. When he got up close to her scalp, he fisted the hair on the back of her head and leaned forward. He stopped an inch from her lips and whispered, "I love your hair, Ruby."

He watched as she visibly swallowed hard. Then, she blushed. "I'm kinda fond of yours too." Staring back at him, she reached up and pulled the hair tie from his hair, letting it fall around their faces.

"Yeah?" His gaze dropped to her lips.

"Yeah," she breathed and ran her tongue along her bottom lip.

He apparently took too long, because she reached between them and gripped his beard to pull him close. Rebel had always been good at taking orders, so he followed her silent command and took her lips in a slow, sensual kiss.

Breaths mingling, tongues caressing, he couldn't get enough of her, and it appeared she felt the same about him.

After a few minutes, he pulled back and cleared his throat. He needed to collect himself or he would be taking her on his bike in the parking lot of the state beach. Rebel really didn't want their first time to be like that. He took a few deep breaths before he slid both of their hair ties in the pocket of his jeans and retrieved the small blanket from his other saddlebag. He held out his free hand to help her off the bike.

When she took his hand and began to dismount, he heard her giggle. "What's so funny, Ruby?"

She looked at him, a grin on her face. "We're acting like teenagers, unable to control our hormones."

He shifted behind her and wrapped his arms around her waist. Holding her close and walking slowly toward the walkway, he asked into her ear, "Something wrong with that?"

She shook her head and turned so she could look at him over her shoulder. "Not one thing."

He pecked her cheek and moved back to her side, shifting one of his arms over her shoulders. When she pressed herself into his side as they made their way down the walkway, Rebel was positive he had never been happier in his life.

Messer

Messer pulled her Land Rover into a spot at the Hen House Inn and let out an annoyed sigh. She hated small towns. While they were great for finding intel, since everyone knew everything about everybody, she found them claustrophobic. And they always seemed to name their businesses corny names that were cutesy and not very professional.

She imagined the person who owned the inn was very nice, but the name made her cringe. Shoving down her disdain for the name of the place, she grabbed her two suitcases and her large duffle from the back of the vehicle and headed inside.

The lobby of the inn wasn't as gaudy as she expected it to be. The wall behind the counter was a nice, muted teal with dark gray pin-striping and the other walls of the lobby, and for as far as she could see down the hallway, were the dark gray with a thick, muted teal, horizontal stripe down the center. All the furniture and the desk were dark gray, and all the detailing was muted teal. It was all very pulled together without being too much.

The woman behind the counter was older than Messer, but she was beautiful and pulled off the teal color of her short hair very nicely. With a smile, she greeted, "Welcome to the Hen House. I'm the owner. People just call me Mama Hen."

"Nice to meet you," Messer said as she stopped at the desk and pulled her small wallet out of her jacket pocket. "I'll need a room. We'll go with two weeks to start."

Mama Hen's eyebrows lifted as she moved to the computer and started clicking away. "That seems like a long time for Warden's Pass. You have family in the area?"

"Something like that," Messer replied and pasted a smile on her face, hoping the woman bought it.

They finished up the check-in, and Mama Hen handed over a keycard. Messer thanked her, then she headed up to the second floor and to her room.

Once inside, she unpacked her suitcase with her clothes by laying it on its back and unzipping it. She wasn't sure what her mission would entail, so she thought it best to stay prepared to leave at a moment's notice.

With that done, she pulled the table and chairs away from the window, not wanting anyone to be able to see her if she was sitting at the table. Then, she pulled the case file and her map of Warden's Pass out of the duffle and laid them out on the table, deciding to grid out the town and make a plan.

Eyeing the location of the biker compound, Messer tried to think of a way to do some recon on the place without them spotting her. From the look of things, it was going to be a challenge, but Messer had never walked away from a challenge in her life. This wouldn't be the first one.

Mama Hen

After the new customer stepped into the elevator, Mama Hen lifted her receiver and pressed the first speed dial number.

"Yeah?"

"Axle, it's Mama Hen."

"I know." Axle chuckled. "What can I help you with?"

Mama Hen ignored his amusement. "A new customer came in. Never seen her before. She was evasive about her reason for visiting and booked the room for two weeks, with the option to extend. Something about her tripped my internal alarm."

"And… How accurate has this alarm been in your past, Mama Hen?"

Mama Hen put her hand to her hip and cocked her head to the side, even though Axle couldn't see her. "I've had to depend on it more times than I could count, Axle Weber, and it's never steered me wrong."

"What *did* you do for a living?"

Mama Hen ignored his question. "Gossip doesn't become you, Axle. I take it you're on it."

With another chuckle, Axle replied, "Yeah. Room number?"

"Two thirteen," Mama Hen answered

"Vehicle?"

Glancing at the screen that showed the view from the security cameras in the parking lot. "Dark gray Land Rover. Parked in the side lot, near the south exit."

"I'll get Keys on it. Might need a room key."

Mama Hen started clicking away, preparing the key. "I'll have it ready for you guys."

"Thanks, Mama Hen."

Bri

The walkway was paved, but it was lined with thick woods, making it feel like they were walking through a cave. The night air was breezy, but the heat radiating off of Rebel kept Bri comfortable. They walked for a few minutes until the trees opened up and revealed a small section of beach that was separated from the next much larger section by a few trees and a rather large hill that jutted out almost until the waterline.

It was the perfect little hideaway for a couple on a bike ride, looking for some privacy. She eyed the blanket in his other hand.

"I come here a lot when I just need to think, or I'm too angry to be around others. With my family being the way it is… was…" He shook his head, and her heart broke just a little for him. For as tough as he was, there was a lost little boy in there who only wanted a stable family.

"So, this is your sanctuary?" She asked as they slowly walked over to a spot near the bottom of the hill.

He nodded. "Yeah. And I wanted to share it with my Ruby." He kissed her temple before he released her and spread the blanket out on the sand.

My Ruby? Bri stared at him for a long moment, trying to decide if she was his or if she even liked him calling her that. Her pussy decided it absolutely did, so she shrugged and let it go.

He took a seat in the middle of the blanket with his knees bent up and his legs open. He patted the spot between his thighs, motioning for her to sit.

She settled there, turned slightly to the side, so she could see both him and the water. After gazing out at the small waves crashing against the sand twenty feet in front of them, she looked at him and pressed a kiss to his lips. When she pulled back, she whispered, "Thank you for sharing your spot with me. Do you want to talk about your family?"

Rebel cupped the back of her head in his hand and kept her close. He shook his head. "Another time." His gaze dropped to her lips.

Bri was a bit ashamed to admit that she was relieved he didn't want to get deep with the conversation. She was in much too good of a mood from their amazing date to taint it with family trauma. She wanted to know about it and be there for him, but their three mini make-out sessions had her body on fire. They needed a release of a different kind.

When he leaned forward and pressed his lips to hers, she could have cried out with joy. Instead, she fisted her hands in the front of his shirt and pulled him as close as she could get him.

Rebel didn't break the kiss when he growled, but she wondered what exactly made him growl. Experimenting, she released his shirt and waited. After a few moments of slow, soft kisses, he ramped up the passion a bit, and she fisted his shirt in her hand again. The growl that came from him was deeper, more guttural.

Unable to stop herself, she broke the kiss and giggled. "Like that, do ya?"

Rebel nipped her chin and nuzzled her neck. "I fucking love when you grab onto me like you can't get me close enough."

"Like this?" She moved her hands to his cheeks and slowly slid them back into his hair and fisted. Within seconds, she was flat on her back on the blanket and Rebel was between her thighs. His kisses got urgent and demanding, his tongue ordering hers to play. She complied, tickling the inside of his mouth the way he was tickling hers.

When they needed to breathe, Rebel dragged his lips along her cheek to her neck, panting and pressing his jean-clad erection against her core. "Fuck, Ruby."

"It's your fault," she whispered back.

Rebel chuckled against her neck as his hand dipped under her shirt at her side. "My fault?"

"Yeah. You started it with your flashy eyes and your kisses and your compliments. Your. Fault."

He hummed and kissed his way down to the skin of her chest, exposed by her V-neck tee. After dipping his tongue into her cleavage, he asked, "Is this where I'm supposed to apologize? Because I have no intention of doing so."

Before she could respond, his hand cupped her bra-covered breast and gave it a gentle squeeze, causing Bri's breath to catch.

"The way I see it." Kiss. "You started it." Kiss. "With this outfit." Kiss. "And your various pairs of boots." His hand pulled the cup of her bra down and his fingers found her hard nipple. As he tweaked and caressed the nub, he kissed his way back up to her mouth. "So, it's your fault," he said against her lips.

Bri's heart was pounding out of control and her breathing was shallow. The more the man played, the more she wanted him to play. "Rebel," she moaned when he pinched her nipple, before moving on to her other breast.

"What do you need, Ruby?"

She huffed out a breath. "Everything. *Something.*"

Smiling, he kissed her again. This time, he didn't take long to work up to passionate. He shot straight there with his mouth as his hand began working the front of her shirt up her body. When he pushed her shirt up past her breasts, he broke the kiss and moved down to her breasts.

As Rebel sucked her right nipple into his mouth, Bri moaned and tightened her grip on his hair, holding him against her. He sucked and licked and kissed the skin around her areola for a while, until he moved over to her other breast. When he did the same to her other nipple, Bri lifted one of her legs and wrapped it around his waist, lifting her hips to press her core even harder against his erection.

Rebel growled against her breast as he slid his hand over her abdomen to the button of her jeans, where he stopped. He lifted his head and looked into her eyes, his own giving off that greenish-gold light.

"Yes?"

Bri nodded quickly, her chest heaving with her accelerated breathing. "Yes."

"Thank fuck," he uttered as he unbuttoned and unzipped her jeans. She helped by wiggling her hips as he pushed them down a bit. His lips returned to hers as he worked his hand into the front of her jeans to cup her core over her panties.

She moaned into his mouth when one of his fingers grazed her clit through the fabric.

He pushed aside the gusset of her panties and caressed her slit. "You're so wet for me."

She nipped his bottom lip. "Your fault."

He grinned and went back to kissing her as he slowly slid one of his fingers into her core. As he fingerfucked her, he made love to her mouth. She appreciated it because she couldn't help the whimpers and moans. At least his kisses were muffling them.

When he added another finger and began to play with her clit with his thumb, she thought her heart was going to pound right out of her chest. The pleasure he was creating inside of her was overwhelming her senses.

He smelled like leather and oak, and she couldn't get enough of it. On top of the hair and beard and sexy eyes, he was smart and sweet. The sound of his voice whispering in her ear sent shivers through her body just like his touch brought her to the brink of pleasure faster than she ever experienced before. One kiss from him had her wanting to strip him naked and taste every inch of his body.

"Yeah, Ruby, ride my hand," he growled against her mouth.

She hadn't even realized it, but she was working her hips with the rhythm of his fingers. Looking into his eyes as she kept moving, she saw the lust and awe and something she didn't quite recognize in his eyes. That was all she needed.

Bri gasped as her pleasure crested and spilled over the edge, her climax rising inside of her. Rebel slammed his mouth to hers and swallowed her cries of pleasure. He kept kissing her as her climax eased, leaving her limbs loose and relaxed, and cupped her core again.

"Good?"

She nodded and smiled up at him. "More than good."

"Good." He went back to kissing her.

Desperate to feel his skin, Bri slid her hands under his cut to grip his Henley and yank it up. Finally, she was able to touch and caress the skin of his abdomen, trace his muscles, and follow his happy trail to the button of his jeans.

Rebel broke their kiss and pressed his forehead to hers. "You… you don't have to."

"You don't want me to?"

He quietly chuckled. "Sweetie, I want your hands all over me, more than I think I want anything else in this world. And, yes, I'm sure that made very little sense. Maybe."

Gazing into his eyes, Bri giggled and unbuttoned his jeans. "I want to."

"By all means."

She had just gripped his zipper, ready to unzip his jeans, when a noise came from somewhere around them. The sound popped their privacy bubble and had Rebel on alert.

His head snapped up and looked around as his hands moved to her chest and began fixing her clothes. Once she was covered, he climbed to his feet and refastened his jeans as he scanned their surroundings.

T.S. Tappin

Rebel

Ignoring the growling wolf inside of him, Rebel climbed to his feet and refastened his jeans. The desire to kill whoever was making those noises was overwhelming. Not only was he worried about Ruby's safety, but he was about to have her hands on him, and this fucker was interrupting their fun.

He felt like they had been in a state of foreplay since the first time he saw her. Would he have went all the way and fucked her for the first time on the blanket? No, probably not, but he desperately needed some relief that didn't come from his hand.

His wolf was prowling inside of him, irritated that he hadn't claimed Ruby, as well as worried for her safety. Rebel took a deep breath as he visually scanned the area, needing to get himself and his wolf under control.

Scanning the tree line, he shifted to the side to look down the walkway a bit. He didn't see anyone. Turning slowly, he let his eyes scan the tree line again, until he reached the hill. When he didn't see anyone, he looked down at Ruby, sitting on the blanket, fully put back together. He put his finger to his lips in a request for her to remain quiet. Once he got a nod from her, he stealthily made his way around the bottom of the hill and came face to face with Elsie and Elfie Kirsh, a married couple from Warden's Pass who had had a problem with the Howlers since the Howlers helped their daughter-in-law, Kathy, escape their abusive son, Ernie.

"You should be ashamed of yourself," the old bitty hissed at Rebel, while clutching to her husband's arm.

"What in the fuck are you doing here?" Rebel could barely get the question out through his gritted teeth. His gut was telling him it wasn't a coincidence.

"We were just walking the beach," Elfie said as he lifted his chin and attempted to look down his nose at Rebel. "This is a public beach. What you two were doing is *indecent*."

Rebel crossed his arms over his chest and chuckled. "You're just pissed that she won't let you touch her like that." Ignoring their gasp, Rebel turned and headed back around the hill to Ruby.

He knew they were following him, but he was over their bullshit. Grabbing the blanket from the ground, he took Ruby's hand and headed for the walkway.

"Miss, you should know better than to *associate* with trash like that."

When Ruby stopped and turned to face the couple, Rebel said, "Just ignore them."

"No." Ruby pulled her hand from Rebel's and finished turning around.

With a sigh, Rebel also turned around. His woman had her hands on her supple hips, looking like she was about to burn the world down with the fire shooting from her stare.

"I don't know *you*, but I know him. Seems to me the words you are throwing at a *good man* make you trash."

"He is a *biker*," Elsie Kirsh hissed the last word like it was a curse word.

Ruby laughed. "Yes. Yes, he is. And what does that have to do with the content of his character?"

"They are criminals," Elfie sputtered.

"Name one law they have broken." She waited a moment, but when the Kirshes didn't have an answer, she added, "The Howlers have done more for Warden's Pass than the entire city council and the police force combined. In my opinion, you should be on your knees thanking them for the service they have provided to our town."

As the older couple scoffed, Ruby turned on her heel, took Rebel's hand, and dragged him down the walkway. Bitching about self-righteous assholes under her breath, she stomped down the path.

Rebel wanted to push her up against a tree and show her just how fucking hot it was that she'd defend him and his club that way, with her high-class, proper language. As she dragged him behind her, he settled for staring at her luscious ass and the way it swayed with every step.

"Stop staring at my ass, Rebel," she ordered.

Rebel grinned. "I can't help it. It's mesmerizing."

That did it. The tension was broken, Ruby burst out laughing.

Chapter Eleven

Niles

When the woman from out of town asked Niles whether he'd seen the newscast and whether he was worried about shifters, he knew she wasn't a friend of the Howlers. He watched the way she had moved through the diner to her table and her body language as she took a seat. She was stiff, controlled, like she kept her emotions locked down. Her mannerisms and way of speech sounded very military to him. If he worked things the right way, maybe he could use her skills to his advantage.

Niles had heard about the townsfolk who wanted to push the Howlers out of town. He talked to Reginald about meeting with them. They sounded like a group of people he wanted to spend time around. If anyone had a reason to want to get rid of the Howlers, it was Niles. They had stolen his family and moved them. Now, he was sure one of those asshole monsters was moving in on his woman and trying to take his place in his kids' lives. That shit couldn't fly.

After eating her lunch, the woman, Stella, had started asking questions of the people eating at the diner. When he heard her ask the person at the next table, he motioned her over.

Now, she was sitting across from him, and he was explaining that the shifters were dividing the town and how they split up his family. Sure, he left out some details, but he told her the important parts.

By the time he was done, they had exchanged numbers, and she had told him to give her a call if he heard anything else. He never did find out why exactly she was in town, but his gut was telling him she was about to be an important part in fucking with the Howlers.

Bri

When Rebel dropped her off at home, he walked her to her front door. Bri invited him inside, but he refused to go further than just inside her living room. That was a disappointment until he scrambled her brains with another make-out session.

She really wanted him to follow her up to her bedroom, but he insisted they wait. She almost pushed the issue until he mentioned wanting to get home to the boys to make sure they hadn't burned his house down. Reluctantly, she nodded and let him walk out her front door.

After she watched him ride away, through the front window, she went upstairs to get ready for bed, thinking how sweet he was to wait on her front porch until he heard the lock engage. She washed her face and brushed her teeth before changing into her favorite set of pajamas — a loose tee and a pair of cotton shorts.

When she climbed into bed, she glanced over at the empty side and wished Rebel was there with her. Sure, she wanted them to finish what they started, but she also just wanted to cuddle with him while she slept. Bri suspected he would be an outstanding cuddler.

With a smile on her face, she grabbed her cell phone off of the side table and sent him a message.

Rebel

Rebel had just said goodnight to the boys and stepped into his bedroom, when his phone vibrated with a notification. Deciding to wait to remove his boots until he knew he didn't need to go anywhere, he pulled his phone from the pocket of his cut and checked it, expecting it to be Axle or another one of his brothers. It was a text from Ruby.

>SINCE I DON'T GET ANY MORE SEXY TIME WITH YOU TONIGHT, WHICH IS YOUR FAULT, I GUESS I'LL HAVE TO HAVE SEXY TIME WITH MYSELF AND TAKE INSPIRATION FROM MY BOOK BOYFRIEND.<

A vision of her having sexy time with herself popped into his head, eliciting a groan from him. With a grin, he crossed the room to his bookshelf and pulled his favorite spicy book out. Quickly flipping to his favorite sex scene, he found the page he wanted from a certain section and took a picture of it. Then, he sent her a text along with the picture.

> >FUCK, RUBY. ALONG WITH THE VISUAL YOU JUST CAUSED, I'LL BE USING THIS FOR INSPIRATION DURING THE SEXY TIMES I'M ABOUT TO HAVE WITH MYSELF.<

After pressing send, he bent down and removed his boots. Then, he hung his cut on the hook by his closet door. Telling himself he couldn't get back on his bike and go back to her house, he forced himself to get undressed and climb into bed. He glanced at the empty side of the bed and sighed. What he wouldn't give to have her there for him to wrap in his arms and hold her while they slept.

Yeah, he was totally gone for this woman, and she didn't even know it yet.

Rebel had just settled back on his pillow when his phone vibrated again on his nightstand. He wouldn't acknowledge the speed at which he grabbed the phone, or what that might mean, to enter his brain. He opened their text string and about swallowed his tongue at the picture of her pretty face with her hair spread all over her pillow that was there waiting for him. It took a second for him to pull his eyes from the photo to look at what she typed.

> > YOU KNOW THERE'S ANOTHER SOLUTION, RIGHT?<

Throwing back his covers and climbing out of bed, he sent his reply.

>I WAS TRYING TO BE A GENTLEMAN, BUT YOU JUST WENT AND KICKED HIS ASS OUT OF THE PICTURE. YOU BETTER NOT START WITHOUT ME. BE THERE SOON.<

Rebel had never gotten redressed so fast in his life.

Bri

Ten minutes later, when Bri opened the door, she barely had time to see who was standing there before Rebel had her up in his arms. With her arms around his shoulders and her legs around his waist, she held on as he kicked the door shut behind him and reached back to turn the lock.

"Uh… hi," she said as he began to climb the stairs with her still in his arms.

"Hi," he said and slammed his lips to hers, taking her breath away with the passion and urgency of his kiss. Forcing entrance into her mouth, he showed her exactly what he planned to do between her legs as soon as they were both naked.

When he finally broke the kiss, it was because they reached the top of the stairs, and he needed to know where to go. "Which room?"

"First door on the right," she breathed against his lips.

Gazing into her eyes, he took a few steps to the door and stepped into her bedroom. Then he turned and pressed her back to the wall next to her door. With one hand on her ass holding her up, he used the other to shove her shirt up. Putting his lips to the skin between her breasts, he kissed his way over to a nipple.

Bri's head fell back against the wall as her eyes closed and she soaked in the pleasure his actions were causing in her. As he sucked and nibbled on her nipple, he pressed his hips forward, letting her feel his hard length against her core. Even separated by clothes, she had a good idea what she was up against.

Against her skin, he growled, "I'm too on edge to take this slow, Ruby."

"'Kay," she mumbled as he moved over and sensually attacked her other nipple. Needing to see what he was doing, she yanked the shirt off and dropped it to the floor. Looking down, she felt her core clench at the sight of Rebel's tongue flicking her nipple.

When she moaned, he let out a growl and turned around. He carried her across the room and tossed her on the bed. While she sat up to watch, he was crossing the room again. He laid his cut out on top of her dresser, before he quickly yanked off his boots and started tossing clothes everywhere in an attempt to get naked. It gave her a chance to take in the tattoos he had. On his left pec was an anatomical heart that had been stitched back together. He had the same design that was on the back of his cut on his back, and it took up a good portion of the area. Under his right arm, on his ribs, he had a simple quote. When he moved a certain way, she was able to read it — *Sometimes the right path is not the easiest.* She liked it, and she liked watching him reveal more skin. The man was hot. He only paused long enough to nod to her shorts and utter, "Off."

She had been so turned on for hours and didn't waste any time shoving her shorts and panties off. When she glanced up, she found Rebel frozen with his jeans half-way off. His eyes were glued to her naked body and were giving off that greenish-gold glow.

"Fuck," he growled.

Bri couldn't help the grin that grew on her face. She scooted back until she could lay her head on her pillow. Then she stretched out and let him look his fill. It didn't take long for him to get with the program and finish undressing.

With a look of pure animalistic lust on his face, he crawled up the bed from the foot, spreading her legs as he went. Growling, he kissed up the inside of her thigh until he got to her core. He shifted her legs up to rest on his shoulders. After shooting a wink up at her, he buried his face in her core and ate like he had been starved.

Licking and nibbling, he brought her to the edge in record time. When he added two fingers to her core and curved them just right, her body arched off the bed and a guttural moan came out of her as her climax washed over her.

"Yeah, Ruby. Give it to me," he ordered and kept up what he was doing until her body collapsed on the bed.

He didn't bother waiting. Before she could even catch her breath, he was over her and kissing along her neck. "Condom?"

With the rest of her energy, she reached out and slapped the top of her nightstand. Chuckling, Rebel pulled the top drawer open. When she saw his brow hike up, she was confused until he showed her what he found — her teal vibrator with its clitoral stimulator and thirteen different vibration settings.

"I've always been good on a team."

Snorting a laugh, Bri wrapped her legs around his hips.

Rebel returned her toy to the drawer and grabbed a condom. After putting on the condom, he gently kissed her lips and lined the head of his cock at her entrance.

"You sure?" The look on his face told her that he would stop if she told him to, but it would take a monumental effort for him to accomplish that. Either way, it didn't matter. There was no way in hell she was turning him away.

"Rebel, fuck me already."

"Yes, Ms. Cooke," he said with a cocky grin and slid inside of her, pulling a groan from both of them.

Once he was fully seated inside of her, he paused and took a few deep breaths. She totally understood because she had never felt so full, but if he didn't begin to move, she was going to riot.

He had just begun to slide out, when his phone rang with a ringtone she had never heard from his phone before.

Rebel's greenish-brown eyes looked down at her. "That's Axle. It ca—"

"I swear to God if you stop right now, I will kill you," Bri growled, surprising herself with the vehemence in her tone.

Rebel grinned. "The whole town could be on fire, and I wouldn't stop fucking you, right now, Ruby." With that, he pulled out and slammed back in, making her moan.

He set a hard and steady pace, curling his hips up just right at the end, hitting her exactly where she needed it. Bri couldn't even worry about what she looked or sounded like. He was scrambling her brain with the sensations he was causing.

When his hand found her breast, and his lips took hers in a sensual kiss, her core clenched hard around him.

"Next time," he whispered against her lips, "I will taste this body from head to toe."

"Yes," she cried out as his hand slid down her body, and his thumb found her clit.

"But this time, I want you to come on my cock, Ruby." Then he kissed across her cheek and down her neck to where it met her shoulder. He latched onto the skin there and sucked, sending her over the edge.

As her body drowned in a sea of pleasure, she heard him call out his name for her and felt him slam inside of her one last time.

Rebel

His heart was still racing as Rebel took care of the condom and returned to her bedroom with a warm washcloth to clean Ruby up. As he wiped her clean, he bent down and traced the tattoo on her thigh, a stack of books with a teacup on top, with his tongue. It was just another sexy secret his beautiful, sweet librarian had. After taking care of her, he kissed her lips.

"Gotta check on what Axle wanted. Be right back."

With a blissfully sated look on her face, she gave him a nod and snuggled into her pillow.

Feeling proud of himself, Rebel snatched his jeans off the floor and pulled them on. He grabbed his phone from his cut and stepped out into the hallway. Unlocking his phone, he pressed redial and put the phone to his ear.

After two rings, Axle answered, "Hey."

"Yeah?" Rebel tried to calm his breathing, but he knew Axle was going to be able to tell.

"I stopped by your place to talk to the twins about prospecting and what that means. They said you flew out of there like a bat out of hell. Everything good?"

"Yeah. Things are good."

He heard the amusement in his president's voice when he asked, "So what ya doing, Reb?"

Rebel huffed out a breath. "I'm at Ruby's. Is that all you needed?"

Axle chuckled. "Yup. Well, and we have church at 10."

"Okay. I'll be there."

"Try and get some rest at some point."

And that's when Rebel hung up the phone on his laughing president.

Rock

After getting the kids in bed and taking a long, hot shower, Rock pulled on a pair of pajama pants and climbed into bed. That was one con to being a parent. He couldn't just collapse naked in bed. If his daughter had a nightmare, it wouldn't be good if she walked in and got a look at her father's johnson.

Once he was in bed, he grabbed his phone off the charger and dialed up Diamond. He needed to check in and see how packing was going, but really, he just wanted to hear her voice. He missed her like hell.

After he claimed her with the club, something shifted in him. He knew in his soul that Lace was happy for them. That helped in dropping the last wall he had up. The fact that his family was supportive of their relationship was the most important thing to him, but truthfully, it was about him opening himself up to the possibility of having a true relationship with her. With a relationship came the possibility of being hurt. That was what had held him back for so long. However, Diamond wasn't Lace. He couldn't keep making her pay for Lace's actions.

When he watched her take that cut from Axle, it was as if his heart was whole again. She accepted every part of him, without hesitation, without an ounce of doubt. It was only fair that he returned that faith.

"Wes," she uttered into the phone in that sweet voice of hers.

"Hey Angel," he replied and relaxed back against his pillow, shoving his free hand behind his head.

"The kids in bed?"

"Yeah. They had a million questions today, but they seem to be excited for you guys to come live with us. Hunter is a bit leery about sharing a room, but we'll make it work."

"Miles and Jenna are over the moon. The second they found out, they started packing their rooms. I've never seen rooms be packed up that fast ever in my life."

Rock chuckled. "I think they kinda like me."

"Kinda? If I told Miles he could change his name to Wes, he would be all over it. Jenna already asked me if she could call you Dad."

Rock's heart clenched hard at that. He cleared his throat, trying to stop the tears that had suddenly appeared in his eyes. "Tell Jenna she can call me whatever she wants to call me."

"That's what I told her."

Needing to change the subject before he ended up sounding like a sap on the phone, he asked, "Where are you?"

"In bed," Diamond replied with a sexy lilt to her voice. "Where are you?"

"In my bed, smelling your sweet scent on the pillow next to me."

"Yeah?"

Rebel's Fairytale

"Yeah. Every time I smell it, I get hard as a damn rock."

The giggle he heard didn't help the fact that he was hard. "Do you need help with that?"

"Diamond, the only help I need is to close my eyes and think of you, but the sound of your voice doesn't hurt."

"Let me listen, Wes."

Not needing any more encouragement, Rock moved his hand from behind his head and slid it into the front of his pajama pants, palming his erection. "You want to hear me come for you, Angel?"

"Yes," she breathed.

Stroking his cock, he asked, "Are you touching yourself?"

"Mm-hmm," she replied.

Rock closed his eyes and pictured his Diamond with one hand teasing her clit and the other playing with her nipple. *Fuck*. That alone could make him shoot like a fucking teenager.

"Slide two fingers in that pretty pussy and fuck yourself for me."

He heard her shifting around. Then he heard her let out the sweetest gasp, followed by a sexy as hell moan.

"Wish I was there, Angel. I'd replace those fingers with my own as I licked and sucked that little clit of yours until you came all over my face. You know how much I love tasting you."

"Wes," she moaned.

Wes quickened the strokes on his erection and tightened his grip. "Fuck yourself harder, Angel. And rub your clit with the heel of your hand."

"I am," she cried. Then he heard her panting heavily, and he knew what that meant.

"That's it, Angel. Fuck yes. Come for me."

She moaned out his name as she did as he instructed. He returned the favor, calling out her name as he reached his own climax, coating his hand and stomach with his load.

"I love hearing you come," she giggled into the phone.

"Soon enough, you'll be watching it too. Love you, Angel."

"Love you, too, Wes."

"I'll be there in two days."

"Okay. Can't wait. Night."

"Night." He waited for her to end the call. Then he set his phone on the nightstand and got back up to go clean up the mess he'd made. When he was done, he headed back to bed to try to go to sleep, hating that he had to do it alone. He couldn't fucking wait for her to be there with him.

Chapter Twelve

Rebel

After following Ruby to work the next morning, he waited while she crossed the lot. She had paused briefly halfway across the lot to text someone, before she waved and continued inside. Knowing she was safe, Rebel headed home. He parked his bike in his usual spot outside the garage, since he allowed the twins to use the other spot in the garage and made his way to the front door. When winter hit, he'd have to pull his truck out and put his bike in the garage for storage. Deciding he needed to start checking over his truck to prepare it for winter, he pulled open his front door.

When he stepped inside, he was confronted with the sight of the twins standing in front of the island with their arms crossed over their chests. On either side of them was Pike and Ranger, both of them grinning like the idiots they were.

Ross glanced over at the clock on the wall before he glared at Rebel. "And where have *you* been all night?"

Rebel sighed and shut the door behind him.

"You couldn't call to tell us you wouldn't be home?" Ryker was trying to glare, but he wasn't quite achieving the effect he was going for.

Ignoring them, Rebel removed his cut and hung it on the hook by the door.

"Cousin, I think it's time for us to have a talk." The demanding tone of Ross's voice made Rebel roll his eyes as he walked across the room and stopped in front of Ross. "When a man and a woman love each other…"

That was all Ross got out before Rebel swung out and cuffed him upside his head with his shifted paw. Ignoring his now whining cousin, he glanced from Pike to Ranger. "What do you two want?"

"Axle told us to be here to pick up the twins, in case you weren't home from your girlfriend's house in time," Ranger said with a grin.

Rebel shot Ranger the finger and stepped around them, headed for his room. "Bring them to the clubhouse. I'll be there by ten."

As he opened his bedroom door, he heard Ranger shout, "Shall I compare thee to a summer's day? Thou art more lovely and more temperate."

Rebel just entered his bedroom and shut the door behind him, not giving Ranger the attention he so obviously wanted.

Freshly showered, Rebel parked his bike in the lot to the clubhouse and made his way up to the room on the second floor that they used for church, what they called their meetings. When he opened the door and stepped inside the room, he saw that all of his brothers were already there and waiting on him.

Taking a deep breath and preparing him for the shit he was no doubt about to receive, Rebel moved over to his usual chair and sat down, between Rock and Rex. He glared at Ranger who was sitting across the table from him with a fucking shit-eating grin on his face.

Axle slammed a fist down on the table to call church in order. "Okay. First… Rebel."

Rebel looked down the table at his president. "Me? Yeah?"

The smirk on Axle's face didn't give Rebel the warm fuzzies. "Anything you want to tell us?"

"Nope." Rebel shot his president a glare.

Unbothered, Axle pushed, "Are you sure?"

"We want to know about the librarian," Pike commented.

"Yeah, Romeo," Trip confirmed. "Tell us about your librarian."

As Rebel took a deep breath and let it out slowly, Ranger took the opportunity to be a dick. "*'O Romeo, Romeo! Wherefore art thou, Romeo?'*" Ranger cooed in a high-pitch voice.

Rebel stood up and headed back around the table, since that was where the door was located, shooting them the finger over his shoulder as his 'friends' laughed their asses off.

"'*Parting is such sweet sorrow*,'" Ranger shouted as Rebel approached the door.

"We're not done, Rebel," Axle said through his laughter. "Sit back down."

"We're done discussing Ruby… for now," Rebel insisted, hand on the doorknob.

Axle gave a nod. "Okay. We have club business, though." He waited while Rebel returned to his seat. "Pike?"

Pike cleared his throat. "Okay. So, I've talked to them and so has Axle and Rebel. We think the best thing for the twins would be to prospect, and they're interested. I would be Ross's sponsor."

"I'll be Ryker's sponsor," Ranger stated.

"Anyone object?" Axle looked around the table. When no one said anything, he gave a nod. "Get them cuts and put them to work."

"Nice," Ranger commented with a smile.

"Emerson," Axle said.

It was like all the happiness was sucked out of the room at the mention of the young wolf.

Days ago, Axle's sister-in-law died in the war with the Hell's Dogs MC. She had married Emerson only weeks ago. The pain and grief Emerson was feeling was something not many of them would ever understand.

"He's not ready," Axle commented. "When he is, I need one of you to sponsor him. We need to keep an eye on him. I think the best way would be to let him prospect."

Top cleared his throat. "I'll sponsor."

"Any objections?"

There wasn't even a cough. The room was silent. They knew the struggle with Emerson was going to be keeping him from doing anything crazy, and the best way to do that was to put him in a position where he would be taking orders from them for most of the day. Eliminating his free time would limit the amount of time he had to drown in his grief.

"I'll update you all when the time comes."

Messer

Looking around the room at the group of wannabe badasses, Messer barely resisted rolling her eyes. The group consisted of the elderly, the weak, and the dumb. If she was reading them right, they were hoping she'd do their bidding.

Messer could play along, but there was no way she was going to be a pawn in their game. She was there for information gathering, and this group of inflated-egos seemed like a great place to start.

"So, what do you think?" The man with the buzz cut and the polo shirt, who introduced himself as Daniel, one of the owners of the hardware store, was giving her an appreciating glance that made her skin crawl. She didn't do pretty boys.

Resisting the urge to roll her eyes *again*, she pasted a smile on her face and fluttered her lashes a bit. "I'm blown away. It's a great plan."

She could almost see the man's ego inflate even more as he straightened and puffed out his chest. "We've already started the boycotting phase. We're boycotting their businesses and any business that they support or that has shown support to them. We also plan to pull funding from places where their *family* members work. They call them family members, but they're really their women."

His brother, Charles, nodded his head and scowled at the floor. "If those whores choose to open their legs to those... *monsters*, they can take the heat for them, starting with that damn librarian."

"Leave it to me." The elderly woman across the room from her had a self-satisfied grin on her face.

Not knowing what the hell they were talking about, Messer just nodded and listened while they shot encouragement around the room at each other.

"Bobby's Bar is a target, too," the woman who introduced herself as Gladys Smith uttered.

Her husband nodded and replied, "Yes, Bobby may not employ them anymore, but he would and has in the past."

"Those *monsters* found *three* of their whores there!" blurted the man who said he owned the largest farm in the area. She was pretty sure his last name was White, and he was married to the librarian harasser.

"Three?" She painted what she hoped they thought was appropriate disgust on her face and held up a hand to her face. "Those women don't realize what they are?"

"Oh, they know," Buzz-cut's brother spat. "They just fall on their dicks and pretend they aren't the disgusting creatures that they really are!"

"Relax, Charles," Buzz-cut said through gritted teeth. "This isn't helping."

"Maybe…" Messer cleared her throat, pretending she was about to volunteer to do something she was scared to do. "Maybe, if I had as much information on them as you know, I could… I dunno… find a way to make them… disappear. I… uh… know some people." She looked over at Niles, the man she met at the diner, and found him giving her a proud grin. He didn't believe her shy, unsure act, but he didn't have any idea who she really was.

The seamstress, Dorothy, leaned forward and smiled at her. "I know more than anyone else here. I'll make you a list of members and their spouses. Their lackeys change all the time, so I don't know about them, but I can get you the rest."

"Do you... do you know what... *animals* they are?"

Dorothy nodded. "Well, most of them."

Perfect.

Bri

Bri was having the best morning. It started with her waking up with Rebel's body over hers. He was kissing along her shoulder and just holding her. The moment she let out a moan and wrapped her arms around him, Rebel shifted his hips between her thighs and moved his lips to hers.

"Good morning," he had whispered against her lips, between kisses.

Not wanting to miss the opportunity, she reached over and snatched a condom from the drawer.

His gravelly chuckle sent pleasure shivers down her spine. He took the condom but didn't put it on. Instead, he climbed out of bed, scooped her up, and carried her to the bathroom.

She had never enjoyed a shower more in her life.

When they were done, he kept her company while she got ready for work. His hands didn't seem to be able to stop touching her though. He would touch her ass, tickle her side, grip her hips, anything and everything.

He stopped her when she went to put on her lip gloss. "Not yet," he mumbled. Then he was kissing the holy hell out of her. After scrambling her brains, he stepped back with a grin on his face. "Okay. Go ahead."

She put her lip gloss on, but her hand was shaking like crazy.

Once she was ready for work, he walked her out to the garage. Then, he went out to his bike and followed her to work, giving her a wink and a smile before he rode away.

Yes, she was having a great morning. Or at least, she had been until Sharon White stomped into the library and went off like a rocket.

The older woman stopped in front of Bri's desk and put a hand to her hip. With her free hand, she wagged her finger at Bri. "I heard from my daughter's friend that you posted about a *biker* leading the teen reading hour."

Bri took a deep breath and let it out slowly, doing her best to remember that she was at her place of employment and needed to remain professional. "Yes, Mrs. White. Mr. Blau is an avid reader, patron, and respected member of the community who has already helped one young man foster his love of reading. I think it's important that young men see other men showing a love for reading and not being ashamed of it."

"But a man of *his sort* shouldn't be around *the children*. Someone in *your* position should know better. Not that it should surprise me that you don't. From what I hear, you are *with* him."

"Ma'am," Bri began, once again, mentally reminding herself that she was at work, "who I date is no concern of yours or the town's."

"I beg to differ! You are a role model, and you're flaunting your sex life with—"

"That's enough. If you have an issue with the programs or how they are run at this library, you are free to take them up with the director, as she has already approved of them and the volunteers helping run them. If you have more commentary about my personal life, know that I have no desire to hear it. It has nothing to do with my job or the library. Is there anything else I can help you with today, or shall I call Debbie Reese and let her know you're on your way to her office?"

"I think I'll call her on my own time and inform her of your *unprofessional* behavior. I'll also be making sure she knows my husband and I, as well as our *well-connected* friends, will no longer be donating to this establishment, as long as you and *that trash* are here."

Bri just gave a nod. "Okay. Have a good day, Mrs. White."

As she watched the woman storm out of the library, she lifted the phone from her desk and dialed the extension for the director. She was fuming at the intrusive nature of the complaint, as well as the disgusting way she was talking about Rebel. Her personal life was her own, and Rebel had done nothing to deserve those comments.

"Hello?"

"We've got a problem."

T.S. Tappin

Chapter Thirteen

Rebel

Rebel was at one of the Howler-owned apartment buildings, helping Trip and Pike change locks, when he received a text from Ruby.

>IF THE **KAREN** WHO CAME INTO THE LIBRARY TODAY HAS HER WAY, I'M GOING TO BE OUT OF A JOB. ALL BECAUSE PEOPLE ARE ASSHOLES. WHISKEY. I NEED WHISKEY.<

As soon as he read the words, his wolf went on high alert. He immediately told his brothers he had to go. He wasn't sure what happened, but his woman needed him. Both being mated to their own wonderful women, Trip and Pike just told him to call if he needed them.

Not sure if she had whiskey, but knowing she wanted it, he stopped by the store and grabbed a bottle on his way to her townhouse. His wolf was pacing, which worried Rebel, since his wolf didn't usually make something out of nothing.

After parking in the driveway and grabbing the bottle from his saddlebag, he made his way up to her front porch, preparing himself for any possible scenario. He didn't know her well enough to guess where her mind was at, but he guessed that the whiskey request meant it wasn't in a great place. When he knocked on the door, he heard her shout, "Come in!"

He opened the door and stepped into her living room to find her pacing the length of it. Her hair was pulled up in a messy bun on the top of her head. She was dressed in a teal and black sports bra and matching booty shorts that made him think things he probably shouldn't be thinking when she was angry or worried. In her hand, she had a short glass with a goldish brown liquid he guessed was whiskey.

After setting the bottle he brought on her side table, he removed his boots and hung his cut on the hook by the door. She looked pissed, *extremely pissed*, but she didn't look hurt, which he was grateful for. Rebel told his wolf to relax.

"Hey," she huffed out, mid-turn.

"Hey," Rebel replied as he slowly crossed the room and leaned up against the side of one of her built-in bookshelves. "So… what happened?"

She huffed out a breath. "Sharon White just stomped in there and basically told me that I shouldn't have you around the kids, and I'm a slut and flaunt my sex life in front of children!" She swung her arms around as she let the words fly, causing Rebel to worry she would spill her drink as he watched it slosh against the sides of the glass.

On the next pass, he took the glass from her hand and set it on the tray on top of the chest she used for a coffee table. "Okay. None of that is tr—"

"I know! I mean, what right does she have to make judgments about anyone else? I have done nothing but be professional! What I do in my time off is none of anyone's business! Except yours, of course, since, ya know, it's with you." Rebel wanted to smile, but he stopped himself as she continued with her rant. "*Flaunt it in front of the children?* Has she lost her *mind?* Not once have I done anything that would be considered flaunting anything in front of children!"

Rebel knew he needed to just let her get it out. She was red-faced and angry. She needed to vent, then he would help her solve the issue. While part of him was pissed to hear that some piece of shit thought they could label her as anything other than a professional, he couldn't change the minds of douchebags. The rest of him was having a hard time keeping his attention off those fucking shorts and that sexy as hell tattoo on her thigh.

"And what she said about you! The *nerve!* I swear to god, if I wouldn't have been at work, I would have made her regret every damn word that came from her mouth! How dare she judge you! Just because you ride a motorcycle doesn't mean you're an idiot or a criminal!"

"I murdered my unc—"

She stopped pacing and pointed a finger at him, cutting off his words. "He deserved it."

Rebel held up his hands in surrender, knowing he wasn't going to win this argument when she was that angry. He was surprised that his wolf had calmed down and stayed that way during the conversation.

She resumed her pacing and her rant. "The things you and the clubs do for this town vastly outnumber what her and her hoity-toity friends have done. They just throw money at things and hope it fixes the problem! And that! She said she wouldn't be donating to the library, and neither would her friends." She huffed out an annoyed sigh. "And of course, she and her friends are the big-name donors, the ones who basically fund the library. Without their money, the library will be screwed."

Seeing where he might be able to help, Rebel started to form a plan in his head.

"I'll lose my job, my home, and my car. The kids will lose their access to books, to services, to a safe place where they can be themselves. The community will lose a valuable resource. And for what? So, some big-haired, scorned hag can throw her weight around!"

Rebel stepped forward, grabbed her hips, and slammed his lips to hers. After kissing her until they both needed to breathe, he pulled back and said, "Now that I have your attention, I think we can help."

Panting, Ruby stared at him, and Rebel watched her pretty gold-flecked blue eyes as she tried to process his words. He mentally patted himself on the back for having that effect on her.

"Wh-what?"

He released her and leaned back against the bookshelves. "The Howlers and the Claws do fundraising events all the time. We also happen to know some very influential individuals and have access to people with deep pockets. So, we'll set up a fundraiser and donate the needed funds to the library. As for what she said about me, I don't care. There's nothing she could say that people haven't already said about me or my club. We don't give a damn what people think." He crossed his arms over his chest. "As for this bitch, I think you called it. She's just a big-haired, scorned hag who thinks she can throw her weight around. She's drunk on her own power and likes to wield that power." He shrugged. "So, we'll take away her power."

She just stared at him for a long moment, and he wondered if he said the wrong thing. Then, she launched herself at him, forcing him to catch her with his hands on her ass as she wrapped herself around him. She slammed her lips to his and forced her tongue past his lips, not that he would have objected to that action at all.

As she kissed the hell out of him, he squeezed her ass in his hands and turned them so her back was pressed against the bookshelf. When she broke the kiss and tilted her head to the side, Rebel took that opportunity to kiss and nip along her neck. He pressed his hips against her core, letting her feel the effect she had on him.

"Rebel," she moaned as he kissed his way down to her cleavage.

"If you want me to stop, you need to say so. Otherwise, I'm fucking you right here," he growled into the curves of her breasts.

"You better not fucking stop." The slight cry to her voice made him grin as he set her on her feet and went to work on removing her sports bra. "I know you didn't go to work dressed like this."

Panting, she shook her head and immediately began removing her shorts. Not wanting to waste time, Rebel yanked off his shirt, removed the condom from his wallet, and unfastened his jeans. Before he could pull out his cock and put on the condom, she dropped to her knees in front of him.

"I was going to do a workout in my spare room, but the anger took over."

"My Ruby was going to do some moves on a pole," he commented, running his fingertips along her jaw as she unzipped his jeans and reached in to pull out his cock.

She grinned, her hand fisting his erection, and looked up at him. "Now I'm going to do some moves on a different one."

His chuckle turned into a groan as she wrapped her lips around the head of his cock and sucked him in. "Fuck! Your mouth is heaven, Ruby."

Ruby wasn't playing games, apparently. She sent a fast rhythm, cupped his balls, and tickled the tip with her tongue on every stroke. If he didn't stop her, he was going to shoot down her throat and that wasn't what he wanted.

Reaching down, he grabbed ahold of her bun and gently pulled it back until she came off of his cock with a *pop*.

"Yeah?"

"If you don't stop, I'm going to come. I want to be in your pussy, not your mouth, when I do that."

The pout she gave had him reconsidering for a moment, but he stuck to his guns and helped her to her feet. Kissing her lips, he gripped her hips and moved until her back was against the wall on the side of the bookshelves. He handed her the condom.

"Put it on me, Sweetie," he ordered against her lips.

With a saucy smile, she did just that.

After kissing her lips, he lifted her again, and she wrapped her legs around his hips. Shifting his hips so that the head of his erection was resting on the edge of her core, he nipped her bottom lip. "Hold on, Ruby. This is going to be hard." When she nodded, he entered her on a hard thrust, quickly pulling out, and slamming in again.

As both of them moaned loudly, he set a fast and hard rhythm and shifted his hands, so one of his thumbs could reach her clit. He made love to her mouth as he fucked her pussy and rubbed her clit.

It didn't take long for her thighs to tighten on his hips and for her fingernails to dig into his back. Then, Ruby broke the kiss and cried out his name as her pussy clamped down on his cock. Rebel didn't bother trying to hold back. He embraced the tingles building in his balls and let the pleasure wash over him, growling as he filled the condom.

Howling inside of him, his wolf was demanding Rebel claim their mate. His fangs slid down, but he stopped himself at the last second. He hadn't even talked to her about mating and what it meant. It wasn't right to do that until they both agreed.

When the climax faded and his fangs receded, he looked down at Ruby and saw her eyes wide. "Ruby… I'm sorry. I… I didn't… My wolf…"

"Let me down," she stated.

Rebel pulled out of her and set her on her feet. "Let me take care of this," he mumbled as he motioned to the condom and went to the half-bath.

While he did his business, he lectured himself about the close call. How did he lose control like that? Claiming a mate wasn't like a ring that you could simply take off. That mark was permanent. It was serious. He knew better than to let his wolf make decisions, especially ones that affected others.

After putting his cock away and refastening his jeans, he decided it was time to explain to her what mates were and what it meant for them. It was a talk he would've had to have with her, anyway. It was just happened a lot sooner than he planned.

When he returned to the living room, he found her wearing his shirt, wrapped in a throw blanket, and pacing the room again. He settled in the same spot he had been against the bookshelves and took a deep breath.

"What the hell was that?" She didn't look at him as she spoke.

Here we go. He opened his mouth and gave her the honesty. "My wolf was demanding that we claim our mate. I lost control and almost did that. I'm sorry. I won't let that happen again."

"Wait. Mate? Your wolf demanded that you *what*?"

"Shifters have mates. It's like their *person*. My wolf has identified you as our mate. You're *my* mate. When a shifter finds their mate, they bite them and claim them, leaving a scar behind, and a bond is formed. It's like a shifter marriage."

She looked over at him like he lost his mind. Her eyes were wide, and her brows were lifted. "Marriage?"

Rebel winced. "We're part animal, Sweetie. We don't make these decisions the same way humans do. But… I'm just going to say it all. It's permanent. I mean, yeah, there have been couples that have split up, but it doesn't end well for the shifter, if they don't find another actual mate. Anyway, it's the person that completes us, fits us, compliments us in a way that no one ever has."

"And you know that how?"

He shrugged. "The same way I can shift into a wolf. Magic."

She dropped the blanket and lifted her hands to fix her bun. It ended up crooked when he pulled on it during her blow job. He made his gaze stay on her face rather than drop to the expanse of her legs on display, because he didn't think getting a hard-on while having that conversation was going to help anything.

"Let me get this straight." She dropped her hands and folded her arms over her chest as she began to pace again.

Not wanting her to trip, he bent down and grabbed the blanket from the middle of the floor.

"Your wolf has declared me your mate. You and your wolf have decided it's me. So, what? I don't have any say in this?"

Rebel swallowed hard, terrified they were about to scare her away. He didn't want to tell her she had an out if she wanted it, but he needed to. "No, Ruby, it's not like that. You have *all* the say. Nothing happens until you approve of it. If you say you don't want us, then we don't get our mate. We aren't forcing anything on you. *I'm* not forcing anything on you. If you tell me to leave, I leave."

He saw her eyebrow pull together. "So… this… attraction between us… is that just your wolf?"

"What?" It was his turn to look at her like she'd lost her mind. "Sweetie, no. Without my wolf, I'd still want to fuck you every chance I got. Without my wolf, I'd still think you are the sweetest, most beautiful woman I ever saw. Without him, I'd still be totally in love with you and your brain. The pull between us is because we are two grown adults who have amazing fucking chemistry."

She stopped and turned to face him. "Is there a time limit on this stuff?"

Rebel's Fairytale

He didn't blame her for not reacting to his declaration. He hadn't planned on confessing all of that when he started speaking. It just came out. It made sense that she had too much else to process from their conversation to be able to even acknowledge his words of love.

"There's no time limit," he told her.

She narrowed her gaze on him. "If your wolf is pushing you, what does that feel like?"

He looked away from her gaze, dropping his to the floor between them. "Don't worry about that."

"Oh no. You don't get to do that. Out with it, Rebel." He saw her feet enter his view, followed by her shins, then her thighs. She gripped his beard and made him look at her. "What does it feel like?"

Gazing into the eyes he loved to the depths of his soul, Rebel took a deep breath and slowly exhaled. "It feels like an itch you can't seem to scratch."

"So… annoying as hell?"

"That pretty much covers it."

She huffed out a breath and shrugged. "Then, I guess I have some stuff to think about."

"I'm sorry," he practically whispered, hating that he added so much more stress to her already very full plate.

"For wanting to spend your life with me? That seems like an odd thing to be apologizing for."

Rebel couldn't help it. He chuckled and pressed his lips to hers. Laying his forehead against hers, he asked, "You want me to go?"

She shook her head. "I just... I need to think all of this through. Is there anything else with this mate stuff that I should know about?"

Rebel sighed and wrapped his arms around her. Holding her close, he answered, "Not really. With the club, there's an extra layer, but—"

She pulled her head back and looked up at him with narrowed eyes. "Out with it, Rebel."

Trying really hard not to comment on how fucking beautiful she was when she was angry or bossy, Rebel shifted his gaze over her shoulder. "Well... Once we claim a woman with the club, she is our Ol' Lady. You would be my property, but I'd be yours, too. And before you yell at me, it's just a term. I don't think of you as a thing, and neither would my brothers."

Ruby rolled her eyes. "I've read motorcycle club romance, Rebel. I know that much."

"You'd get a cut like mine that would say *Property of Rebel...* and my mating mark."

"And what would you get?"

Rebel gave her a kiss on the lips, soft and sweet, trying not to get his hopes up. "I would get your name on my body, most likely my neck, and something else involving your Ol' Lady name somewhere on my body. That would probably be your choice."

When Ruby smiled up at him, he knew he was swaying her a little in his direction.

"And I would have a patch on my cut that read *Property of Ruby*."

She smoothed her hands down his bare chest. "I like the sound of that."

"Good." He kissed her forehead. "Now, grab a book and a blanket, and get snuggled up on the couch. I'll get you some tea."

Turning, he went to the kitchen and prepared her a cup of mint chamomile tea. When he returned to the living room, she had done what he said and was snuggled up at the end of the couch with a blanket and a book. He handed her the tea and shifted. He heard her gasp and looked up at her.

The cup in hand started to tip as she stared at him with her mouth open and her gaze darting all over his wolf form. She jolted and set the cup of tea down on the side table. When she looked back at him, she asked, "Can I touch you?"

Without answering her, he lifted his front paws and used them to lift himself up onto the cushions.

"If you leave fur behind on my couch, you're cleaning it up."

He huffed a snort — A wolf version of a laugh as he settled his body on his stomach with his head in her lap. The giggle she gave was music to his ears, but the loving way she ran her fingers through the fur behind his ears was the sweetest touch he'd ever received.

T.S. Tappin

Chapter Fourteen

Rebel

When he woke up the next morning, light was shining through the thin curtains of the window behind her couch. He was on his side with his back to the back of the couch. Ruby was in his arms, facing away from him. The blanket was shoved down to their feet, and his tee that she was still wearing had gotten pushed up, revealing her bare ass to him.

Moving his hand from her waist, he caressed the cheek of her ass as he kissed along her shoulder. "Ruby," he whispered. "Sweetie, wake up."

"No," she grumbled and scooted back, rubbing her ass against him.

"I have to get going, soon."

In response, Ruby rolled over and wrapped herself around him, her arms around his neck and her top leg over his hip. "No," she mumbled into his ear.

Quietly chuckling, Rebel palmed her ass and held her against him. Kissing along her neck, he used his tongue and teeth to pull a moan from her.

"I like waking up with you."

She was holding on tight to him, Rebel liked it. If he had his way, she'd never have to let go. "I feel the same way… especially when you're wearing my shirt and your bare ass is in my hands."

He smiled when he heard her giggle.

They laid like that for a few minutes, just soaking it in. His heart was full, and his wolf was content, even if he still wanted Rebel to claim their mate, and soon.

"You work today?" He kissed the underside of her jaw.

"No, but I have to go in for a meeting with the director after lunch."

He hummed against her skin and lifted his leg, forcing hers apart a few more inches. Sliding his hand along her ass and down between her legs, he uttered, "So… what you're saying is you have time to kill?"

"Something like that."

He circled her entrance with the tip of his finger as he teased the skin of her neck with the tip of his tongue. "I might have a way to take care of some of that."

"Does it involve me moving? Because I'm quite comfortable." Her hips had started moving with his finger, trying to get him to penetrate her.

"Yes, but I'll do all the moving if you want me to."

"You drive a hard bargain."

"I'm trying to drive a hard something else." He nipped her jaw. "You want me?"

"What do you think?" She shifted her arms, allowing her to look down and press her forehead to his.

Gazing into her gorgeous eyes, he slowly slid his finger inside of her wet, hot pussy and began to lazily fuck her. When she began to pant, he kissed her lips. "Yeah, I think you do, but I need to hear it, Sweetie."

In a whisper, she replied, "I want you, Rebel."

Rebel didn't waste time. Wrapping his arms around her, he climbed off the couch and carried her up the stairs to her bedroom, where he knew there was a box of condoms. He was going to make love to her, let her see in his eyes what he felt in his heart while he made her feel as good as he could. He didn't have much to offer her, but what he did have, his heart and his found family, was all hers. She just needed to reach out and take it.

Rebel knew it would take time for her to process what she learned and make her decision. He'd give her time, and he'd be there when she was ready. Until then, he'd show her what she'd be missing if she walked away.

Starting with really fucking great sex.

Rock

Rock was able to get Ranger and Brute to come with him to help Diamond pack up and move. He and Brute were in the box truck, with Ranger following them on his bike. The plan was to pack them up that day and the next morning, and return to Warden's Pass tomorrow.

One more day, then Rock would have his family all in one house. He couldn't fucking wait to have dinner around the table with his woman and all their children. He wanted his woman in his bed every night, and he wanted his life to finally be healthy and happy, not full of deceit and drugs. One more day, and he would have everything he ever wanted.

Seeing his exit, Rock turned on the blinker and veered onto the exit ramp.

"How excited are you, right now?" Brute asked, quietly.

"Pretty fucking excited," Rock admitted, allowing a smile to grow on his face.

"I like Diamond," Brute told him and patted him on the shoulder. "She's a good woman, a good mom."

"Wait until you spend some time with her kids." Rock chuckled and took a left. "Miles is gonna be one of us. He's determined. Sweet Jenna is just full of smiles and optimism."

"Well, I'm looking forward to getting to know my new niece and nephew. Did you warn Diamond her babies are about to get spoiled to all hell?"

Grinning, Rock nodded. "She's aware. I think it's about time those kids see what it means to have a real family. They deserve it."

"Uncle Brute's on it," Brute said in that low, deep voice of his.

Rock took a right onto Diamond's street. When he got to the house where Diamond was renting the upstairs, he parked at the curb and killed the engine. Ranger rounded the truck on his bike and parked in front of the box truck.

When Rock climbed out of the truck, Ranger gave him a grin and called out, "Let's do this. It's time to bring our family home."

"Damn straight," Brute agreed.

Unable to hide his happiness, Rock smiled and led them up to Diamond's apartment. He knocked on her door before he opened it with his key and stepped inside.

He had just opened his mouth to call out for Diamond or the kids, when a screeching bundle of pink and purple charged him. "Weeeeeeeessssss!" The bundle stopped right before she ran into him and looked up. "Wait. I mean… Dad." Then, Jenna giggled and wrapped her arms around Rock's waist.

Rock bent down and scooped her up into his arms. "How's my Jenna?"

"I'm happy. I'm getting a new sister and a new brother and a new dad." She gave him a huge grin. "And a new room!"

"Yup. Do you want to meet some of your new family? These two are my brothers. This is Ranger." He pointed in Ranger's direction. "And this is Brute." He motioned to Brute. "You can call them by their names or uncle or whatever you want. Okay?"

T.S. Tappin

Jenna nodded and blushed. She leaned closer to Rock and looked at them before she hid her face in Rock's neck. "Hi. I'm Jenna."

As the men greeted Jenna, there was a shout from the other room. "Mom! Rock's here! Come on! We gotta go!" Then, Miles ran into the living room. He stopped running as soon as he got into the room. He lifted his chin and started walking like he was cool.

Rock bit the inside of his cheek to hold back his laugh. "Miles. Good to see you." He held out his free hand to the little boy.

Miles took his hand and shook it. "Good to see you, Rock."

Rock introduced Miles to Ranger and Brute. Just like he expected, his brothers knelt down and pulled Miles into conversation. Seeing it, Jenna kissed his cheek and asked to be put down. Rock chuckled but set her on her feet.

Knowing they were good and would be occupied with his brothers, Rock went in search of his woman. He glanced in the kitchen, but she wasn't there, so he reversed course and went to her bedroom. He turned the knob and stepped in, closing the door behind him.

There she was, standing in front of her dresser, pulling clothes from the drawers, and packing them in an open suitcase on the floor. When he turned the lock on the door and it clicked, she looked into the mirror above the dresser and smiled at the sight of him.

Rock took six steps across the room and up behind her. Sliding his arms around her waist, he kept his gaze locked with hers in the mirror as he lowered his head and used his chin to move her curls away from her neck. With wet kisses, he left a trail up her neck to her ear.

"God, I fucking missed you," he whispered in her ear and pulled her body back against his, tightening his arms around her.

She dropped the clothes in her hands and covered his arms at her waist with her hands. Turning her head to look into his eyes, she replied, "I missed you, too, Wes."

He gently kissed her lips. "Need you."

Against his mouth, she said, "Back left pocket."

He hiked a brow and moved his left hand to the pocket in question. Sliding his fingers in, he felt the familiar foil of a condom package. Pulling it out, he grinned at her. "My Diamond was prepared for me."

She bit her bottom lip for a moment. "You'll find out how prepared in a minute."

Rock groaned and went to work getting her pants down. As soon as he had access, he slid his right hand down and between her thighs, finding her core wet and hot, ready for him.

"Told ya," she breathed and tried to spread her legs a bit for him, but she was hampered by the jeans and panties gathered around her thighs.

Thanking the gods she had yet to put shoes on, he shoved the pants and panties down her legs until she could step out of them. Then, he unzipped and unfastened his jeans, shoving them down to his knees.

After rolling the condom on, he gripped her hips and took a step back, taking her bottom half with him. "Hands on the dresser, Angel." As she complied, he lined up his cock to her entrance, keeping hold of her hip with the other hand. "Spread your legs for me, Diamond."

She slid her legs wider and tilted her hips for him, looking over her shoulder, giving him a sexy smile. Rock grinned back at her as he slowly slid inside of her, eliciting a moan from both of them.

"Home," he growled, pulled out and slammed back in. As he set a steady, hard rhythm with his thrusts, he slid his hand from her hip up her back over her shirt and into her hair. Fisting it in his hand, he bent forward and kissed along her shoulder.

"Wes," she breathed and worked her hips in rhythm with his.

"That's it, angel," he panted against her skin. "Work yourself on my cock. Make us both finish, Diamond."

He slid his other hand around her waist and down to play with her clit, loving each and every noise that came from her sweet mouth.

"Gonna make love to you every night. You hear me?"

She nodded as much as his grip on her hair would allow and replied, "Please."

He hardened his thrusts and slid his fingers down to feel where he was entering her, while the heel of his hand pressed and rubbed on her clit.

Rebel's Fairytale

"Rock," she gasped as her muscles contracted hard on his cock. He released her hair, moving that hand back to her hip, and watched as she threw her head back in ecstasy. Her core began to milk him as the sweetest sound he ever heard came out of her mouth, triggering his own release.

Slamming inside, he groaned, "I fucking love you."

"Love you, too," she panted back.

Then, they heard a knock on the door.

"One second," Rock called out and prayed it wasn't one of the kids.

"No need to hurry," Ranger said with amusement in his voice. "We're taking the kiddos for ice cream. Miles found Diamond's keys for us. She good with us taking her Jeep?"

Diamond was giggling as she leaned back against him, his cock still buried inside of her and twitching. She nodded.

"Yeah. Take it."

"We'll make a lot of noise when we get back."

Then, they heard Ranger shouting to the kids about what flavor ice cream he wanted as they left the apartment.

"Have I ever told you how much I love your brothers?"

"Can you *not*, when I have my dick inside of you?"

That intensified Diamond's giggles.

Rebel

Rebel entered the club house and waved at the few brothers who were scattered around the main room, before he headed down the hallway to Axle's office. The door was closed, so Rebel gave the door a few knocks with his knuckle and waited.

"Yeah," Axle called out from the other side of the door.

"Rebel," he replied.

"Come in," Axle ordered.

Rebel opened the door and stepped inside. What he found on the other side of the door was Axle sitting in his office chair with Gorgeous sitting on his desk in front of him. Thankfully, they were both clothed.

"Hey Reb," Gorgeous, Axle's mate, said with a smile and slid off the desk. After giving Axle a kiss, she rounded the desk and approached Rebel. She patted him on the arm as she passed.

"Hey Gorgeous."

"I'll leave you boys to gossip," she commented with a giggle as she left the office and shut the door behind her.

Rebel chuckled as he took a few steps and sat down in a chair across the desk from Axle.

Looking over at his president, he was happy to see the man had a slight smile on his face. They had been put through the ringer, lately, especially Gorgeous. It was good to see a moment of happiness for them.

"How's she doing?"

The smile slowly faded from Axle's face, and Rebel felt like an ass. "She's... really good at putting a smile on her face and pretending she's not dying inside."

"How are *you* doing?"

Axle shook his head and crossed his arms over his chest. "I feel like I failed her... and Emerson. The only one who can get him to eat is Gorgeous, but I don't like her being around him right now, because he's not... nice."

"His mate died," Rebel said, cautiously.

"I know." Axle winced. "Doesn't mean I like him being an ass to Gorgeous."

"I doubt she takes it personally. Let her take care of him. It probably helps her."

"Yeah." Axle cleared his throat. "You said you had a problem we needed to address."

Rebel ran through what Ruby had told him about Sharon White and her outburst at the library. When he was done, Axle's brows were pulled together, and his eyes were practically shooting fire.

"They can say whatever the hell they want to say about us, but we will not stand by while they ruin the reputation of a good woman, especially not one who is family."

Rebel bit back the grin. He knew Axle would respond like that. "She hasn't accepted she's my mate, yet. She knows. We had... a talk, last night, but she's processing."

Axle jerked back and threw up his hands. "What is there to process? You love her. Your wolf loves her. From what I hear, she's pretty damn into you."

Rebel chuckled. "I seem to remember a time, not that long ago, when you had to do some convincing of your own with the woman who just walked out of here."

Axle barked a laugh. "True." Then, he sighed. "Okay. So, we need to figure out how to replace the funding."

Rebel nodded and cleared his throat. "Well... some of it. I have savings, and I—"

"Shut the fuck up," Axle said and waved off his words. "*We* will figure it out. I'll call church for tomorrow, like three. Rock and the guys should be back by then. Get us the figures. Or... pull Keys in. I'm sure he can get what we need."

Rebel choked down the sudden emotions that flooded him. As much as he felt like the club was his family, sometimes he forgot how all-in they were when one of them had an issue. Ruby may not have accepted them as *hers*, but they had accepted her as part of them.

"I appreciate it."

"Just another chance to remind outsiders what happens when you fuck with our family." The evil grin that appeared on Axle's face both warmed Rebel's heart and terrified him in equal measure.

Chapter Fifteen

The next morning... Diamond

Diamond and her cousin, Ann Marie Akton, sat on Ann's porch and enjoyed the view. Diamond's apartment was upstairs from Ann's, so it gave them the perfect view to watch as Rock and his friends carried furniture and other heavy stuff across the yard to the box truck, while the kids carried lighter things. With the men shirtless, the view was mesmerizing.

"Lord have mercy," her cousin breathed from Diamond's right. "You're moving to a place where you will see these men on a regular basis?"

Diamond chuckled at her cousin's question. "Well, Rock I'll probably see *naked* every day, but I doubt I'll see Ranger and Brute half-naked often."

"Even clothed, they are a sight to behold. If this is the scenery, I might have to visit soon."

As Ann spoke the words louder than was necessary, Ranger was heading back toward the house. He glanced over and shot Ann a wink as a grin grew on his face. "I've got a place for you to stay, Sweetheart."

Diamond rolled her eyes and laughed.

"Watch yourself," Ann warned. "I just might take you up on that."

He bit his bottom lip and let his gaze rake over Ann. "Don't threaten me with a good time."

"Keep it in your pants," Rock gritted out as he passed Ranger. "Little eyes and ears." Then, he nodded toward the kids still standing at the back of the truck with Brute. "Just give her your number already and get back to work. We have church at three. You can flirt later."

"Yes, sir," Ranger commented and gave Rock a mock salute. When Rock reentered the house, Ranger came over and handed Ann his phone. "Text yourself."

With a cheeky smile on her face, Ann took his phone from his hand and did as he asked. When she handed him his phone back, she uttered, "Now, don't be expecting any strings. I don't do entanglements."

"Oh fuck," Diamond cursed under breath. "You basically just said *I dare you*."

Ann shot her a look. "What?"

"That's what your words translate to in biker speak."

A feeling of contentment and love filled Diamond's gut as Ranger ruffled her hair in a brotherly way and commented, "That's what I heard."

Bri

The meeting with the director the day before was nothing special. Debbie just wanted to know exactly what was said and what was done. She said she had spoken with Sharon White, but Sharon wasn't forthcoming with the story, only wanting to complain about Bri's love-life. Debbie informed Bri she had told Sharon that Bri's love-life had nothing to do with her employment or the library, and it wouldn't be discussed further, which Bri was grateful for. However, they were both bracing for measures to either pull funding or a drop in donations.

Bri felt like it was the perfect time to take a few days vacation, considering she had some thinking to do, on top of the issue with the library scene. Debbie agreed. They also decided to put a hold on the teen group until everything blew over, but Bri suspected the teens, especially Derrick, weren't going to be happy about that. What teenager didn't want to go to a reading group led by a biker? The boys wanted to be him, and the girls and a few of the boys wanted to stare at him.

When Bri finished her workout, doing a routine on her pole in her second bedroom, she took a quick shower to wash off the sweat. After washing up, she wrapped herself in a towel and headed into her bedroom to find her phone. She found it was on her nightstand and checked it, smiling when she saw a text from Rebel and a few from Allie and Liz. Deciding to check her friends' messages later, she opened the message thread with Rebel and read.

>I'M HAVING A COUPLE OF THE GUYS OVER FOR A BONFIRE TONIGHT. WOULD LIKE IT IF YOU WERE HERE. THINK PIXIE AND SUGAR WILL COME WITH THEM.<

With a smile, Bri typed out a reply.

>WOULDN'T MISS IT. SHOULD I BRING SOMETHING?<

His reply was quick.

>BESIDES YOUR SEXY ASS AND SWEET SMILE? NO.<

She rolled her eyes, but she loved his words. Rebel had a way of making her feel beautiful and desired with just a few words or a look.

>WHAT TIME SHOULD MY SEXY ASS AND SWEET SMILE ARRIVE?<

Another quick reply.

>COME AT 6:30 AND I'LL MAKE YOU DINNER FIRST.<

She bit her lip as she sent her reply.

>I'LL BRING DINNER. SEE YOU AT 6:30<

The heart she got in return made her own beat a little harder.

Everything he had told her about mates, Ol' Ladies, and love had her mind swirling. She knew she had to process it and make some decisions, but how did she do that when she couldn't stop questions from piling up?

Most of her questions could be answered with one word — Magic. She knew he couldn't answer those questions any more than she could. She wondered how much of an impact his wolf had on him and his desire for her, but he insisted he would still want her if his wolf wasn't a thing. Not wanting to start a relationship on doubt, she felt the need to believe him on that. Following that train of thought, she believed that he loved her, too. Hell, he had said as much during his rant about how much he wanted her.

The man was practically everything she would have said she wanted if she would have been asked to compile a list of attributes she wanted in a man. His rugged, sexy exterior hid a deep intellect and kind soul. He was capable of violence, but he wasn't quick to act, and generally lived his life with generosity and gentleness. He brought her tea when he barely knew her. The way he was with that teen was just who Rebel was. From what she knew of the Howlers, they all operated with the same mindset.

Rebel was so focused on giving his cousins a safe place and some stability, something they had never experienced, even though they were adults. Not many men would toss aside their bachelor ways to take on supporting two grown men and do it without an ounce of regret, or expectations of a return on the investment.

The biggest shocker for her was the list of things they had in common. She loved books, and so did he. She had a corny sense of humor, and Rebel had shown her he wasn't averse to a stupid joke. They both wanted to belong, to have a support group around them, to have a family they could depend on.

When you took their similarities and his heart, added his considerate personality and his amazing body, and topped it with the way he fucked her, she felt silly even having to think about whether to be with him for the long haul.

The fact that he was a shifter was obviously a bit crazy, but it was a good kind of crazy. What self-respecting romance reader wouldn't jump at the chance to be on the arm of a sexy biker shifter? It wasn't a difficult choice when she simplified it like that.

Still... He said the mating was permanent. If by some crazy chance, he turned out to be someone completely different than she thought, she couldn't just walk away. Could she?

She briefly thought about the Ol' Lady stuff and shrugged. If she came to the conclusion she would accept the mating, the Ol' Lady status came with it. Therefore, she decided it all boiled down to the mating.

As she dressed, she let herself imagine a life with him and what it would entail. She had just finished throwing together a Chicken Pot Pie Casserole when she came to the realization that she was already pretty attached to him and couldn't imagine a day when she'd want to walk away.

Deciding to let that marinate for a while, she did a quick job of applying a natural look to her face and did her hair. Once she was done, she noticed she had fifteen minutes to get to Rebel's. Grabbing her purse and the casserole, she headed out to her car.

She was on her way to Rebel's house when she heard the notification from her phone. She finished the drive and parked in his driveway next to where he normally parked his bike. Checking her phone, she saw a text from him.

>I'M RUNNING LATE. SORRY! WILL BE ABOUT 30. LOCK CODE FOR THE GARAGE DOOR IS 83572. DOOR TO HOUSE FROM THERE WILL BE UNLOCKED.<

She sent him a text to let him know she would be fine until he arrived, put her phone in her purse, grabbed the casserole she had prepared, and headed inside.

Rebel

They had to push the meeting back until six, since loading up Diamond's stuff took the guys longer than expected. Axle said Rock had mentioned something about Ranger and his damn flirting.

After texting Ruby the door code, so she could get in his house, Rebel told the twins to get to work cleaning up the clubhouse and showed them the storage closet where they kept the cleaning supplies. Then, he headed up to church.

Everyone was already there when he arrived, so he skirted the table and took his seat.

"Okay. Now that the man of the hour has arrived, let's get started," Axle said and slammed the side of his fist onto the table. "Ruby was confronted at the library by Sharon White. After throwing some fucked-up words at Ruby, Sharon threatened to withdraw donations and fuck with funding for the library. That can't fucking stand."

Dragon's growl through the room wasn't a surprise, but it was Pike who asked, "What in the fuck did that bitch say to Ruby?"

Fuck. The vehemence in his brother's voice warmed Rebel's heart. His family was already in *protect Ruby* mode.

"Most of it had to do with us and the usual bullshit," Axle answered in a calm voice, "but she capped it with calling out Ruby's love life. I won't repeat the fucking words she used or what she insinuated."

"Fuck that shit," Skull blurted. "Okay, yeah, we'll figure out funding for the library. I think that's a given. But I won't stand by while some bitch talks shit about my sister."

Agreement sounded around the table.

"But is she our sister?" Axle looked down the table at Rebel and raised a brow.

Rebel sighed and rolled his eyes. "I have something to raise at the table that needs to be handled before we make any decisions about the rest."

"You have the floor," Axle said with humor in his tone.

After shooting him the finger, Rebel announced, "She hasn't accepted that she's even my mate, yet, and I don't know that she will, but just in case… I want to claim Ruby at the table as my Ol' Lady."

"Vote." Axle's one word was met with a chorus of *fuck you, of course she is, duh,* and a few other shouted statements in the affirmative.

Rebel's Fairytale

Rebel couldn't stop the grin from forming on his face. "Thanks, my brothers."

Axle's hand came down on the table again. "Good thing I already ordered the patch. Well, now, that it's official, what are we going to do about the library and the assholes fucking with us and our family?"

The rest of the meeting was about numbers and plans, along with a good amount of anger about what was said to his Ruby.

Once the meeting was done, Rebel left the twins at the clubhouse and headed over to the salon to talk to the women about what to get for Ruby. He wanted to make sure he had anything she would need to be comfortable at his place if she stayed overnight.

As he crossed the street, he noticed Ranger and Trip around Dragon's bike, but there was no way he was getting in that mess. Whatever they were doing wasn't going to sit well with his brother.

When he came out of the salon with more bags than he expected and a list of tea flavors to get at the grocery store, he was not at all surprised to see Bullet attempting to hold Dragon back from kicking the shit out of Trip and Ranger. He also wasn't surprised that Dragon was directing most of his anger toward Trip. Crossing the street, he looked at Dragon's bike and saw what was causing the problem. There was a sticker of some kind on the side of the tank of Dragon's bike.

Reading the sticker when he got close enough, Rebel sighed and set his bags down by his bike. He sent a quick text to Pike, since Pike was the sergeant at arms. Part of his duties was club security. The situation seemed to call for it.

"I will fucking kill you," Dragon growled, his eyes flashing green light in Trip's direction, signifying how fucking pissed Dragon was.

"It's a cling!" Ranger shouted.

Dragon's glare shifted to Ranger. "And you think that makes it *better*?"

Ranger shrugged and started backing away.

Trip kept a few bikes between him and Dragon, because while he was an idiot, he wasn't *that much* of an idiot.

"No harm, no foul," Ranger insisted.

"It's a joke, Dragon," Bullet said, calmly.

"You don't touch a man's bike," Dragon argued. He looked at Trip again. "I will break your fucking fingers."

The gleam in Trip's eyes let Rebel know Trip was about to say something to make the situation worse. In an attempt to prevent it, Rebel headed his way.

"That's fine. I don't need my fingers to fuc—"

Rebel covered Trip's mouth and dragged him away as Dragon let out an angered growl and shoved Bullet aside.

"Do you have a motherfucking death wish?" Rebel shoved Trip back and stood between him and Dragon, Ranger and Brute joining him.

Rebel's Fairytale

Pixie

After parking her car on the curb in front of Rebel's house, Pixie grumbled to herself about Sugar's insistence that she apologize to Ruby for spying on her and Rebel. Pixie thought Ruby wasn't upset in the least, but Sugar had been relentless. So, Pixie caved.

Pike thought it was hilarious that Sugar was making her apologize. He was lucky she hadn't left the compound before he could get in the car. He knew she was going to go and asked her to wait for him to finish church. Now, she was wishing she'd left when he was busy with his brothers.

Pixie crossed the front yard and up the front steps, with Pike on her heels. She knocked on the front door and crossed her arms over her chest.

Pike stopped behind her and put his hands to her hips as he lowered his head to her ear and whispered, "Relax. It's just a courtesy."

Pixie scoffed, hiding the effect his voice in her ear had on her body. "I doubt Ruby was even offended."

"That's not the point." Pike chuckled and kissed her temple. "Pixie, it won't hurt you to apologize."

"Whatever."

The front door swung open, and Ruby waved them in with a smile. "Hi. Rebel isn't home yet. He should be here soon."

"That's fine," Pike said and gave Pixie a bit of a shove to get her moving into the house. "We're here to talk to you first, anyway."

"Me?" Ruby's eyes widened, and she led them through Rebel's living room to his kitchen. Once there, she approached the coffee pot and began making fresh.

Pixie slid onto one of the stools at the island, and Pike did the same on the stool next to her. "Yes." She let out a sigh. "If we offended you in any way by our spying, I am sorry. It was my idea. We shouldn't have invaded your privacy."

When she finished, Ruby whipped around and looked at her with a smile on her face. "Offended? Pixie, I thought it was hilarious and adorable. You were only trying to find out what was going on with him, and I think you did it with the best of intentions and hope for his happiness. I'm not offended at all."

"Was Rebel?" Pixie winced as she thought about Rebel being angry with them. She liked Rebel, and her mate was close to him. It was important to Pixie that Rebel wasn't upset with her.

Pike snorted a laugh. "Annoyed? Yes. Offended? Not even a little bit."

Ruby nodded. "That's what he said." Then, she realized what she said, and her cheeks reddened. "I mean... That's what Rebel said... uh... told me." She huffed out a breath. "I mean... Rebel told me that he was annoyed, but he wasn't angry or upset."

When Ruby finished speaking, Pixie looked over at Pike to find that his face was red too, but because he was trying so hard to keep from laughing. She kicked his shin under the ledge of the island but looked back to Ruby. "I'm glad. We really do only want the best for him. And we were so excited that he found someone he cares about."

"So, we're good." Ruby smiled. "Would you like some coffee? Pop? I haven't found any tea, but I've only been here a couple times."

"I'll have water, if you don't mind," Pixie replied.

Pike pulled his phone from his pocket and was reading the screen as he mumbled, "I'm good, Ruby. Looks like I need to go help Bullet keep Dragon from killing Trip and Ranger. Something about a sticker on his bike that says *I'm a good boy.*" He chuckled as he stood. He was still chuckling as he kissed Pixie's temple and took her keys from the spot on the island where she set them.

"That Ranger is a trickster, isn't he?"

"Trip isn't any better." Pixie laughed and shook her head. "Those two drive Dragon up a wall regularly."

Ruby walked over to the refrigerator and grabbed a bottle of water from inside. She handed it to Pixie and leaned down to rest her elbows on the top. "I'm still learning about all of you, but from what I know, you're all family to each other. There's bound to be some rivalry and playful ribbing."

Pixie nodded. "So, how did you meet Rebel?"

Ruby's cheeks blushed, but she smiled. Then, she told Pixie the whole story — the scene she was reading with the pink hand towel, the fact that she was eating gummi bears, that she looked up and saw him, that she immediately proceeded to choke on a gummi bear, that Rebel saved her, etc.

By the time Ruby was done with her story, Pixie had a million ideas running through her head. First of all, how freaking adorable was that?! Secondly, she needed to read this book as soon as possible. Thirdly, no wonder he called her Ruby with the way she blushed. And last but not least, how soon could she get her hands on enough pink hand towels to pass out to the Shifty Sisters?

"I can see your wheels turning," Ruby commented.

Pixie gave her a smile. "I was just thinking about how adorable that story is. I love that."

Ruby nodded. "It's pretty awesome."

"Well, I'm glad you two found each other."

Pixie made a mental note to find the towels and put together a plan of action.

Chapter Sixteen

Rebel

While Rebel, Ranger, and Brute kept shifting to stay between Dragon and Trip, Trip couldn't seem to keep his idiot mouth shut.

"You need to relax, man. Maybe we should call Kisy out here."

"Fuck," Rebel mumbled under his breath and braced for impact.

Ranger's, "Shit," and Brute's, "Here we fucking go," weren't a surprise at all.

Bullet wrapped his arms around Dragon's waist from behind and started shouting for someone to get Axle.

In the hubbub, Pixie's car shot into the parking lot, and Pike climbed out of the driver's side. "Dragon," he said in an authoritative tone as he left her car running and stormed toward the fight.

Dragon ignored Pike, his eyes locked on Trip, steam practically shooting out of his ears. "You don't fucking deserve her."

"And we're back to where we started," Bullet hissed, using all of his might to keep Dragon from advancing. Bullet's face was beet red from the effort, his arm muscles straining to maintain hold.

"What in the fuck is going on out here?" Axle stormed out of the clubhouse as Pike reached Dragon.

Standing in front of Dragon, Pike put his hands to Dragon's shoulders and shoved. "Fucking stop it!"

"Fucking baby," Trip commented as he approached Dragon's bike.

"Don't you fucking touch my bike again," Dragon bellowed and shoved Pike aside, sending him to his ass on the ground.

Trip reached down and yanked the cling off. That fact must not have registered in Dragon's head, or it didn't matter if it did, because Dragon just dragged Bullet with him as he stormed toward Trip, shoving brothers out of his way.

Rebel shifted between Dragon and Trip again. Just as Dragon reached out to shove him aside, Axle came from the side and tackled Dragon and Bullet to the ground.

With Axle laying over Dragon, Bullet on his legs, and Pike moving to hold his shoulders down, Dragon's chest was heaving with his anger. Axle moved to straddle Dragon's chest and glared down at the man. In his alpha voice, a voice they didn't hear often, Axle ordered, "Lock your motherfucking ass down, or we'll put you in that god damn cell again."

Dragon was shaking with his anger as he closed his eyes and visibly strained to get some kind of control back. It took a good five minutes. During that time, Rebel dragged Trip as far away from Dragon as he could.

"You need to stop bringing up Darlin' every time you two are beefing," Rebel told him.

Trip shrugged.

"Seriously, Trip, he's going to end you over a fucking comment, one of these days, and you'll only have yourself to blame."

With a roll of his eyes, Trip nodded. "Fine. I'll keep her out of it… and I'll apologize."

"Not now," Rebel warned. "Shit. Not now."

From the front of the clubhouse, they heard Kisy's voice. "Not that I'm against a bunch of men in that position, although I'd like it more if you all were naked, but why are you on top of my mate?"

And with that, the tension was broken as the group of grown men devolved into laughter.

Bri

As Bri was still recovering from the shock of Pixie telling her how Sugar and Siren got together, the front door opened, and Rebel stepped through, carrying quite a few bags.

"Hey," he said with a smile. He moved into the kitchen and rounded the island. After setting the bags down on the top, he kissed her lips.

Bri kissed him back before she motioned to the bags. "I told you I'd make dinner."

"This isn't dinner." He started removing things from the bags and setting them on the tiled top of the island. "Hey Pix. Pike will be here soon."

"I figured. Are Trip and Ranger still breathing?"

"By a miracle, yes."

They kept talking, but Bri wasn't paying attention. She was distracted by what Rebel was unloading, box after box of different teas — Earl Grey, mint, chai, chamomile, green tea, and more. From the next bag, he pulled out a set of mugs that were teal and had various quotes about books on the side. He removed bathroom products from the third bag. He had gotten her favorite shampoo, conditioner, and a few hair products she had in her bathroom. There was also a straightener, a curling iron, a blow dryer, a brush, a comb, a toothbrush, her brand of toothpaste, and a variety of things to use to pull her hair back.

Bri was stunned and touched by the gesture. It didn't feel presumptuous, though. It felt like Rebel's way of letting her know he wanted her to be as comfortable at his place as she was at her own. Rather than laying down expectations, he was doing what he could to make sure she was taken care of in the ways he could.

Without giving a damn that Pixie was in the room with them, Bri turned to face him, reached up, and

Rebel's Fairytale

cupped his face in her hands, and pulled him to her. Giving him a deep, wet kiss, Bri ignored the cheers coming from Pixie and whoever was in the living room.

When Rebel wrapped his arms around her and pulled her until she plastered to his body, Bri let him. Taking over the kiss, Rebel began moving them out of the kitchen and toward his bedroom door. Bri broke the kiss, suddenly aware of the people watching them, and dug her heels in to stop him.

"Wait," she breathed against his lips.

Rebel's eyes were giving that greenish-gold light. "You can't kiss me like that if you don't want me to drag you to my bedroom and fuck you ten ways 'til Sunday."

Bri giggled, but she felt her cheeks heat up.

"Don't mind us," Pike said.

When did he get here? She glanced around Rebel to see Pixie, Pike, Siren, Sugar, and Ranger standing there.

"We'll wait," Ranger added with a grin on his face.

Bri pressed her face into Rebel's neck and groaned. She felt his chest moving with his laughter.

"Ruby, it's okay. Nothing to be embarrassed about."

"Seriously," Siren began, "we all do it. Do you know how many times church has been delayed because Axle's been busy in his office?"

Bri lifted her head and glanced over at them again.

Ranger's phone started ringing. He pulled it out of the pocket of his cut and looked at the screen. "Fuck. It's like he knows when we're talking about him." He pressed *answer* and put the phone on speaker. "Yeah, Pres?"

"You need to lay the fuck off of Dragon," Axle growled from the other end of the line. "You and Trip are going to end up dead. Do you understand that? That man could kill you without breaking a fucking sweat!"

"Uh… yeah, Ax, I hear you. By the way, you're on speaker."

There was a pause. "Who are you with?"

"I'm at Rebel's, so him, Ruby, Sugar, Siren, Pixie, and Pike."

"Hi, ladies. Sorry you had to hear that, but I'm in charge of a group of adolescents who can't seem to understand consequences."

Bri laughed with the other two women, while the men all rolled their eyes.

"Ranger, steer clear of Dragon. I mean it."

"You got it, Pres."

"And Ruby, know that we're taking care of the library issue. Nothing to worry about on that front."

A little surprised, Bri jolted and replied, "Uh. Okay. Thanks?"

"Have a good night." Then, the line clicked, and Ranger shoved the phone back into his pocket.

Bri looked at Rebel and raised a brow. "Something we need to talk about?"

Rebel gave her a smile. "Yeah… a lot, actually, but it can wait until later. We will have dinner and fun with our friends first."

Bri was curious about their plans to save the library, but she knew it was something she didn't want to discuss with an audience, so she shelved the discussion and decided to focus on the dinner aspect of the evening.

Letting go of Rebel, she rounded him and headed for the oven. "Dinner will be done in twenty minutes. Hope you all like Chicken Pot Pie Casserole. I hope I made enough."

"There are a couple frozen pizzas in the freezer if we're still hungry," Rebel told her as he moved to the refrigerator and grabbed a few bottles of beer. "Sugar, what can I get you to drink?"

After getting the oven going and setting the timer, Bri returned to the island and looked at all the stuff Rebel had bought for her. He really was a generous and thoughtful man. As he talked with his brothers and the women, Bri leaned into his side. He shifted his arm around her shoulders, allowing her to wrap her arms around his waist.

Soaking in the family vibes rolling around the room and the easy way they all included her in their discussions, Bri felt her resistance crumble a little more and her heart warm to the idea of accepting Rebel as *hers*.

"You good, Sweetie," Rebel whispered into her ear.

She smiled at him and nodded. "Yeah."

Niles

Sitting in his mother's car down the street from the house where the wife-stealing asshole lived, Niles watched as the prick backed Mary up to the side of the box truck and kissed her. He couldn't believe his wife was being such a damn slut. It didn't matter that they were divorced. She took some vows, and he was going to make sure she honored them for the rest of her damn life.

When his kids ran out from the front door, Mary and the prick broke up their make-out session. The prick rounded the back of the truck, where Jenna ran up to him and wrapped her arms around the prick's legs. Looking up at him, Jenna smiled and said something.

The prick threw his head back and laughed before he bent down and lifted Niles's daughter into his arms. It was at that moment that he knew he'd have to end the fucker's life, but he'd make him suffer first.

"Why are we just sitting here watching that couple?"

"That's my wife and my kids," Niles told Stella.

"Then, why is she making out with the hot guy?"

Niles shot her a glare. "He's not *that* hot."

Stella shrugged. "Looks pretty hot to me."

"Whatever. She divorced me, but that doesn't mean shit. She's mine. And they are my kids. He shouldn't have his hands on them."

"If you say so."

"He's a Howler," he told her.

"What?" She looked over at him, suddenly alert. "Seriously?"

Niles nodded. "He goes by Rock. He has two kids of his own."

"What else do you know about him?"

"Do you mean do I know if he's a shifter? No, I don't. But he's one of them, so I assume he is."

Stella raised her phone and took a picture. When Niles looked at where her phone was pointed, he saw Mary grinning at the prick as he grabbed a box off the back of the truck and carried it toward the house. Yeah, she would pay, too.

Bri

Rebel was sitting on the ground in front of the chair Bri was in. He was between her legs, with his knees bent and up in front of him.

Her phone buzzed in her pocket. She pulled it out and saw who texted her. With a smile on her face, she replied to the text and returned her phone to her pocket.

As Rebel took another drink of his beer, Bri glanced over at Ranger to see him looking at his phone and smiling. She bent down and slid her arms around Rebel's neck. Pressing her face to the side of his head, she let out a sigh.

He reached his free hand up and gave one of her forearms a squeeze. "Glad you're here, Ruby," he whispered and turned his head to kiss her cheek.

As he nuzzled against her neck, Bri watched as Pike shifted Pixie's legs until they were resting on his lap, removed her shoes, and began rubbing her feet. She looked over at Siren and Sugar, and saw Siren wrapping a blanket he grabbed from inside around Sugar's shoulders. He bent down and kissed the top of her head.

"Pixie, your water is low. I'll get you more. Sugar? Ruby?"

"I'm good," Ruby replied.

Sugar handed him her glass. "Another margarita. STAT," she said with urgency.

Ranger chuckled. "On it, doctor! *'To serve is beautiful, but only if it is done with joy and a whole heart and a free mind.'*" Then, he jogged to the house.

She almost snorted when Ranger quoted Pearl S. Buck. The look the men gave him was hilarious. "He didn't ask about you guys," Bri mentioned to Rebel.

Rebel shrugged. "We're capable of getting off our asses and getting our own."

"So are we," Bri pointed out.

"Yeah, but you shouldn't have to," Rebel said with finality, nipping her jaw.

Bri turned her head and kissed his lips. "I'm figuring out that you Howlers take pride in spoiling the women in your lives."

"As we should."

Rebel's Fairytale

"I think I want to do a full overhaul on the kitchen," Sugar commented from her seat on the other side of the fire and looked over at her mate.

Siren shrugged and took another drink of his beer. "Okay. Whatever you want."

Sugar's gaze shifted over to Pixie. "That was easy."

"Why wouldn't it be?" Pike raised a brow. "When was the last time Siren denied you something you wanted? I would bet good money that he hasn't since you mated."

"Not one fucking thing," Siren confirmed and reached over, wrapping his hand around Sugar's thigh. "She wants to tear the house down and rebuild? Sure, babe, whatever you want. New car? You got it. Twelve kids? Get naked. We got work to do."

Bri giggled as Sugar's eyes almost bugged out of her head. "*Twelve kids*? Have you lost your damn mind?"

"Just blinded by love, Sugar," Siren replied with a smile.

As Rebel quietly chuckled, Bri watched the two give each other a look that could rival the heat given off by the fire in the middle of their circle of friends.

※※※※※※※

After the twins got home, they were exhausted and went to bed. Rebel and Ruby walked their friends out and said their goodbyes. She was leaning up against the door jamb, watching Rebel give Sugar and Pixie hugs, when Ranger stepped outside and pulled her into a hug.

"Glad my brother found you, Ruby. You're good for him. And thanks for the quotes."

As he released her, she replied, "No problem. How did you get my number, anyway?"

Ranger shrugged. "Keys. Hope you don't mind."

"I don't."

"Meant what I said. You're good for Rebel."

Bri smiled at him. "He's a good guy. You all are."

Ranger winked at her.

"I noticed how they take care of their women like they are the most precious thing in their world. Is that a shifter thing?"

Ranger shrugged again. "Yeah, but it's more a Howler thing. Our women are the most precious thing in our lives. Our sisters are cherished and our Ol' Ladies are revered. Shifter or not, it's how the Howlers operate. I'm sure Rebel's the same way with you."

As Bri felt her cheeks heat again, she nodded. "He seems to thrive on doing everything he can for me."

"Well, get used to it. All the older Howlers I know are still doing those things for their Ol' Ladies after decades."

She raised a brow. "And you expect Rebel and I to still be together decades from now?"

Ranger looked at her like she had a flash of stupid. "Uh… yeah," he said in a way that clearly stated he meant, *Uh… duh.*

"Why is my woman's face red, Ranger?" Rebel approached them as Pixie's car backed out of the driveway, and Siren roared away on his bike with Sugar curled around him.

Ranger chuckled. "When *isn't* her face that color?"

Then, the two did a handshake, man hug thing, before Ranger jogged over to his bike and took off.

Once he was gone, Rebel turned to face her and smiled. "Any chance I could convince you to stay?"

T.S. Tappin

Chapter Seventeen

Rebel

Rebel cupped Ruby's face in his hands and pressed his lips to hers for a soft kiss. "Please? I missed you last night."

"You did?"

He gave her another soft kiss, lingering there for a little longer. "Yeah. I don't like sleeping away from you."

Sliding his hands back until his fingers were tangled in her blond locks, he felt his wolf give a low growl of approval at the look of bliss on her face as her eyelids lowered.

"Please?"

"I… I suppose I could."

Rebel turned and started backing into the house, taking her with him, kissing her lips. When her hands landed on his chest under his cut and slid down to his abdomen, where they fisted in his Henley, he growled into her mouth and deepened the kiss.

Ruby broke the kiss and whispered against his lips, "Like that?"

Rebel reached behind her, shut the door, and locked it. "Fucking love that," he answered, took her hand, and started pulling her toward his bedroom.

"We have stuff to talk about," she reminded him.

Rebel stopped and looked at her. "Yeah, we do. Can it wait until the morning, though? We've had such a fucking fantastic night. I don't want to bog it down with serious talk."

"And sex isn't serious?"

The smirk on her face had his cock twitching. "Yeah, but… it's… that's different."

She giggled at his stammering. "I was kidding, Rebel. Yes, we can have our talk in the morning."

"Good." He started walking again, dragging her to his bedroom. He opened the door and pulled her inside before he shut and locked the door behind them.

When he heard her gasp, he looked to see what caused it. *The pole in the front area of the room*. He forgot that he installed that with everything that had happened that day. In order to fit it in his room, he had to move around his furniture and relocate his desk and bookshelf to the guest room.

Rebel had considered installing it in the guest room, but then, he thought about one of the twins walking in on her doing her exercises. The thought had his wolf enraged, so he figured that wasn't a good idea and did what was necessary to install it in his bedroom.

"You… there's a pole," she said and pointed at it. Two seconds later, her arms folded over her chest, and she narrowed her eyes on him. "You aren't expecting me to perform for you, *are you*?"

Rebel gave her a grin. "I mean… I wouldn't *stop* you, if you felt so inclined, but no… I don't expect it. I installed it so you had a place to do your exercises while you were here… if you wanted to."

"Well, that's good," she said, still giving him sass, but her face began to turn his favorite shade of red again. "But if anyone is giving anyone a show, it would be you giving me one."

His wolf growled inside of him, and Rebel agreed. As his eyes flashed greenish-gold light, he removed his cut and hung it on the hook by his door. Then, he bent down and quickly removed his boots. As he crossed the room, headed for the pole, he yanked his Henley off.

"Wh-what are you doing?" He noticed how Ruby's voice lifted an octave.

"Giving you a show," he answered as he reached over and turned on the speaker system.

Bri

As Rebel walked away from her, Bri couldn't believe what he was about to do. In a million years, she never would have expected an intellectual biker to bust out with a pole dancing routine, but yet, there he was. She realized how crazy that sounded, since she was a librarian and could do the same thing, but that wasn't the point.

After getting a song going with a decent beat, he winked at her. He approached the pole, but as he passed it, he reached out with his right hand and grabbed it. Leaning to the left, he let his momentum swing him around the back of the pole and back around to the front. When he was facing her again, he kicked his right leg up in the air, swinging himself upside down, and wrapped it around the pole. Smiling at her, sending a shiver of desire down her spine, before he pointed his left leg and arm out in the air, away from his body and the pole.

Bri's legs began to shake, feeling weak from watching him move with such grace and strength that she was forced to sit down or risk her legs giving out on her. Not taking her eyes off him, she reached back and felt around until the bed hit her hand. Then, she sat down on the edge of the bed. She was mesmerized by him as he moved with the beat, rolling his hips as he readjusted.

After moving his arm, he leveraged the bottom half of his body out and spread his legs in a V in the air. Pressing her legs together to try to alleviate the ache he was creating there, Bri's mouth dropped open. She knew he could move, and she knew he was strong, but this was more than her body and brain could process. He made it look so easy, and she knew it was anything but easy.

She was beginning to understand the reason male dancing shows and clubs were so successful. It wasn't about skin or nakedness. It was about the moves, the grace, the raw power they exhibited with their body alone.

Using his core strength, he held himself in the move longer than she would have been able to, running his free hand down the center of his bare chest to the waistband of his jeans before he again wrapped his leg around the pole again and swung himself around it.

After a few maneuvers, he positioned himself upside down, with his spine against the bar. Holding himself up with only his arms, he spread his legs and leaned his hips forward until his feet were level with his head. After holding the move for a moment, he brought his legs together and back up to flatten them against the pole.

He continued adjusting his hold and maneuvering his body for a few more minutes, twisting himself into moves that were way past a beginner level. She had a brief thought that he had to have more than a basic knowledge of the craft, but it was brushed away when she noticed the sweat glistening on the skin of his chest, arms, and back, accentuating all the sexy muscles that she loved.

Once he had thoroughly blown her mind and made her wet for him, he maneuvered himself upside down with his back to the pole, holding himself up with one arm. Then he flipped off of the pole and landed on his feet. With his chest heaving and his eyes glowing, he turned to face her.

Rebel

When he was done, he let go of the pole and turned to face Ruby. Even though his eyes were shining that light, he didn't have a problem seeing the sexy as hell look on her face. She was sitting on the corner of his bed, her cheeks the wonderful pink he loved so much, and she was biting her lip. As he moved over to the stereo system, he chuckled to himself, well aware that he had blown her mind. He turned off the music and faced her again. Gazing into her eyes, he asked, "What do you think?"

"I think… I think… How do you know how to… Wow."

Chuckling, Rebel approached her and stopped between her knees. Reaching down, he slid his hand along her cheek and into her hair. "When you spend time at a strip club and the dancers are your friends, there's a chance they might take that opportunity to teach you some things." He shrugged. "I'm a good student, and I enjoyed it."

Staring up at him and listening, her arms unfolded, and her hands pressed against his abdomen.

Using his grip on her hair, he tilted her head back and gazed down at her. "You never have to give me a show, Ruby. Just being around you is enough of a turn-on for me." He took one of her hands and pressed it against his jean-covered erection.

"You're making it really hard to be rational about our relationship," she whispered as the fingers of her other hand absently traced his abdomen.

"Don't be rational," he whispered back.

"I have to be."

"Says who?" He bent down and took her lips in a deep but slow kiss. "I'm not pressuring you, Ruby. I promise. Just know, I'm here when you're ready. And, until then, I'm going to treat you as if you're already mine, so you know what you'd be getting."

When she laid back on the bed and started scooting up until she was fully on the bed, Rebel followed her, crawling until his hips were between her thighs, and he was kissing her chest along the V-neck of her shirt.

"Rebel," she breathed, her hands gripping his shoulders.

"What, Sweetie?"

"We both have way too many clothes on."

Chuckling, he gripped the hem of her shirt and shoved it up until it was at her shoulders. As she let go of him and removed it the rest of the way, he kissed between her breasts as he unzipped and unfastened her jeans.

They separated long enough for both of them to get naked. Then, he was back between her thighs and sucking one of her nipples into his mouth as she arched off the bed and let out a moan.

It was the sweetest fucking sound he ever heard. His wolf loved it too, which is why he was doing the low growling thing and pacing inside of Rebel.

His hand slid between them, and Rebel slid two fingers into her wet, hot core. Fuck, she felt so damn good to him. Every instinct he had said to slam inside of her and fuck her until neither of them could breathe, but he tamped down those instincts.

"Need you," she gasped as he curled his fingers just right.

"You're going to do what I tell you to, tonight, Ruby. And right now, you're going to come on my fingers." He bit down on her nipple and quickened the thrust of his fingers, shifting his hand so the heel was rubbing against her clit.

"Rebel," she shouted as her nails clawed into the skin of his back.

Rebel released her nipple and kissed over to the other one. Giving it the same treatment, he soaked in every moan and gasp his woman gave him. When he felt her core begin to contract around his fingers, he released her nipple and ordered, "Give it to me, Ruby. Now."

With a low-keening sound coming from her lips, she threw her head back and did as he commanded. He kept up his ministrations until Ruby's body relaxed back on the bed. Then, he pulled his fingers from her core. Gazing into her sated gold-flecked blue eyes, he lifted those fingers to his lips, slid them inside, and sucked off every bit of her juices.

When she bit her bottom lip, Rebel growled and reached over to his nightstand. He grabbed a condom and lifted up on his knees. As he rolled it on, he let his gaze travel all over her body, appreciating every curve, every dimple, every freckle.

"You're so damn beautiful."

She lifted her foot and traced his abdomen muscles with the tip of her big toe. "I could say the same to you," she replied with a smile.

Wrapping his hand around her ankle, he lifted her foot to his face and nipped her big toe. As she giggled, he pressed his lips to her ankle, then the inside of her calf, then the inside of her knee. He worked his way up her inner thigh until he reached her core.

Using his lips and his tongue, he cleaned her of her juices, making sure not to miss a drop. Then, he crawled over her, taking a hold of one of her knees and positioning it by his ribs.

After giving her a deep kiss, he looked into her eyes and whispered, "I'm going to fuck you now."

Breathing heavily, she nodded and wrapped her other leg around his hip.

Rebel reached between them and lined himself up with her core. "I want to make you feel good every night for the rest of our lives," he told her as he slid inside of her, making her moan. "Fucking love making you moan like that, Ruby."

When she started moving her hips, he pulled out and slammed back in. "Fucking love feeling this pussy around me." He pulled out and slammed in again, this time harder and faster. Increasing the speed with every thrust, he bent down and kissed along her shoulder, letting all of her noises wash over him.

When she started contracting around his cock, he pulled out and grabbed her by the hips. Flipping her over, he forced her on her knees and reentered her from behind. Kissing up her spine, he fucked her like it was the last time he'd ever be inside her pussy.

"Yes, Rebel! Yes!"

Following his lips with his hand, he slid it up her spine until he could fist it in her hair. Forcing her to turn her head, he nipped her jawline. "You feel so goddamn good."

Ruby slid her hands up above her head and pressed them against the headboard, bracing herself and giving herself leverage to push back against him with every thrust.

"Yeah, Ruby," he growled and nipped her shoulder. "Work yourself against me." He slid his free hand around her hip and began circling her clit with his middle finger. Almost immediately, her core began to tighten around him, flexing and releasing. His wolf was demanding he claim her, snarling and pacing. Rebel put his mouth to her shoulder and sucked, sending her over the edge. Hearing her moan with her orgasm sent him over. Slamming inside, he let go.

As pleasure coursed through him, he released the skin of her shoulder and nuzzled his face into her neck. As they both slowly came back down, he let go of her hair and leaned to the side, bringing both of them down on the bed, so he wasn't crushing her. His hand was still cupping her pelvic bone and his cock was still inside her, and he was in no hurry to change that.

Rebel's Fairytale

His wolf was snarling at him, pissed he didn't claim her, but he told his wolf to shut the hell up.

"Well... that was... intense," she panted out, trying to catch her breath. Her words made his gut tighten.

Kissing up her neck, Rebel asked, "Too intense?"

She turned her head to look over her shoulder at him. When her gaze met his, he saw the sated look in her eyes, and his gut unclenched. "No. No, not too intense. I like it when you just take over."

Rebel gave her a smile and nipped her earlobe. "Anytime you want me to, I will. I like taking care of you in all ways."

"Like the tea?"

He shrugged. "You like tea. I wanted to be prepared."

She smiled. "That was very nice of you, Rebel. Thank you."

"Again... anytime, Ruby." Then, he kissed her shoulder. "Let me take care of the condom."

Rebel slid out of her, moaning at the sensation and the shivers it sent through his body. As he climbed off the bed and headed for his bathroom, he took in the sight of her laid out on his bed and bit back the groan the visual caused. He never wanted to leave it.

After taking care of the condom and cleaning up, he wet a washcloth and returned to the bedroom. Bending over her, he watched her face as he slid his hand with the washcloth between her thighs and gently, slowly cleaned her. Her thighs spread a bit, and she bit her bottom lip as her eyes slid closed. Yeah, he liked taking care of his woman.

He tossed the cloth into his hamper before he yanked the comforter out from under her. Sliding into bed behind her, he wrapped himself around her and settled in, pulling the comforter over them.

"I love sleeping in your arms," she said, sleepily.

He waited while her breathing evened out. Then, he buried his nose in her hair and whispered, "I love you."

Chapter Eighteen

Bri

When Bri woke up, the first thing she noticed was there was a hand between her legs and a hand cupping her breast. Glancing over her shoulder, she smiled when she saw a sleeping Rebel cuddled up behind her.

As much as she liked the visual and being in his arms, she had to use the restroom. Carefully, she slid out of his grasp. She was almost to the edge of the bed, when two hands grabbed her hips and pulled her back against Rebel.

"Where do you think you're going?" Rebel sleepily asked against her neck.

"I gotta use the restroom," she replied and smiled as his lips left soft, wet kisses on her skin.

"I guess," he grumbled and let go of her. "Hurry back."

Ruby turned enough to kiss his lips, then she climbed off the bed and went to his bathroom. When she was done taking care of her morning business, she returned to his bedroom, only to find that Rebel had drifted off back to sleep.

She found her panties and pulled them on. Then, she snatched up one of his shirts and pulled it over her head, thankful that it almost reached her knees. As quietly as possible, she left the bedroom and headed to the kitchen with the intention of making some tea.

She had just reached the kitchen counter when the twins came out of the hallway and stepped into the room. She froze and stared at them, unsure what to do.

"Morning," Ryker commented as Ross just grinned.

"Morning," she replied. "I was going to make some tea."

"Sounds good. We have to grab some breakfast before we head to the compound."

That's when Bri noticed the cuts they were wearing. On the front right panel was the Howlers logo. The left had a patch that just said *Prospect*. When Ross passed her, she saw that it also had the Howlers logo larger on the back, just like Rebel's, but it didn't have what Rebel had told her was the top and bottom rockers.

During one of their casual conversations, he had told her that some clubs don't even give the club's colors until the prospect patched in. After some questions, she found out that those words translated to some clubs don't give the prospect the large logo on the back of the vest until they have earned their full membership to the club.

The nerdy part of her loved that club life practically had its own language. It was neat that they had their own set of rules, words, and way of doing things. Her curiosity had her peppering him with questions until a grin appeared on his face. She had blushed which had led to them making out on the couch.

"So, you're… prospecting for the Howlers? Is that what it's called?"

Ross nodded as he grabbed a box of cereal out of the pantry. "Yup."

"And that means you have to do everything the members tell you, right?"

It was Ryker's turn to nod. "Yup. I think bathrooms at the businesses in the strip mall are on the agenda for the day."

"Ew. Bathrooms." She turned and grabbed the kettle off of Rebel's stove, moving to the sink to fill it.

"Part of the gig. If it earns us membership to the club, it will be worth it," Ross said as he grabbed two bowls from the cupboard.

Ryker grabbed the milk from the refrigerator and turned around. "So… you're moving in?"

Bri almost dropped the kettle into the sink at Ryker's question. "Wh-what?" She shut off the water and turned to face him.

Staring at the stuff Rebel bought her the night before still on the counter, he nodded to it. "Do you need help grabbing your stuff? I'm sure we could call Axle and let him know we're helping you and Rebel."

"N-no. No." She shook her head, took a deep breath, and swallowed hard. "Uh… no. Rebel was just making sure I had… stuff here… in case…"

"Oh." Ryker shrugged. "I don't know why you guys are waiting. You're mates, but that's your business."

"W-would you care? When we get to that point, would it… bother you guys?"

Ross looked at her like she lost her mind. "Why would we care?"

"I don't know. I just… wouldn't want you to feel like I'm… invading your space."

"Nah. We're good," Ross said and set the bowls on the top of the island. As he filled the bowls with cereal, Ryker retrieved spoons from the drawer.

Neither of them seemed bothered at all. They just asked her life-altering questions while they acted like they asked her what the weather was going to be like for the day.

"You guys approve… of me, don't you?" Her question was quiet, but she really wanted to know. Bri suspected that was what the whole conversation was about — the twins giving their approval. She just needed clarification.

She set the kettle on the burner and turned the burner on while she waited for their answer.

"Ruby," Ryker said, softly.

She looked over and saw both of the twins staring at her. "Yeah?"

"You don't need our approval," Ross began, "but you have it."

They both smiled at her, and she smiled back through her happy tears.

"Why in the hell are there tears in my woman's eyes?" Rebel's voice, rough with sleep, rang through the room. Then, he was standing next to her and wrapping her in his arms.

"Because she's a woman, and that's what they do when you tell them you wouldn't mind it if they moved in with you and your much-loved cousins," Ryker answered as he poured milk in their cereal.

Rebel looked over at her and kissed her lips. "They freak you out?"

"A little, but it's okay."

"We were just saying we'd help if she was moving in." Ross took a bite of cereal. "We weren't demanding that she promise to do it right now."

Rebel kissed her lips again and grinned.

When the whistle from the kettle sounded, she turned off the burner and moved it over. Rebel had grabbed two of the new mugs he bought and quickly washed them, while she grabbed the box of chai tea from the island.

Ryker snorted a laugh. "You two already move like a long-mated couple."

Once the twins were gone and Rebel had whipped them up some omelets, the two of them settled on two of the stools at the island and ate their breakfast. As he ate, Rebel used his free hand to keep a physical connection between them. He brushed her hair out of her face. He caressed her back. Rebel gripped her thigh. Anything he could do to keep them in contact, he did.

She loved that about him, his need to touch her. He wasn't selfish with affection, but he also seemed to recognize when it was bordering on too much. He would pull back and give her a bit of space. How Rebel managed to read her so well boggled Bri's mind.

When she was finished with her omelet, she took a sip of her tea and sighed. "Okay. Talk time."

Rebel nodded, still chewing his last bite. He grabbed their plates and forks, and carried them to the sink. When he returned to his stool, he began, "I talked to the brothers. Part of the money needed at the library will come from the club businesses. For the rest, we're going to do a charity carnival at the compound. All the proceeds will go to the library. Either way, the library will not lose one cent of donations, no matter what the dissenters do."

Bri stared at him for a long moment, trying hard to wrap her mind around what he was telling her. "Just like that?"

He shrugged. "Yeah."

"Rebel, it's a lot of money."

"It isn't the first time the Howlers have done something like this for the town. You've been here long enough to know that."

She nodded. She *had* been in town long enough to know that the Howlers were an integral part of how certain services and business remained functioning. When she moved to Warden's Pass five years before, she was surprised by the number of services offered in a town of that size, but it didn't take her long to figure out how. The Howlers were how. They took care of Warden's Pass the same way they took care of each other and their families.

"You all don't deserve what they are doing."

He reached out and tucked her hair behind her ear. "Neither do you." He sighed. "I need to tell you something, but I don't want you to freak out."

She narrowed her eyes on him. "What?"

"I claimed you as my Ol' Lady to the club." When she opened her mouth, with the full intention of telling him she hadn't agreed to anything yet, he held up a hand. "I know. And like I said last night, I'm not trying to pressure you. The fact of the matter is no other woman will be my Ol' Lady no matter what you decide, and that is what I've decided. They would have done it, anyway, but claiming you to the club just solidifies their commitment to treating you like they would Sugar or Pixie or Gorgeous. They already feel that way about you. I just made it official."

"So, they'll hate me if I don't agree?"

He shook his head. "Nah. They'd never hate you, Ruby."

She wanted to be irritated about it. She wanted to tell him he was being pushy, but he wasn't. He hadn't asked for anything from her. He gave her the facts and told her to take her time. Just because he was sure didn't mean he was demanding she feel as comfortable with things. He was doing what he told her he would. He was showing her what things would be like while allowing her time to make up her mind.

"I'm *really* not trying to pressure you," he said, quietly and dropped his gaze to his hands in his lap.

"How nuts is your wolf being?"

Rebel chuckled. "He's being a demanding dick, but I'll survive."

Wishing she could just throw caution to the wind and accept what he was offering, Bri leaned forward and pressed her lips to his. When his tongue slid along her bottom lip, she opened and let him inside. Within minutes, she was in his arms, and he was carrying her back to bed.

"Rebel!" She laughed. "We can't spend all day in bed."

"Why the hell not?" He tossed her on the bed and grinned down at her as she bounced and settled.

⁂

Bri was nervous about walking into the tattoo shop, not because of it being a tattoo shop, but because she was meeting up with what Pixie had referred to as a meeting of the Shifty Sisters. Ruby didn't quite understand what she meant by that when she got the text, but she assumed Pixie was referring to what Rebel called the Ol' Ladies. They were important to the club, so they were important to Rebel, and she didn't want to screw up and make things awkward.

She wasn't one of the Ol' Ladies, so she certainly wasn't one of the Shifty Sisters. Bri was confused about getting an invitation, but she was going because she really liked them and hoped to make some new friends.

Pixie, Sugar, and Mary, who Rebel told her was now called Diamond, were all wonderful women, and Bri had started building a friendship with them. As someone who was very selective with her friends, she was hopeful that the others would be just as kind.

Taking a bracing deep breath, she pulled open the door to the tattoo shop with the logo in bright purple and pink on the glass.

As soon as she stepped inside, Bri was assaulted with the noise from all the women. The cheers of welcome and laughter made her smile.

She clocked Pixie, Sugar, and Diamond sitting on a couch in the lobby. They waved her over. As she approached, she looked around and saw several of the other women scattered around the room.

She gave a slight wave of hello to them, a little intimidated by the sheer number of them. She wasn't normally freaked out by women, but these weren't just any women. If things worked out with Rebel, they would be a part of her life on a regular basis. The situation had her a bit on edge.

"Relax," Pixie told her and patted her hand. "They all already like you."

"They don't know me."

Sugar shrugged. "You put a smile on Rebel's face. That's all they need to know."

Diamond nodded. "The Howlers and the Claws have welcomed me with open arms, even though they barely know me."

"Oh! By the way, I have gifts for everyone," Pixie exclaimed and pulled a large Howlers tote bag out from next to the couch.

The Shifty Sisters gathered around the couch. Bri noticed the curious yet suspicious expressions on the faces of the women.

"Okay. So, you know how I relayed the story of how Rebel and Ruby met?" Pixie grinned. "I read the book she was reading when it happened. And, let me tell you, it's a must read. Anyway, back to the presents." She yanked a pink bundle from the tote bag and held it up. "I bought all of us pink hand towels!"

As she giggled, she started tossing pink bundles to each of the women in the room. When she dropped a bundle in Bri's lap, she felt her cheeks heat up.

"And that is why he calls her Ruby," Gorgeous said and gave her a sweet smile.

Bri huffed out a breath and looked around at the women. "Can we talk about that?"

Rebel's Fairytale

The few women who were standing about the room were suddenly sitting in chairs near the couch, staring intently at her. She hadn't even seen most of them grab the chairs.

"Uh... Rebel mentioned that the nicknames had some significance. And since he goes by a nickname, too, I tend to believe that to be the truth."

Darlin' nodded. "First, if Rebel said it, you can count on it being the truth. He's a very honest man. Second, the men don't go by nicknames. They go by road names. Lastly, if they give you a name, it is way more respectful than calling you by your given name. It's a sign of acceptance, of belonging. It's how the Howlers show you that they think of you as family. It's how they claim you as one of theirs. And when they do that, they are acknowledging that they are yours as well." She smiled. "Rebel calls you Ruby because he cares very deeply for you. The guys call you that because they respect Rebel and like you. We call you Ruby because you're one of us now."

Bri took in everything Darlin' said and let the sense of belonging wash over her. Just as Rebel had told her, she suddenly had more friends than she knew what to do with. It would take some time to get used to.

As for the nickname, there were far worse things to be called than Ruby. The fact that Rebel appreciated the almost constant state of red to her cheeks was something that made her almost giddy inside. She noticed him doing little things with the sole intention of making her blush. Her favorite was the way he kissed her, like he would die without his lips pressed to hers. If that's what she got for letting him call her Ruby, she would drive down to the courthouse and change her damn name.

Looking down at the hand towels, Ruby thought about Rebel lounged on her couch, reading a book, as she was getting ready to meet up with the women. He looked like he belonged in her space, like his rough, masculine body and sharp intelligence was made to be in her life. She suddenly realized what the weird feeling was that had been sitting in her gut. It was the feeling that something big was happening, something life-changing.

"I think I might like it around here," she said and smiled.

A loud whoop sounded as the women celebrated her words.

Sugar slid an arm around her shoulder. "We kinda like having you around here."

"Now, Diamond," Gorgeous blurted, "it's time for you to get inked!"

"What are you getting?" Pixie asked Diamond with an excited smile on her face.

Diamond grinned. "Rock requested that it says *Rock's Reward*."

When she finished speaking, the women in the room let out a collective sigh.

"That's so sweet," Ruby commented.

"When you get yours, what will yours say?" Diamond asked.

Ruby felt panic rise in her. "Not sure we'll get there, but… I don't know."

"Whatever." Pixie waved away her words. "You are *sooooo* getting there."

"By the way," Darlin' said as Diamond and a few of the girls moved down the hall toward one of the work rooms, "what are you doing for Rebel's birthday, tomorrow? I know the club is having a big party for all the birthdays of the month, next week, but are you doing anything?"

"What?" Ruby pulled out her phone and unlocked it. She pulled Rebel's text string up and sent him a text.

>It's your birthday tomorrow? Why didn't you tell me?<

"It's Rebel's birthday, tomorrow," Darlin' repeated. "You didn't know?"

"No," she mumbled as she read his reply.

>It's just another day.<

>Bullshit. How old are you going to be?<

Ruby let out a little growl, making Darlin' and Gorgeous laugh.

>29. Seriously, Ruby, it's not a big deal.<

After rolling her eyes, Ruby sent a reply.

>We're having a get together at your house, tomorrow night, at six.<

She didn't even wait for his reply. She shoved her phone in her purse and huffed out a breath. "I can't believe he wasn't going to tell me about his birthday."

T.S. Tappin

Chapter Nineteen

Rock

Sitting at a table in the clubhouse with Rebel, Pike, and Siren, Rock was sipping a beer. His kids, all four of them, were in the cafeteria room with Axle, and he was helping them make personal pizzas. Axle was excited to introduce Nugget to Miles and Jenna, and also to start building a bond with his newest niece and nephew. Rock thought it was adorable, not that he would tell Axle that, and he wasn't about to turn him down.

They were discussing the plans for the carnival and what needed to be done when the front door opened, and Diamond walked in with Gorgeous, Ruby, Pixie, and Sugar behind her.

His eyes locked with Diamond's, and he asked, "You done?"

She nodded and bit her bottom lip, making him want to suck on it. "Want to see it?"

"Yes." He set his beer down and stood.

"I can show you right here," she said and started to lift her shirt.

"Not here," Rock blurted. Then, he cleared his throat and rounded the table, ignoring his brother's snickering. When he reached her, he took her hand and led her down the back hall to the women's bathroom.

After knocking on the door, opening it, and calling out to make sure no one was in there, he dragged her inside. He shut and locked the door. "Okay. Let me see," he said as he turned to face her.

Diamond bit that bottom lip again, driving him fucking crazy. Then, she pulled her shirt up from the bottom and showed him the bandage just above the waistband of her leggings.

Crouching down, Rock carefully peeled the bandage back and looked over the tattoo. Below the Howlers logo, in bold script, were the words *Rock's Reward* with a diamond for the *o*, the apostrophe, and inside the *a*. He fucking loved it. After replacing the bandage, Rock placed a soft kiss over it. Then, he gripped the waistband of her leggings and yanked down.

"Rock," Diamond gasped out and gripped his shoulders as he went to work on removing her shoes, leggings, and panties.

"I'm going to show you how I feel about it, and you're just going to let me," he said as he kissed his way up her thighs. When he got to the apex, he lifted one of her legs over his shoulder and dove in.

He'd been with her enough times to know exactly where and how to lick and suck. Holding her up with one hand, he used two fingers of his other hand to help bring her to her first orgasm.

Once he had licked her clean, he stood and gripped her hips. Lifting her to the edge of the counter, he kissed her lips. Then, he went about pulling out his cock and slipping on a condom he retrieved from his wallet.

His woman was going to feel boneless by the time he was done with her. Then he'd feed her, rehydrate her, and do it all over again.

Rebel

When Ruby walked in with the Ol' Ladies, Rebel's first thought was that he liked that. Seeing her with the other women of the club family made his heart clench with happiness and rightness.

His second thought was *Oh shit. Ruby's pissed.*

The other women went to their men, but Ruby stopped just inside the door. As he approached, she crossed her arms over her chest and glared at him.

"It's not a big deal, Sweetie," he said quietly.

"Not a big deal? It's your birthday, Rebel."

He leaned forward to kiss her, but she turned her head. He kissed her cheek instead and fought the smile that threatened to appear on his face. "I should have told you. I'm sorry."

"Yeah, ya think?" She rolled her eyes. "I guess I forgive you, but I'm still irritated."

"Does that mean you aren't coming home with me?"

She shifted on her feet and dropped her gaze to his chest. "I didn't say that. But I'm *not* staying the night. That's your punishment for keeping it from me."

As much as he didn't like sleeping away from her, he wouldn't push her on it. After all, she was mad because she wanted to celebrate him. How could he fight her on that?

"So, you're saying I'll have to fuck you before I follow you home?"

The corner of her mouth twitched as she fought her smile. "You think you can fuck me until I forget?"

Rebel shrugged. "Sounds like a viable plan to me."

The Next Day... Ruby

Still a little irritated with Rebel that he didn't tell her it was his birthday, she had used her annoyance to her advantage. Like always, when annoyed, she was quick with her decisions, efficient in her movements, and could organize like a motherfucker.

That was how she managed to get everything she needed for his birthday party within an hour, except for his present. His present took her longer to figure out. Bri didn't want to get him something stupid. She wanted it to be a gift he appreciated, enjoyed, cherished.

She decided on a signed copy of the book she was reading when they met, but it was going to take a few days to get to him. So, she printed the order and put it in a box. Then, she did something she *never* thought she would do in her life.

Dressed in her favorite set of black satin and lace lingerie, her leather jacket, and her heeled boots, she set up her phone on a stand and took a video of her doing a routine on her pole. When she was done, she took screen grabs of her favorite, most flattering moments, and printed them out. After putting them in a small photo album, she wrapped it.

When she arrived at his house, she was nervous. Would he like the gifts, or would he think they were stupid? She was glad she decided to show up a couple hours early to set up. It would allow her time to get over the humiliation if he didn't like them.

As she approached his front door, she gave herself a pep talk. He thinks you're beautiful and badass, because you are! You're a badass babe and you're hot, and you're not going to be embarrassed.

She lifted her hand to knock on the door, but it was pulled open, and Rebel was standing there in only a pair of those tear-away sports pants, looking scrumptious.

Tearing her eyes away from his bare abdomen, she looked into his eyes. "Hi. Happy birthday."

He smiled at her and kissed her lips, taking the bags from her other hand. "Thanks, Sweetie. You already told me that, this morning when you texted me."

"I know, but now I'm in person." She let him take the bags and turned around to go back to her car to get the rest.

"Where are you going?"

"To get the rest," she answered as she crossed his porch to the stairs.

"I'll get it." Then, he was walking around her, hands free.

She waited on the porch, while he opened the passenger door and grabbed the remaining two bags and the cake.

"This all?"

"For now."

He closed her car door and headed toward the porch.

Once they were both inside, she tried to grab the original bags he took from her from the floor by the door, but he let out a growl. Shrugging, she left the bags there and followed him to the kitchen.

She started unpacking the bags, setting plates and cups on the top of the island. "Your present is in the gift bag. It might be a good idea to open it before anyone else gets here." She didn't look at him because she was still steeling herself for his reaction.

When the bags were empty, she finally looked up and saw him staring at her. "What?"

"I wasn't going to open it until you were done." He nodded to the stool next to him. "Come. Sit." Then, he reached for the gift bag. It was dark green and had silver stripes on it.

Taking a deep breath, Ruby rounded the island and slid onto the stool next to him. She tried really hard not to fidget as he pulled out the first small box and pulled off the ribbon. He lifted the lid and pulled out the folded piece of paper.

The look on his face was amused and curious. He unfolded it and read what it said. Then his eyes shifted to her. "Ruby," he breathed, before he leaned toward her and took her lips in a slow, sweet kiss. "That's perfect, Sweetie. Thank you."

"That's… not all."

"You really didn't need to get me anything but thank you." He reached in the bag and pulled out the wrapped album. He pulled off the plain green wrapping paper and revealed that it was a 5x7, dark green album. "You've got my attention," he mumbled as he set aside the wrapping paper.

Ruby held her breath as she watched him open the cover. His eyes looked over each photo before he flipped to the next. Ten photos, and no response. She couldn't read his expression. It was completely blank. When he slowly closed the cover and still didn't say anything, she slid off the stool.

"Well, ya know, it was just an idea. No biggie." She turned to go back to setting up his party, trying her best not to be upset, when he grabbed her wrist. She stopped moving and looked back at him.

He was staring up at her, that golden-green light coming from his eyes. "Ruby," he said, his voice more growl than human voice.

"Is that… good… or bad?"

"Ruby," he said again, and pulled on her arm, forcing her to return to his side. He released her wrist but only to wrap that arm around her waist. Then, he opened the cover again and ran his fingertips over the photo. "Fucking beautiful."

"You like?"

His hand slid up to fist in her hair. Then, he forced her head down the few inches he needed for him to take her lips in a scorching kiss. Using his teeth and tongue and lips to drive her crazy. Without breaking their kiss, he started unbuttoning her shirt.

When she needed to breathe, she broke the kiss and asked, "I'll take that as a yes."

"Hot as fuck," he growled out and stood. Gripping her hips, he lifted her and headed for his bedroom.

"What about the ice cream?" she asked in a moment of panic.

"Fuck the ice cream," he replied and tossed her onto his bed, immediately pulling off her shoes.

"Why do you always toss me on the bed like that?"

"It makes your tits bounce," he answered matter-of-factly, and began pulling off her jeans and panties.

Once he had her naked, he shoved down his own pants and climbed in bed with her. Instead of over her, like she expected, he relaxed next to her with his back to the headboard. Rolling on a condom, he ordered, "Climb on."

Ruby rolled over onto her knees and crawled over to him. Throwing her leg over him, straddling his thighs, she looked down into his eyes. "I'm glad you like them."

"I fucking love them, but no one else on this earth will ever see those fucking photos."

When she smiled down at him, he gripped her hips again and lined her up with his erection.

"Hold on, Ruby. It's going to be a rough damn ride."

T.S. Tappin

Chapter Twenty

Reginald

Reginald couldn't believe he was spending his Monday night in that stuffy room at city hall, listening to the room of assholes bitch and moan about his request. It was simple. The Howlers wanted the necessary licenses and permits to throw a charity carnival. They should deny them. There wasn't much to it but a vote.

Yet, the council was going on and on about legalities and suitable reasons. He was tired of it.

"I'm sure there's a damn reason," he barked.

Timothy McCallum let out a deep sigh. "We can't deny them just because you have a bug up your ass. Frankly, I don't get what you could possibly have against them. They have been known to keep this town going when we were on the verge of bankruptcy. How many times have the Howlers donated money or made purchases that have kept a business or service from going under? More times than I can tell you. They are a vital resource and good citizens."

"They are a *nuisance* and a *danger*, especially to the children of this town," Cordelia Philips insisted and slammed her hand down on the table she was sitting at.

"How?" Ariella Cordova asked with a hefty dose of doubt in her voice.

Reginald stated, "They have roughed up and assaulted numerous members of this community. They have so many businesses that it stops others from being able to make it in this town. And they are literal *monsters* capable of hurting our children!"

Ariella shook her head. "They roughed up men who had used their fists on the women they were supposed to love or on their children. The danger to the children are men like the abusers they rescue the women from. As for the businesses, they employ more members of Warden's Pass than anyone else. And they give back to the community. I vote yes on the permits and licenses, and you won't change my mind."

"Same," McCallum agreed.

As Reginald listened to his fellow council members approve of the licenses and permits for the charity carnival, he mentally took down names of his enemies. If it was the last thing he did, they would all regret that decision.

Rebel

With his woman bouncing on his dick, Rebel was in motherfucking heaven. He had his arms around her and his hands gripping her ass cheeks, helping her keep up her rhythm, not that she needed his help.

"Fuck yes," he growled as she ground down on him, while leaning forward and shoving her breasts in his face.

"Rebel, I'm gonna," she panted out.

Rebel leaned back further, using the headboard as leverage to thrust up into her on her downward strokes. "Give it to me, Ruby."

Three bounces later, she stayed down and threw her head back, crying out his name. *Fuck*! She was the most beautiful creature he had ever met. The sight of her experiencing ecstasy had his own climax coming over him like a freight train. That was when his wolf got loud, demanding their mark on her. To appease his wolf, he bent forward and sucked the side of her breast into his mouth. He sucked for all he was worth, while he rode out his pleasure.

When they were both through it and panting as they tried to regain their wits, Ruby had her face buried into his neck. "Happy birthday."

Rebel barked out a laugh and gave her ass a slap. "Best fucking birthday ever. Shower time."

Ruby was off of him quick and shaking a finger at him. "Oh no! I'll shower in here, but you aren't joining me. We'll never have things ready by the time they get here."

Rebel climbed to his feet. "What is there to do?"

"I have to unpack and prepare the snack platters. I have to set out the cups and plates and utensils. The chili. It's still in the pot in the trunk of my car. It needs to simmer to warm."

Rebel approached her and kissed her lips. "Let me take care of the condom. Then, I'll go get the chili and get it simmering. I'll shower in the twins' bathroom. Is that okay?"

Ruby ran a hand down his chest and nodded. "I think that would work."

"Then, you better take your hands off me. I'm not responsible for what happens while you're touching me."

Ruby yanked her hand back, causing him to laugh again. Then he kissed her lips and went into the bathroom to take care of the immediate business.

Pixie

When Pixie and Pike arrived, Ruby's cheeks were beet red. She had a small green album in her hand as she opened the door for them. She waved them in and told them she would be right back. When she returned, the album was gone.

"What was that?" Pixie asked with a grin.

"Nothing," Ruby said and grinned back.

Rebel's Fairytale

"I'm guessing a birthday present we aren't allowed to see," Pike uttered on a chuckle as he headed for the refrigerator and grabbed a beer.

Ruby just cleared her throat and moved over to the stove to stir whatever she was making in a giant pot. "Hope you guys like chili. I started it earlier and am just warming it up."

Pike walked over and looked in the pot. Letting out a groan, he commented, "You're quickly becoming one of my favorite Ol' Ladies. Don't tell the others."

Ruby giggled as Pixie rolled her eyes at her mate.

"Where's Rebel?" Pike grabbed a spoon from the counter and tried to steal some chili, but Ruby slapped his hand away.

"In the shower." She nodded toward the hall. "And you can wait just like everyone else."

"Meanie," he said and took the stool next to the one Pixie was sitting on.

Out of the blue, Pixie thought of the pink hand towel situation and looked over at Ruby. "Do you have the hand towel here?"

Ruby narrowed her eyes on her, but answered, "Yes." Then, she crossed the kitchen and pulled the hand towel out of a bag on the counter.

Pixie giggled. "Pike, I need you to do me a favor." She proceeded to tell him her plan, but Pike almost immediately began shaking his head. "Please. Pretty please." Pixie stared into her mate's eyes and stuck out her bottom lip.

"It would be hilarious," Pike mumbled as he glared at Pixie.

"Yes, it would be. And... it would be fulfilling a fantasy of Ruby's."

"Hey," Ruby whisper-shouted from across the island, trying hard to hold back her laughter, "don't bring me into this."

"Did you or did you not choke on a gummi bear because you were reading a scene about a pink hand towel and looked up and saw Rebel?" When Ruby's cheeks turned bright red, Pixie grinned. "I rest my case."

Pike let out a deep sigh and stood. "Fine. But if he kicks my ass, you're kissing it better."

Pixie patted his ass as he stepped by her. "I'll even throw a blow job in there as a bonus."

As Pike passed Ruby, he took the hand towel from her hand. When he walked out of the room and down the hall to the twins' bathroom, Ruby tossed a kitchen towel at Pixie and hit her in the face. "You're a wicked woman."

Pixie knew Rebel wouldn't think it was that funny, but in the end, he wouldn't be mad. The truth of the matter was, she just wanted to give Ruby a little fun and bond with her a bit. Their men were close, and Pixie wanted her and Ruby to be close too.

Pike returned to the kitchen with a stack of towels and plopped them down on the kitchen island. "I'd hide those if I were you."

Pixie watched as Ruby snatched up the pile and rushed them off to Rebel's pantry. She had just closed the pantry door when they heard the shower turn off. A minute later, the bathroom door opened, and Rebel came storming out of the bathroom, grumbling about the twins and laundry, when he entered the kitchen. Three steps in, he stopped and looked around.

Standing there with nothing but a pink hand towel covering his junk, he looked at Pike and mumbled, "I thought I smelled pussy." Then he kept walking, passing Pixie and Pike seated at the island.

Pixie tried to get a peek at Rebel's bare ass, but suddenly, her mate's hand was covering her face. "Hey!"

"Woman, you are not looking at my brother's ass," Pike growled.

When he finally removed his hand, Pixie and Ruby looked at each other and burst out laughing.

Three minutes later, Rebel stepped out of his room, fully dressed, and said, "I don't know where we got a pink hand towel from, but if you think I don't know what you were doing, you're wrong." He held up a book, and sure enough, it was the book that contained the pink hand towel scene.

With a smile on his face, Rebel rounded the island and came up behind Ruby. He moved her hair from her neck and placed a kiss there, while Ruby's face turned the color of a tomato.

T.S. Tappin

Rebel

How they ended up playing that dice game with the pad of goals and the cup, Rebel didn't know. It wasn't very biker-esque, but it was making the women happy. There was more giggling going on around the table than he had ever heard.

He was glad he spent his day finding a dining room table and carting it home. Ruby had offered to let him borrow hers. That was when he realized he was going to need one with his Ruby in his life. She was a people person, and he would have guests over every weekend if it made her smile the way she was at that moment.

The four women were sitting together at one end of the table, trying to whisper to each other, but all the men, except Rock, had shifter hearing and could hear every word they said.

Rebel did not want to know Rock could do that with his tongue, but he did, and there was no way to erase that knowledge from his brain.

When Pixie started to describe some move that Pike did with his hips, Rebel stood. "I think I need some fresh air."

"Me too," Siren said and followed him toward the back door.

"Wait up," Pike said with a grin on his face.

Rock looked confused, but he stood and followed them.

When they were all on the back deck, Rock shut the door and looked at them with a question on his face.

Pike pointed to his ear. "Shifter hearing. And... bravo, brother."

Rock's face broke out in a grin. "I don't know what for, but thanks."

"I can't believe these fuckers interrupted me finding out exactly what move was Pixie's favorite, but I'll just experiment later until she tells me."

Rebel just grinned. Yeah, he'd have company every weekend.

Niles

They thought they could just take over this town and do whatever the hell they wanted, and Niles wasn't going to stand by and watch it happen. He had plans, good plans, plans that would let them know exactly who the fuck they were messing with.

He climbed out of his mother's car and slammed the door shut. As he walked back to the trunk, he thought about the look on Mary's face as she watched that fucker carry boxes into his damn house, and the way his daughter ran up to that fucker and hugged his legs. That shit couldn't fucking stand. He had to do something.

The Howlers were nothing but a group of bullies and thieves, and he was going to put an end to their bullshit.

He opened the trunk and grabbed the shopping bag. After slamming the trunk shut, he stormed down the alley to the library. He set the bag down on the ground and removed one of the cans from inside. Shaking it, he edged toward the front corner of the building and looked around to see if anyone was there. The parking lot looked like a ghost town, and no one was on the streets or in front of the houses across the street. *Perfect.*

Taking a deep breath and preparing himself to get it done and get it done fast, Niles rounded the corner and began leaving the message on the brick of the building in hazard orange.

When he was done with the front, he switched out the cans for the lime color and went to the back of the building. He left his message there, before he grabbed the cans and bag, and hopped back in his mother's car. He peeled out of the alley and headed out of town for the night.

If Mary was going to cheat on him with the fucker, he was going to go find him some pussy in Grand Rapids. Then when she had suitably paid for her misdeeds and apologized, he'd take her back, and life could go back to normal.

Chapter Twenty-One

Ruby

Waking up in Rebel's arms was an amazing feeling. His hold on her let her know he was happy to have her there, even in his sleep. He always held her, but usually one of his hands was cupping something, a breast or between her thighs. She loved it.

This morning, she was on her back with him almost laying on top of her. One of his arms was straight on the bed, half under her pillow. His other arm was wrapped around her waist, and his head was using her breasts as pillows.

She wished she could just enjoy it, but a phone was ringing, she thought it was hers, and her bladder was screaming. Running her fingers through his hair, she softly said his name.

"No," he mumbled into her breasts. "No wake up."

"I gotta pee. And I'm pretty sure that was my phone ringing."

Looking down her body at his face, she saw when he opened his mouth and sucked the skin of the side of her breast in.

"Rebel," she breathed and laughed.

"Don't want to let you go."

"I have to go to the bathroom and answer my phone, but I promise I'll come back."

He huffed out a sigh and slowly rolled off of her. "Fine. Hurry."

After climbing off the bed, she headed to the bathroom. As she passed the bed, she glanced over at him, taking in the fucking beautiful visual he presented. His hair was loose and messy on his pillow. Laying on his back, he had the blanket pulled up only so far to cover his privates, leaving his sexy abdomen, chest, and arms on display. *A work of art*.

Smiling, because he was hers, she entered the bathroom and took care of business. Then she washed her hands and brushed her teeth. As she made her way back through the bedroom, she snatched one of his shirts from the floor and slipped it on.

"Fuck," he groaned. "I like you wearing my clothes."

Giggling, she shook her ass at him a little as she left his room to go find her phone. It didn't take her long because it started ringing again.

Snatching it up from the top of the island, she pressed *answer* and put it to her ear. "Hello?"

"Bri, I need you to come to the library right away."

It was Debbie, her boss.

"Um… okay. Is everything okay?"

There was a deep sigh. "No. Someone vandalized the building. The police want to speak with you. They went by your home, but you weren't there. I told them I would contact you."

Vandalized? "Oh, wow. Um… Yeah, I'll be right there. Give me fifteen."

"See you soon."

Ruby ended the call and let out a deep sigh. *Who in the world would vandalize a library?* Sure, Sharon White was angry, but Ruby couldn't see the older woman vandalizing a building. Throwing a fit? Protesting? Sure. Absolutely. But vandalizing? No.

Setting her phone back down, she returned to the bedroom to get dressed, her mind still on the phone call.

"There's my Ruby," Rebel sleepily said as he watched her move around the room. "Get back in bed."

"I can't," she mumbled and gathered her clothes from the floor. She piled them on the bed and began pulling on her panties. Then she pulled off his shirt and grabbed her bra.

Rebel sat up. "Why? What's going on?"

"I have to head to the library." She fastened her bra and adjusted the straps. Grabbing her shirt, she put it on and started fastening the buttons.

As he slid off the bed and onto his feet, Rebel asked, "What's going on? They need you to fill in or something?"

She shook her head and pulled on her jeans. "Someone vandalized the building, and the police want to speak to me."

"What?" Rebel snapped into action and started getting dressed. "Vandalized, how?"

She shook her head again. "I don't know, but I'll call you when I know more."

"I'm going with you," he said as he fastened his jeans.

"No. It's my job, Rebel. I need to handle this on my own. Just let me go alone."

He just stared at her for a long moment as she slipped on her shoes. She saw it in his face that he was warring with himself. The protective side of him wanted to be there with her to make sure she was okay, but the man she loved wanted her to have her independence.

Loved? Did she love him? Yes. She didn't know when that happened, but it did.

"You don't have to handle things on your own anymore," he said quietly.

She nodded. "I know. And I appreciate your support, but this is my *career*. I wouldn't tag along on a job site for you. That would be inappropriate."

He sighed and approached her. After cupping her face in his hands, he gently kissed her lips. "Okay. Just promise you'll call and tell me what's going on as soon as you can."

"I promise." She let him kiss her again. Then she rushed to the bathroom to brush her hair and pull it back, since she didn't have time to shower.

Once she was done, she rushed through the house, grabbing her phone and purse, and hustled out to her car.

Rebel

As soon as Ruby left, Rebel finished getting dressed and brushed his teeth. He pulled his hair back into a man bun and headed out to the kitchen. Leaning against the island, he called Axle.

"Yeah?"

"Someone vandalized the library last night. Ruby just got called down there to talk to the police. She just left. Have you heard anything?"

Axle sighed. "That must be why I got a call from the WPPD. Leaving now to head downtown."

"Do we have anyone on the library?"

After a chuckle, Axle replied, "Since I know you're heading there to check on your woman, I guess it's you."

"When Ruby gets pissed at me," Rebel began with a smile, "I'm blaming you."

"What's new? Everyone blames me. Okay. Keep me updated. I'll do the same."

Rebel ended the call. By the time he made it out to his bike, he received the group text that Axle had just sent to all the brothers.

>VANDALISM AT LIBRARY. HEADING TO TALK TO POLICE. REBEL GOING TO LIBRARY. KEEP EARS AND EYES OPEN.<

After shoving his phone in the pocket of his cut, Rebel removed his handgun from the built-in holster and put it in the hidden compartment on his bike. Then, he started it up and headed for the library, hoping Ruby didn't get too pissed when he showed up.

Ruby

Standing next to her car in the parking lot of the library, Ruby was stunned. She couldn't believe what she was seeing. In bright orange spray paint, the words *LIBARYAN IS MONSTER LOVER. PROTECT THE CHILDRENS.* were spread across the front.

The police only let her into the parking lot when they recognized that she was the librarian and one of the detectives said to let her pass the barrier.

So many conflicting emotions were coursing through her system. She was angry that someone damaged the building without any care for the fact that children would see it. The fact that it was directed at her was hurtful, but to insinuate that she would somehow be a danger to children was the biggest insult anyone could have thrown at her. Add in the fact that they were calling Rebel a monster and that left her feeling protective and full of rage. Embarrassment was a lesser factor, but it was still there, along with concern for her job.

"Bri," she heard her boss call from near the front door.

Taking a deep breath and preparing herself, Ruby shut her car door and stiffly walked over to her boss and the detective she was talking to.

Her boss, Debbie was a middle-aged woman, with dark brown hair cut in a short, stylish cut and dark brown eyes. She was short with plenty of curves, but she never displayed them. She always dressed in slacks and a nice blouse, with a suit jacket over it. Ruby thought she looked better without the jacket, but she wasn't about to comment on someone else's style.

When she reached her boss, she asked, "Is it just outside? Was the interior damaged?"

"Just outside. Bri, this is Detective Hank Wilson. He has some questions for you." Debbie motioned to the man standing next to her. "Detective, this is Brianna Cooke."

Detective Wilson held out his hand, and Ruby took it. He was younger than Ruby expected, maybe in his early thirties. His hair was dark, almost black, and it was slicked back, giving him a greasy look. His dark blue suit was wrinkled. She could tell with one look that he thought he was pulled together and had a misguided confidence, but he looked like a disheveled mess to Ruby.

After shaking hands, he let her hand go and began, "Sorry we have to meet under these circumstances. Also sorry I have to do this when I know this is quite a shock for you, but in order to find the perpetrator or perpetrators, we need to act fast."

Ruby gave a nod, staring at the ugly words across the brick of the building. "Of course," she mumbled.

The detective asked her all the expected questions about her contact information, full name, Sharon White, the complaint, her understanding of what the message said, and came around to the questions Ruby really didn't want to answer. Not that she suspected the Howlers of having anything to do with it, but she also didn't want to bring them into something they had no involvement in. She was feeling protective of Rebel and his family.

"And how are you connected to the Howlers Motorcycle Gang?"

"Club," Ruby corrected. She fought the urge to glare at the detective and cleared her throat. "I am dating Port Christopher Blau. He goes by the road name Rebel."

The detective nodded while he wrote on his little notepad. "And is Mr. Blau a... what do they call them?"

Ruby's eyes narrowed on the detective, and she reminded herself that telling off the detective wouldn't help the situation. "Shifters," she said through clenched teeth. "They are called shifters. And whether or not Rebel is a shifter is no one's business."

"I disagree, Ms. Cooke." The detective cocked an eyebrow. "The vandal obviously has a problem with *shifters*, as well as you. The most logical connection would be if your boyfriend was a shifter."

"I am," Rebel said as he strolled up next to her. "If you have questions about me or my club or shifters, you can direct them my way."

When he stopped next to her, Ruby was irritated. She thought he understood that she needed to handle this on her own. "Rebel," she said on a sigh. "I thought I told you to let me handle this."

He gave a nod, but replied, "Axle sent me. He's heading downtown to talk to the police, at their request."

She put her hands to her hips and stared into his brownish-green eyes. "And you didn't have any say in that decision?"

He just shrugged.

She didn't believe for one minute that he didn't have anything to do with Axle's decision, but now wasn't the time to argue with him about it. She shelved it for another time and turned back to the detective.

"I don't know who did this. The only person I've had any confrontation or issue with is Sharon White, but to be honest, I don't believe she would do something like this."

The detective nodded and again verified her phone number in case he had further questions. Then he handed her his card and turned to face Rebel.

"Mr. Blau, if you wouldn't mind answering some questions for me, I would appreciate it." Then the detective and Rebel walked off.

Glaring at the Howler's colors on Rebel's back, Ruby went to follow them, but Debbie grabbed her arm to stop her. "Bri."

With a deep breath, Ruby turned to face her boss. Remembering that she was dealing with her place of employment, she pushed aside her issues with Rebel and uttered, "I'm sorry, Debbie. I don't know who did this."

"I know. I don't hold you responsible, but..."

Ruby nodded. "You think it would be best if I wasn't here until they figured it out."

"I'm not forcing you to take leave. And if you decide you don't want to do that, I will stand behind you. But, Bri, this isn't all of it."

"What do you mean?"

"There's more on the back."

Debbie held up her phone and showed Ruby a picture of the back of the building. In lime green paint were the words *WE KNOW WHAT YOU MONSTERS DONE*.

Rage, pure rage filled Ruby at the words. The asshole or assholes pulled the Howlers into this. It was a clear message to and about the Howlers. And she would guess the words on the front of the building were only there to incite the Howlers into doing something they could get in trouble for. She didn't like being a pawn in someone's game.

"This is bigger than you. And I'm worried for your safety." Debbie looked sincere. Her brows were pinched together, and there were frown lines around her mouth.

"I understand your concern, but..." Ruby took a calming breath. "I'm not letting some idiot with fifteen dollars' worth of spray paint and terrible penmanship keep me from my job. Again, if *you* tell me I need to stay home until this is handled, I will. If you are expecting me to make this decision, it's going to take a lot more than the scrawlings of a lunatic to force me out of my job, even temporarily. So, let me know what you decide."

Then she turned on her heel and stormed back to her car. She was too angry to stand there any longer. She needed a minute to pull herself back together.

Rebel

Standing with Detective Wilson near the opening of the alley behind the library, Rebel was already over the man's bullshit. He wasn't trying to find out who did it. He was trying to find a way to blame it on the Howlers.

Letting out an annoyed sigh, Rebel met the detective's stare and in a firm tone reiterated, "The Howlers have nothing to do with this."

The detective stared back. "You say that, but how could you know what the other members have done?"

Irritated as fuck, Rebel reminded himself that it wouldn't be right or beneficial to punch the detective in the face, no matter how satisfying it would be. With narrowed eyes, Rebel asked, "Have you ever been part of a brotherhood, Detective?" He crossed his arms over his chest and clenched his jaw for a moment. "I *know* my brothers. If they would do something like this to a *library*, they *wouldn't* be a Howler. We wouldn't stand for that."

The detective tried to bully him into changing his answer by attempting to stare him down, but all it did was make Rebel want to laugh in his face. The man wasn't as intimidating as he thought he was.

"Have you had any... *confrontations* with anyone? Or have you heard of any of your *brothers* having a confrontation with anyone?"

"Since the town hall, I had some comments thrown at me at the grocery store. But other than that, not that I'm aware of."

The detective narrowed his eyes and shot back, "Would you tell me if you did?"

"Are you insinuating that a member of the Howlers MC would obstruct an investigation?" Siren strolled up and stopped next to Rebel, staring hard at the detective, with his hands in the front pockets of his jeans. He was giving off the appearance of being cool, calm, and collected, but Rebel knew Siren was seething inside about the whole damn situation.

"Troy," the detective said on a sigh, "I simply asked a question."

Ignoring the use of his real name, Siren continued, "Well, I hope you know I would take great offense to that... if that's what you were insinuating. As a former member of the WPPD, as well as a former member of

Rebel's Fairytale

the WPFD, I take it as an insult if you were to imply that I would be a part of something *illegal*. We are upstanding members of this community, and will be treated as such, or you can speak to our attorneys. Is that understood?"

The detective's face turned a darker shade of red, and he slammed shut his little notebook. As he slid the notebook back into his suit pocket, he said, "I'm thinking I should probably speak directly to your president."

"You do that," Rebel said and gave the detective the fakest smile he could muster.

When the detective stormed off, Siren asked, "Do we have any idea what this is about?"

Rebel turned to look at the fucked-up bullshit painted on the back of the building again. "Well... I'm assuming it has to do with the woman who tried to get Ruby fired."

"I got a call from a friend of mine on the council." Siren let out a sigh. "They tried to deny our request for permits and licenses for the carnival. I think we have a group of people in this town who want us out. We need to know who else is involved, besides Sharon White."

Rebel nodded. "Yup. Time for recon. Anyone find out who the woman at the Hen House is?"

"Yeah. Keys said she's some former member of military and law enforcement. Known for breaking rules. Unemployed as far as we know. And she recently opted out of her lease on her apartment in Chicago. Name's Stella Messer." Siren took out his phone and snapped a few pictures of the vandalism and the area.

"We need an inside man," Rebel mumbled, trying to figure out who could do it.

"We could talk to Bobby. He could pretend to be *fed up with our shit*," Siren mused. "Or one of the prospects."

"We'll bring it up to Axle," Rebel decided.

Together, they headed around the building the long way, ignoring the police officers when they yelled at them about staying away from the crime scene. As far as Rebel was concerned, the fuckers could kiss his ass.

Chapter Twenty-Two

Ruby

Ruby was pissed off on multiple levels. She was mad at the idiot who dared to vandalize the library, pulled the Howlers into it, and used her as a pawn. She was mad at the town for not seeing the Howlers for who they are and not as monsters. But at the forefront of her mind, she was mad at Rebel for not respecting the boundary she set.

After he spoke to the detective, he came to the parking lot and tried to talk to her, but she wasn't about to argue with him in front of her boss, the police, and the town who had lined up on the edge of the property to gawk.

He must have sensed that, because he kissed her cheek and told her he'd see her at her place.

Without saying a word, she got in her car and drove home. Now, she was sitting in her garage, trying to find some calm before she went inside and let him in the house.

After ten minutes, she climbed out of her car and made her way inside and to the front door. She unlocked and opened it, not at all surprised to see him standing there, waiting for her.

She just turned on her heel and went to her kitchen, knowing he would shut and lock the door behind him.

"Ruby."

Ruby approached the refrigerator and pulled out the carton of eggs, the butter, and a container of already chopped veggies. "What?" She turned and slammed the items down on the counter with more force than was probably smart before she turned to grab a pan out of the cupboard.

"You seem... madder than... I expected."

Ruby shot him a disgusted look and slammed the pan down on her stove top, the movement causing a great *clang* to echo in the room. "Of course, I'm mad." Grabbing a bowl from another cupboard, she started forcefully cracking eggs into it. "For one thing, they defaced a building that children frequent. They dragged me into whatever their damn problem is and put my job at risk. My boss didn't demand I take time off, but she sure as hell was trying to get me to agree to it. The idiot with the paint also dragged you and the Howlers into this mess, which I don't fucking like one damn bit. And I specifically asked you to not show up there, told you I didn't want to have you there while I was dealing with something that had to do with my *career*, but you showed up anyway."

"Sweetie—"

Rebel's Fairytale

"Don't Sweetie me, Rebel," she blurted and pointed a finger at him. "I asked you to let me handle this, but you didn't give me that. You said you would, but you didn't. You lied."

"Axle sent me," he insisted and grabbed the butter off the counter, opening it and slicing off a pad to put in the pan.

She watched him drop it into the pan and turn on the burner, then she returned to the eggs. "And how exactly did that go down, Rebel? If I had to guess, you called Axle, and Axle said go down there because you want to, anyway? Am I close?"

She glanced at him and saw him wince, before he replied, "The Howlers were already in it. When I called him, he was heading to the police department at their request. He needed someone to go look at the vandalism, and yeah, he sent me because of you, and because I wanted to be there with you. You can be mad at me for that, but I can't apologize. I won't."

She finished with the eggs, retrieved the milk, added some to the egg mixture, dumped in the veggies, and began to whisk before she responded. She knew if she didn't take a minute, she was going to come off meaner than she intended to be. "So, you won't apologize for crossing a boundary I set, and you agreed to? Noted."

She felt him against her back before she saw his hands come around and take the bowl and whisk from her hands. After setting them aside, he wrapped his arms around her and kissed the side of her head. "I didn't think about it that way. Yes, of course, I'm sorry for that. *Gods, Ruby*. I'd never want to cross a boundary with you. I love you. I wouldn't ever do anything to intentionally hurt you."

Ruby felt her anger at him waning, but she wasn't letting him off the hook that easily. She stepped out of his arms and turned to face him. "In the future, if you have to choose between a boundary I set and an order from your president, what are you going to do?"

Rebel's gaze dropped to the floor. He scratched at the beard hair at his jaw and sighed. "It depends, Ruby. I'm being honest, here. If it has to do with your safety, I'm going to do whatever keeps you safe. If that means you're mad at me for keeping you safe, then I can live with that. If there's a way I can respect your boundaries, and not do damage to my club, I'll always take that route… unless it has to do with your safety. And believe it or not, Axle wouldn't expect me to cross a boundary with you to follow an order. I can go to him with it and figure something out."

"So, I'm priority?"

He looked confused for a moment. "Well… yeah."

She nodded and went back to whisking.

"Do you forgive me?"

She let out a deep sigh. "Yes, but I'm still mad."

"Fair enough. Now, what else are you mad about? Because if you beat those eggs any harder, we're not going to end up with omelets."

She stopped what she was doing and moved to the pan. Dumping half of the mixture into the pan, she answered, "Like I said, I'm pissed at this asshole that did this to the library. I mean... they put my job in jeopardy. They exposed kids to something scary and unnecessary. They caused damage to that beautiful building. But more than anything else, I'm pissed off that they would try to accuse our family of doing something malicious or—"

"Our?"

At his question, she turned and looked at him. "What?"

"You said *our family*."

She was confused for a moment until she thought over what she had said. As her heart began to race and anxious excitement built in her stomach, she met his gaze again and confirmed, "Yes, I did. Of course, they're our family. I'm your mate."

His eyebrow lifted as a smile grew on his face. "Are you?"

Rebel

Rebel tried not to get his hopes up as he stared at her and waited for her response. Was his mate finally accepting their bond? Had he finally proven himself? He tried really hard not to be pushy, but it had been difficult. His wolf and his heart already thought of her as theirs.

While he waited for her answer, his wolf stood, his tail swishing, as he whined. *I know, buddy. I know. I want it, too.*

Without another word, Ruby took two quick steps toward him and grabbed his cheeks. She pulled him toward her, pressing her lips to his. He groaned the second her tongue caressed his bottom lip. Rebel opened to her, but he let her continue to lead it. He didn't know where she was taking them, but he sure as hell liked the path.

Still kissing him, she put her hands to his chest and pushed. He allowed her to push him up against the wall and didn't fight it when she tried to remove his cut. He let it fall off his shoulders but caught it before it hit the floor. Without turning away from her, he reached out and dropped it on the counter.

She broke the kiss and tore his tee over his head. Then her lips and tongue were on his chest and working their way up.

"Ruby," he groaned and tangled the fingers of one hand in her hair. The other hand he wrapped around her and pulled her as close as she would allow.

When she reached his neck, she ran her tongue in a circle over the area where his neck and left shoulder met. "This is where, right?"

As the realization dawned, he swallowed hard and nodded. "Yes."

She slid one hand down his chest, his abdomen, and over the waistband of his jeans to tease his erection through his jeans. It felt incredible to have her take the lead and touch him like that. He'd let her do anything she wanted to him. When she began to stroke him through his jeans, he let his head fall back against the wall and moaned.

That was when she struck. Her human teeth broke skin, but barely, just enough to let him know her intention. She was claiming her mate.

He gasped her name as pleasure shot through him. The second her teeth released his skin, he gripped her hips and lifted. Carrying her over to the counter, he set her on top and started removing her clothes.

"The stove," she breathed.

"What?"

"The stove is on."

That's when Rebel remembered the omelet. He reached over and turned off the burner. When he turned back around, her shirt and bra were gone.

He cupped her breasts in his hands and gave each a sweet, soft kiss, before he sucked a nipple into his mouth and looked up at her. Her eyes drifted closed, and her mouth dropped open. Moving over to the other, he did the same thing with that breast, before kissing a path up to her mouth.

"You claimed me," he said against her lips.

"I did. That's what the bite means, right? I bit you, so you're mine."

He grinned. "That's what that means." He ran his tongue over her bottom lip before he sucked on it. "It's my turn to claim you."

"Will it hurt?"

"I hear it doesn't, if the match is a good one." He cupped her legs behind her knees and forced her legs around his hips. Wrapping his arms around her, he told her, "Hold on, Ruby. This is something that needs to happen on a soft surface."

As he lifted her, she threw her arms around him and laughed.

He carried her up to her bedroom and laid her out on her bed. Stripping her of the rest of her clothes, he threw the clothes and shoes over his shoulder, not giving a damn where they landed. As she grabbed a condom from her drawer, he removed his boots, socks, and jeans.

Climbing onto the bed, he kissed his way up the inside of her left leg. When he reached her core, he gave it love, but he didn't linger. It was evident that she was just as ready as he was, and frankly, he didn't want to risk her changing her mind. Part of him worried he'd still lose her somehow. He wanted the mating officially done.

He kissed the rest of the way up her body, only veering off to give each of her breasts some more love before he made it to her lips.

"Put it on me," he growled and pressed his lips to hers.

As she opened the condom and quickly rolled it on to his hard length, he kissed all over her neck and shoulder.

Surprisingly, his wolf was quiet. He suspected it had to do with the fact that she bit him, but he didn't question it too much.

When she was done putting the condom on him, she wrapped her legs around his waist and lined him up with her core.

"Fuck me, Rebel. Claim me," she whispered into his ear, making his eyes glow and a growl to work its way up his chest.

Not needing any further encouragement, he slid into her on a hard thrust. She moaned as he pulled out and slammed back in. There were no sweet words or soft touches. It was pure heat and intensity.

Each thrust had her moving up the bed until she lifted her right arm and braced herself against the headboard. Rebel took her mouth in a deep, wet kiss as one hand worked between them and played with her clit.

Four thrusts later, he felt her climax gathering, her core tightened, along with her legs. He didn't let up what he was doing as he let his fangs slide down. He looked into her eyes to make sure she wanted it.

After the wonder of what she was seeing passed, she smiled and nodded. That's when he struck. The second his fangs slid into her flesh, she reached her orgasm and cried out his name.

Euphoric.

He could feel her sliding into her designated spot in his heart, binding them, joining them, making each of them whole. As his wolf howled his joy, Rebel released her flesh, gave it a lick to seal it, and threw his head back. He howled as he reached his pleasure and came. Happiness filled him as ecstasy flowed through his body.

He'd barely come down from his high, his fangs having just receded, when he heard the answering howls from his brothers. He smiled and laid his forehead to hers.

Ruby giggled. "Was that the Howlers?"

"Yeah. They're happy for us."

"That's so cool," she breathed, gazing up at him with happiness in her eyes.

"I love you," he expressed and kissed her lips.

"I love you, too, Rebel."

"As much as I'd love to just lay here with you all day and do this over and over, we have to go to the clubhouse."

Her expression changed to confusion. Her brows came together, and her smile faded. "Why?"

He shrugged. "Tradition." He slid out of her, eliciting a moan from both of them, and got to his feet. "But first, shower time."

When they were getting dressed, he noticed a text from Axle on his phone.

>Church, as soon as Rebel's done. We'll give him ten minutes. That ought to be enough<

Rebel snort laughed and sent a reply to the entire club as he told Ruby to wear her leather so they could take his bike.

>Fuck all of you<

Once they were both dressed, he took her hand and led her out to his bike. After he helped her put on her helmet and climbed on the bike, he held out his hand to her to give her something to hold on to as she climbed on. Then, they were off.

When they walked into the clubhouse, the main room was filled with Ol' Ladies. He grinned through all the cheering and whistles, kissed his Ol' Lady, and headed up to church.

He barely stepped into the room before the razzing started.

"Uh… Rebel, what's on your neck?" Pike pointed to the left side of his neck, where Rebel knew Ruby's bite mark was still visible.

"Yeah, Rebel, what's that?" Siren grinned at him.

"*You* are supposed to bite *her*," Bullet told him like he was talking to a kindergartener. "Did your dad not tell you that?"

Ranger shook his head and sighed. "I think I should have that talk with the twins. Wouldn't want them to get confused too."

Rebel shot him the finger as he rounded the table and took his seat. "Stay the fuck away from the twins when it comes to mating or sex advice."

"You don't trust me?" Ranger put his hand to his heart. "For shame!"

Chuckling, Axle slammed his hand to the table. "Okay. Enough. Congrats, Rebel. We're all happy for you."

Congratulations rang out from around the table. Then Axle got to the meeting.

Chapter Twenty-Three

Ruby

Ruby wasn't fond of being the center of attention, but she supposed she asked for it by leaving her love bite on Rebel. If she knew anything about the women around her, they would take that as a sign that she was one of them, which she supposed she was, now.

Smiling, she took a seat at the closest table. To her right sat Pixie and Sugar. To her left was Butterfly and Kisy. The other women were giving her grins and sweet smiles. Kisy, on the other hand, leaned forward and met her stare.

"What?" Ruby didn't know what the woman's problem was, but her stare was making her uncomfortable.

"You bit him?"

Confused as to where this was going, Ruby slowly nodded. "Yes."

"You bit him, so he's yours." Then the crazy bitch smiled. "Niiiiiiice." She extended her arm and hand which was balled into a fist.

Ruby chuckled as she bumped Kisy's hand with her own fist.

Butterfly snorted a laugh. "You *would* think that's nice. You licked Dragon in front of the entire club to claim him."

"Yeah… and?" Kisy shrugged.

"Don't forget about breaking Pumps's nose," Pixie added with a grin.

Ruby shook her head and laughed. "You are all a bit insane, but I think I like it."

Sugar giggled. "Well, that's good, because you're stuck with us now."

Ruby's phone buzzed with a text message. As she pulled her phone out of her purse, she laughed at what she saw on the screen.

Rebel

"So, having Bobby be the insider is out," Axle said with an annoyed sigh. "They hit his bar while the police were at the library. I don't think it's the same person. This time, they actually knew how to spell."

"What did it say?" Rebel asked as he looked down the table at his president, irritation building in his gut. They fucked with Ruby and Bobby, two people whose only crime was being connected to them. That shit was bonkers.

It was Skull who answered. "*'Monsters gather here'* was painted along the front in lime green."

Pike nodded. "He's pissed. I had to talk him out of storming down to town hall and laying into anyone he could find. Bobby said something about hearing some rumors that a few of the members of whatever group is responsible for this are on the town council. He said he'd keep his ears open for more information, but he made it clear he's on our side in this. I still don't feel right asking Bobby to stick his neck out even further for us."

The entire club murmured sounds of agreement.

"Are we sending someone over to clean it up?" Ranger asked.

Axle shook his head. "After Pike talked him down and talked some sense into him, he decided it wouldn't be a good idea. He doesn't want to draw any more attention to his bar. And I can't say I blame him." Another sigh. "Think on other options. Come to me if anything clicks."

There was more agreement around the table.

"Now… for the fun stuff." Axle stood and approached the shelving unit in the corner. After opening the doors, he pulled out a familiar looking cut and shut the doors. "Should I even bother trying to give this one myself?"

"I'll do it," Ranger said and stood, holding out his hand to take the cut.

"Wait!" Pike shot to his feet. "I want to do it!"

"No way!" Ranger glared at Pike.

"Why would you get to do it?"

Ignoring the two idiots, Rebel got to his feet and headed for the door, following Axle out of the room. Pike and Ranger continued arguing all the way down the stairs. By the time they got to the main room of the club house, Pike and Ranger were shoving each other. It wasn't long before both of them were rolling around on the floor.

Rock shook his head and approached Axle. "Give it to me."

Axle went to hand over the cut, when suddenly, Pike and Ranger stopped fighting, Ranger pointed a finger at Rock, and warned, "Don't you even think about it."

Rock chuckled and held up his hands in front of him.

Ranger hopped to his feet and snatched the cut from Axle's hand.

Rebel just stepped around the idiot, shaking his head, and walked over to Ruby's side. He bent down and kissed her lips. "They need you on your feet, Ruby."

"Why?"

"You'll see." He smiled at her and took her hands, pulling her to her feet. Then he moved behind her and wrapped his arms around her waist, letting her rest back against him.

His wolf was perfectly content, lounging, tail swishing. Their mate was claimed and safe in his arms. Rebel and his wolf were happy.

Rebel's Fairytale

The Howlers lined up in front of her and the Ol' Ladies stood off to the side. Right in the center, Ranger stepped out in front of Axle and grinned.

"I'm so excited," Ranger expressed and wiggled his eyebrows, making all the women laugh.

"This is fucking serious," Pike grumbled.

Ranger flipped him off. Then, he took a deep breath and looked into Ruby's eyes. "Axle will have to get over allowing me the honor of doing this. And it is an honor, Ruby." He winked at her. Raising his voice a bit, he said, "By tying yourself to Rebel, you tied yourself to us and to our pack. By having his back, you have ours. We're a package deal. And we understand we're getting more out of the deal than you are. You will never need for anything for long. You will never want for anything for long. You will never suffer again. And if for some reason you do," the room filled with growls and hisses, making Rebel even more proud of his family, "the one who caused it will suffer far more for their efforts. I'm honored to call you my sister."

He pulled his phone from his pocket, pushed a few buttons on the screen, and then read, "*'My bounty is boundless as the sea, My love as deep; the more I give to thee, The more I have, for both are infinite.'*"

Rebel looked at him like he lost his mind. *Why in the hell did he keep quoting Shakespeare and other classic literature?* When Ruby giggled, Rebel stepped to her side and looked at her face. She winked at Ranger, making Rebel wonder what the hell that was about.

"For you," Ranger said in a ridiculous pompous voice and handed her the cut.

Giggling, but with eyes full of tears, Ruby took the cut and slipped it on. She looked down and ran her fingers over the patches that read, *Rebel's OL* and *Ruby.*

"You look good in that, Ruby," Rebel commented and nipped her earlobe.

She looked up at him. "Love you."

"Love you too. Now, you wanna tell me why you winked at Ranger and why you… the quote…"

He was confused, but his gut was telling him there was more to the story.

Giggling, she held up her phone. Glaring at him from the screen was a text string with Ranger's name at the top. "Where do you think he was getting the quotes?"

"High five," Ranger called out.

Ruby turned and slapped her palm against Ranger's. "You did such a great job with that one. I'm impressed."

Ranger gave her a ridiculous bow. Then, the club bombarded her with hugs and shots.

Remembering all the times he saw Ruby sending mysterious texts, and all the times Ranger had tortured him with ridiculous quotes, Rebel smacked her ass and laughed as he realized she had been bonding with his brother for days, and he was clueless about it.

While she was busy drinking with her new sisters, he approached Ranger and gave his shoulder a squeeze. "Thanks, brother."

Ranger shrugged. "She's a good woman. Getting to know her wasn't really a hardship."

"Still... I appreciate it."

"Love you, man."

Rebel shook his head and sighed. "You just had to make it awkward, didn't you?"

Niles

The evening after he skipped town, Niles ran out of money. He had spent hours at the strip club in Grand Rapids, but it was basically a bikini bar, so it wasn't like he saw much. He tried to talk his way into going home with one of the dancers, but she was an uptight bitch, like she had a right being self-righteous when she flaunted her body for money.

Stupid bitches always thought they could look down on him, and he was fucking sick of it. He just needed his Mary back. He'd teach her how to be a proper wife. Then his life would be on the right track.

It wasn't his fault that he was living on his mom's couch and driving around her car. Mary had left him paying for everything. There was only so much he could do on a part-time maintenance worker's pay. If Mr. Henderson hadn't been a dick at his last job, it wouldn't have been a problem. Just because he flipped off a homeowner, the bastard canned him, like he was the only one who had ever had a bad day.

Still fuming about the way his life was going, Niles wasn't paying much attention as he flew past the *Welcome to Warden's Pass* sign. He didn't notice the police car until it was behind him with the lights flashing. Cussing, he gunned it.

The last thing he needed was to deal with some pigs after the day he'd had. *Fuck that.* He'd just lose them and swing back around to his mom's. He could hide her car in the neighbor's garage for a while until the police forgot about it.

Niles could have done it, too, if that fucking deer hadn't darted out in front of the car at the exact wrong god damn time.

Niles hit the deer going sixty in a forty, sending the smashed-up car fishtailing. Eventually, it rolled and continued to roll until it ended up in the ditch on the side of the road.

The next thing Niles remembered was waking up cuffed to a hospital bed. *Fuck!*

"Well, welcome back, Niles." The officer grinned down at him. "The car was totaled, by the way, but don't worry. We were able to save the cans of spray paint from the trunk. You know… the spray paint you used on the library."

"I don't know what you're talking about," Niles mumbled, his head throbbing.

The officer chuckled. "Yeah. Tell that to the judge."

Rebel

Sitting around the clubhouse with his brothers, Rebel watched as Ruby hung out with her new sisters. Siren somehow talked Sugar out of shots. They were entering another time of uncertainty in the club. The last thing they needed was a bunch of drunk Ol' Ladies to look after.

Siren took a seat across from Rebel and let out a sigh. He looked confused as he gazed across the room at his woman.

"What's up?"

Siren's gaze shifted to Pike at his question. "That was too easy," he mumbled.

"What?" Rebel asked.

"Talking her out of shots. She's drinking a caffeine-free pop."

Rebel's eyes widened as he looked over at Pike. Pike had the same look on his face, and Bullet whistled low and asked, "Is she preggo?"

Rebel had never seen Siren move so fast. One minute, he was sitting in his chair. The next, he was at his woman across the room, and had his nose buried in her neck. They watched as Sugar glared at him and shoved him away. They had a whispered conversation that was so light, even their shifter hearing couldn't pick it up, before Siren nodded and kissed her.

As Siren made his way back to the table, he shook his head. He plopped down in his chair. "She said she's not pregnant, yet."

"Yet?" Pike smiled at Siren. Siren's answering smile told them everything they wanted to know. He loved the idea of being a dad, and the possibility was more real than it had been the day before.

"Pike, what's up with the pink hand towels? A stack of them showed up at our house, and Butterfly said Pixie gave them to her. She started giggling when I asked about them. Nothing in our house is pink, except those damn hand towels."

"Same with Sugar," Siren said with a nod.

"You too?" Rock took one of the open seats.

"Gorgeous got some, too, but she likes pink so I didn't think too much about it. I am *now,* though."

Rebel and Pike locked eyes. They were both trying to hold back laughter. They managed it for about three minutes before Pike and Rebel were wheezing with laughter, and Rock and Siren groaned.

"What in the hell is wrong with you two?" Axle demanded as he looked at them like they grew extra limbs.

"Inside joke," Pike managed to squeak out between wheezing laughs.

Axle just shook his head and walked away, headed for his woman, while shouting, "Gorgeous! We're throwing out those damn towels!"

Ruby

When Rebel stopped his bike in front of Allie's house, Ruby grudgingly unwrapped her arms from

Rebel's Fairytale

around his waist and slid off the back. She was wearing her property cut from the club and wanted to show Allie. She didn't want Allie finding out from someone else. Her bestie would have been pissed.

Rebel got off the bike and slid his arm around her waist as they headed for the front door. She loved how he felt the need to touch her at all times. He was good about giving her space when she needed it, but he made it clear that touching was his love language.

The little brick house had a small square stoop and two steps. The one-stall garage wasn't much smaller than the house itself. It was the perfect home for a single woman with no kids. Allie had finished the basement and turned that into her bedroom, leaving the bedroom on the main floor to be her office. Working from home, that was essential. It allowed her to shut the door on her day when she was done and give her some separation in her life.

They were halfway up the front walk when the front door flew open, and her bestie was standing there with her hands on her hips.

"Bish," she breathed and stared at Ruby with wide eyes. "I freaking told you!"

Ruby giggled and nodded. "You did. I guess we're official now."

"Ruby, we were official the second I saw you," Rebel said and shifted his arm up to her shoulders. Leaning toward her, he kissed her cheek, causing Allie's eyes to bug out, and her lips moved in an *awww* as she met Ruby's gaze.

"I had no say in it?"

He chuckled. "You had say. Your red cheeks told me everything I needed to know."

Ruby rolled her eyes, but she couldn't help the smile that grew on her face. "You gonna let us in, Bish?"

"Oh! Right!" Allie moved back, motioning for them to come in. When Ruby went to pass her, Allie stopped her and gave her a hug. "I'm so happy for you, Bri."

"Thanks, Allie."

"You think you can set me up with one of those Claws?"

Rebel burst out laughing as he stepped around the two of them. "I can make sure you're invited to some events, but the rest is up to you… and them."

"Fair enough." Allie's gaze locked on Ruby's. Then she mouthed *He's hot. Way to go!*

They spent the next hour hanging out at Allie's. Ruby was grateful to Rebel for humoring her best friend and answering her questions. It seemed to Ruby that he felt the same way about her friends that she felt about the Howlers and the Claws — They were important to her, so they were important to him.

As they climbed back on his bike, Ruby hugged him tight and told him, "Thank you. I love you."

Looking at her over his shoulder, he replied, "You never have to thank me for treating our family the way they deserve. And I love you, too."

Then he faced forward again and started his bike.

Chapter Twenty-Four

The Next Day... Niles

After being discharged from the hospital with only bumps and bruises, Niles was brought to jail, it took a day for him to get himself released from there. He had a court date for the vandalism and another for the reckless driving, but he managed to weasel out of the evading charges, claiming he was just in a hurry to get home and hadn't seen the cop. He wasn't sure they believed him, but he didn't give a damn.

Niles had shit to do. First stop, he had to check on his kids. Since they were now living in that fucker's house, he needed to make sure they were being treated right. After that, he had to meet up with Stella and plan what to do next.

Climbing into the passenger seat of his sister's car, he told her to take him to the fucker's address, but his damn sister started pitching a fit. She took him, but she yapped the whole time about responsibilities and getting his life together. Then, she started harping about replacing their mom's car. He wasn't replacing shit. The woman was his mom. It was her job to let him use her shit.

He just ignored his sister until they arrived. Having her stop down the street, he ordered her to wait for him, and the bitch better or he'd teach her the lesson her husband should have — Women are meant to do what they're told.

After giving her a look that clearly emphasized his point, he got out of the car, jogged down the block, and snuck up to the fucker's front window. Looking inside, he saw pillows, blankets, and furniture rearranged in the living room. It looked like someone had built a fort.

A few seconds later, his little Jenna came into the room with a smile on her face and a bowl of popcorn in her hands. She was followed by another little girl and Mary. They were all laughing.

He made his way around the side window and looked in, where he saw Miles sitting at the table with another little boy and the fucker. It looked like they were playing some kind of board game.

Niles really wanted to take that fucker out, but it wasn't the time. First, he needed to get his kids and his woman out of the house. The need to get revenge was growing ever stronger with the passing days, though.

As he made his way along the side of the house, back toward the road, he tripped on a rock and just barely missed banging into the side of the box truck. When he looked at where he tripped, he noticed that lying next to the rock he tripped on was a pocketknife.

He picked it up and examined the handle. The name *Hunter* was etched into the end of the grip. With the knife in hand, he rounded the box truck and approached the fucker's bike. Without hesitation, he slammed that blade into the side of the back tire.

With a grin on his face, he jogged back to his sister's car and got in. "Let's fucking go," he ordered.

Rock

After kissing Diamond's lips for longer than he should have, Rock forced himself to walk out the door. He had to meet up with a contact about a woman in town who was looking for a way out of her marriage with a controlling dick of a husband.

He thought about putting the meeting off, but Diamond insisted that he go. Pressing her forehead to his as she straddled his lap and looked into his eyes, she whispered, "If you didn't go, you wouldn't be the wonderful man I fell in love with. You know it will bug you if you don't. So, go."

She was right, so Rock had said goodbye to his family and headed out. When he rounded the box truck, he knew something was off, but he didn't know what it was until he approached his bike. He saw the knife sticking out of the tire before he noticed the odd angle at which his bike was sitting.

Yanking the knife out, he noticed it was the pocketknife he had given Hunter for his birthday. Hunter had lost it during the move and was worried Rock would be disappointed. Rock wasn't, and he was happy he could give the knife back to Hunter, but he wondered how it ended up in his tire.

Who in the fuck had been on his property and when? Rock didn't like that shit at all.

Putting the knife in his pocket, he called Axle and put his phone to his ear.

"Yeah?"

"We've got a motherfucking problem. Someone was on my property and used my kid's pocketknife to flatten the rear tire on my bike."

"Fuck," Axle barked. "I'll send Score with the truck to bring it in. And Keys will be over to put up cameras. I know you don't want it with the kids getting older and getting closer to shifting age, but for now—"

"No, do it. I have a meeting. Need security for a couple hours," Rock growled, trying to keep his voice down so his family didn't hear.

"You got it, brother. I'll see who is available and keep Diamond and the kids safe. Give me ten."

"Thanks." Rock ended the call and sent a text to his contact that he would be late.

He didn't know who in the fuck did it, but he wasn't about to let anyone put his family in danger. He may be a human, but that didn't mean he couldn't fucking protect his family. Rock would give his life to keep Diamond and the kids safe, if that's what it would take.

A few minutes later, Brute and Brute's younger brother, Matthew, a Howler prospect, showed up. Seeing the two of them, Rock knew his family was in good hands. Borrowing Brute's bike, he took off for his meeting.

Rebel

Ruby had just fallen asleep in his arms, when Rebel heard his phone vibrate on the nightstand in her bedroom. Carefully, so as not to wake her up, Rebel reached over and picked up the phone. Checking the notifications, he saw a group text from Axle to the club.

>TIRE SLASHED ON ROCK'S BIKE IN HIS DRIVEWAY. HEADS UP. THEY'RE RAMPING UP THE BS<

Rebel cussed under his breath. Letting out a deep sigh, he sent a reply asking if Rock needed help.

>SCORE IS GRABBING HIS BIKE. BRUTE AND BRO ARE THERE.<

Feeling better, knowing Rock was taken care of, Rebel returned his phone to the nightstand.

"Rebel," Ruby mumbled and rolled over to face him.

"It's okay." Rebel settled back on the pillow and wrapped his arms around her, pulling her close. "Go back to sleep."

"What happened? That wasn't a happy sigh," she said into his chest.

He kissed the top of her head. "Someone slashed a tire on Rock's bike, but he's got help."

"Who would do that? Who would do all the things that have been happening? I don't understand people."

He tightened his hold on her. "Yeah, me neither."

"We'll get through this." She placed a soft kiss on his chest. "Our whole family will."

He smiled into her hair. "That's right. We will."

Holding his woman tight, he closed his eyes and sent up some thank yous to the gods for sending Ruby into his life.

Chapter Twenty-Five

The Next Day... Ruby

It was time for her to return to work. Ruby wasn't about to let some vandals keep her from her life. She loved her job, and she was going to keep doing it. She loved Rebel, and she wasn't about to let these idiots put him down. Ruby loved her new family, and she would stand by them. With her head held high and those thoughts in her head, Ruby entered the library.

Before getting to work, she went down the hall to Debbie's office. She wasn't surprised to see the woman behind her desk. Until things calmed down, Ruby suspected Debbie would be a constant presence on her shifts. Any meetings Debbie had would happen when Ruby wasn't working or would happen at the library until further notice.

Ruby didn't give a damn. She wasn't doing anything where she would need to worry about who was watching, and she knew that Debbie wasn't there to *keep an eye on her*.

"Hey Bri," Debbie said and gave her a soft smile. "Welcome back."

Ruby leaned against the door jamb and smiled back. "Hey. What's going on with the investigation?"

Debbie nodded. "They found the guy. Niles something or other. Not sure what his connection to you or Sharon is, yet, but Detective Wilson said he was looking into it. Unfortunately, the man is out on bail, but at least we know who he is."

"Niles?"

"Yeah." Debbie sighed. "I heard about some other spray paint vandalism around town. This isn't specific to us. They know he didn't do that tagging, but I didn't hear this from the detective. I heard this at the grocery store, so I dunno."

Ruby sighed. "It happened. The connection is the Howlers. I don't know who this Niles person is, but I'll mention it to Rebel."

"Bri," Debbie began and looked away from Ruby, "I want to ask you to reconsider—"

"With all due respect, Debbie, I'm not ending a relationship in my life just because a small group of townspeople have a problem with my choice of partner." Ruby straightened. "If the same group came into the library and demanded you end your marriage with your partner, would you even consider ending it or going on leave from work over it?"

Debbie shook her head. "No. You are correct. Sorry."

Ruby gave a nod. "I'm going to work now."

"I'm here if you need me."

Another nod, then Ruby headed out to the main area of the library. On the way back to her desk, she sent a quick text to Rebel.

>THE SPRAY PAINT GUY WAS ARRESTED. NAME IS NILES SOMETHING. HE'S OUT ON BAIL.<

Rebel

Helping Axle and some of his other brothers with setting up the carnival, Rebel didn't immediately check Ruby's text. About ten minutes after he heard the notification, he pulled his gloves off his hands and grabbed his phone from his pocket.

Reading the text, his brows drew together. *Niles? Who is Niles?*

Approaching Axle, who was talking to Siren, Rebel asked, "Hey. Do we know a Niles?"

"That's what I was just asking," Siren replied. "Niles Flynn."

"Why?" Axle looked from Rebel to Siren, a scowl on his face.

"He vandalized the library," Rebel said.

Siren nodded. "Was arrested with the spray paint in his possession. He's been released on bail."

"What did you say his name was?"

They all looked over at Rock. Siren was the one to answer. "Niles Flynn."

Rock started cursing up a storm as Axle, Siren, and Rebel just watched and waited. When he was done, he told them, "He's Diamond's ex."

"Fuck," Axle cursed.

Messer

Sitting in the backroom of the hardware store with the group of lunatics, Messer wasn't surprised they were unsuccessful in achieving their goal of running the Howlers out of town. From what she had witnessed, they had no idea what they were doing. They thought they were being stealthy but speaking out in a town council meeting wasn't stealthy, neither was tagging a library or a bar, without taking the necessary steps to get rid of evidence.

They were losers, and incompetent in her opinion. Hell, they hadn't even given her much knowledge on shifters. What she learned, she had figured out herself.

The Howlers weren't all shifters. Some of them were humans. Beside the few instances where they had roughed up a shitty husband or boyfriend, there weren't any known violent or aggressive incidents. That didn't mean the Howlers were violent or aggressive, it only meant they were good at hiding it if they were. It also meant they were good at stealth, unlike the group in front of her.

She also learned that Axle Weber was the president of the club, and the Howlers had a close ally club in the Tiger's Club MC, which was led by Crush Welles. Both of which were well known in the community. Axle was more liked, but the only negative she heard about Crush was that the woman was cranky.

Dealing with townsfolk like the people around Messer, she understood how a woman would end up cranky. That didn't mean she felt sympathy for the two presidents, though. They were both shifters. Violent or not, they had the ability to potentially hurt people or kill them. They were a danger, a threat to humanity.

She was going to have to let go of this group, though, and proceed on her own. The only semi-useful one was Niles Flynn. He at least had some information on the Howlers. It wasn't much, but it got her started.

As Daniel Williams, one of the brothers who owned the hardware store, yelled at Charles Williams for vandalizing Bobby's Bar, knowing the bar had cameras, Messer considered her next move. The carnival was probably her best bet of getting close to the clubs. Since it was being thrown at their headquarters.

"I wore a bandana covering my face and a hoodie," Charles grumbled at his brother.

"Oh? The bandana hanging out of your back pocket?" Daniel's voice rose with his anger. When Charles blushed and dropped his gaze, Messer knew Daniel was right. Daniel turned his attention to Niles. "And you! Why in the hell would you keep the paint in the car you were fucking driving? I swear to fuck you both are idiots!"

Yeah, it was time to break ties with these fools.

Matthew

Matthew Waters couldn't fucking believe it. Finally, it was his turn. He hadn't pressed the issue about his prospecting time being drawn out. He had to take a break just over a year ago to take care of some personal shit, and that had meant he started his time over when he returned. The Howlers had been understanding about the whole situation. They didn't have to let him return to prospecting after his break, but they were gracious to give him another chance. Matt didn't know if that had anything to do with his brother, Brute, or his brother by choice, Rock, but it didn't matter to him either way. He wanted to be a Howler.

Being called into the church room for the Howlers was a damn trip. He'd wanted to be welcomed into that room for so damn long. Hell, they didn't even let prospects clean in there. Having Axle personally call and ask Matt to meet him there at four was the closest he'd felt to being a member. It was either really good or really bad but, following the advice Kisy and Butterfly had given him while they hung out at the bar, he was thinking positively and manifesting that shit.

Taking a deep breath, Matt knocked on the door and waited. When he heard Axle call out, he twisted the knob and pushed the door open. Leaning his head in, he looked around, his gaze landing on Axle sitting at the head of the long table. "Pres?"

"Come on in," Axle told him.

Rebel's Fairytale

As Matt stepped through the door, he took in the other two people in the room, Pike and Keys. The presence of the two men didn't give him a clue which way the conversation was going to go. When you're talking about the sergeant at arms and the tech guru of the club, shit could be really good, or they hacked into your shit and found something you should be ashamed of.

Taking a few steps toward them, Matt was wracking his brain, trying to think if he had ever done anything too embarrassing. He didn't think so. *Think positively*, he reminded himself and waited for further instruction.

"Have a seat," Axle said and motioned to the seat to his left.

Matt took the seat. Pike and Keys sitting across from him.

"Look. I know your path in the club has been… unconventional," Axle began. Leaning back in his chair, Axle folded his hands behind his head and sighed. "Normally, we wouldn't ask this of someone until they were a member of the club, but you're a special case. It's pretty much a given you'll join us. Once all of this shit is over, we'll do the vote. But we need to ask something of you. It's dangerous and could put you in the path of… Well, I'm just going to say it." He straightened in his chair and let his hands fall to the top of the table. "We need someone to get close to the outsider who came to town and find out everything you can about her."

Without even having to think about it, Matt nodded. "Yeah, I'll do whatever you need me to." The Howlers were important to him, and he already considered them family. If they needed his help, he'd give it without question.

Axle and Pike both smiled at him. Pike nodded as Axle replied, "Yeah, kid, you'll be a good addition to the club."

"I appreciate that."

"Keys, give him the rundown on Messer."

Chapter Twenty-Six

Two days later... Diamond

The kids were full of energy and driving her bananas. All of them were excited about the carnival. In an attempt to get them to run off some of the energy, Diamond piled the kids into her Jeep and headed to the park near the elementary school.

Rock was busy with his brothers, setting up for the carnival. Not wanting to bother him while he was busy, she didn't bother calling him to let him know they were going to the park. They would be in a public place. She figured they would be okay. Diamond justified her decision by making a promise to herself that they wouldn't be there long.

As soon as she put the Jeep in park in the lot next to the park, the kids had their belts off and were out of their seats, running for the playground.

Diamond had always liked that park. It was in the center of a wide-open space, surrounded by a four-feet tall chain-link fence, with walk-throughs at various points to give access to the parking lot or the school.

The park structures weren't anything fantastic, but they were the standard items you'd find at any self-respecting park — a swing set, a slide or two, a jungle gym, and most importantly, benches in the shade for parents to chill on.

After turning off the Jeep and climbing out, Diamond headed to the benches while she smiled at her children running amok. They were great kids, but anytime four young children were put together without a chance to expel some energy, it was a recipe for disaster.

They had been there for about thirty minutes when Mia asked to go to the bathroom, which was in the building on the opposite side of the park from where she parked. Taking Mia's hand, Diamond told the others to keep an eye on each other and to stay by the play structures, while she took Mia to the bathroom.

Letting her go by herself wasn't an option. Anyone could be in that bathroom. Diamond wasn't a helicopter parent, but she erred on the side of caution when it came to the kids, especially after what was happening in Warden's Pass recently.

After Mia was done and had washed her hands, Diamond again took her hand, and they headed back to the boys. As they approached the play structures, Diamond searched for the other kids within the structures and didn't see them. It wasn't until she scanned the outer area that she found them.

Rebel's Fairytale

Her heart jumped into her throat as she saw Hunter throwing punches and kicks at a grown man who had a hand on an upper arm of each of her biological children and was trying to pull them toward a running car in the parking lot.

"Miles! Jenna!" Diamond let go of Mia's hand and took off, running faster than she ever had in her life. Her eyes never left her babies. She was halfway to them when she realized who the man was — her ex-husband, Niles. Panic filled her at the sight. He was trying to take away her babies.

When she reached them, she stepped in front of Niles and tried her best to force him to let go of her kids. Slapping, punching, clawing — Nothing was out of the question. Eventually, he let go of Miles in order to grab Diamond by the hair.

"Fucking slut," he growled at her as he yanked her around by her hair.

During one of the spins from his ministrations, she saw Hunter and Miles forcing Niles's fingers off Jenna's arm. When she was free, the three kids ran back to the park, where Mia was standing, watching, with tears running down her face.

"I'll call Dad," Hunter yelled.

"Stupid fucking whore," Niles continued to shout at her as he repeatedly swung and hit her in the face, sending shocks of pain through her head.

Diamond was having trouble gaining her balance. Every time she thought she found it, he would yank her hair again and pull her around. She was pretty sure she lost some hair in the process, but she resisted the next pull and maintained her balance, allowing her a split second to kick out and hit him right between his legs.

As he let out a loud wail with pain, his hold on her hair loosened. She yanked herself free and took off for the kids. "Run!" Waving her arms in an attempt to get the kids moving toward the bathrooms, she kept shouting to them, "Run!"

She had just caught up to the fleeing children when the sound of motorcycles filled the air. Glancing back, she noticed the car and Niles were gone, but the parking lot had a whole pack of Howlers on their bikes.

Rock was off of his bike and sprinting their way.

"Kids! It's okay. You can stop." She came to a halt and bent over, putting her hands to her knees. Her head was throbbing, and her face felt like it was twice the size it normally was, and she was pretty sure she had a bald spot on the back of her head.

"Diamond! Kids!" Rock slid to a halt at the group of them. After checking over the kids and kissing the top of each of their heads, he turned to her. The pain that filled his expression when he looked at her told her everything she needed to know about her appearance.

"That bad?"

"Come on, kids. Let's go get in the Jeep, while Dad takes care of Mom," Brute suggested.

As Brute and his brothers took the kids back to the parking lot, Rock carefully cupped her face in his hands and gazed down at her, concern written all over his face. "Angel," he breathed and ran his thumbs softly over her cheeks. "Who did this? Hunter said he never saw the guy before."

"Niles," she choked out as tears filled her eyes. She wasn't crying because of the pain, though. She was crying because she knew she'd never have to deal with situations like that by herself ever again. Rock had her. Rock would *always* have her.

"I will kill that motherfucking piece of shit," Rock vowed through clenched teeth. "Are you hurt anywhere else? Do you need a doctor?"

She shook her head and allowed him to pull her into his arms. "I just want to go home."

"Come on, Angel." She felt his lips softly touch the top of her head and let out a sigh. She was safe.

At The Same Time... Ruby

Ruby was beat. Rebel was insatiable the night before and kept her up for hours with her thighs around his head for a good portion of it. After he finally slid inside of her, it took another thirty minutes before he was satisfied.

He left her boneless and happy as she drifted off to sleep while he used the restroom to clean up. She vaguely remembered him returning to wipe her clean, but she had been well on her way to dreams by that point.

When she woke up, he gave her *that look*, and it took everything in her to slam the bathroom door in his face, because she had to get ready for work. His chuckles came through the door as she climbed in the shower.

They were like newlyweds without the wed part. Well, in the shifter and biker senses, they were married. It was just the human definition that was missing. She briefly wondered if he'd want that, or even if she wanted that, as she drove to work.

Her day was ordinary in the sense that nothing crazy happened, but the library had been a lot busier since the vandalism. People showed up to gawk like they do as they pass an accident on the side of the road. Ruby just kept her head on her job, except for the stray thought about Rebel, and got through the day.

While she loved the way they spent their evenings, she was sorely lacking sleep. With Rebel and the clubs setting up the carnival, it would be the perfect time to get in a nap.

After getting in her car when she was done for the day, she sent a quick text to Rebel.

>SOMEONE KEPT ME UP ALL NIGHT. I'M GONNA GET IN A NAP. CALL ME WHEN YOU'RE DONE.<

His first reply came quickly.

>YOUR FAULT.<

That was followed by another. When she read it, she couldn't help but smile. She may have mated a biker, but she mated a sweet one.

>SLEEP WELL, SWEETIE. LOVE YOU.<

Putting her car in gear, she headed home. Ruby couldn't wait to change and climb into bed. She was pretty sure Rebel had left one of his Henleys in her room, and sleeping with his scent around her sounded like heaven.

After parking in her garage, she shut the large door and moved to the entrance to her kitchen. Yawning as she stepped inside, she didn't see him. One minute, she was thinking about her pillow. The next, she was face first against the wall with her hands held behind her back.

"What the hell?" She tried to pull her hands away, but the grip tightened.

"I have a knife. Don't make me use it," an unfamiliar voice said into her ear.

Ruby swallowed hard and felt panic rise in her system. "What do you want?" Her instincts were telling her to fight, get away, but that was her panic talking. She needed to focus and remember what to do. Over the years, she had read a book or two about hostage situations. She knew there were recommended dos and don'ts, if only she could remember what they were.

"You'll find out soon enough," the man said as she felt a scratching material rub against her wrist. *Rope*? Then, her hands were tied together. Grabbing her upper arm, he yanked her through her kitchen to her dining area and forced her into a chair.

As she stared up at the man, she noticed he looked vaguely familiar. She couldn't quite place him, but that wasn't necessarily important at the moment. She needed to focus on keeping herself alive, unharmed, and getting through this.

Bits and pieces of things she had read started to trickle through her brain. *Talk to them. Build rapport. Get them talking.* Right. Okay. She could do this. "Do I know you? You look familiar. Or… you don't have to answer that, if you don't want to."

The man started to pace in front of her, his knife in a sheath attached to his belt. She couldn't see the whole thing, but it looked like it could do plenty of damage. Fear and panic began to rise again, but she did her best to shut it down and focus on the situation at hand. If she were to make it out of this, she would need to know what he looked like so she could tell the police, so she watched him and clocked every detail she could. He had sandy blond hair, an average build, was probably in his mid-thirties, and was dressed in jeans and a dark blue polo. It was the polo that was snagging her focus. *Why?*

"That's not important. What's important is you need to know who you're attaching yourself to. Those *things* aren't human. I know they look like it most of the time, but they ain't. Do you understand?" He stopped and looked at her, his brown eyes wide and wild. "Do you?"

Ruby thought it best to just nod, so she did.

"Good. Listen. I know they go around town pretending to be *good citizens* and all of that, but they are *monsters*! You can't forget that! And you can't let

Rebel's Fairytale

children around them! If a child got hurt, the blood would be on your hands! Do you want that? Do you?"

As the panic gave way to anger, Ruby took a deep breath and told herself to keep it in check. The last thing she needed was to enrage the psycho. *Don't psych up the psycho. Don't psych up the psycho. Don't psych up the psycho.*

"Do you!"

Ruby shook her head. "No. No, of course, I don't want that."

"Good. And really… you're a *librarian*! You shouldn't be hanging out with *bikers*. They're *criminals*! And you're just giving up your beauty to them! You're tainting yourself with their *slime*! I get it, though. I do." He started pacing again. "I did it, too. Minx had me… brainwashed, years ago. I thought she was perfect and beautiful and… I wanted to marry her. Then, she just left me. Me! Can you believe that? She just ended it. No reason. No explanation. She was just done! She tainted me! But I got clean, Bri. I got clean… and you can too. You can. I'll help you get clean. I'll help you cut them out of your life."

The panic began to rise again. She didn't want this man helping her do anything. "I appreciate that," she managed to croak out through the bile rising in her throat.

"Yeah, we'll cleanse you," he said, almost like he was talking to himself. "We'll cleanse you. We'll erase them. It'll be like they never existed."

Ruby fought back tears as she realized how deranged of an individual she was dealing with. She sent up prayers to the gods that she got out of this alive. Maybe Rebel would come over to check on her. Maybe the neighbor would hear something. Maybe the gods would protect her somehow. Until they did, she'd have to find a way to protect herself.

Rock

After settling Diamond in bed with pain reliever and ice packs, Rock stormed down the stairs and into the living room. He motioned with his hand to Brute, who stood up from where he was playing dolls with Mia and Jenna on the floor, and followed Rock out to the front porch.

"What's up? How's sis?"

Rock swallowed hard. "Stronger than most of us," he answered, putting his hands to his hips and staring down at the boards under his feet. "I have to kill him. I have to, Brute. And I get it if you don't want to be a part of that, but—"

"Fuck you," Brute said and glared at Rock. "Fuck you and fuck that bullshit."

Rock fought back the smile that wanted to grow on his face. They didn't share blood, but they were brothers all the same. "I'm just saying—"

"I know what the fuck you're saying, and my response stands. That's my sister up in that bed with those fucking ice packs, and I'll avenge her if I want to.

If you don't like it, you can fuck right the hell off." Brute took a few steps away and turned to glare at Rock again. "*I'm just saying*… Fuck that shit."

Rock held back the smile, knowing it would just piss Brute off, and asked, "Okay. Then, what are we going to do?"

Ruby

Ruby didn't know how long had passed, but her arms were starting to ache from being in such an unnatural position. She attempted to move them a little to alleviate the pain, and as she twisted her wrist a little, she noticed the rope wasn't as tight as it was when he first forced her into the chair.

Hope bloomed in her chest. If she could get free, she had a better chance of making it out of the situation alive. She needed a plan, though.

The man had been quiet for a while now, pacing in front of her and muttering to himself. She was only half paying attention to him, while she tried to look around the room casually. Ruby needed a weapon, in case she got free. She knew there was no way she'd make it to the front door or the garage door before he caught up to her. No, Ruby couldn't just run. She needed a way to protect herself.

She knew she had a metal letter opener in the shape of a dagger by her chair in the living room, since she had a tendency of curling up in her reading chair when she went through her mail. However, that was too far away. The bat she kept in the corner behind the front door was practically useless to her from that distance.

Glancing to her right, her gaze landed on the wood block on the counter that was full of knives. She quickly looked away from it, not wanting Psycho to realize what she was staring at. If he knew she saw the knives, he'd surely hide them. She couldn't have that.

While they weren't right next to her, they were within a couple of yards of the chair she was sitting in. If she were to wiggle her hands enough to pull them out of the rope, she could wait for the right time, when he wasn't paying attention, and get to the block. Ruby would have to time it just right, but it was possible. Whether it was doable was still up in the air.

She tried to remain calm, but she knew her chest was heaving with the adrenaline and hope coursing through her veins. *Please don't notice. Please don't notice. Nothing to see here. Keep up your pacing.*

The noise of kids shouting rang through the air, and Psycho jumped. Ruby knew who it was. The woman who lived in the townhouse down the block had five kids. When she was trying to get some cleaning done, she sent all of her kids out to play, and they tended to play catch in the street. She wasn't about to tell him that, though.

Cursing under his breath, he turned to face the living room and slowly headed for the door, careful to stay out of the view of the front windows. When he was almost to the door, Ruby wiggled her wrists for all she was worth. Eventually, the rope gave way and fell to the floor. She had just stood and took her first step toward the knives, when Psycho looked over his shoulder at her.

Now or never, Ruby told herself as she bolted for the counter and the block of knives. She had managed to get there before Psycho grabbed a handful of her hair and yanked. Her hand was already firmly around the handle of the chef's knife, when he yanked her back, so the knife slid out of the slot and came with her.

"Bitch! I was trying to help you!"

"Fuck you! And fuck your help! *You're* the monster," Ruby shouted, adjusting her grip on the knife as she turned and shoved it into his gut. Not wanting to risk it, she yanked it out and shoved it in again, as Psycho's mouth fell open, his eyes widened, and he looked down at where she stabbed him.

Yanking out the knife, she ran for the front door, only to stumble to a stop when the door flew open, and Rebel stepped through.

Panting, she came to a stop and said, "Well, it's about fucking time you got here." Then she dropped the knife to the floor.

T.S. Tappin

Chapter Twenty-Seven

Rebel

After tossing the football with the neighbor kids for a few minutes, Rebel jogged his way up to Ruby's front door and used the key she gave him the day before to unlock it. He did not expect to see Ruby on her feet when he stepped inside. He didn't expect to see her holding a knife and covered in blood. He *really* didn't expect Charles from the hardware store to be coming at her with another knife. Yet, that's exactly what Rebel walked in on.

Without a moment's thought, he shoved her out of the way before his wolf took over, and he lunged at Charles. Charles screamed like a little bitch, but he still swung out with his knife-hand before Rebel's paws hit his chest. Luckily, his knife missed Rebel. As they fell to the floor, Rebel locked his jaws around the man's throat and shook for all he was worth. He heard the crunch, but he didn't stop. *He couldn't stop.* He had to end the threat. Ruby was in danger, and Rebel had to protect her.

The next thing he remembered was Ruby on her knees in front of him while he was still in his wolf form and her hands combing gently through his fur.

"Good job, Rebel. It's done. You did good. Come back to me, now." Her eyes were filled with tears, but there was a soft smile on her face. "Come back to me, mate."

Rebel took a deep breath and allowed himself to shift. As soon as he was in his man form again, he pulled her into his arms and held her tight. Looking around the room, he saw all the blood and the rope on the floor behind a chair that was facing away from the table.

"What happened here?"

She let out a quiet sob. "He was here when I got home."

"I'm so sorry, Ruby. Damn it. I'm so sorry I wasn't here to protect you."

She pulled back to glare at him through her tears. "I'm not an invalid. I can protect myself, Port Christopher."

He snorted a laugh at her use of his real name. "Yes, ma'am."

She nodded, and then her glare faded, and her tears intensified. "But I *really* don't want to be here, right now… or ever… I don't think."

"So… don't be."

"What?" She looked at him confused as he cradled her in his lap.

He shrugged. "Don't be. Move in with me. We can discuss it more later, if you feel it's necessary."

"*If I feel it's necessary?* Uh… yeah, it's definitely necessary."

Rebel rolled his eyes. "Okay. But for right now, just stay with me. I have to call Axle and get a clean-up crew in here."

"What are we going to tell the police?"

Rebel looked her square in the eye and prayed to the gods she didn't fight him on his answer. "Not a damn thing."

He could practically see the million questions spinning in her brain as she stared at him, but he didn't have time to go through them and explain everything. They could do that later, when they weren't sitting next to a dead body, and she wasn't covered in blood.

"Ruby, I know you have questions, but for now, I need you to just trust me. I'm going to call Axle while you head upstairs and get cleaned up. Then, you're going to leave here with me. You'll stay with me for now. And we aren't calling the police."

"But—"

"Ruby, the second you leave this house, this becomes club business. What you have to know about that is I won't be able to share a lot of club business with you. Some of it isn't legal, and we keep it from the Ol' Ladies to keep you from getting into trouble if the police ever get involved. That's all I can tell you right now. Okay?"

He knew she wasn't really okay with it, but he let out a sigh of relief when she nodded and climbed to her feet. He noticed how she did her best to avoid looking at the dead guy a few feet away.

"Call Axle from upstairs," she said in a quiet voice. "I don't want to be alone."

Climbing to his feet, Rebel replied, "I can do that." He took her hand and led her up the stairs. "Come on. Let's get you cleaned up."

He washed his hands in her bathroom and waited for her to step in the shower. Thankful that the majority of blood didn't stay on him when he shifted back from being in his wolf form, he returned to her bedroom and sat down on her bed to call Axle.

"Yeah?"

Rebel could hear the sounds of metal hitting metal in the background and knew Axle was still working on carnival setup. "Charles Williams was in Ruby's townhouse when she got home. He tied her up. I don't know what his objective was, but he's dead on her floor with two stab wounds and a broken neck."

There was a brief pause. "Shit. Give a guy a fucking warning."

"Sorry, Pres. Don't have time for that. She's cleaning off the blood right now. Then, I'm taking her to my place. We need clean up." He looked down at his jeans and saw a few areas where blood had transferred from Ruby. "And I need some clothes."

"Yeah. On it. Was it her?"

"The stab wounds? Yeah. The broken neck? No."

"Sounds like you found a good mate. I'll take care of it. Any idea how he got there?"

Rebel sighed. "No. I didn't see any strange vehicles on the street, but I also wasn't expecting to walk in on this."

"I'll get Keys on it. Take care of your mate, Reb. Don't worry about a thing. Someone will be there soon with clothes."

"Thanks, Ax." Rebel ended the call. After a moment of quiet thought, he stood and started packing her clothes into the suitcase he found on the top shelf of her closet.

Rock

Standing in his garage with Brute and Pike, Rock ended the call he just made to Ginger and took a deep breath. After letting it out slowly, he said, "Okay. So, this is the plan. I'm going to have the kids go to Ginger's house for a couple days. She can take them to the carnival. Rex and Top volunteered to help her keep an eye on the kids. Then, we'll have Diamond hide out in the house, while we have one of the Claws dress up like Diamond and drive Diamond's Jeep out to the cabin. We'll hang back and let him follow her, since he's been watching the house and following her for a couple days. He vandalized the library, too. He doesn't know we know, but he's not very good at being stealthy. On the path to the cabin, we'll block him in and take him out."

"Sounds good. So, who is going to dress like Diamond?" Brute asked.

Rock thought about it and replied, "Well, I think height-wise and body type, probably Nails. She'd have to… enhance some stuff, but she could pull it off. Think she would?"

Pike nodded and pulled out his phone. "I'll call her and ask, but I'm sure she would."

"Or," Diamond said as she stepped through the open garage door, "and this is just a thought, but you could just let me do it. No, I amend that, you could ask what in the hell I think, since it's my ex-husband and my life that is on the line."

Rock took another deep breath and looked up at the rafters, not wanting to snap at Diamond, because none of it was her fault.

"Don't you start that shit, Rock. You told me I was strong. You sat there and told me that I could do anything. You fostered me finding that strength within myself. Now, you want me to go back to being weak? I don't fucking think so."

Pike and Brute pretended to be awfully interested in the go-cart in the corner. *Fucking traitors*.

"Angel, I'm just—"

"Taking my choices away. I know."

Fuck. That made it sound like he was no better than her piece of shit ex.

Rebel's Fairytale

"Diamond," Rock said on a sigh and put his hands to his hips.

"I'm doing it, Rock. Give me a gun, if you feel the need to, but I'm doing it."

The last thing he wanted to do was agree to allow her to put herself in danger, but she wasn't wrong. If he didn't agree to her performing the mission, it would be like he was telling her she wasn't strong enough. In an effort to keep her safe, he would be sacrificing her self-esteem and her trust in him. Rock had to let her do this. He had to let her be bait, but he didn't have to let her do it without safeguards.

"Do you even know what you're insisting on doing?"

"I've been listening since you were on the phone," she answered and crossed her arms over her chest, staring him down, daring him to say one damn word to her about it. He wasn't that stupid.

"Okay. Then, do you have any ideas about how to put a seed in his ear that you're going to go hide away at a safe house until everything calms down?"

She nodded and shrugged. "He's been following me. So, I'll go for a late lunch with the girls and make sure I mention it *louder than I should*. Either way, he'll either hear that, or he'll just follow me."

Pike walked over and came to a stop next to Rock. "She's good at this," he told Rock. "Maybe we should talk to the Claws. They could use another member working with Nails and Ginger with security."

Rock glared at his friend.

Diamond giggled. "I'm good being an Ol' Lady, but my services are at their and your disposal." Then, she fucking winked... *winked* at Pike.

When Pike chuckled, Rock knew his unhappiness was showing all over his face.

Messer

Messer didn't look forward to making the call, but she had to do her daily check-in. Commander West hadn't been happy with her lack of new information the last couple days. She really needed to figure out a way to get close.

At least she could tell him what her plan was to change that.

"Elite Messer," Commander West said into the phone as he answered it.

"Commander, I think I have a way to get close to them and try to gather intel. They are throwing a town carnival on their land, tomorrow. Proceeds are going to the local library, since the group I had been talking to had caused some issues there. I'm going to go to the carnival and try to find an in."

"Sounds promising."

"From what I understand, most of them will be there."

"Good. I need something, Messer. We all have people to answer to."

"Understood," she replied.

"Check in tomorrow." Then, he ended the call.

Rebel's Fairytale

She was sure the carnival saved her ass. That went a lot smoother than the call the day before. She had heard whispers and rumors of a carnival, but no concrete information until she saw the flyers on the light posts in town earlier that day. Not having much information before, she hadn't wanted to mention it to him until she could confirm details.

With a sigh of relief, she slid out of her vehicle and started across the parking lot. The owner was behind the front desk as she came in through the door. Instead of the welcoming smile from the first day, the woman was looking at Messer as if she was trying to figure her out.

Good luck with that, Messer thought as she gave the woman a forced smile and headed down the hallway.

It wasn't the first time the owner looked at her like that. It had only increased in frequency the longer she was there.

Messer couldn't worry about some woman with nosy habits. It wasn't as if the hotel owner was a threat. What was she going to do? Tie her up with hotel towels and torture her with toiletry items until Messer broke?

Nah, she wasn't worried about the hotel owner.

On the second floor, she approached and entered her room. Walking over to her table, she dropped everything on the top and pulled her phone from her jacket pocket. Pulling up the encrypted video app, she did as she always did and checked to make sure all the cameras she had set up in her room were still working.

Instead of the screen filling with various boxes of different views of the room, she was greeted with an error screen.

"Fuck," she cursed under her breath. She'd have to redo all of her security measures. It wasn't the first time the connection had gotten interrupted with the wireless cameras on a job. It was a flaw to the programming that they hadn't figured out, yet. It was just frustrating.

After sulking about it for a few seconds, she set her phone down and got to work.

Niles

Niles was still pissed as he sat in a car down the street from the fucker's house. Since his sister refused to let him borrow her car, he had to steal one. He was aware of a family on his mom's street who was on vacation for a couple weeks. The car would be ditched long before they realized it was gone.

He was grateful for people who still didn't have video cameras. It made things easier. He was dealing with enough bullshit.

Niles had been sitting there for a couple hours, and the sun had just gone down, but he had yet to see his kids or Mary. He couldn't believe that bitch took a cheap shot at his dick. All Niles wanted to do is get his family back together. And sure, he lost his temper when she confronted him, but she should know better than to push him to that point by now. She ruined his entire fucking plan. Now, Niles had to wait for another opportunity, but he could be patient.

Another half hour passed before the front door opened and kids started streaming out of the house, followed by Mary and the fucker. He watched as all four of the kids climbed into her Jeep and buckled themselves in. After the fucker loaded backpacks in the hatch of the Jeep, he followed Mary to the driver's door and gave her a deep kiss before she climbed in.

Niles was fucking furious. How dare the fucker kiss his wife in front of his kids! He would make the fucker pay for that shit.

As Mary backed out of the driveway, Niles started the stolen car and put it into drive. He waited until she got to the other end of the block, before he pulled away from the curb and followed her.

Ten minutes later, he watched as she pulled into the driveway of a tan ranch-style house with a black metal sculpture of a motorcycle attached to the front.

The kids climbed out of the Jeep and grabbed their backpacks from the back. Mary followed them to the front door, where a red-haired woman, who looked to be maybe ten years older than Mary, was standing.

Mary and the woman talked for a minute. Then, Mary kissed the heads of all the kids and returned to the Jeep as the kids went inside the house with the woman.

As Mary left the ranch style home, Niles considered finding a place to force her off the road and take her, but those thoughts were dashed when one of the damn Howlers came riding up on his bike and appeared to be following Mary.

Damn it!

Ruby

Relaxing on Rebel's couch, curled up in a throw blanket, Ruby sent texts to Liz and Allie. She was vague about what was going on, but she wanted to let them know she wouldn't be at her townhouse for a while. They weren't happy with her answers, and she knew they would demand details at the next download day, but they were appeased for now.

Snuggled up, Ruby watched Rebel moving around his kitchen. He was such a good man, and she wasn't sure he knew it. He was always trying so hard to do the right thing and strived to be the man he wanted to be, that she was pretty sure he missed the fact that he already was that man.

The adrenaline had begun to wear off, making her hands shake and her tears build again in her eyes. She couldn't believe what happened. It was almost like it was a dream, a nightmare really.

Things like that happened in books and movies. She didn't expect it to happen in real life, and especially not to her. Thinking back on it, she couldn't quite believe she was able to actually stab someone once, let alone *twice.*

She hadn't really thought about it at the time. She just acted. It was self-preservation that kicked in and caused her to do something she normally wouldn't have even considered.

Watching Rebel attack and end the man's life should have been more traumatic to her in the moment, but instead, she had just been grateful that he was there and worried about his mental state. That was the second man she had seen him take out in defense of people he cared about. That couldn't be an easy thing to live with.

When she wasn't a shaking mess, she would need to check in with him about that and gauge where he was at emotionally. To a man like Rebel, it would weigh on him at least a little bit. She needed to keep an eye on that.

There was a loud noise as Rebel dropped something in the sink. Ruby instantly jumped and let out a shout as her heart rate picked up and her breathing became shallower.

Fuck! She took a deep breath and let it out slowly. You're okay. It was Rebel. It's okay. Everything's fine. You're safe.

"Ruby," Rebel said, softly.

She opened her eyes to see him standing a few feet in front of her with a mug in his hands and a worried expression on his face.

"I'm so sorry. I didn't mean to startle you."

She shook her head. "It's okay. I'm okay."

He held out the mug to her. "Chai. It will help with the adrenaline crash."

She nodded and took the mug from him. Cupping it with her hands, she put it to her lips and took a sip. "Thank you."

Rebel lifted the edge of her blanket and slid in next to her. Wrapping an arm around her shoulders, he leaned in and kissed her temple. "Things are going to be tense for you for a bit, but it will fade."

She nodded again. "I know."

"I'm so damn proud of you, though. You defended yourself. I knew you were strong, but yeah... I'm just fucking proud of you."

Looking over at him, she gave him a smile. "I wasn't going to let him win."

"Damn right," he mumbled and returned her smile.

She let her gaze travel over his handsome face. From his golden green eyes to his soft lips and full beard, he was so damn handsome. Knowing there was an intellectual behind the leather and badass only increased his hotness factor. The fact that he was willing to lay his life on the line for the people he cared about just sealed the deal that he was her perfect mate.

"I love you," she whispered.

His eyes softened as he cupped the back of her head. He leaned in and said, "I love you, too, Ruby," against her lips before he took them in a deep, slow kiss.

By the time he broke the kiss, her hands had settled, but her heart was beating fast for another reason. She didn't push for more, though. Instead, she just cuddled into his chest and sipped her chai, letting both of them soothe her frayed nerves.

Chapter Twenty-Eight

Rock

Rock knew he was in the doghouse. He knew that even though he agreed to not stand in the way of her doing what she felt was right, he had still implied that she wouldn't be able to handle it and had also tried to take away her choices.

While he thought his intent was important, it didn't excuse his behavior. He fucked up, and he needed to make it right. For once, he was happy the kids were gone for the night. It would make it easier for them to make up, whether they did that through fighting or fucking.

After his shower, he returned to the bedroom to find her sitting up in bed, reading on her e-reader. A bit of a win surged his system to know that he had bought that for her as a congratulations gift when she secured her job at the store. She had mentioned that it was hard for her to read on the phone because the screen was so small, so he made sure she had what she needed to get her fix. Along with the e-reader, he sent her a gift card to her favorite online bookstore to stock up.

He was thanked with a sexy pic of her holding the e-reader in bed, wearing nothing but her panties. Not that he needed a thank you, but it was the best thank you he ever received.

After he let himself remember that and appreciate it, he leaned against the door jamb and crossed his arms over his chest. "Diamond."

She didn't look up from the screen. "What?"

"I'm sorry. I just—"

"Leave it at *I'm sorry,* or you might fuck it up, Rock." She still didn't look at him.

Fuck! She was so damn gorgeous, even when she was pissed at him. Her full, sexy lips were pursed, making him want to nibble them until they relaxed, and her curls were begging for his hand to fist in them while he fucked her slow.

Get your mind back to the issue, Rock!

"I *am* sorry. I shouldn't have made a plan without discussing it with you first."

She nodded, eyes still on her e-reader. "That's better."

Rock fought the smile that threatened to grow on his face. "I promise not to make plans about anything that has to do with you without discussing it with you first."

Diamond was quiet as she turned and set her e-reader on the side table. Then, she looked over at him and smiled. "There it is. Welcome back, my love."

Giggling, she pulled back the blankets and raised a brow in invitation.

Despite his recent decisions, Rock wouldn't classify himself as a stupid man. Without hesitation, he dove into that bed and set about ravishing his woman.

Axle

The knock on Axle's office door pulled him out of his concentration on paying the bills for the club house, the apartment building, and the auto shop. He shut the laptop and called out, "Yeah?"

The door opened and Pike looked in. "You busy? Dan Williams is here."

Oh shit. "Okay. Show him in."

Pike looked down the hall and made some hand movements. A few seconds later, a disheveled and anxious Daniel Williams stepped through the door and eyed Pike curiously as Pike came in behind him, shutting the door.

"I need to talk to Axle alone," he told Pike.

Pike just chuckled and leaned back against the door, crossing his arms over his chest.

"He's not going anywhere," Axle said and pointed to one of the chairs across the desk from him. "Sit. Tell me what you want."

Daniel took a seat and cleared his throat. "I… uh… My brother and I… Well…"

"You what?"

The man cringed. "Chuck wasn't a fan of... you guys. He started... doing things and saying things. And... I found a note from him, but he's missing. I don't know what he's going to do, but I fear it has something to do with your club. I'm... I'm here trying to stop him. He's... gone off the rails... and I can't stop it."

Axle actually felt bad for Daniel. The man looked conflicted. He had loyalty to his brother, but he also knew what was right and wrong, and was trying to stand up for what was right. That took guts when dealing with someone so close to you who was intent on doing the opposite.

"You no longer have to worry about Chuck."

Daniel's brows pulled together. "What?"

"You got the note with you?"

After a nod, Daniel pulled the folded paper from his back pocket and handed it over to Axle. Axle unfolded it and read:

> I FIGURED OUT HOW TO FIX THINGS. I'LL TAKE CARE OF THEM. YOU DON'T HAVE TO WORRY ABOUT IT. I WON'T LET THEM DO TO HER WHAT THEY DID TO ME. THEY WON'T GET AWAY WITH IT AGAIN. I'M GOING TO SAVE HER.

Axle refolded the note. "You no longer need to worry about Chuck." He locked eyes with Daniel. "He will no longer be a problem for you or for us."

Daniel stared at him for a long time. Slowly, tears built in his eyes. "He did something stupid, didn't he?"

"Something monstrously stupid."

Daniel nodded and sniffled. "He's not coming back."

Axle didn't confirm or deny.

Rebel's Fairytale

Looking like he was in a daze, Daniel stood and made his way toward the door. Pike stepped aside and let him leave. Axle didn't know if he realized he left the note behind or not, but he wasn't about to point it out.

He reached down and took the bag out of his metal trash can. He used the lighter from his desk drawer to light the corner of the note on fire. Then, he dropped it into the metal can and let it burn away.

Axle looked over at Pike. "Give him a few minutes. Then, go question him on who he's working with. Make sure we have all the names. This shit needs to end."

Pike nodded and left the office, shutting the door behind him.

Axle was shutting down his computer and getting ready to call Rebel with an update on Ruby's place. Before he could head up to his room at the compound to snuggle his daughter, fuck his woman and get some sleep, there was a knock on the door. Biting back the groan, he called out, "Yeah."

"Dragon," Dragon's voice said through the door.

Shit. It wasn't something he could put off until the morning. He had sent Dragon and Keys on a local mission. He needed to know what they figured out.

"Come in."

The door opened, and Dragon stepped in, followed by Keys. After shutting the door behind them, they each took a seat across the desk from him.

"What did you find out?"

It was Keys who spoke first. "Well, Dragon entered the room with the key from Mama Hen. He told me about the cameras he found and the brand. I was able to break the encryption on them and the app she used. Then I deleted any footage of Dragon in her room."

Dragon added, "I searched the stuff in her room. Didn't find much. Clothes, bathroom shit, and the cameras. Then, I found a locked metal black suitcase slid under one of the beds."

"Get it open?"

Dragon shot him a look that made sure Axle knew he was offended by the question.

"Right. And what was in it?"

"Weapons. A lot of silver bullets and blades."

Axle rolled his eyes. "Ah… so we're werewolves who shift on the full moon and are allergic to silver?"

"Apparently."

"There was also a polo shirt in her clothes with a logo on it. One I hadn't seen before. I took a pic and sent it to Keys."

Keys nodded. "It took a lot of searching and some looking around on the hidden channels, but I found a posting about an academy for hunters, and not the deer hunter variety."

Shit.

"I haven't been able to track a location or the money backing it, but apparently, they are recruiting people to go to this academy and train to hunt shifters down.

Looks like this is the group the champions told us about."

"And one of them is in our town."

"Looks like it," Dragon confirmed.

"This is bad," Axle breathed out on a sigh.

"Yup," Keys agreed.

"Let's hope the prospect does a good job and can get us more info."

"We patching him in?" Dragon asked.

Axle nodded. "I'm bringing up the vote first church after the carnival, but he can't wear colors until he's done with the mission."

"Well, he has my vote," Dragon said and stood.

"By the way," Keys said as he straightened, "I changed the code so that when she gets the cameras back up and running, I'll get a copy of the feed."

Axle grinned at him. "Glad you're on our side."

He returned the grin and followed Dragon out of the office.

Rebel

Warm. Rebel was so warm and comfortable. He was lying on his back with his woman's naked body wrapped around him. It was motherfucking heaven.

His phone vibrated again on the nightstand, letting him know what brought him out of his sleep to begin with. Carefully, he grabbed it and checked to see who was calling him.

Axle.

With a sigh, he carefully extracted himself from Ruby's hold and sat up. Turning and climbing to his feet, he answered it. "Yeah?"

"Hey. Sorry to call so late, but I thought you'd want to know that they cleaned her place and got rid of his car. It was parked a couple blocks away in an empty storefront parking lot. Anyway, it's all taken care of. They said most of the blood was on the linoleum. There were a few spots on the carpet, and they cleaned it up, but as long as we keep her from being connected with his disappearance, there's no reason to be concerned with it."

Rebel nodded even though Axle couldn't see him. "Yeah. Thanks, Pres. I appreciate it. I know she does too."

"No need. We're family."

"I'm trying to talk her into moving in with me. So hopefully, the place won't be her home much longer."

There was a smile in Axle's voice when he replied, "Shacking up is good."

"I think so. Anyway, go to your woman and sleep."

"Eventually," Axle replied and ended the call.

Chapter Twenty-Nine

The next morning... Diamond

Taking a deep breath, Diamond entered the diner and made her way over to the table that Sugar, Pixie, and Kisy were sitting at. Sitting down in one of the empty chairs, Diamond smiled at each of them.

"Hey."

They all smiled back and settled into easy chit-chat about the weather, their men, and upcoming birthdays. Not long after she sat down, a person entered the diner from the rear door and slid into a booth in the corner. They were facing away from her and were wearing a hoodie with the hood up, so she couldn't see what they looked like. The person did have the general body type and size of Niles, though, and she reminded herself not to panic or make anything too obvious. *Play it cool, Diamond.*

After the ladies placed their breakfast orders with the server, their conversation shifted to the carnival.

Diamond took the opportunity to bring up the reason she was there.

"Well, I hope you all have fun at the carnival," she let her voice rise a bit, "but considering what's been going on, I'm going to go away for a while."

"I'm so sorry that happened to you at the park," Pixie said on a sigh. "You're still gorgeous, though."

Diamond gave her a soft smile. "Thanks. I'm just going to go to one of the safe houses for a bit. Rock has a lot on his plate, and I don't want him worrying about me on top of everything else."

"When are you leaving?" Kisy asked and leaned in, seemingly focused on what Diamond was saying, but the sly glance over her shoulder told Diamond Kisy was also paying attention to the other people in the diner.

"Tomorrow afternoon. I'm going to help out with one of the carnival food trucks for a while in the morning, then when Gorgeous comes to relieve me, I'll head out."

Diamond was so glad that the women were given a heads up about the conversation from Axle and their men, otherwise she knew they would have challenged her on that last bit.

"Right," Sugar said, softly. "Are you sure you want to go to the safe house though? Alone?"

Diamond shook her head. "Rock has a lot going on. It will be easier, and he will know I'm safe up there. Besides, I can't complain about having a few moments of peace. I love our kids, but they can be a noisy bunch."

"I get that. I can convince Dragon to let me come stay with you, or…" Diamond leveled a look at Kisy before Kisy let out a resigned huff. "Are you leaving from the carnival?"

Diamond shook her head. "I'll go home first and grab my bags."

"That makes sense," Pixie commented, but her eyes bugged out a bit. Diamond knew she didn't approve of their plan. It was dangerous, but Pixie also knew it was going to happen anyway, and she was trying to let Diamond know she hoped their plan worked, just like the texts she sent her before they arrived. Diamond appreciated the women for even putting themselves in that position. She really hoped her goal was achieved, and it wasn't just a waste of time.

After a brief silence, she redirected the conversation away from her plans.

They ate and finished out their conversation, then Diamond said goodbye to the three of them and headed out to her Jeep parked at the curb right in front of the diner.

Niles

Sitting in the corner booth, facing the wall, Niles listened carefully as Mary talked to those biker sluts about her plans as he repeatedly waved the server away. It was like his prayers were being answered.

She was going to give him the perfect opportunity to get her back.

Once he had her back, he'd show her what she did wrong and teach her how she was going to behave from now on. She had a lot of making up to do to earn his forgiveness, but he was willing to let her do it. Someday, they will be happy again.

Yeah, he'd get her back. Then, he'd start working out how to get his kids back. Once all of that was done, he would start developing a plan to take out the fucker who tried to step into his spot in his family.

It wouldn't do for him to just work with his comrades and push the Howlers out of town. No, that wouldn't be enough. He needed to kill the fucker. He wouldn't be happy until the fucker was no longer breathing.

Double-checking that the hood on his sweatshirt was still fully up and hiding his face, he slid out of the booth and headed for the rear exit of the diner. He had plans to make.

Rebel

Sitting on one of the stools at the island in the kitchen, Rebel watched as Ruby stood at the stove and stirred the homemade chicken noodle soup she was making. The twins were ordered out of the kitchen because, while they had been trying to help her, they kept getting in her way.

They were worried about her. Rebel had noticed the creased brows and the forced smiles as they looked at her. The twins cared about her nearly as much as he did. Rebel wondered if she realized that. Probably not.

Either way, she'd learn eventually. They were a package deal.

"If you keep staring at me like I'm dinner, I'm going to burn your dinner."

Rebel grinned. "Then I'll just have to eat something else."

She looked at him over her shoulder and smirked. "But I was planning on serving you that for dessert."

"I'm a growing boy. I need seconds." He winked at her.

"Ew," Ryker called down the hall. "Can you at least tell us to leave the house before you two start that? We do not want to hear it."

And that's when Ruby started giggling over her pot of soup, Rebel laughing with her.

Ruby

After Rebel and the twins spent an hour eating the hell out of the soup she made and showering her with compliments, Ruby relaxed in the tub for a little while. She let the hot water soothe her while listening to music through headphones with her eyes closed.

After a few minutes, the air was filled with the smell of her favorite candles — tropical fruits with a hint of sugared citrus. Confused, she opened her eyes to find Rebel lighting a row of tea light candles on the counter of the sink, after he lit a couple on the edge of the tub.

When he was done, he looked over at her, smiled, and shot her a wink, before he dimmed the light for her and left the bathroom. Ruby laid there, smelling her favorite scent, and wondered why it took so long for her to find him.

By the time she got out of the tub, she was fully ready to cuddle up with Rebel and see where the night took them. After thinking about all the ways she tried to make her life better, easier, she wanted to find a way to do the same for him. She knew he didn't need that and would probably tell her that her presence was enough, but she wanted to give him more.

After drying off, she wrapped a towel around her body and went into the bedroom. With his hair pulled back in a man bun, Rebel looked sexy as hell, lounging on the bed, in a pair of loose pajama pants and nothing else. His shoulders were to the headboard, his ankles were crossed, and there was a book in his hand.

She unwrapped the towel and hung it on the hook next to the dresser. After opening the top drawer, she reached in to grab panties, but stilled when she felt Rebel's breath against the skin of her neck and shoulder when he said, "You won't need those."

Smiling, she tilted her head to the side, giving him more access. Rebel took the hint, lowered his head, and gave his mating mark a slow lick. Her core clenched in reflex, and a moan escaped her mouth.

His hands landed on her hips and pulled her naked ass back against his body, letting her know he was ready.

"I want to make love to you."

She reached up and back, cupping the side of his face with her hand. "That sounds nice."

"Nice?" He chuckled. "That's one way to describe it." Then, he scooped her up into his arms and kissed her lips as he carried her over to the bed. Laying her down, he came down with her, holding himself over her on bent elbows.

After kissing her until her brain was mush, he worked his way down her body, leaving a trail of kisses down the center of her until he reached her core.

"Spread for me, Ruby," he said, softly.

Her chest heaving with anticipation, Ruby slowly bent her knees and spread her thighs, displaying what he wanted.

His eyes glowed that beautiful light as he dropped between them and pressed his lips to the top of her slit. After giving her clit the sweetest kiss, he moved lower and slid his tongue as deep as it would go into her core.

Ruby moaned and reached down, taking hold of the hair on the top of his head and holding him to her as he proceeded to fuck her with his tongue.

"Fuck," he growled against her. "I love the way you taste. Could spend my life right here." Then he kissed his way back up to her clit.

"Rebel," she said and gasped as he sucked on her clit and slid two fingers into her core, curling them just right, and took over where his tongue had left off.

For ten minutes, he brought her to the brink over and over, and would back off, only to start again. Her grip on his hair got tighter and tighter each time. He must have finally taken the hint, because he really got to work and didn't stop when her core clenched around his fingers.

Pleasure coursed through her body, stealing her breath, and her hips had a mind of their own as she ground against his face and beard.

When she came back down from the high, Rebel lifted his head and grinned at her as he ran a hand over his face and beard. Crawling up her body, he uttered, "I love it when you do that… rub yourself against my face. And I fucking love how your cheeks get pink when I make you come." He bent down and kissed across one of her cheeks as one of his hands cupped her breast and gave it a gentle squeeze.

"Rebel," she began, wrapping her legs around his hips, "if you don't get a condom and fuck me right now, I'm going to do it myself."

Rebel chuckled as he reached over and grabbed a condom from the bedside table. "My woman is greedy."

"I just know what I want."

"Good thing I like giving you what you want."

She watched as he rolled the condom on. "Good thing."

As he pressed his lips to hers, he lined his cock up with her pussy and slowly slid inside. After bottoming out, he pulled out and slid back in, a little faster. Once he had a steady rhythm going, he broke the kiss and said against her lips, "I love you, Brianna Cooke. I'll always be by your side."

Ruby wrapped her arms around his shoulders. "I love you, too, and I think I like having you there at my side."

He spent the next twenty minutes gazing into her eyes, giving her soft and sweet kisses, before following that up with deep ones, but his rhythm remained the same. Reaching between them, he used his thumb to caress her clit until she threw her head back and cried out his name, as her body was overcome with pleasure and the love he was showing her.

"Yes," Rebel breathed and dropped his head. Sucking on his mating mark, intensifying her orgasm, he slammed inside her and trembled as his own pleasure rushed over him.

T.S. Tappin

Chapter Thirty

The next day... Rebel

Rebel kept his eyes on Ruby as she prepared herself for the carnival. He knew she was conflicted and still upset about what happened at her townhouse. He tried to talk her out of going to the carnival, but he didn't push too hard.

He had pressed his luck when he practically demanded Ruby take the day before off and relax at home. She had shot that idea down and made it very clear that she needed the schedule and normalcy of her life. Rebel was going to challenge that, but she added it would look suspicious if she took a day off. The last thing they needed was people wondering what happened to make her take a day off, especially after she had been so adamant about not taking leave after the spray-paint incident.

He had to concede her point. Recognizing that Ruby was a grown woman who had been taking care of herself for a long time, Rebel had kissed her and followed her to work. He stayed in the parking lot until the twins showed up and camped out in the corner of the lot on their lawn chairs.

Ruby had yet to comment on the presence of various Howlers at the library. He doubted she was oblivious to their presence, but she hadn't mentioned it. Maybe she just recognized that it was his way of compromising. If she wanted to work, he was okay with that, but he was keeping her safe until the situation calmed down.

Even though he knew she was capable of deciding what was right for her, he was still worried about how she was going to handle being at the carnival. All the people and noise were bound to be a lot.

"Are you sure you want to go?" Leaning against the door jamb to the bathroom, he watched her as she pulled her hair back in a ponytail and secured it.

"Yes, Rebel. I need to be there. It is to benefit the library, *which I work for*, and it's because of me that the library needs the fundraising in the first place."

"Ruby," he admonished, "it's *not* your fault. It's that bitch Sharon White's and Niles Flynn's fault, along with whatever band of idiots decided to take up their misguided cause."

She nodded. "That doesn't mean I feel less responsible."

"Well, I can't change how you feel." He sighed. "No one would blame you if you wanted to have a quiet day."

"I feel like I need to be there, Reb." She looked over at him. "Okay?"

He gave a nod. "Just promise me you'll tell me if it becomes too much, and I'll get you out of there."

She gave him a soft smile that made his heart race a bit faster and made him want to drag her back to bed. His wolf growled inside of him in commiseration.

"Promise me," he repeated.

"I promise."

"Good." He leaned toward her and kissed her lips. "You look beautiful in that, Sweetie."

She looked down at her skinny jeans, heeled boots, and solid dark green buttoned blouse. "Thank you."

"Please wear your leather. I love the way it looks on you, but we're also taking the bike."

Giggling, Ruby stepped past him and retrieved the leather from a hook on his bedroom wall. When she slid it on, she looked at him over her shoulder and winked.

He let out a growl and came up behind her. Giving her ass a smack, he lowered his head and nosed away the jacket and shit. When it was exposed, he gave his mating mark a suck, grinning when she let out a quiet moan.

Messer

After looking at the map of the town and where the compound was located, Messer decided it would be best to just walk to the carnival, instead of driving a few blocks and trying to find parking. From what she could tell, the Howlers were using the fields just outside of the compound fence line as parking and for some of the rides. The walk wouldn't be much shorter than it would be if she started walking from the hotel.

As she headed down the hall that led out into the lobby of the hotel, she saw a new face behind the counter. It was a pretty blond woman with a slight wave to her hair, bright blue eyes, and a welcoming face. That was dimmed when her blue eyes narrowed on Messer. Okay, maybe her judgment of the woman was wrong.

The woman put her hands to curvaceous hips and watched Messer as she approached the front door. Messer wondered where the owner was, but that thought was fleeting as she stepped outside and headed for the carnival.

Thirty minutes later, she had arrived at the carnival and already indulged in an elephant ear from one of the food trucks. She rarely ate fried food, but she couldn't resist them. They were just too damn good.

Telling herself she didn't need another one, she strolled around the carnival and casually watched the members of the Howlers and the Claws interact with townspeople. From what she could tell, most of Warden's Pass seemed to like the clubs and trusted them.

During her time in the town, few people had negative things to say about the clubs, except for the misfits she met through Niles.

Rebel's Fairytale

Whether or not the town thought they were a danger didn't erase the fact that they could change into predatory animals and were capable of doing grave harm to anyone around them. There was a reason people didn't cuddle up with wolves.

"It's insane, isn't it?"

Messer had to fight the shiver the sexy deep and gravelly voice caused as it registered in her ear. She turned and looked at the man who had just spoken to her. He was close, so she stepped to the side and faced him.

Holy hell. She let her gaze run over him and wondered if she was dreaming. He was... *perfection.* With smooth, medium to dark brown skin, a bald head, and intense dark brown eyes, she felt like someone had pulled all of her favorite things from her brain and stuck them all in one man. They even added in the bulging muscles all over his body, testing the limits of the clothes he was wearing, and the trimmed goatee around his soft-looking lips. She wanted to nibble on them.

After swallowing hard, she asked, "What?"

"The fact that they look like ordinary people, but when the mood strikes, or maybe it's the moon, they can turn into vicious animals and tear you apart."

He was looking off at something. She followed his gaze and found that he was looking at Axle Weber, the president of the Howlers, who was holding a baby in his arms and was kissing the lips of a pretty, curvy blond woman.

"Do you know them?"

The man shook his head. "No. I just heard about them from a news report and through stories from people who had been here before. I had to come see for myself." He was quiet for a moment, and Messer wondered what his intentions were. Was he a possible ally, or was he the type who would become a shifter fanatic? Then he spoke again. "It makes you wonder… why hasn't someone just started taking them out? I mean… they could be a real danger to the population."

Taking a chance, Messer replied, "Maybe someone plans on it, but they don't have enough information about them, yet."

The man nodded. "True. Knowledge is power, and all of that."

"What's your name?"

"Matt. What's yours?" He smiled and held his hand out to her.

There was no way she was giving this man her real name. "Chantel." She took his hand and shook it. "Would you be interested if someone was looking for help gathering information on them?"

Smirking, Matt raised a brow. "Maybe." Then he bit his bottom lip for a moment and released it. "If that someone looked like you, the probability would greatly increase."

"Good to know." She started walking away and wasn't surprised at all when he followed her. Hell, she'd give it a shot. Two sets of eyes were better than one, and he couldn't be any worse than Niles.

And if she was able to get a few orgasms out of the deal before she left, she wouldn't object to that either.

Rebel

Ruby didn't like it, but Rebel had insisted on sticking close to her at the carnival. When they arrived at just before eight in the morning, he had approached Crush and Pinky, who were in charge of job assignments, and requested he be assigned to whatever job they were putting Ruby on.

With understanding in her eyes, Crush had changed the names on the assignments sheet and instructed him to the numbered duck booth. It was probably one of the most laid-back games they had set up. No loud noise. No sudden movements. It would help to keep Ruby from being startled or triggered.

It was a small kiddie pool, the hard-sided plastic ones you could get from any dollar store, filled with water and rubber duckies. On the bottom of each duck was a number. If you picked a duck with an odd number on the bottom, you won a prize. Since it was for charity, and they bought the small stuffed animals in bulk, Rebel was pretty sure every duck had an odd number on it.

Looking at him with narrowed eyes when he returned, Ruby allowed him to take her hand and lead her over to one of the food trucks where they were providing breakfast burritos and coffee for all the workers. He got them fed and supplied with caffeine before they had to be at their booth at nine.

Most of the morning was relatively calm. They had many kids and parents show up at their booth to play the game. Ruby really liked helping the kids pick out their prize when they won. Seeing her eyes light up when talking to them had his heart aching. It was so full of love and pride for her that it almost hurt.

It wasn't until just after lunch that she started to get jumpy. He didn't know exactly what set it off, but he noticed her hands began to shake and the smile on her face began to look forced.

When she began to talk to the winner of the game about their prize, Rebel waved over Ross and quietly told him to notify Crush that they needed to be relieved from duty.

Within a couple minutes, Ross and Ryker showed up and told Ruby they wanted to give out some stuffed animals for a while. He was positive Ruby saw through the twins' declaration, but she didn't fight it. She just gave each of them a hug and told them to make sure they gave out the best ones first.

Once they told the twins how the game worked, Rebel took her hand and led her to the apartment building. She didn't say a word as they entered and climbed the stairs.

When he stopped at a door and pulled his keys from his pocket, she finally asked, "Where are we?"

"Members from each of the clubs have rooms here. Downstairs are the Claws' rooms. Up here is for the Howlers."

"But... you have a house."

He finished unlocking the door and opened it, motioning her in. After she stepped through, he joined her and shut the door behind them.

"Yes, but we have parties in the clubhouse often. Sometimes, things get… chaotic, and being on a bike is not a good idea."

She laughed. "So, basically, you guys get drunk and need a place to sleep it off."

He grinned at her. "Yeah. Well… and some members don't have houses, so they just stay here. I lived here until I became responsible for the twins. Then, there's the obvious doghouse situation for the mated members."

She was still smiling, but she raised a brow. "Rather than sleep on the couch?"

"Something like that." He moved over and sat down on the edge of his made bed, glad that he had the twins come and clean up the room. He reached out and grabbed her hand, pulling her until she sat on his lap. "You were getting jumpy."

She nodded and let out a sigh. "It was too much stimulation."

"Understandable." He caressed her cheek with a knuckle. "You've earned some grace, especially with stuff like that."

"How do you not…" She winced and shook her head.

"What, Ruby?"

She took a deep breath and let it out slowly. "I keep thinking about the moment the knife went into his gut.

Then, the sight of your wolf latched onto him and shaking your neck crosses my mind. I just… How do you not… get lost in… knowing you took a life?"

He wrapped his arms around her waist. "You didn't take his life, Ruby. I did."

"He would have died from those stab wounds."

"But he didn't. He died from me snapping his neck."

She looked into his eyes, those gold-fleck blue orbs full of concern for him. "How do you not get lost in the fact that you took a life?"

Rebel didn't look away from her eyes when he answered, "I feel guilt for my uncle, because there was a time in my life when I loved him, but more because of the twins. I don't like that I took Charles's life, but I don't let myself focus on it. My uncle would have tried to kill me and would have made the lives of his sons hell again. Charles was trying to take your life. That is reason enough for me to justify both actions. I did it to protect my loved ones. If I'm on this earth to do anything, it's that. You stabbed Charles to protect yourself. He put himself in that position by entering your home."

"It's that simple?" She reached up and ran her fingers through his beard.

He shrugged, closed his eyes, and savored the feel of her fingers through his beard. "Yeah."

"What if I need more time to get to that point?"

Opening his eyes, he met her gaze and replied, "Then, I will be here to help you. We're going through

Rebel's Fairytale

this together, just like everything else for the rest of our lives, Sweetie."

She pressed her forehead to his and sighed. "My sexy, sweet biker."

"And if my sweet side doesn't do the trick, I can always just fuck you until you can't think."

She giggled and wiggled her hips. "You mean to tell me that's not a cucumber in your pocket?"

He gripped her hips and pulled her down harder. "Your fault," he told her and nipped her bottom lip.

Niles

Niles didn't see the point in going to carnival. Since Mary was just coming back to the house to get her bags, he parked the stolen car down the block and waited. When he saw her Jeep turn onto the street a little after two, he slid down in the seat, so she didn't see him.

He watched while she went into the house and came out a few minutes later with a suitcase, a duffel, and her purse. She put them in the back of her Jeep and got back in.

He looked around to see if she had a bodyguard tailing her. Surprisingly, she didn't. Niles wondered if she even told the fucker she was going, but it didn't matter.

When she backed out of the driveway, he started the car. He waited until she reached the stop sign at the end of the block before he put the car in drive and pulled away from the curb.

They drove through town and turned onto the highway road that took them out into the country. Approximately a half hour later, she turned the Jeep onto a dirt path barely wide enough for the Jeep.

Pulling off to the side of the road, Niles waited a few minutes before he also turned onto the dirt path. The automatic headlights on the car turned on as soon as he entered the thick woods that surrounded them. He was about a quarter mile from the highway road when he saw the Jeep stopped on the path, with nothing around them but trees. You could barely even see the sky through the canopy.

He stopped the car and tried to figure out what was going on. Did the Jeep get stuck? Was Mary lost? He started to get excited that she might have just made this easy for him, but that hope was dashed when the fucker and two other men stepped out from the woods and stopped between his car and the Jeep.

Realizing he had been set up, he put the car in reverse and turned to look over the seat to back down the path to the highway. That's when he saw the large truck parked at an angle on the road, blocking any chance of escape.

Fuck!

Rock

Standing in the middle of the path, staring at the outline of Diamond's piece of shit ex through the windshield of the car Rock was sure was stolen, he let a smile grow on his face. The fucker had no idea what he was about to go through.

Lifting his left hand, he made sure the fucker saw the tattoo on his ring finger, before he crooked a finger, and motioned for the idiot to get out of the car.

It took another couple of minutes, but the man finally realized there was no way to avoid what was about to happen. Niles opened the door and slowly got out of the car, leaving it running. Not taking his eyes off of Rock he rounded the car to the hood and stopped there.

"What?" The man tried to sound tough, but he really sounded panicked. Rock could understand that. He *should* feel panicked.

"You put your hands on my kids, then on my woman. I don't like that." Diamond had gotten out of the Jeep and fitted herself to Rock's side. Rock slid his arm around her shoulders and held her close.

"They aren't your kids. They're *mine*! *She's* mine!"

Rock tsked and shook his head. "That's where you're wrong. You see… they *were* yours, but you put your hands on them. Then they ceased being yours. You relinquished any hold you had on them with your actions. Then, I met them. And we realized she was meant to be with me all along… so were Miles and

Jenna. They are *my kids*, and she is *my woman*. You will never be near them again."

The man's face was red and twisted with anger. His hands were balled into fists at his side. His chest was heaving, and his breaths were harsh coming from his lungs.

"This is the part when you ask why."

"Why?" Niles growled.

Rock grinned. "You hooked up with that ragtag group of assholes trying to scare the *monsters* out of town, but there's something you didn't realize. We're only *monsters* when assholes become violent and force our hand. I might not be able to shift and tear you apart, even though you've most definitely forced my hand, but they can." He used his free hand to motion to Brute standing to his left and Siren standing to his right.

"No," Niles said. When Rock's brothers shifted into a large brown bear and a full-grown lion, the idiot's voice became shrill. "No! No!"

Then, like the fool he was, he did the number one thing you're not supposed to do when dealing with predators — He ran.

As the bear and lion took off after him, Rock turned Diamond around and led her to the passenger side of the Jeep. After getting her settled into the seat, he rounded the vehicle and got in the driver's seat. Putting the vehicle in drive, he glanced over at her.

"You okay?" Rock watched her face for any sign of distress.

Diamond looked over at him and gave him a sweet smile. "Yeah, Wes, I'm good. Let's go enjoy the carnival with our kids."

"Remind me to never piss you off," he joked and chuckled.

She raised a brow. "Think my brothers would chase you down like they're doing to Niles?"

He nodded. "Yeah, I'm positive they would."

She giggled. "Smart men."

He hit the gas and headed down the path to the turnoff that would take them the long way back to town, knowing Brute and Siren would take care of Niles and the car. "I'm pretty sure they are more scared of pissed off women than of each other."

"They should be."

He reached over and took her hand in his. "Seriously… you okay?"

She sighed. "I would have liked if he would have just left us alone, but that was never going to happen… So yeah, I'm okay."

Lifting her hand to his lips, he kissed the back of it. "Time to have some fun with our kids."

T.S. Tappin

Chapter Thirty-One

Next night... Axle

After the two-day carnival had wound down, Axle was in his office crunching numbers in between bites of his burger that Gorgeous had brought him. She had insisted he take a break and eat, since it was close to midnight and he hadn't eaten since lunch, but he told her he would when he was done.

Ten minutes later, she showed up with a plate that held two cheeseburgers with the works and half of a plate of fries. Then, she kissed his lips and told him she was heading home. She was such a good woman. He'd won the jackpot with her.

His wolf gave a low howl in confirmation as Axle thought about his woman and took another bite of his burger. Without her, he'd be lost.

Chewing, he turned his attention back to the books. He'd have to go over them again to double check, but it looked like they managed to raise half of what the library needed to maintain the same budget. They didn't just want to replace any donations that were lost with Sharon White and her friends. The Howlers wanted to give the library enough to survive even if all their donations disappeared.

Ruby was family, and the Howlers took care of their own. If they could make sure she could continue the career she loved and was damn good at, they would.

Covering the other half wouldn't be too difficult. He had already been in contact with Xander, who was pissed and said he'd use his influence and his wallet to save the library if they needed him to.

Hell, Mama Hen had called and asked if she needed to set up a continual donation with the library to help out.

Axle had already spoken to each of the members individually, as well as asked Crush to do the same with the Claws, to find out what they felt comfortable donating.

Truth of the matter, they had achieved their goal. He would share the news with Rebel in the morning, after he gave the totals another run through.

He closed the laptop and the books and focused on finishing his food. Axle had just popped the last fry into his mouth when there was a dock on the door.

"Come in," he called out and wiped his face and hands on a napkin.

The door opened and Keys walked in, carrying his laptop. He shut the door behind him before taking a seat across the desk from Axle.

"I found what we need to get the assholes to back off."

A grin grew on Axle's face as he rounded his desk and took the chair next to Keys as Keys set his laptop on the desk and started it up.

An hour later, Axle sat back in the chair and let out a whistle. "Shit. I've said before. I'll say it again. Glad you're on our side."

Keys chuckled. "I'll put together a *presentation* for each of them. When are you wanting to do the visits?"

Axle sighed. "Church in the morning. We'll decide then."

After a nod, Keys shut down his laptop and headed out. Axle closed up his office and headed out to his bike. He wanted to be home and in bed with his woman.

Raghnall, God of Wisdom

Raghnall, God of Sapientiam, also known as the God of Wisdom, was rereading his favorite book again. He had no idea how many times he had read it, but it always inspired him and reinforced the mission he and his brother Colvyr held dear — The Gods should protect the humans where they could, without taking away will or using unnecessary force.

He flipped the page, but the knowledge that his champion, Ordys, was in his realm divided his attention. Three minutes later, there was a knock on the door to his library.

Honestly, it was one of many libraries he had in his slice of the Locus Deorum — Place of Gods. He had one on every floor of his three-story home, and the basement was full of bookshelves jammed with his collection.

Not getting up from his favorite reading chair, he opened the door with a flick of his finger. "Ordys, you may enter."

"Thank you." Ordys came to stand in front of him and cleared his throat. "I did as you asked. After finding out the goal of this group, I came up with a plan I think you will approve of."

"Thank you, Ordys." Normally, he wouldn't have needed Ordys to do any research, but it wasn't as easy as it used to be to see into the human world.

His parents had reinforced the shield between the human world and Locus Deorum. Aella, the God of Chaos, had been using their champions and some magic to try to break through the cell they had been put in. If Aella managed that, the human world would be in danger. Aella wasn't known for great discretion or control. Their impulsiveness had started wars, caused illness, ruined truces, inspired greed, and many other things that changed the course of history.

His parents didn't like Aella being locked up, but they appeased Colvyr and Raghnall, knowing they had the best interest of the humans in mind.

"And what did you find out?"

"The Black Forest Academy is what you think it is — a training academy to create soldiers to hunt down shifters and eradicate them. I have no doubt that when they find out about the others, they will be added to the list of those they will hunt down."

"And the plan?"

Ordys looked at him, his stare as clear and sure as it always was. He was Raghnall's favorite because he always did his best to succeed in his missions, but he understood that sometimes the plan needed to change in the middle of the action to make that happen. He also didn't put humans in danger, unnecessarily.

"I would like to take a few champions and infiltrate the academy to find out what they know and what they are planning. Once I know as much as I can, I should be able to warn the shifters they know of and help set up safe houses and safeguards."

Raghnall nodded. "Your base… where will it be?"

"Warden's Pass."

"Yes. I like this." Raghnall smiled. "And I'll just pretend it has nothing to do with that beautiful woman that has been in your thoughts so frequently when you visit."

Ordys smiled back. "Kitty. Yes, she has some to do with it, but it's not serious. Mainly, it's because Warden's Pass is a known shifter location. It will be easier to protect if I'm already there."

"Have you picked the crew you are taking with you?"

"Yes. I think Vega, Ember, and McKenna will be enough. Any more than that, it increases the risk we'll be discovered."

"I expect updates as often as you can manage."

Ordys gave a nod and headed out of Raghnall's home.

Chapter Thirty-Two

Axle

The following morning, during church, Axle gave Rebel the news that they had raised what they needed to in order to save the library. They also discussed what Keys had learned and made a plan.

After church wrapped up, Axle got on his bike and headed for town with Pike, Skull, Dragon, and Keys. They pulled into the parking lot of the office building that held Smith & Smith Accounting and backed their bikes into a row on the side of the building.

As a unit, they headed for the front door. Skull snorted a laugh. "We're going to stick out like a sore thumb in here."

In a rare moment of humor, Dragon shot back, "What do you mean? I wore my best blue jeans and my newest tee."

Laughing, they entered the building, walked right past the lobby security, and approached the bank of elevators. Pike used the toe of his boot to push the *up* button.

Dragon stared down the security guard who looked to be in his early twenties and no more than a hundred and forty pounds. The man was shaking, which made sense. Instinct alone would tell him that Dragon would squash him like a bug on the bottom of his steel-toed boots.

When the elevator dinged, Dragon winked at the security guard, and Axle wondered what *exactly* Kisy did to the man to pull that side of him out. Then, he realized he didn't want to know.

They piled into the elevator, and Keys pressed the appropriate button as Skull asked, "Uh… anyone see a weight limit sign? We're not exactly light."

"Speak for yourself, Hefty," Keys replied. "And the weight limit is twenty-five hundred pounds. It says it on the sign behind your bald head."

"Give the man a patch and, all of a sudden, he gets mouthy," Pike said with a grin.

They were still laughing when the doors opened, and they stepped out into the lobby of the fourth floor. Skull winked at the receptionist and told her. "No need to tell the bosses we're here. We'll announce ourselves."

As the receptionist stood and sputtered a response, they took a left and walked down until they came to the door of the corner office. Without knocking, Dragon turned the handle and swung the door open.

Rebel's Fairytale

"Reggie, my man," Axle said as he followed Dragon and Pike inside the room, with Keys and Skull coming in behind him.

"What is the meaning of this?" The older man stood from his seat at the head of a conference table and scowled. The three other suited men just looked over at the Howlers.

Axle walked over and took the chair at the other end of the table. Leaning back and getting comfortable, he grinned at the fucker. "I don't mind if we have this meeting with your associates here, but you might. Your choice, but you have thirty seconds to make it, before I just start talking."

"I will call the police on you!"

"Twenty-eight seconds."

"You can't just barge in a man's office!" The man was spitting all over the other suited men as he shouted.

"Twenty-four seconds."

"I mean it! I'll call the police."

Dragon leaned back against the wall next to the door and crossed his arms over his chest. With a shrug, he said, "Call 'em. Want me to do it? I bet they'll be *real* interested in what we have to say."

With a huff, he waved the other suited men out of the room. When his eyes locked on the receptionist, who was standing in the doorway and nervously wringing her hands, Axle spoke up. "Don't you even think about threatening that woman or her job."

"Go back to work," Reginald Smith grumbled.

When the receptionist walked away, Pike closed the door and turned the lock as Skull took the seat to Axle's left.

"What do you want?" The man returned to his seat.

"Well, a little birdie sent us some financial paperwork. Now, I don't know much about all of that. I'm just a dumb ol' biker president, but my brother, Keys here, now *he's* a certified genius. He was able to read those financials, and wouldn't you know it, he discovered some interesting information about town funds mysteriously disappearing and the same amounts appearing in your accounts under *miscellaneous payments.*"

"You can't just access my financial accounts!"

"How we got that information is the least of your worries," Skull told him.

"That's right." Axle straightened the chair and rested his elbows on the table. "You see… we're willing to forget all about this… as long as you lay off our clubs and our families… and return the money, of course."

"Of course," Pike said on a nod.

Keys set his laptop down on the table. "Would you like proof? Because I have plenty."

Ten minutes later, they were back on their bikes and laughed all the way to their next stop — The White Farm.

Ruby

Laying back against Rebel's chest on the couch, Ruby let out a sigh. She wasn't even paying attention to the movie that was playing on his television. She had been thinking about what to do with her townhouse. Rebel told her the townhouse was clean, but every time she thought about going back there, her stomach twisted, and her heart started to race.

Nope, she couldn't live there anymore. She would have to sell it or figure out how to put it up for rent. Did she want to keep it? Did she want to deal with renters and contracts?

"What's going through that gorgeous brain of yours, Ruby?"

Along with hearing his voice, she felt the rumble through his chest. She liked that.

"I can't go back to my townhouse."

He started playing with her hair. "So don't."

"I need to figure out what I'm going to do with it."

"Sell it if you want."

She sat up and turned to look at him. "What if I don't want to sell it?"

He shrugged. "Then don't."

"It can't just sit empty, though. I'd have to figure out how to rent it out, contracts, leases, maintenance, and all of that stuff."

A smile grew on his handsome face, framed by that full beard and sexy golden-green eyes. "Has Kisy ever told you what she does for a living?"

Ruby thought for a minute and realized it had never come up in their conversations. "No, actually."

"She works for Howlers Properties, specifically Howlers Property Management. You need to talk to her."

She cringed. "I don't like feeling like I'm taking advantage of a friendship." She watched as Rebel rolled his eyes. *Rolled his eyes!* "I know you didn't just roll your eyes at me."

Rebel chuckled. "You are a member of the HTC family, Ruby. You wouldn't be *taking advantage* of anything, except family benefits."

She liked the sound of being a part of their family, and truthfully, Ruby felt it every time she was around them. They truly welcomed her with open arms. With them, acceptance was easy. They didn't try to get her to conform to what they wanted her to be. She didn't feel the need to try to fit in. Ruby was just one of them, and that was the end of it.

Rebel sat fully up and reached out. Caressing her cheek, he whispered, "Just stay here with me, Ruby. I like having you here."

The words made her heart skip a beat. She loved that he was so willing to have her around as much as possible. Her presence didn't seem to bother him at all. Same with the twins. They all just acted like she had always been there. It was nice, but a part of her worried they were just putting on a front because they knew she had been through something traumatic.

"Just like that?"

"Yeah. We'll go get your stuff and bring it here. You can make this place feel more like home to you. The twins wouldn't care. As a matter of fact, I think they would like having a feminine touch to the place."

"Are you sure about that? You're *positive* the twins won't care?"

Ross stepped into the open archway between the living room and kitchen areas. "Twins won't care about what?"

A moment later, Ryker stopped next to him.

"Ruby is considering moving in with us."

Ross looked confused, but it was Ryker who asked, "She didn't already move in?"

"Yeah," Ross began, "I thought she already did. The other day… you brought stuff." He shrugged. "Nah, we don't care. Need help packing or moving? We got you."

"For real," Ryker said and nodded. "And you won't even have to have Rebel or one of the guys order us to do it. We'd do it for you."

Her eyes filled with tears, and that irritated the hell out of her. Ruby was really sick and tired of the waterworks. Yeah, sure, she'd been through a lot, but she wasn't what she would call a crier.

Through her misty eyes, she stared at the boys. "I fucking love the Blau family and the Howlers. Seriously."

Both of the twins blushed, which sent Rebel into a cackling fit, almost falling off the couch.

Axle

When Axle and the others pulled up to the White Farm, they parked their bikes near the house. They checked the house first but didn't get a response. Glancing around the property as they walked, they made their way to the largest barn, the one closest to the house, and stepped through the wide-open doors. At first, they didn't hear anything but the horses in their stalls.

As they walked through, noises in the far room caught their attention. Skull began to quietly chuckle as they approached the door to Jeffrey White's office. Without knocking, they swung the door open and got an eyeful of Jeffrey White and Dorothy Jones, naked and fucking on the couch across the room.

"Fuck," Axle barked and looked away.

"Well, that takes one stop off our list," Keys commented as his eyes dropped to the floor and stayed there.

"How dare you just walk in my office!" Jeffrey shouted as he climbed off of Dorothy, his sister-in-law, who let out a scream.

"I think I'll wait out here," Pike commented. "I think you're safe, Pres."

"Yeah. Same," Dragon called out. Then, the two traitors stood on either side of the door like they were bouncers at a club.

Axle rolled his eyes. "Get your motherfucking clothes on."

"What in the hell are you doing here?" Jeffrey was frantically yanking on his clothes, not bothering to help Dorothy untangle her clothing at all.

Skull snorted. "You'll find out as soon as your balls are covered."

It took them a few minutes, but when Jeffrey and Dorothy were finally covered and seated on the couch, Axle began. "Well, honestly, Jeffrey, we came here to tell you that if you didn't lay the fuck off of our clubs and our family, we would let everybody know about your debt from your porn addiction. I have to tell you, Jeff, I've seen my fair share of porn in my day. I mean, there's nothing wrong with it, unless it gets to the level at which you've found yourself." Axle tsked. "Mortgaged the farm to pay off your credit cards? Only to do the same thing three years later?"

"Damn," Skull commented. "How many hours do you have to spend watching porn to rack up *that* kind of debt?"

Keys set his laptop on Jeffrey's desk and opened it. "It wasn't just pre-recorded stuff. It was cam girls and special requests. Hold on. I'll pull up what I found, and you'll see what I mean."

"No!" Jeffrey jumped to his feet and waved his hands.

Suddenly, Pike and Dragon were standing between Jeffrey and Axle.

"I wasn't gonna..." Jeffrey swallowed hard. "I... Proof isn't necessary." He swallowed hard. "What do you want?"

"I already told you," Axle replied and smiled. "Back off. Leave the Howlers, the Claws, and anyone who might be connected to us alone. Or... we'll send drives with this information to every member of your church, as well as your wife... just in case she doesn't already know."

"Okay." Jeffrey nodded. "Okay. Yeah. I can do that."

Skull lifted his hand with his phone screen showing Jeffrey's direction. Axle didn't have to look to know what he was showing Jeffrey. It was a photo of him on top of a naked Dorothy on that couch.

"We'll also throw that in with the drives... to be thorough. I'm sure she'd be interested in knowing what you and her sister are up to."

Jeffrey's face turned red with anger, but he gave a nod.

"You can't let them do that, Jeff," Dorothy practically screamed.

"No shit, Dor! Fuck!"

"And don't think we planned to leave you out," Axle looked at Dorothy and scowled. "You think we don't know what you tried to do when my dad and uncles finally let you know your ass would never be an Ol' Lady? You think we don't know about those shipments of *specialty* pillows you were sending and receiving

Rebel's Fairytale

from Indiana? We knew someone was giving those fuckers information for years, but we were having trouble figuring out how they knew so much about our clubs."

"I wouldn't do that!"

Axle raised a brow. "Really? I have to say I was a little surprised to find out that one of the fuckers who were killed in that tragic accident at their clubhouse was your biological child. I mean… wow. And that info probably would've died with him, but you see, not all their members died. No. And the one who survived had gained the confidences of the higher members. One of them got chatty when he was drinking, and he laid it all out. We didn't know which woman in Warden's Pass was the bio mom until we tracked down the birth certificate for the fucker. And there you were… in black and white."

Keys turned the computer to show her the open birth certificate file.

Dorothy's eyes widened, then they filled with tears. "That means nothing!"

"Hmm…" Skull tapped the tip of his finger to his chin. "I wonder what her friends down at the church would think about the fact that she had a kid and shipped him off to live with his biker dad who ran drugs?"

"I'm kinda curious if there are any leftover remnants of her drug running days in that hoarder's paradise she calls a house. Bet it's real tough to clean," Dragon uttered. "I bet the PD would be curious, too."

"Oh, most definitely," Keys said and nodded. "Especially when they get an anonymous file full of proof of unaccounted for money in her accounts, and the pictures I found of her sitting on the lap of her biker lover while he was wearing his cut."

"Jeffrey!" Dorothy stood and turned to look at her lover. "Are you just going to stand there and let them—"

"Shut the hell up, Dor, before you set them off."

"*Now* you're learning," Pike said in a cheery voice.

"I'm sure your best friend, Sharon, would also be interested in this picture," Skull said and pointed to his phone, "since it's her hubby you were boinking. Don't forget about that."

The older woman started to pout. When she realized not one man in the room gave one shit she was upset, she asked, "And I just have to back off?"

"Yup." Keys shut his laptop and picked it up.

"By the way, Jeffrey," Axle began as he headed for the door, "you're gonna have to rein in your wife, too."

Jeffrey gave a nod, and plopped back on the couch, defeated.

"We have a deal, Dorothy Jones?" Skull asked for clarification.

"Yes," she said on a sob.

"Great. We'll just hang onto the info in case you have a change of heart."

⥺⥰⥼

Rebel's Fairytale

After they parked on the side of the main building of Kirsh Inc, Axle told the others to wait outside for him. Pike started to argue, but Axle shut him down. His presence alone would be an interruption to the norm inside the plant. They weren't there to cause a spectacle. They were there to relay information to Elfie Kirsh to get him to back the hell off.

The only way Pike agreed was if Axle had a call with Pike open on his phone the entire time. Sure, he could have used his Alpha voice and ended that argument, but he didn't like to do that. Rolling his eyes, he called Pike on his phone and Pike muted his end. Axle carefully put his phone in the pocket of his cut and headed inside.

When Elfie entered his office fifteen minutes later, Axle was sitting in his desk chair with his booted feet up on Elfie's desk, waiting for him. The man stopped just inside the doorway and stared.

"Well, hello, Elfie. How's your wife? No, not Elsie. The other one." Axle grinned. "Yeah, we know. We know about Francine. We also know about the three kids you had with her — Ricky, Elliot, and Louisa."

Elfie quickly stepped inside and shut the door behind him. "Where did you find out about them? How?"

"That's not important." Axle shrugged and kept smiling. "What is important is what we can do with that information."

"What do you plan to do with that information?"

"Nothing…" Axle dropped his feet to the floor. "As long as you leave the Howlers, the Claws, and anyone associated with us alone. Do you understand?"

Elfie swallowed hard. "Elsie can't… find out."

"Yeah." Axle looked around. "This is a mighty fine business you set up for yourself. It would suck if you had to sell it off to pay her what's owed to her as well as alimony."

Elfie flinched. "Yes. I will lay off."

"And you'll get your wife to lay off."

Nodding, Elfie agreed, "Yes."

"Great." Axle got to his feet. He pulled a 4x6 picture out of his back pocket and laid it carefully on Elfie's desk. It was a picture of Elfie, Francine, and the three kids. "You can keep this. We have more."

As Axle passed Elfie, he patted him on the shoulder. Then, he exited the office and made his way out of the building, smiling and waving at the various employees he came across. There would be rumors of Kirsh's association with the Howlers by the end of the day.

Chapter Thirty-Three

Ruby

After a morning of packing, Ruby was sent to the diner to have lunch with the girls, while Rebel and a group of the guys moved her furniture and boxes. She wasn't about to fight them on it. If they wanted to do the heavy lifting, who was she to stop them?

Sipping her tea, while sitting at a table in the diner, Ruby listened as Kisy and Butterfly argued about whether or not Kisy should wear a black wedding dress. When Pixie offered she should also wear stilettos with it, Butterfly choked on her sip of pop.

Kisy was cackling so hard her face had turned red, and she couldn't breathe. Which is why Ruby was startled when Kisy was suddenly on her feet and shouted, "Ordys! Welcome back, Fucker!"

Then there was a deep chuckle and a handsome man with dark brown hair and eyes, a killer muscular body, and golden-brown skin stepped up to the table.

"I was only gone for a few days, maybe a couple weeks, and I told you I would be back. Just had to pack up. Think your man will still be okay with a houseguest until I can find a permanent place to stay?"

"You need a place?" Ruby looked up at him. "I have a two-bedroom townhouse I'm looking to rent out."

"And you might have an in with the property management company handling it," Kisy said with a grin. She playfully elbowed him in the ribs. "Besides, do you really want to hear the… *nightly noises* at our house?"

Ordys grinned. "That's a good point." He held out his hand to Ruby. When Ruby took it and gave it a professional shake, he said, "I'm Ordys."

"Ruby… uh… Bri Cooke, but they call me… Ruby." She cleared her throat. "Ruby is fine."

As the other women giggled, Ordys gave a nod. "And which of the lovely gentlemen bikers granted you with that very appropriate name?"

That's when Ruby realized how hot her cheeks felt.

"She's with Rebel," Kisy told him. Then she turned to face Ruby. "Ordys is a dragon shifter and champion to Raghnall, the God of…" Her brows furrowed together in concentration.

"Wisdom," Ordys supplied.

Kisy snapped her fingers. "Yes! The God of Wisdom."

Ruby had no idea what in the hell Kisy was talking about. *Gods? Dragon shifters? There were dragon shifters?* Had she stumbled into a fantasy novel? Well, apparently so. Her man could turn into a wolf. It may have been fantasy, but it was also reality, and her brain was having trouble reconciling those two facts.

"But don't ask him for a ride. Ordys would give you one, but Rebel would probably act like Dragon about it and throw a tantrum about you merely asking."

Butterfly snorted a laugh and turned away from them.

"God of Wisdom?" Ruby was staring at Kisy and Ordys.

Ordys looked down at Kisy. "You all didn't explain the Gods to her?"

"Look here, Mister." Kisy put her hands to her hips. "Things have been a little crazy around here, and we might have been busy. And honestly? That's Rebel's responsibility."

"Facts," Pixie blurted and took a drink of her water.

Butterfly had returned to the conversation and nodded. "But we really have been dealing with some serious stuff."

"Yeah, I know. It's part of the reason I was gone. Once I set up a permanent residence, I'll be heading out of town for a bit to help with that." When Kisy's eyes narrowed in curiosity. He shook his head and chuckled. "You're not peppering me with questions again."

Ruby raised her hand. "Can I? Because I have a shit ton of them swirling in my brain."

"Sure." Ordys said, an expression on his face Ruby would have labeled amused.

"Can you shift into a *real* dragon? What color are you when you shift? Do you breathe fire? Is it breathing fire or shooting fire? Do you have a horde or a cave somewhere? Are you drawn to shiny things? How big are you when you shift? Are the Gods real? Like are they corporeal or—"

Kisy put her hand over Ruby's mouth. "Geesh. Let the man answer."

Ordys chuckled. "Yes. Dark Green. Yes. It's not really breathing but… breathing works. I have savings, but I don't have a cave of gold and treasure hidden away somewhere. It depends on the shiny. Approximately nine-feet tall. The gods are real. They can be corporeal if they want to be."

Ruby tried to pull Kisy's hand off her face, but the bitch had a grip.

Kisy smiled at Ordys. "I'll have her make a list if she has more questions."

"She'll have more questions," Butterfly uttered with a nod. "She's a librarian."

Kisy smiled. "Dragon is across the street. And I'll get with you after lunch about renting Ruby's place."

With a grin on his face, Ordys said, "I missed Warden's Pass."

Still holding a hand over Ruby's mouth, Kisy shouted, "Kitty, Ordys said he missed you!"

Rock

When he got out of his new SUV, with the much needed third-row seating, and helped Diamond get the kids out, Rock was waiting for the front door of the house to open and family to start streaming out. It took longer than expected, but as the last child climbed out, Rock heard, "Wes, it's about time you brought my new grandbabies and daughter to see me."

He looked over at Diamond and smiled before he called back, "Yes, Mama Nia, I know."

"You are just a handsome young person," his mom said to Miles as Rock took Diamond's hand. He led her up the front walk toward where Mama Nia was greeting the children, with the rest of the family behind her on the small porch. They looked like sardines jammed there. "And you! Goodness! You're gorgeous!"

"Mama Nia, this is Miles," Rock put a hand on Miles's shoulder. "And the gorgeous one is Jenna. Kids, this is Mama Nia. She's the one who will spoil you, but we don't sass Mama Nia. Understand?"

Miles gave a serious nod as Jenna giggled and covered her face with her hands.

"Mama Nia," Mia said in her little girl voice that was unnecessarily high, but Rock loved the sound to depths of his soul, "we get to have sleepovers *every night*!"

"Well… that just sounds like a grand time." She tapped Mia on the tip of her nose with the tip of her finger. "Why don't you and Hunter introduce them to the rest of the family, while I say hello to Mary?"

"She goes by Diamond," Hunter said and smiled back at Rock. "Right?"

Diamond giggled as Rock grinned at his boy. "That's right."

"Well, she's as pretty as one," Mama Nia said as she approached them. "And I already know you're as strong as a diamond." Mama Nia took Diamond's face into her hands and let out a sigh. Rock loved his chosen mother even more as he watched her interact with his woman. As a smile grew on her face, she whispered, "Thank you for bringing my boy back to life."

Rock's heart clenched as he watched two of the most important women in his life hug and start what he knew would be a bond stronger than steel.

He felt a hand land on his shoulder and looked over to see Pops grinning at him. Pops cupped Rock's neck with his other hand and gave him a nod, as pride radiated from him. "You did good, son. You did good."

"I did, didn't I?" As they both chuckled, Pops slid his arm around Rock, and they headed for the house, leaving the women to finish their moment alone.

Rebel

While getting his second tattoo inked into his skin, Rebel could hear Ruby talking with the other Ol' Ladies in the lobby of the tattoo shop. When they started talking about how sweet he was, Ginger snort laughed from her seat next to him.

He looked over at the woman working on the tattoo of the red-riding hood on the back of a wolf. Ginger was still focused, but there was a smile on her face.

"What are you laughing at?" He smiled and joked, "Don't be fucking up my ink."

Ginger stopped and looked at him. "If you question my skills, I can always have one of the newbies come in and finish up."

Rebel shook his head. "No… No one is questioning your skills, oh mighty ink master."

After rolling her eyes, she went back to work. While Ranger could tat, as well as a few of the Claws, Ginger was by far the best artist they had. Hell, it was common for people to come from across the state just to have her work on them.

"She's not wrong, though," Ginger uttered as she went back to work. "I heard about the little things you do for her. You *are* sweet. There's nothing wrong with that."

"I just want her to be happy and safe."

"You're good at that, too." Ginger added the word *Ruby* in flowing script, along the edge of the hood. "I think the two of you are perfect together."

"I happen to agree." He was smiling when he looked over at the mirror on the wall and saw the name *Brianna* inked into the left side of his neck in bold black script with red stone accents. *Fuck*! He liked the look of it.

T.S. Tappin

"You asking her to marry you? Or are you satisfied with the shifter and biker commitments?"

"I want it all," he said. "I'll ask soon."

Ginger stopped working and wiped the tat clean. When she looked over at him, she said, "I'm happy for you, Rebel. Your mom would be, too."

Feeling choked up at the memory of his mother, Rebel just nodded.

Ruby

After getting her tattoo, later that day, Ruby couldn't wait to show Rebel. She loved it. It was the perfect design to show what their relationship began and where it was headed. It didn't bother her nearly as much as she thought it would that she had a man's name tattooed into her skin. To her, that just proved that her heart was all in. She hoped he liked the ink as much as she did.

With hope in her heart, she said goodbye to the girls and made her way up to their room in the apartment building on the compound, where he was waiting for her.

Stepping through the apartment door, she saw him sleeping on the bed and let out a happy sigh. He looked so peaceful. As quietly as possible, she shut the door and made her way over to the bed. She crawled onto the bed and cuddled up to his side.

After a few minutes of watching him sleep, she was startled when he said, "This feels a little weird... you watching me sleep."

She giggled.

He opened his eyes and looked over at her. "You get it done?"

She nodded and smiled. "Wanna see?"

"Yeah."

She sat up and turned her back to him. Carefully, she pulled her shirt off and let him see her new tattoo. On her upper back, on the left side, there was a deep red book. The cover had the Howlers logo on it, and the title was *Rebel's Fairytale*.

A few moments later, she felt his lips against her spine, working their way up her back.

"You like it?" She liked the feel of his lips on her skin and hoped that was an indication of his approval.

"Yeah, Ruby, I like it." He moved until his legs were around her hips, and he wrapped her arms around her waist. "I'm about to heal this."

"Heal it?"

"My shifter saliva will heal it." He kissed her skin just below the tattoo. "Then I'm going to show you just how much I like it."

Ruby looked at him over her shoulder. Looking into his eyes as his tongue came out of his mouth and licked along her tattoo. Shivers ran through her body. It was the sexiest thing she ever saw. Her throat went dry as she watched him repeat the movement, over and over again, until he had thoroughly covered the entire tattoo.

"Get ready, Sweetie. This will not be gentle."

Chapter Thirty-Four

Two days later... Ruby

Ruby called lunch with her family a success. Her dad and brother were insistent that she was rushing things, but they had also told her they trusted her judgment and would give Rebel a chance to prove he was everything she declared him to be. Her mother just seemed curious.

After they heard he was a biker, Ruby fully expected her dad and brother to judge him harshly without knowing anything else about him. She was happy they seemed to understand not all bikers were the same.

Explaining the dynamics of the club and how they were a family, Ruby knew she had fallen into gushing about the Howlers, the Claws, and the Ol' Ladies, but she couldn't help it. She hadn't only fallen in love with Rebel, she'd fallen in love with every single one of them. They were her family, too. She went from having one brother and no sisters to having a shit ton of both. Ruby knew when her parents and brother saw how she was treated by her new family members, they would put aside any misgivings and accept Rebel and his family with open arms. She couldn't wait for that.

They had ended the lunch with a promise to have dinner together soon. She told them she would talk to Rebel about having dinner at home, because she would like them to have a chance to spend some real time with him and the twins.

Excited and filled with hope, Ruby entered the house through the front door and stopped dead in her tracks at what she saw.

In the wide-open area between the living area and the area that held the kitchen and dining room, two large lions were rolling around on the floor in something. She couldn't quite see what it was, but it looked like dried oregano.

"What is going on?" she asked as she shut the door behind her and tried hard not to laugh. She assumed the lions on the floor were Pike and Siren.

Rebel and the twins were standing on the other side of the lions. They were all bent over, their faces red, laughing so hard that sound no longer came out of them, and they were wheezing.

After a few moments, Rebel was able to pull himself together long enough to explain, "We got the cat stuff. Bleu doesn't care about it, but apparently, Pike and Siren *really* like catnip."

Ruby could no longer hold back her giggles. As she further studied the scene, she saw Bleu, the cat from the library, sitting on the island in the kitchen, looking down at Pike and Siren on the floor.

"You brought the cat here?"

Rebel's expression clearly meant *Duh*. "She needed a home. She couldn't just keep living at the library." He looked nervous, rubbed the back of his neck, and looked around. He shrugged. "I guess I should have asked first."

Ruby smiled. "It's fine." She looked back down at the lions on the floor. "I take it that's catnip they're rolling around in."

Rebel snort laughed. "Yes. I sent the twins to go get cat supplies and told them to get catnip. I figured we could use it to… I dunno… try to convince the cat to like me. The twins came back with a large bag of it. The second Pike and Siren smelled the catnip, they started rolling around on the floor in it and eventually shifted."

She crossed the room and carefully stepped around the lions, so she didn't accidentally step on a tail or something. After approaching Rebel, she pressed her lips to his and smiled at him. "I'm glad you adopted Bleu."

He blushed and shrugged again.

Damn. He was so cute when he got nervous or embarrassed.

The twins finally pulled themselves together and greeted her. After giving her hugs, they asked her about her lunch and her family. While explaining what happened, Ruby walked over and picked Bleu up.

Petting the gray cat, she talked with Rebel and the twins and watched as the lions continued rubbing and rolling their bodies around in the catnip.

It wasn't until Ross came out with the sash from a robe and dangled it over the head of one of the lions that Rebel finally intervened. As the lion started batting at the sash, Rebel uttered, "I think it's time we clean this up. We should probably call Pixie and Sugar, too." Even though he was taking care of his friends, there was humor still in his tone.

Ruby bent down and kissed the top of Bleu's head. "Catnip not your thing? Or are you just too dignified to lower yourself to rolling around on the floor with those alley cats?"

Pike shifted back and shot her a playful glare, his eyes a bit glazed. "Hey," he protested, but he immediately lost interest in her or her words as he rubbed the side of his face against the floor.

"How did you get the cat here?" Ruby asked Rebel.

The twins started laughing again as Rebel scratched at his beard and answered, "Well... I had Pike put the cat in one of those baby-carrier things that you wrap around your torso. Bleu snuggled right in there and didn't seem to mind when Pike started his bike. So... yeah... that's how she got here."

When Ruby started giggling again, Bleu meowed, started purring, and began rubbing her face against Ruby's cheek.

Rebel's Fairytale

After Pixie and Sugar came to collect their men, since the men were too high on catnip to ride their bikes, Ruby helped Rebel and the twins clean up the ridiculous amount of catnip and fur that was spread across the floor.

Once that was done, Ruby found a spot in the laundry room for Bleu's new litter box. Then she filled and set out the cat's food and water dish in the kitchen, before she dumped the rest of the dry cat food into a resealable container and put the cat treats in the pantry.

While she did that, Rebel had taken all the cat toys out of the packaging and also put together the six-feet-tall cat tree, while Bleu watched him with distrusting eyes from across the room.

While he finished that, Ruby went into their bedroom and got in an hour of exercise before heading off to the shower. She dressed in one of Rebel's tees and a pair of her leggings. Not planning to go anywhere else for the night, she was all about being comfortable.

When she stepped out of the bedroom and was strolling toward the kitchen to make some tea, she glanced over at the floor and stopped. In the middle of the living room floor, Rebel was sleeping on his stomach with his cheek resting on his folded arms. Curled up and sleeping on the center of his back was Bleu. As carefully as possible, she retrieved her phone from her purse and snapped a picture.

Staring at the two of them, her heart felt too full, overflowing with happiness, love, and contentment.

T.S. Tappin

Rebel

When Rebel woke up from his impromptu nap, he didn't open his eyes. It was the sound of Ruby's voice that had woken him. She was talking with Ross. He just laid there and listened for a moment.

"I'm sorry all that happened to you," Ruby said softly. "It's amazing to me that you and your brother have turned out so kind, and I'm happy to see you both on a different path."

"Thanks." Ross sighed. "It's because of Uncle Thrash and Chris. They saved us... more than once."

A lump formed in Rebel's throat at Ross's words.

"If it wasn't for them, who knows where we'd be. I just. There was a time that I had a hard time controlling my anger and... Chris suggested I start a journal and get the feelings out. I'm not one to write a journal. It's not my thing, but I started trying to write poetry about it and found out it helped."

"Art has a way of helping people connect with what they are feeling inside."

"This isn't art," Ross said on a quiet laugh.

Rebel opened his eyes and watched the two of them at the kitchen island. Ruby reached over and pointed at an open journal in front of Ross. "An expression of emotion in a creative way is art, and Ross, you are *really* good. I'm not saying you need to show these to anyone else, but I am saying you shouldn't stop if it helps you. I'm also saying you should be proud because not everyone can do what you've accomplished in those poems."

As Ross nodded, Rebel noticed him visibly swallowing hard, seeming to be overcome with emotion. "Thanks, Rubes," he choked out.

Fuck… He loved her even more now, and he didn't think that was possible.

T.S. Tappin

Chapter Thirty-Five

Two weeks later... Rebel

Rebel parked his bike next to Ruby's car and headed for the front door of his house. As he walked, he decided it was time to get his truck out of the garage, but when winter hit in the next couple months, the twins would have to start parking next to the garage, so Ruby's baby could have their spot. No way was his woman going to park her badass car out in the elements. He wouldn't have it.

Making a list in his head of what he needed to do on the truck as he entered the house, it took him a minute to register what he was seeing. On the far wall the room, the only wall that had been bare when he left, were floor to ceiling built-ins.

He blinked, then stared, at what he knew hadn't been there that morning. The twins had been busy at the clubhouse, so he knew they didn't suddenly take up carpentry.

It was as he was pondering it that Ruby walked into the room, slapping a new battery into her power drill, wearing a sports bra and a pair of jean shorts, with a brown leather tool belt around her waist. On her face was a pair of safety glasses, and her hair was pulled up into a messy bun on the top of her head.

She was covered in saw dust and sweat. The only thing he could think was *Holy motherfucking shit balls, my woman is a knock-out!*

"Oh, hey."

"You... there... shelves." He pointed at the wall that was apparently turning the room into the mini-library he always wanted but never had the time to create.

She smiled. "Yeah." As she stared at him, her smile faded. "Crap. I should've asked first, huh?"

"To build shelves in your own home?" He cleared his throat as her face turned red and she bit her bottom lip. "Uh... Ruby... you've got five minutes to get in the shower and rinse off that saw dust."

She smiled at him as she started backing toward their bedroom. "Why?"

His eyes shone golden-green light at her. "Reasons."

She giggled as she turned and ran. With a grin, Rebel chased her.

―――――――

Two hours later, Rebel and Ruby were wrapped up in each other and the sheets on their bed. Running his fingers through her hair, he thought about what Ginger had asked him while he got his tattoos. The idea of declaring his promises to her in front of their family and friends sounded wonderful. He wanted to give her that day, that moment. He wanted to show her she was worth it all. She had given him what he needed for his life and his culture. He wanted to give the same to her.

"Ruby."

She tilted her head up to look at him and smiled. "What?"

"Marry me."

For a long moment, she just stared at him. He watched as her eyes filled with tears. "You want to marry me?"

He nodded and leaned down to kiss her lips. After a slow, soft kiss, he whispered against her lips, "Your fault."

She giggled. "Yes, I'll marry you… not that you asked."

Rebel chuckled. His woman was a smarty-pants, and he fucking loved that about her. "Brianna Jeanne Cooke, would you please do me the honor of marrying me and becoming my lawful wife, therefore, making me the luckiest man on this planet?"

Grinning, she replied, "I love you."

He rolled on top of her and kissed her lips. "I love you, too."

T.S. Tappin

Ruby

As Ruby watched Rebel and the twins rake leaves and bag them up, she sipped her vanilla chai and grinned. Every time Rebel turned his back on the twins, one of them would rake leaves at him. The fifth time, Rebel turned and tackled Ryker. Laughing, the two of them wrestled in the leaves.

Shaking her head and giggling, Ruby pulled the throw blanket tighter around her shoulders.

It was strange how quickly her life changed. In a matter of weeks, she went from a librarian with a quiet life to the mate to a wolf shifter who was guardian to two other wolf shifters, a cat mom, and had anything but a quiet life. There were always people around, always something going on.

Ruby loved every second of it. When her library and her job were in jeopardy, her new family had stepped up and made sure she could feel safe in her career. When her home was violated and she was attacked, Rebel and his club stepped up, cleaned it up, and wrapped her in their collective arms. She felt happy and a part of a family of choice who truly understood the meaning of support.

As Rebel glanced over at her, smiled, and winked, Ruby's heart clenched and so did her core. The man was sweet and sexy, naughty and nice, bad boy and intellectual. He was everything she ever wanted. He just happened to get growly and furry on occasion.

Rebel's Fairytale

As she watched her boys, the slider opened and closed behind her. Then her two best friends, Allie and Liz, walked up and stopped next to her. Without looking over at them, she greeted, "Hey."

"Hey," Liz replied. "Damn. You are surrounded by hot men."

Allie chuckled. "Wait until you meet the rest of the Howlers."

"She's not wrong," Ruby said and took another sip.

"Right. Well… you ready to explain how you managed to meet a man, shack up, and get engaged in a month and a half?" Liz asked.

"Look at the man," Allie told her. "Do you blame her?"

T.S. Tappin

A Glimpse at What's to Come...

Ordys

After filling out the applications for the Black Forest Academy for all of them, Ordys prepared the crew with what he knew of the academy as well as had each of them study the layout. Ember and McKenna hadn't fought alongside the Howlers and the Claws in the war, so they weren't as familiar with shifters beyond the champions. Ordys caught them up on what shifters could and couldn't do. There wasn't much difference between them and shifters, but he wanted his crew to be as prepared as possible.

It only took a few days before each of them received a phone call from an individual who didn't do anything but give them an address and a date to arrive. Each of them were arriving on different days and at different times. Ordys was relieved to know he was going in first. As team leader and lead champion, he didn't think it was right for one of the others to take the risk of being first to arrive.

On the day of his arrival, he climbed out of the truck in the parking lot of the place and looked around. It looked like a boarding school, which made sense, since it used to be.

Grabbing his bag from the back, he headed for the front door of the building in front of him. When he stepped inside, he was greeted by a man in a black cargo pants, a black polo shirt with the BFA logo on the right sleeve, and black combat boots on his feet. In white thread on the left front of the shirt was the name *Hawkin*. The man was standing with his head held high and a look of pure professionalism on his face.

The name made Ordys pause. He would have to research to see if this guy was connected to Milhawk Investigations.

They were not fucking around at this academy. It wasn't a group of ragtags, well… not *all of the*m were. They were training soldiers, and it would be smart to take them seriously.

Ordys held out his hand to the man. "I'm Otis Belnak."

"Hunter Belnak, welcome to Black Forest Academy."

Katana

As she pulled into the parking lot of the only hotel in town, The Hen House Inn, Katana's stomach filled with butterflies. She had heard the town was shifter-friendly. She hoped that was the case, but she also hoped they didn't hate witches.

Her pride had tolerated her while her mother was alive, but they made it clear she wouldn't be welcome once her mother was gone. She supposed she should be grateful they allowed her to stay long enough to go to her mother's memorial. The day after, they stood across the street from her mother's home and watched as she packed up her car with her belongings and left.

The house belonged to the pride matriarch and would be cleaned and given to someone else. There had been nothing left in Bryxton Falls, California for Katana.

Most of the shifter world was unaware of the existence of witches. Her father had witch-genes in his bloodline, but it had been dormant for him. When she was five and floated the cereal box across the kitchen to her with only a flick of her finger, her father almost lost his shit, until her grandmother let him in on the family secret.

By then, her parents had already established themselves in the town and in the pack. Reluctantly, the pack allowed them to stay, but they didn't hide their disdain for Katana or her father.

Her father died when she was sixteen from what her mother told her was a freak accident in the kitchen of the pride community center, but Katana had never believed that.

Shaking off the sad thoughts of her father and his death, Katana grabbed her suitcase out of the backseat of her car and headed for the lobby.

When she was greeted by the smiling face of the woman with bright teal hair behind the counter, Katana sent up prayers to the mother and to whatever god was up there that this would be a safe place for her to start over.

"Welcome to The Hen House. Everyone calls me Mama Hen. You new to town?"

Katana nodded. "Yeah. Starting over. Heard about this place and thought it might be a good place."

"Oh, Warden's Pass is a great place to start over. Where'd you hear about us?"

Katana eyed the woman and took a chance. "On the news."

She saw the moment the woman put two and two together. "Yes. We are a safe place." Then the woman grabbed a notepad, wrote something on it, and pulled the page off. After folding it in half, she handed it over to Katana. "Let's get you checked in. Then I want you to get settled, relax, and call that number tomorrow. My niece, Kisy, will make sure you have everything you need."

"She's shifter-friendly?"

Mama Hen barked out a laugh. "Yeah. You could definitely say that. She mated a wolf."

Relief flooded Katana at the woman's words. "Okay. Yeah. I'll do that."

The woman chatted with Katana as she checked her in. By the time Mama Hen handed over the key card, Katana felt like she knew the woman all her life.

As she turned to grab the handle on her suitcase, she heard the sound of motorcycles outside. Glancing through the front windows, she saw a group of at least a dozen bikes ride by.

"And *they*, my chicken, are the Howlers. You'll be getting to know them soon."

T.S. Tappin

QUOTES

Ranger was on a roll! With a little help from everyone's favorite librarian, he threw out some quotes to throw Rebel for a loop. Here are the Quotes used in this book:

'O Romeo, Romeo! Wherefore art thou, Romeo?'
—WILLIAM SHAKESPEARE
ROMEO AND JULIET, ACT 2 SCENE 2

'Parting is such sweet sorrow.'
—WILLIAM SHAKESPEARE
ROMEO AND JULIET, ACT 2 SCENE 2

'My bounty is boundless as the sea, My love as deep; the more I give to thee, The more I have, for both are infinite.'
—WILLIAM SHAKESPEARE
ROMEO AND JULIET, ACT 2 SCENE 2

'To serve is beautiful, but only if it is done with joy and a whole heart and a free mind.'
—PEARL S. BUCK

Find her on the Web:

TikTok: Booksbytt
Instagram: Booksbytt
Goodreads: T.S. Tappin
YouTube: Books by TT
BookBub: T.S. Tappin
Website:
www.tstappin.com
Merch Store:
Books-by-tt.creator-spring.com

Any emails can be sent to
Booksbytt@gmail.com

About the Author

T.S. Tappin is a storyteller who spends most of her days playing chauffeur to her children (Tyler, Gabby, & Hailee, not to mention all of Hailee's friends who also call Tara "Mom"), strong (probably stronger than he wanted) partner to her significant other (Mark), cuddler to her American Bulldog/Pitbull (Champ), or cleaner of other people's messes (for work and at home). Reading and Writing are her favorite ways to spend her spare time, but she doesn't have much of that with three busy teenagers in the house. She loves every moment of it. She's that mom in the stands yelling and cheering and generally making an embarrassment of herself. She's a very proud Wrestling-Baseball-Softball-Dance-Cheer-Theater-Robotics-QuizBowl-DECA-Esports-Choir-NHS-Rockstar-Crew Mom!

For More Information

On the Howlers MC or Tiger's Claw MC, go to www.tstappin.com or find T.S. Tappin on TikTok or Instagram using the handle BooksByTT.

Your honest review would be appreciated. This book is on Amazon, GoodReads, and BookBub.

If you have any questions, T.S. Tappin can be reached at BooksByTT@gmail.com

Thank you for Reading!
Dream Big. Dream Often. Dream Always.

Printed in Great Britain
by Amazon